GUY
of
WAERING

A Tale of Rodina

Keith Mancini

authorHOUSE®

AuthorHouse™ UK
1663 Liberty Drive
Bloomington, IN 47403 USA
www.authorhouse.co.uk
Phone: 0800 047 8203 (Domestic TFN)
       +44 1908 723714 (International)

Published by AuthorHouse 05/17/2019

ISBN: 978-1-7283-8853-3 (sc)
ISBN: 978-1-7283-8854-0 (e)

Print information available on the last page.

For my wife.

Acknowledgments

Guy of Waering is loosely based on the legend of Guy of Warwick. Once considered one of the nine worthies alongside figures like King Arthur, the legend of Guy has faded from the minds of many. By recreating the story in the fictional land of Rodina, I hope to do my part in keeping the legend alive.

I would like to thank all those who read, and offered feedback, and those who supported me along the way. Will Lyall for the cover artwork. My family of course, who mean more to me than I could ever have imagined. A special thanks to Justin, whose continued support and employment means that I have been able to support my family whist writing this book, and to anyone who has bought any positivity to my life, no matter how small, it is appreciated.

Finally, to those who have kept the legend of Guy alive throughout the centuries. While Guy may be only a single character in the tales of Rodina, his is the story through which I get to introduce the world.

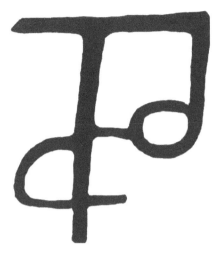

Saxon Rune carving above the entrance to Guys cave.

www.keithmancini.com

Waering –
Spring 911 NW

1

Guy approached the eastern gate of the walled town of Waering. He was dressed in a simple leather and linen outfit of natural colours with burgundy beading and accessories. He had finer outfits, and some in green, but none fit him so well as that one. It was tailored to him and seemed to hide his size, for Guy was both tall and broad. The gate was still open, and the guards barely nodded at him as he passed through. As a former steward's son, he was a privileged nobody; they could ignore him without the threat of punishment. Not to matter, they would be greeting him with more warmth when he was betrothed to the earl's daughter.

He had dreamed of his return for days, and it was no mistake for it to coincide with the earl's weekly feast. It was time to put his plan into action.

The banquet hall was hot, busy, and loud. The regular gatherings were attended by normal townsfolk, those who deserved to be recognised, and socialites looking to further themselves by being around the earl. Guy found himself with the townsfolk, feeling overdressed and out of place. It was perhaps too much to imagine a seat at Earl Rohaud's table, but at least he had a seat, and with it a route to Phylissa. The feasts created a constant buzz among the townsfolk and maintained the earl's popularity as a man of the people. The pre-meal excitement was notching and the great fires in the hearth added an unwelcome heat on a fine spring evening. He could smell people, and worse still, he was melting under his leather jerkin. Guy worried that despite his soak in the springs, he may end up smelling like the villagers around him. He had not pictured that when he dreamt of the evening.

Despite the noise and joyful bustle surrounding him, Guy felt eyes on him, a gentle touch in contrast to his surroundings. His head turned to scan the balconies. A wash of emotions rolled through him as his eyes rested on Phylissa. A simple spring gown of yellow gave her a soft golden glow. Gone from his mind was the crowd, all was calm, quiet, like time had someway paused. In a glorious moment he took in the beauty of her pale skin, blue eyes, and elegantly braided black hair before their eyes met. Even from that distance he could see them shine, so full of life, and something else, that he hoped was love. He saw a smile spread, starting from her eyes lighting up her whole face. As he inhaled he felt his smile match, if not surpass hers. He couldn't help it, didn't want to. A man though, he reminded himself, should not stand in public wearing such a smile, especially when her father was standing beside her. He managed to restrain his smile before meeting the eyes of the earl and he nodded a greeting. Earl Rohaud, courteous as ever, nodded back a smile of sorts, but nothing compared to the smile Phylissa flashed him as she turned to follow her father from the balcony.

Guy took a seat on a communal bench next to an excited miller, who smelt like he had been lugging sacks of flour all day, perhaps all week. It was the miller's first feast, though it looked as if he had supped his fair share already. His enthusiasm was contagious and despite himself Guy nodded a polite smile. Carry on like that and the miller's first feast would also be his last. The earl liked moderation from his people.

The room fell silent and all heads turned in anticipation. A burly porter announced Earl Rohaud, his son and daughter, the sheriff, and two other guests who were members of the council. The earl was greeted with a standing ovation. Guy joined in, his eyes seeking out Phylissa. Within the hour he would have spoken with her, and maybe even her father, if the situation allowed. Her eyes found him eventually. He would never tire of that moment, the happiness of recognition, of togetherness. He sat with the others as the earl waved his thanks and the dignitaries took their seats.

The seat beside the earl was empty, as ever, in memory of his wife. There were a further five empty settings. Earl Rohaud stood, thanking everyone for being there and their contribution to the town before inviting old Mr Slobone, the glass smith, to join the top table in appreciation for the stained glass feature in the Eastern gatehouse. There was polite applause as the crowd moved to let him dodder through. The pastor and two town guards followed.

'Master Guy,' he heard as the crowd quieted, he looked to the earl who spotted him quickly. 'Master Guy has returned to us from battling rampant boars in the villages.'

'It was just one boar my lord,' he called awkwardly across the room.

'Even so, a formidable one I hear, the size of a bull?'

'Maybe a young bull my lord,' Guy called out, polite laughter rippled through the hall.

'You are too modest Master Guy, I have seen the beast's skull.' The crowd had quieted the instant the earl began to speak, and it remained so. Expectant eyes turned to Earl Rohaud, but he did not elaborate, he let the eyes rest on him for a moment before he reached behind the table and hoisted the beast's boiled skull before him with both hands, and some degree of effort. Even from where Guy sat, the size could not be ignored, when seen against the earl's body. Gasps from the crowd caused his blood to run cold and his ribs throb in remembrance. It had been larger than Guy could ever have imagined a boar could be, it had almost killed him.

'Behold,' the earl boomed, 'The skull of the beast killed by our very own Master Guy, a brave and noble act. Come and sit at my table and tell us about it.'

As Guy stood there was applause, genuine applause, and some cheers. It would appear that news of his deeds had spread beyond the castle walls. By the time he approached the table he was feeling beyond uncomfortable. He had always drawn attention because of his size. At times he longed to be invisible, anonymous, normal. The fact remained that, even at his young age, he was well known in the town, he could not change what was. The only remaining seat was between the earl's daughter and a councillor. Phylissa's eyes sang songs of joy to him as he sat beside her. She was genuinely happy for him. *Beyond that of a friend?* She had to know how he felt. Surely she would have withdrawn from their friendship if she did not feel the same.

Finally seated, still flush with embarrassment, Guy tried to relax as the eyes of the room moved away from him. It felt like he was sweating even more than before. He settled his breathing and calmed his pounding heart. There was a hand on his arm, and he looked to Phylissa, surprised at the physical contact in public. With so many people there, someone had to notice.

'Hoy,' she said smiling.

'Hoy.'

'I'm glad you made it back in one piece, and the talk of the town indeed.'

His bruised body throbbed in reminder as she moved her hand away. His mind fogged and he could not find words with which to reply. A true man he may be, but Phylissa always made him feel like a confused puppy. The harder he tried to speak, the more aware of it he became. The more aware he became, the harder it was. It had all been so much smoother in his dreams. He had been confident, charming and everything was as it was meant to be. But there, as moments passed, it was the other side of the coin. Her look faded from happiness to something else. What was wrong with him? He had to say something.

'I'm going to ask your father for your hand tonight,' were the words that left him. Without intent they escaped and time slowed again, the words hanging between them. The reaction of Phylissa did not slow, a look of shock was quickly controlled.

'You *cannot*,' she hissed in a whisper.

'What do you mean?'

'You cannot ask my father today. Do *not* ask him, do not even speak to him. I will explain later.'

As she turned away, it was more than a physical removal. That was it, he knew that she would not speak to him again at the table. Guy felt as if the chair had been removed from beneath him, and with it his innards. A hollow storm began, distant inside him. His mind was racing with no guidance, and no answers. Had she been promised to someone else? Did she not love him? The meal became a blur. He controlled himself, as far as he was aware, even when the earl encouraged a villager to tell the story of how a heroic Guy had danced with the boar. How he had injured it with his two pronged spear before facing the beast head on.

The boiled skull of the beast was to be proudly staked above the village gate, and the beast's innards had been scattered across the boundary to ward off others who would cause harm. The villagers had eaten the boar in a big celebratory feast, but Guy had already departed. Earl Rohaud declared that the villager's proposal to change the name of the village to Boarton was approved. The entire room was on its feet in applause for Guy and the earl. In that instant though, Guy felt distant. It was as if a theatre troupe was performing a production of that very moment, and someway he watched himself dining and laughing from the other side of the stage. Events had gone so differently in his dreams. That was not how things were supposed to be.

When the meal was over and Guy had made it to the castle walls, he let go of the control he had fought so hard to maintain. Bent over, he breathed deeply, unable to feed his body enough air, his vision blurred and his guts emptied themselves as the world slowly closed in on him. One thought penetrated the haze.

Get home.

2

Not a star in the sky, Guy woke in darkness and without blanket. Cold, he lay, unable to get his bearings, confused and anxious. His dreams had failed him in the most spectacular fashion. He had foolishly felt that he was ready for any outcome, but he had not considered such abrupt a scenario. *What had he done?* There was a hole in his memory, and he did not know where he found himself. Pulling his knees to his chest he started to weep. He didn't know why, it just came naturally. For the first time since his father's death he let tears and sobs escape him freely until nothing more came. At which point he sat, curled aball, in total darkness. He did not know where he was, but that didn't matter. At that point nothing mattered.

So dark, so quiet, so closed in, it was the longest night in the history of Rodina. His mind had broken, and it had left him in darkness. He could not tell if his eyes were open or closed. *Was that a voice?* His mind had not plagued him with its tricks for some time, it had broken. There it was again. A soft distant echo as a woman called his name. Wary, he turned towards the sound, at least with his mind's eye, for he had forgotten what it was to move. A flicker of light shook his mind alive. His eyes were open. The light was moving towards him. He was helpless to stop it, to stop his name being softly called. Panic had frozen his body. *What was going on?* Someway his mind was working well enough to remember panic, but nothing else. Transfixed he gazed waiting, locked in himself.

His eyes finally forged an image in the flickering of the torchlight. Whoever she was, she wore a bonnet. She was kind and had come to fix him. The face was talking but he could not understand, she reached out to him, he could not move. She was going to fix him.

Perhaps he had died after all and a deliverer had come to guide him. He had to help her. He did not want the darkness any more. He tried, he tried more than anything, but his mind was so disconnected from his body nothing happened. His deliverer was encouraging him he could hear, but as he congratulated himself a distant jolt ran through him. Another one, closer. His deliverer was suddenly screaming at him, slapping him, he could see, yet still his body refused to move, or even feel. He saw a fist and a blinding crack of pain shot through his face. Then, nothing.

Phylissa was sobbing into his chest, his nose throbbed and was bloodied, yet was still assaulted, as he realised he was sat in his own filth. It made him retch. He doubted that he would experience more fear or confusion if he had been woken from death itself. He did not know what was happening, where he was, or when it was, but Phylissa was there, and that was all that mattered.

'Guy,' Phylissa called out as his body convulsed. He tried to speak but could not. She poured from a water skin over his mouth, the cool liquid returned life and feeling as it ran down his face and absorbed into his mouth and beyond. Phylissa kept repeating his name, more relieved than panicked. Phylissa, it was really her. He felt a smile start from deep inside, one of recognition and joy. When it reached his mouth he winced, his lips splitting. 'Let's get you cleaned up.'

Together they eventually sat him up. Disconnected from his surroundings he could do little but watch her. He tried to help as she pulled his jerkin and shirts from his bulk. It took a while, but there was no hurry. He found himself gazing at her as she led him over to a pool, there were candles, but it took him some time to realise where they were. He saw as she began cleaning him. She was in the spring too, still covered by her small clothes. He could see though. Her wet undershirt clung to her breasts. He gazed at them moving as she cleaned his chest. Her fingers explored the bruise that covered most of his left side. She probed the dark purple mass until he winced.

'The boar?' she asked. He managed to nod. 'You should be more careful.' Their eyes met and smiled at each other. Once Guy was washed, she moved away and stood in the spring, the underclothes showing him the curves and contours of her body. 'We need to talk.'

It was rare indeed for Phylissa to be so serious, he took a breath. 'You have been gone for two days. Have you been sat in here the whole time feeling sorry for yourself?' Guy gave her the only look that he could, one that made it clear that he did not know. It was all he could do, he was unable to talk.

They sat sharing a blanket as the silence continued. She had said nothing since, and he had watched as she washed his clothes which were laid out on the rocks. More than aware that he was still naked he felt vulnerable.

'Guy, you must let me speak, and hear what I say.' Guy looked round to her, he would listen. 'My brother has black lung, and will unlikely see next summer. I am to be father's heir.' She paused for a moment to let the words sink in. 'He knows of our affection, but he will want a good marriage for me now. My father will insist on a favourable match. While my brother remains in good health, I know he will wait and let me find my own. But there will come a point...' she trailed off. 'I have always loved you, even when we were children I dreamed that we would be together. You must know this.' Guy did not even know what expression was on his face, she continued without waiting for it to change. 'Sitting here feeling sorry for yourself for two days will not get you my hand. Come back in white and ask for it. Then we can be together.' She slipped from beneath the blanket, took a candle and her clothes and headed away. 'Your horse is outside by the way. It brought me here.'

'I will return a better man, one you can marry,' he called after her, at least in his mind.

He sat alone under the blanket as candles danced light around him. *Come back in the white of a tournament knight. How the fuck was he going to do that?*

3

It was overcast as Guy rode out of the town's northern gate, a chill in the southerly wind caused an uncomfortable tension in his neck and shoulders. Poor Charger looked more like a pack horse than a warhorse, with stuffed saddlebags and bundles of equipment strapped to him. His plod was slower than usual by way of protest and Guy could almost feel the extra effort it required to carry the load. Though his mind was yet to fully recover, he had the arrogance of youth with him. He fought the urge to look back at the town of Waering. Instead he rode purposefully, imagining the eyes of his love watching him leave from the castle tower. He may well be riding to his death, but he wanted to leave good memories for those that he left behind.

As soon as the town walls were out of sight Guy dismounted to save Charger from carrying his weight. His kit would make the journey difficult enough. He had packed hastily, not knowing what he might need, and as a result had taken more than he would ever require.

His mother's response to his departure had surprised him. He had expected tears and an emotional farewell, but she had been stronger than he had. She must have known that the day would come when he would step out into the world. She had added to the already excessive payload, and given him her fortune. A dozen each of copper and silver, a dozen gold too. He could buy a house and a full suit of armour, and still have gold to spare. He had to assume that she'd had the coin since his father's death, and had never used it. A dozen gold, it was more than most saw in their entire lifetime. 'A knight needs coin' she told him as she pressed the pouches into his hand.

He was heading to Boarton as his first stop and would reassess his kit whilst he was there. He could not walk to where he was heading, that would take him forever, and he did not have forever to spare.

The journey to Boarton had taken its toll on the overloaded Guy and Charger, and it was relief indeed when he saw the wooden village walls appear in the distance. By the time he had arrived there was a small gathering at the village gate, beneath the boar's boiled skull, to welcome him. Their kindness and generosity of spirit lifted him, an impromptu feast was declared and a young ox slaughtered. Despite wanting to stay at the inn, it was insisted on that he stay the night as a guest of the owner of the ox.

For a small village it was a good sized house. It had enclosed gardens and two floors, and though it clearly belonged to someone of importance within the village, it retained a rustic simplicity. Stable boys took Charger to the block and promised to bring Guy's kit to the house. Ordinarily he would have seen to his own kit. Trust was something that had to be earned, but he could see the excitement of the young boys. They had probably never seen a beast like Charger before, who was hands taller than any other horse in the village. They would not steal his things.

The night passed in a rowdy and joyous fashion as Guy was treated to a song one of the villagers had written. It was the first song made for him, and it was a proud Guy who laughed and smiled along with the villagers. He had perhaps supped too much, and shared things that he should not have, but he was relaxed, happy, and in the moment. He had drunk through his mind's mischief and had forgotten his broken mind. Neither the past nor the future mattered, just the faces of ecstasy in the firelight, a timeless moment.

The morning after was a different matter, stale ale swirled in his belly, and his head felt as if a mountain bear held it avice with its claws. His kit was strewn about the place but his purse was intact. The leather bound roll of gold coins cried out from inside him, they were definitely still present. He would have to find a different way of hiding his bounty, it was just plain uncomfortable. He managed to remove the roll just before ox and ale poured out of his arsehole. He pitied the poor wench that would have to empty the chamber pot. It had made his eyes water, and the stale ale in his belly expel itself from his mouth. He felt a splash on his face as he hurled into the chamber pot, but chose not to look at his hand as he wiped it away. Finally empty, and with liquid leaking from every orifice on his face he put down the chamber pot and stumbled back to the straw cot. Clammy, he lay, his entire body swirling in discomfort as he considered the lesson he could take from it. A knight should be able to take his ale, but should be suspicious when the ale is cloudy. He was feeling cloudy, and he didn't like it.

He was collected not long after, and taken to break his fast with his hosts and a few of their friends. On the way, despite the servant's protestations, he emptied his own chamber pot, grateful that there was nothing else inside him to escape. The sight and smell of that chamber pot would remain with him for a long time. Fried pork, bread and a chilled water that had been steeped with dried fruits replenished Guy to the extent that he treated the table to a recounting of his fight with the boar. They hung onto his words as if he were the greatest narrator in all of Rodina. After complimenting the juice, it was not long before the servant girl returned with three full skins and a satchel of dried fruits so that he could make his own. Overwhelmed at the host's generosity, and the goodwill the village had shown him, Guy thanked them. For a moment he felt as if he was one of them, that he might have belonged. Perhaps these were his people, their simple lives seemed to make them happy. Even the servant girl had a different demeanour to those in town. He enjoyed a quiet moment as the others talked around him, but he heard nothing. He was drifting again. He snapped himself out of it by announcing that he must leave and telling them of his quest to become a knight. Moans of disappointment turned into expressions of curiosity and support. He loved these people.

He took his host back to his room. His earlier expulsions still lingered in the air despite the bunch of lavender that sat by the open window, he was impressed with the servant girl. Guy had laid the kit he was taking with him out on the cot. His sword and spear, a single change of clothes, rollmat, provisions, and a few other essential items. He added the flasks and satchel to the pile.

'I have a favour to ask of you. My quest will be long and hard and I fear I have bought too much kit. Could I ask you to care for some of it while I am gone? I leave you my armour, it is too big and cumbersome for this journey. If after a year I have not returned for it, then it is a gift for you and the village, the other things too.'

'I will have it cleaned and cared for as if it were my own,' his host offered, not appearing to be put out in the slightest. Guy smiled and nodded his appreciation. He felt more accepted by these people, who gave no thought to what colour he wore, than he did by most in Waering. When the colour of your clothes did not matter, the person inside them became more important. These backward villagers may have the right of it after all, though they could learn how to make a decent ale.

It was mid-morning when he left, significantly lighter of load. A good crowd gathered to see him off and he felt important. Some of them called him Sir Guy as he rode off. He liked the sound of that, and it was with high spirits that he headed away from Boarton trying to remember the song from the night before.

The high spirits remained as he sat atop Charger, riding through noonshine, dreaming into the afternoon of knights and Phyllisa, his estate and his future. It was only when he steered Charger off the track to find somewhere to camp that the reality of his situation began to creep up on him. He made camp easily enough, but he still knew the area. Would he fare so well in lands that were new to him? After feasting on a couple of dusk caught rabbits he sat on his rollmat staring into the fire. Sleep was hard to find. There was a sense of doom within him, and the night's peace was unattainable. Some of that village ale would have seen to that, but he had none, and deep down was grateful. His stomach was still not right. Perhaps that was adding to the dread he could feel building inside. He cursed himself for his arrogant display at the village, he had played on their support and goodwill when deep down he was just a country boy who had no idea how he was going to make it. It could take decent squires several years to become a knight, and he was not even a squire. He would have to seek out an act of honour and chivalry so bold that it could not go unrecognised, and then he had to win a tourney. His mind flashed through infinite scenarios, and none, not even the most optimistic yielded success before the earl married off Phylissa. He questioned whether it was even worth taking such a dangerous path. He should be happy with his lot, and live a safe existence. Danger could take a life all too quickly, and he liked his life, he liked his dreams. He could not return to Waering though, he had been a fool to announce his intentions. Waves of despair started rolling through him, until he realised he was heaving sobs out into the darkness. So soon after falling apart in the caves he was crumbling again. In despair he called out. '*What have I done?*'

Blind to everything but the glowing embers of the fire, calm flames danced in his eyes.

The other side of despair bought with it a simple truth. He was just a man in the night, a part of nature. The vastness of the open sky reminded him of his place in the world. He was young and stupid, and had put too much importance on his own existence, when in fact, he was no more important than the birds that slept in the trees, or the water that trickled in the stream. The power of nature seeped into his being, as it did everything else, and it gave him strength. This was no time for despair. This was the time to define who he was. No more dreams, no imaginings, just the bare reality of the man he would become. Guy felt a connection with the world, for his path was true, and it was one of love. He felt a deep natural strength form at the centre of his being, a strength that, though faint, went beyond the physical. He sat absorbing this feeling, allowing it to spread through his entire body until the sun rose. Only then did he feel the chill of the night in his bones. He stood, bent his knees a dozen times, turned at the waist and rolled his shoulders before flexing his entire body from the inside out. Where once there had been a soft living dreamer, there was a strength developing, the strength of a survivor. He would survive this journey, or die trying.

4

The next few days passed without event, but each step saw Guy get stronger, he was training twice a day, both body and technique. He had taken to running alongside Charger for part of the day. It had been years since he had run, but he could maintain a steady pace, and when he wound that big body of his up, Guy could really move. He had passed into the next county and found himself further from home than he had ever been, in the Vale of Varen, the garden county of Rodina. Food was plentiful and the weather had been fine. He bathed in a stream after his exercise as a brace of spring rabbits cooked above the fire. He was becoming much more aware of his body, as he explored the natural strength that he had been developing within him. His significance had faded, his dreams seemed unimportant, he was not important, he was just a part of this world, the same as a tree or a rock. Through the entirety of Rodina his problems did not matter, and neither did he. All that mattered was becoming a knight. It was liberating.

Guy set some water to boil and gnawed on one of the rabbits as the spring evening air dried his skin. He had not realised how hungry he was, the exercise he assumed. After picking the first rabbit clean Guy placed the carcass in some hot water. He had to stop himself from finishing the meat on the second one, instead saving some for the pot. He reluctantly placed the second rabbit in along with some roots and some fragrant leaves. These little things, Guy was learning, could make a big difference when on the road. They could bring a smile of enjoyment that could make the aches of travelling fade away, even if only for a moment.

As the moon rose Guy stared into the fire and found himself assessing his situation. Alone in the night he could not hide from the truth, and for the first time, he did not want to. He realised that he had never really tried at anything before, he had bluffed his way through life with his size and strength. Becoming a knight was not something he could do half arsed, it had to be all or nothing, and he had to become a knight to win Phylissa's hand. There in the solitary abyss with the moon and the stars as his witness it became his all. He would dream no more. Guy committed in the night and there was no turning back. Everything he would do from then on would be towards becoming a knight. Nothing else mattered.

Back in Waering everything had mattered, the colour of the clothes, manners, etiquette. He could understand that his mother had done the best that she could for him, in the world that she knew. He was not in that world any longer, he was in the real world, where all that really mattered was to keep moving forwards and to try and see tomorrow.

He checked on Charger, topped the pot with water and set it over the embers before adding a good sized log to see the fire through the night. He lay under his simple tarp and stretched his body looking up to the stars. Even laying the right way could make the body stronger, his natural energy flowed unhindered. His awareness was focussed on his body as it started to relax, his breathing steady. A peaceful, determined sleep found him swiftly.

It was the birdsong that woke Guy, and he lay for several minutes as they called to each other. He considered why they felt the need to announce themselves each morning? Perhaps they too were happy to see a new day and their song was one of celebration. When he finally opened his eyes the day had barely begun, a silvery purple sky greeted him. He enjoyed waking up with the world, it was a natural way to live. He scooped some liquid from the pot into a wooden cup and set it to cool while he splashed stream water on his face before stretching his substantial body to see in the new day. His body was still getting used to sleeping on his back, but he knew it was better for him than sleeping curled aball as he used to. He arched and stretched, felt the muscles tighten, forcing a deep crack from the base of his spine. Smaller ones followed as he exhaled and rolled his neck. Throughout his life he had walked unnaturally, hunched over, trying not to stand out. He was starting to walk like a man, upright. Not proud, but accepting who he was and his place in the world. His body would get used to being strong. His sipped from the wooden cup before bending his knees and completing his morning exercises. He did more stretching than usual that morning, it felt like the right thing to do.

He bound his ragged feet as best he could and pulled on his boots. He conducted a quick check to make sure that he had collected everything and hidden the fire, before urging Charger to join him as he started down the road with a slow trot. It always took him a while to get going and that morning was no different, the pain of his blistered and battered feet made him stronger with every step that he took. As he approached the end of his run for the day, he rounded a corner in the road panting. Sweat poured off him as the springtime sun shone. Guy was grunting with effort as Charger found things much easier beside him. A wagon in the road had become de-wheeled ahead of him and he had slowed his run to a walk before he reached the family who seemed unable to refit it, even though the wheel did not appear to be damaged. He approached them, trying to appear friendly, which was difficult panting as he was with spittle flying from his mouth. The family shared concerned glances before the man stepped forward, his hand hovering by his sword.

Guy held open his hands. 'Hoy' he called, 'No threat here. It looks like you could use a hand,' he said between gasps for air. The man stood firm. Guy stopped. 'I have refitted many a wheel, we can have you back on the road in no time.'

'I have no coin,' the man said in expectation of a charge.

'You do not need coin to fit a wheel, just strength and teamwork. What is your load?'

The man assumed a defensive pose again. 'My load is for the markets of Varen.'

'I don't want your load, or your coin, I just need to know if it is heavy.'

'Sacks of grain,' the farmer answered, starting to relax.

'How many?'

'Two dozen. Should we unload?'

'Let us try one time first. Get the wheel ready, and do not try to put it on until you are sure.'

Guy took charge of the situation, giving them each a task. The woman would keep the horses calm, the boy was to help his father with the wheel and the old woman would tell them when to put it on. Guy crouched, feeling the weight. Two dozen sacks of grain would indeed be a test of his strength. Searching for a secure grip that would not impede the refitting of the wheel, he checked that everyone was ready. He lifted briefly, his muscles burnt like hot knives but it moved. 'Let's go now,' he called and lifted again, the cart rose with him slowly. His face became purple with effort and his body quaked under the strain, still he lifted.

'Now,' the old woman called, and within seconds the wheel was sliding down the axle. He held until the wheel slid into place and then lowered the cart collapsing on the ground. The old woman rushed to him, quickly followed by the man and his boy, but Guy was fine and they soon calmed and thanked him while the old woman marvelled at his strength as he gulped as much air as he could. Never had she seen such strength and she had lived among farmers her whole life, she had said proudly, and it was known that farmers were strong men. The farmer ignored the old woman's sleight and offered Guy a water skin. It was good clean water and he drained it all, his body absorbing, rehydrating. His breathing was finally beginning to return to normal. He was happy to have helped. It wouldn't get him a knighthood, but it was the kind of thing a knight should do.

'Will you join us to Varen?' the farmer's wife asked. 'We could do with someone like you. You hear stories of bandits on the road to Varen.'

The husband laughed. 'We travel this road four times a year, and we have yet to see a bandit.'

'You hear stories though.'

'That's true,' he looked to Guy. 'What about it. Will you see us safely to Varen? When we have sold the grain I can give you coin.'

'There is no need for coin. I could do with a night not sleeping on the floor. I will join you. How far is it?'

'Two days, unless the wheels come off again.'

Guy showed the farmer a technique he knew where a rope was coiled three times around the axle and through itself to hold the wheel in place. It was self-tightening and would not easily be worked free.

5

They paused for a noonshine of simple bread and cheese before departing, it was good bread and good cheese. Guy offered the last of his fruit water to accompany the meal, he was relaxed as they ate. It was comforting to be with people, good honest people of the land. As they set off he winced as his blistered feet sent bolts of pain through his body. He caught it quickly, accepting it, but not before both women had noticed. They washed and cared for his feet in the back of the wagon for the afternoon while Charger plodded alongside. Guy looked over at him, trying to take his mind off the agony of his feet. There was more pain with their attempts to heal him than if he had sprinted bare foot over broken pottery for the entire day. Charger looked content though, and that made him smile. Charger had two speeds that he was comfortable with, eyeballs out, and a gentle unhurried plod. Anything in between was an inconvenience, he wasn't built for roaming.

The farmers insisted on making camp that night, they saw to Charger, cooked, and took care of everything, insisting that he stay on the cart. They told him that the herbs they had used on his feet needed time to work effectively. They did not let him walk at all, making him sleep on the grain at night. The old woman had taken away his boots. She had actually poured a few drops of blood from them when she had removed them, a sign perhaps, that he should not overdo his quest to find strength. She had returned from the stream shaking her head at him. 'These are no boots for running in,' she told him, 'not even for walking such a journey. These boots are good for nothing but covering your feet.' The farmer and his wife were nodding and shaking their head at the same time. He had never considered that there were different types of boot. He was happy when he found a pair that fit him. 'Keep running in these boots and you will break your feet for good. Young people today, no regard for the future…'

'Mother!' the farmer's wife interjected, 'Be nice to our guest,' the old woman protested a little, but fell silent. 'Ash, why don't you take him to see Jethro when we get to Varen? If you will not take coin for escorting us, then perhaps you will allow us to introduce you to the best boot maker in Varen. He will make you some boots you can run in.'

'Yes of course,' the farmer agreed. 'I should have thought of that myself.'

'Why would you?' the mother in law chimed, 'A man such as you'.

'Mother!' the farmer's wife called out again. 'We shall not bring you with us again if you cannot behave yourself.'

The old lady excused herself and within minutes was snoring. The farmer and his son exchanged glances and chuckled, everyone joined in, except the old woman who was oblivious.

While the farmer's wife put their son to sleep, Ash senior hopped up onto the cart with a skin of wine to share with Guy. He poured it into carved wooden cups and handed one to Guy who thanked him with a nod. 'Why does the old woman dislike you so?'

'She doesn't dislike me as such. Sure I am not a big strong farmer man, but I have my strengths. What she does not like is that her daughter is happy with me. Marriage, it would appear, was not so kind to her. That is what she dislikes. Sure she speaks with a mouthful of venom, but oft times the receiver of the words is not the target, it is just a way for her to let it out. She is bitter at her own life, not at me or my wife. And she loves Little Ash more than she would ever admit. Besides, she has no one else.'

Guy supped his wine thinking how considerate a man the farmer was, and how no one other than his wife and son would ever really appreciate him. *Did a man need the appreciation of others?* The farmer didn't seem to, as long as he fulfilled his basic task of feeding and providing for his family. He was happy with his lot in life, which was what Guy wanted. The problem was that it was the earl's daughter he wanted to provide for, and he had to become a knight to do that. He talked with the farmer into the night, taking the opportunity to learn of love, and more, through another's eyes. His own views did not matter because they were not based on anything real. Once they had drained the skin the farmer bid Guy good night and headed off into the darkness. Moments later he heard the farmer's wife giggle, an intimate noise that only the farmer should hear. He soon found sleep imagining Phylissa's giggle as he made her happy.

Guy awoke to the smell of meat cooking. He was stiff from his night on the sacks of grain and his mouth was dry from the wine. He sat and stretched, trying to ease the numbness, and let the energy flow through him. The farmer's wife was on him in an instant making sure he did not walk. She unbound his feet, looking at the wounds. The sharp pain of exposed flesh in the morning air shot up his legs as the air brushed a chill over his feet. It was too early to hide the wince as she prodded at them. Satisfied, she removed a small pot from her pocket and applied more balm to his feet. It burned and yet was cooling at the same time. She applied it thickly to the worst of his blisters with a thin layer over the rest of his feet.

'We will let them breathe today,' she told him, 'So no walking, you do not want to get dirt in them, they might get infected.' Guy could only nod. She handed him a pot, 'For you to make water.'

Della left him and returned to the fire. She returned a few moments later and swapped a carved wooden plate of food for the pot. She nodded. 'It is heavy, that is good. Make sure you drink today.'

As he ate the others packed up the camp in an organised, efficient manner. Everyone had their jobs, and did them without prompting, even the boy, Little Ash. When they set off the farmer and his son walked alongside the horses while the women sat atop the cart. The old woman was telling Guy what a real man was like. He only half listened, his mind had its own concerns. What knight allowed a family to care for him and provide for him because of blisters? He should be embarrassed. Convention said that he should be the one providing for them. He should be offering them protection, not some lame passenger. Someway he was able to accept their help and kindness, a knight should also be humble. Knighthood was revealing itself to be a complicated affair with many contradictions. What Guy took to be the ethos was the underlying code of honour and chivalry, being a good person, and doing good deeds, even if those good deeds were sometimes the most terrible things in the world. His thoughts were not helped by the old woman's perpetual monologue on what a real man should be. It was a distorted view, and in no small part aimed at her son by law. He did not rise to it, in fact it appeared as if everyone else could not even hear the old woman. It was when she asserted that a real man should beat his wife if she got out of line, that Guy could take it no longer.

'These words you speak tell me that I am not a real man,' he said, the rest of the family looked round, they were listening now. 'And furthermore, if this is a real man that you describe, I do not think that I wish to be one.'

'Pah, what do you know about it?' the old woman spat, but they were her last words for some time, and the entire party continued in silence, save for the farmer occasionally pointing out animals or plants to his son. Guy felt bad, he was essentially their guest, but Gods she had been grating at him. He had no idea how the farmer put up with it, the constant belittling and put downs. The farmer was indeed blessed with patience.

The dappled sunlight through the woodland kept him distracted, a whole new perspective presented itself as birds and small mammals frittered among the treetops. He could set traps in the trees, he thought to himself, catch a few squirrels.

'Whoa!' the silence was shattered by a man's voice, not the farmers. 'What do we have here?' The farmer eased the boy behind him. Ahead were four men, partly armoured and each bearing swords.

'Just a farmer on his way to Varen, to sell grain.'

'Then you must pay your tax to get there.'

'I have no coin until I sell the grain,' the farmer replied, more confident than when he had spoken the same words to Guy.

'Surely you bought a little something for the taxman, you know you have to pay taxes. No coin? Well perhaps we will have to take this giant horse of yours, or perhaps the woman. We'll leave the old one for you.'

The farmers hand hovered by his sword, One of the men walked up to him, unthreatened, and spoke of the things they were going to do to her. In a flash the farmer had the attacker by the hair, a short knife pressed into his throat, blood trickled down his neck. 'Tell your men to stand down.'

The surprised tax collector soon recovered his wits, and a sharp crack of his head saw the farmer collapse on the floor, holding his face, as a blinding pain consumed him. The other bandits made a move for the cart. Little Ash ran off into the woods. The man thought about chasing him as he examined the blood from the knife wound on his fingers, but found more interest in Della, the farmer's wife, he left the farmer lying in the road and turned to the cart.

The bandits had not noticed Guy as he lay on the sacks of grain, he had slowly worked his spear towards him remaining undetected. His heart was pounding in his chest. These men would likely kill them all. He let instinct be his guide and launched the spear at the man who approached the cart. He was already reaching for his sword as the bandit lurched backwards, shocked, as Guy's two pronged spear slammed into him. Guy leapt from the cart, sword in hand, blocking off the path to the farmer's wife. He felt no pain in his feet, and no fear in his heart. One of the men was trying to pull the old woman from the cart, as she did her best to beat him off. Della tried to help, they were on the other side of the cart though and Guy could do nothing to assist them. His immediate concern was the other two men that approached, looking like they were going to fuck him up. As one engaged him the other went for the farmer's wife, reaching into the cart to grab her. It was he who screamed though as she plunged a small knife of her own into his chest. It was not enough to kill him, but the shock did its job and he pulled back. The old woman had been pulled from the cart and the bandit, still angry at his bleeding neck, stood above her, about ready to introduce her to his boot. The old woman looked pleadingly up at him, only to see a sword emerge from his throat. As the man collapsed and slid from the sword, farmer Ash was standing behind, his weapon dripping blood. In that moment Guy knew that Ash would hear no more stories about real men.

Realising that it was best to eliminate the threat, both remaining men concentrated on Guy. They pinned him against the cart without making contact. It had been reduced to simple parried blows, but in a more coordinated attack both went at Guy in quick succession, as he engaged one, the other sliced his arm. Ignoring the pain he pushed back the attacker and moved into space he stood waiting, grateful that he had escaped. They came again only this time he was ready, he parried the initial blow, turned on his feet and connected the pommel of his sword with the face of the bandit who had sliced his arm. There were cracks, Guy hoped they were the sound of shattering teeth. Turning again he moved towards the other man, there was fear in his eyes, but he was not backing down. Guy feinted, and then struck at the opening, slicing thigh. Again, he picked off his opponent, almost at will, striking three more blows before using all his power to bring the sword down on the man, cutting from the shoulder half into his chest. His sword was lodged in the man as he fell to his knees. The farmer called out, and Guy turned to see the bloody faced bandit charging at him. Unarmed, he prepared to dodge, to take him head on. *To do what?* It had not gone well for him last time. The best approach was still making its way to him when the man was thrown forward, landing on his face, an arrow coming from his back. Guy looked to the cart, to see the Della with a bow in her hand. He nodded silently to her. The farmer was stood over the bandit in a flash, his sword at his throat. He did not hear what the farmer said just before he pushed the sword into him and watched a life fade away.

It was Guy who moved first, helping the old woman to her feet. She was as tough as old boots, and he was sure that it would take more than being pulled from a cart to cause her harm, despite her age. Guy looked next to the woods, to see if there was any sign of the boy.

'Do not worry about Ash,' called the farmer, who hugged his wife, 'He will come back soon enough.'

The old woman spat in the dead face of the man who had pulled her from the cart as Guy retrieved his weapons. His spear first, it came free with a squelch as he stood on the man's chest to pull it out. The sword was a different matter. After cutting through the leather armour, a shoulder and ribs, it had become stuck in the chest bone and spine. Guy was shocked at the damage he had done. It took a few moments of wrenching to free the sword and the pool of blood he stood in continued to grow. He put his weapons back in the cart, and concealed the bodies in the undergrowth, stripping them of anything of value. There was over half a dozen silvers in coin, and the intact armour would likely fetch at least another two, the swords were basic and not well maintained, he left them with the bodies. He gave it all to the farmer as the women cleaned and covered any evidence of the encounter. It was a silent party that continued on down the path once Little Ash had returned. The boy had ran until he realised he was not being followed, then turned back hiding in the trees and seen the fight.

A little over an hour later they came to a stream and the old woman called a halt. She said that they should make camp nearby and clean up. She looked at Guys feet, and then his arm.

'They need sorting out,' she said. There was no arguing with her, but while they made camp Guy persuaded them to let him take the bow and get some food. Once Della had quickly bound his arm, he eased his feet into his boots and headed off into the woods. Not only was he going to hunt, but he had to make more than water. Besides, he had never killed a man before, and he needed a little time to himself.

6

It was close to two hours later when Guy returned, and not yet mid-afternoon, he carried a young boar over his shoulders. He was more at peace with his actions than he had been when he left. There was no option but to engage the bandits to save the women. He had not intended to kill the men, and that was the crucial factor in his mind. He had thought of the men's families, and children left fatherless, as he had been. But it had been their choice to try to steal and more. They were not good men, possibly real men, but not good ones. He was greeted by the entire family on his return, the farmer took the boar from him, and the women gave him something to drink and fussed over him while Little Ash sat quietly carving a piece of wood. Before he let the women take him to the stream to tend to his feet, he put some of the dried fruits from Boarton to steep in some freshly boiled water as it cooled. He had missed the refreshing juice.

The women sat him on a rock, his feet dangling in the chill water of the stream. He wanted to dive in, and cleanse himself of the deaths that he had caused. The farmer prepared the boar with his son as the women took a foot each. To his surprise the balm applied earlier had formed a barrier over the worst injuries, and once it had been washed off, his feet were no worse than before, if anything they were better. The old woman told him that the balm was her recipe as she applied thick layers to his feet, she said that it would keep the wounds clean and quicken the healing. The farmer's wife cleaned the cut on his arm and applied some balm before re-binding it. He had to stay on the rock until the balm on his feet had dried, but for once he did not mind, it gave him time to think. It was a beautiful spot, the stream brought with it a myriad of wildlife, from dragonflies and colourful birds, to small mammals he had never seen before. He cleaned and sharpened his sword, losing himself in the activity.

They came to check on him occasionally bringing him water and bits of food, staying for a few minutes each time to chat, never once mentioning the confrontation. It was Little Ash who bought it up first. After wandering over and looking at the stream in silence for a few moments he finally spoke, without turning to look at Guy.

'I saw you kill those men earlier,' a silence passed. 'They were bad men.'

'They were,' Guy agreed.

'They want to thank you but they don't know how,' the boy said. 'I told them we should just say thank you, but they say that is not enough.'

'There are no thanks required,' said Guy not turning to look at Ash. 'They would have killed me just the same as your parents. They would have taken my horse. Besides, they helped me as much as I helped them. Were it not for your mother I would be dead. If anything I should be thanking her.'

'Without you, my whole family would be dead.' The words hung in the air a moment until they both turned to face each other. 'Thank you.'

Guy had nothing to say, and nodded at the boy who got up and went back to his family. A silent tear rolled down Guy's face, he did not know why. He would have to learn to keep himself together if he was to be a knight.

It was some hours later and the sun was starting to slide towards the land. He had been staring out at the stream. *Had he drifted off again?* Whatever dreams he had been having were not the fluffy dreams of love that he used to have. These dreams came with a dose of reality, and a natural sense of his insignificance. He remembered not his dream, nor had any residual feeling from it. He was the same as before, struggling to feel anything. It was the approach of the farmer's wife that had disturbed his peace. He looked round to see her carrying linen wraps. 'Can I look at your feet?' she asked as she approached.

'Of course,' Guy replied and swung round to face her. There was silence as she examined his feet, save for the occasional sound of approval.

'I want to thank you for what you did for us today,' their eyes met. 'I hate to think what would have happened were it not for you.'

She had him as a captive audience, but he did not feel uncomfortable. He let her thank him. She started to bind his feet, securely, but not tight.

'You are not the only one who wants to offer thanks,' Guy began. Their eyes met again, and this time she was the captive audience. 'You saved my life today, I owe you my thanks.'

'You owe me nothing, which is what I would be without you.'

'Oh I don't know about that, I think between you, you and your husband would have probably been alright.'

The awkward sharing of gratitude over, a smile spread over her face as she pulled two large pieces of leather out of her apron pocket.

'We have made these for you,' she said proudly, and set about tying them to the soles of his feet. They curled up around his feet but still left them open to the air. 'These mean that you can come and join us for dinner. They are waiting for us.'

She led him over to the camp where as usual the rest of them were working in harmony to prepare the meal. As Guy sat down the farmer handed Guy one of the carved plates with some boar, and a bowl with roots and greens. The old woman dipped cups in the pot of juice and handed them around. The boar tasted fantastic, so juicy and succulent. Had he been alone, he would have been close to finishing it on his own, he certainly had an appetite. They ate, drank and even laughed, Guy, conscious more than ever of Little Ash. The day's events would be bound to have an effect on him, but his parents were trying hard to make things appear normal, even the old woman made an effort, though she remained the quietest of them all, which was unusual. She was generally one of those women who thought that because she was old, people should listen to her regardless of what she was saying.

It was not until Della took Little Ash to sleep, and the old woman stood to retire herself, that she decided to share her views. 'Master Guy,' she called back, 'I thank you for your assistance today. I shudder to think what could have happened. You are a good man. You both are.' With that she disappeared into the night.

Guy managed to count to five before turning to the farmer with a mock shocked expression. The farmer nodded and almost smiled. 'I think she just paid you a compliment.'

'I believe she was thanking you for your help.'

'They may have been the words she used, but not the message she was passing.'

'I'm just glad she's alright. Listen Guy, I want to thank you also, you saved my wife from a fate worse than death itself, but I wonder if I could ask for your help one more time?'

'Of course.'

'I have never killed a man before. I don't know how to process it. I mean I know I had to, it's just… we didn't even bury them,' he trailed off. They sat in silence for a moment.

'I had never killed a man before either.'

They shared a glance in the firelight. Guy saw a troubled, yet justified look in Ash's eyes. He wondered what the farmer saw in his. 'But think of this, it is not as if you set out to do them harm. You were protecting your family.'

They talked as they shared the farmers wine, exploring their new bond. They were connected now, to a greater degree than all save two in his life. It was selfish to think, but it was a good first kill, a chivalric one. Somehow the contradictions made a little more sense in his mind. He sent the farmer off to bed where his wife was probably waiting to thank him herself, and told him that he would keep watch that night. It would be good for Guy, he would be expected to keep watch as a knight. He would use it as training.

He kept watch diligently, perhaps too eagerly, but his regular patrols were more to stop the night's mischief from disturbing his mind than a celebration of his recovered mobility. He was letting himself get weak travelling with the farmer. He was supposed to be making himself strong, instead, he was being served as if he were the Lord Knight himself. Had he not been with them though, they would probably be dead. He was being too harsh on himself. He had gotten carried away with developing his natural strength, as he got carried away with most things. It was turning into a long night. He got up for another patrol. He carried a torch with him, it was a patrol that he wanted people to see, if there were indeed people to see it. He thought not, but he carried his sword regardless. It had taken some cleaning, and with every stroke on the stone his mind had flashed images of it slicing through a man. The images were still there when he blinked. He was partly happy to be on watch, for left untamed in sleep, the night's mischief could cause him ill. His stomach growled, and for the first time he felt tired. It washed over him in an instant, all energy vanished in a heartbeat of realisation and all that remained was a little ball of natural energy deep within him telling him to sleep.

A whistle pierced the darkness, and he could hear footsteps approaching, his hand gripped his sword, wishing it were free. The whistle again, then his name whispered in the night, the farmer. He did not relax his grip until he saw Ash approaching, relieving him of watch duty and telling him to sleep. The world was telling him to sleep, and sleep he did. It was not a good sleep, haunted by visions of the day, both real and imagined. His mind swirled unabated trying to process, trying to understand. Guy squirmed helpless as the night's mischief played puppeteer with his mind.

He awoke with a start, he had been slicing through a man, his sword stopped when it met the chest bone, but he man he sliced into was himself. The shock of seeing his own eyes wide with the realisation of death removed him from sleep. It was about to get light. The farmer came over to him, crouching beside him.

'Bad dream?' Guy simply nodded, the farmer nodded back. 'I hope it gets better, for both our sakes'

'So do I.'

Guy sent the farmer back to his wife, he could probably sleep for another hour if the dreams let him. He tied some traps and set out to catch breakfast. Dawn was almost as good a time for catching rabbits as dusk, if he could find their tracks. He looked up in the trees as he followed them seeing the potential, another source of food. He was not really built for climbing trees any more though. In his youth he had been a better climber than boys much older than him. He stuck to ground level though, and without straying too far from camp set half a dozen traps that he hoped would yield something. His feet were less painful, though his body was tired and heavy. He felt the need to bend his knees a few times and get some energy flowing. Back at camp he did just that, and stretched and drilled. His heart was pumping, his breathing hard and fast, but he was happy. For the first time in days he felt the energy flow through him. He would suffer later, he thought, but they were only half a day from Varen, so he could be in a cot when exhaustion came. There was an optimism to the morning, he was about to complete the first part of his journey, it was about to get interesting. Once the sun was up, he knew the farmer and his wife would be watching him, that was fine though, he didn't mind any more. He had always seen exercise as a private thing, but it was not as private as seeing the farmer's wife atop Ash on his first patrol, he had felt that they knew he was watching, but they had carried on regardless.

They started to move as he rebuilt the fire for morning, and he was out checking the traps by the time they were up. When he returned the well-rehearsed routine was under way, Guy could not help but admire it. *That was what a family should be*, he thought to himself as he returned to the camp with a trio of rabbits. Working with each other, for each other. No one expects anything, so everything is given with love. Even the old woman seemed back to herself talking poor Little Ash into a trance. The boy seemed to be blocking her out whilst maintaining the pretence of interest. With a woman like that, he guessed that you soon developed your coping strategies. That morning though, her talk was not of real men, but of good men.

Despite the slick preparations, breakfast was a leisurely affair, the farmer tended to the horses while the women saw to Guy's feet and Little Ash carved some wood. They were pleased with his feet, and after reapplying the balm and binding them with fresh wraps their attention turned to his arm, both women wincing as they removed the bandage. The wound was angry and still weeping, He had tried to ignore the pain, but in truth it hurt like fuck. Guy could not help but wince himself as they prodded it.

'This needs sewing,' said the old woman. Guy tried to protest, claiming that it would not be his last scar. The old woman prodded his arm, 'Then you should learn how to care for your wounds you daft boy. What if it gets infected?'

'I'm a quick healer, it will be fine.' She prodded him again, with less patience.

'This is being sewed, and that's that. Della, go and get my things.'

'Yes Mother,' she replied laughing, and that was that.

The half hour that followed was the most painful in Guy's memory as they scraped and cleaned the wound. The old woman scorned him occasionally for moving, or acting like a child. He was sure they cut some flesh at one point, but all he felt was pain, and he knew better than to watch. When the women were finally satisfied that the wound was clean the pain stopped getting worse. It became more of a dull throb than the searing explosions of pain that had ripped through him when they had cleaned it. 'Now keep still, this may hurt a little,' the old woman said, as she mixed together a concoction that made his eyes water. Guy tried to brace himself as she loaded a flattened stick with her mixture, but as she pressed the stick into his wound, his whole body convulsed, consumed by incredible pain. He doubted it would hurt more if they were removing his arm with a jagged wood saw. His breathing was heavy and it took all his will not to pass out, that would not be knightly. Finally, the wound was packed with the mixture, and they rubbed the area a few times. As he got his breathing back under control, aware of the watching Little Ash, he tried to show that it was not so bad. He realised that it was not actually painful any more, in fact he couldn't feel much of anything, glancing round at his arm, he saw that Della was almost a third of the way through sewing the wound. He was watching the needle go into his flesh, but he could not feel a thing. Panic awoke within him for a moment, fearing a repeat of his broken mind. *Could the pain have broken him again?* The sense of detachment concerned him, memories of the caves and Phylissa thrust forward dominating his awareness, screaming at him that he was broken, and there was no one to put him back together this time. His panicked eyes caused the old woman to chuckle, 'Do you like my ointment? It stops pain and aids healing. It is made with garlik, tea tree and willow bark, mandrake and a few other plants. A knight should know his plants.' Guy simply nodded, entranced by the farmer's wife sewing up his arm while he felt nothing, it was precise, neat stitching. A small part of him wanted to keep the scar natural, it would have been a badge of honour.

Della finished the sewing, applied some balm to the wound and bound it in fresh wraps. 'Keep it bound for three days, the stitches for at least a week. When they start to itch you can take them out, if the wound opens, sew it back up.'

He thanked the women, and went to pack his equipment. Charger had been spoiled the last few days, carrying no load, but that morning he was going to carry their kit. As he packed, Della approached him handing him a satchel and two pots of the balm. 'Please take this,' she said, 'It is not much, but it can keep you well, plus you will need it on your feet for a few days. While my mother may claim these balms as her own, they fetch us more coin than the grain we sell. She doesn't know so keep it to yourself.'

Della explained the various herbs, balm and threads to him and told him how to use them before leaving him to prepare. In a way he was sad to be leaving them, if they could make him a knight he would stay, but they couldn't, so when they reached Varen they would have to part, and Guy would seek out someone who could.

An hour into their ride and the road was showing more signs of activity, more carts and riders heading to and from Varen. Occasional houses and small settlements, inns and people selling their wares on the roadside were becoming more common. Guy started to relax. There would be no bloodshed that day. Riding Charger he had become more than conscious of the roll of gold coins hidden within him, and for once was grateful for his size. He imagined for a moment how uncomfortable it would be for the farmer to conceal such a bounty.

He could not help but smile to himself as they crested the hill and Varen spread out before them in the valley below. It was an incredible sight, the walled city seemed to glisten in the sunlight. It spread over a greater distance than Guy could comprehend, and the green of the spring growth surrounding it would feed those within, and probably more. The sun bounced off the streams that had been cut into the land, fed by the mighty River Serpent which formed the rear defence of the city. Excitement rose in Guy, Varen was the first city he had seen, and it was not even among the most impressive cities in Rodina, he imagined that his journeys as a knight would take him to those in good time.

They entered the city gates without so much as a glance from the guards, they must be familiar with merchants arriving with escorts. Even so, it surprised him, he was used to drawing attention wherever he went. *It might be nice to be anonymous,* he thought to himself. He escorted the farmer and his family to the millers, where they would sell their grain and have residence for their stay. Declining the offer of a place to stay himself, he announced he would have to depart. The whole family came to wish him well, the farmer clasping his arm, gaining assurances that Guy would come and see them when he was passing, and offering one last thank you. Guy nodded to them and was about to turn to Charger when Little Ash ran over to him and held out the wooden figure that he had been carving.

'This is you as a knight,' the young boy said, 'I want you to have it, so that you remember us. Will you come and see us when you are a knight? I have never met a knight.'

'Of course I will,' Guy replied as he ruffled the boy's hair. 'You be good for your parents, and I will see you one day soon.'

Guy turned to Charger and gave a final wave as he led the horse away. He hoped that he was hiding his emotions, he had been fine until Little Ash had given him the figure. It should not have been so hard to say goodbye to people that he had met only days before. It had not been as difficult saying goodbye to his mother. The deed was done though, and soon he was surrounded by the bustle of the city. The miller had given him directions to an inn that had good food and good stables and it wasn't long until he saw the sign for the *Four Kin Inn*.

7

Guy stood quietly waiting for the thin and tiny elderly lady behind the small wooden counter to finish what seemed to be occupying her, the freshly polished wooden panels smelled sweetly of oil. Without looking up she reeled off a list of prices.

'It's two coppers a night for a room, one for your horse, another for a meal, though looking at you it should perhaps be two. Anything else you might want will cost you extra.'

Guy not wishing to argue, though the prices seemed steep, placed a silver coin on the counter.

'I'll take two nights.'

'Up the stairs, last door on the left, the key is inside,' she informed him, never once lifting her eyes from her task, and never once making to give him any change, 'Cause any trouble and you will have to answer to me.'

'I wouldn't dream of it,' Guy replied.

'I'm going to be keeping my eye on you.'

Guy waited for a moment, ready to flash a smile. The woman never gave him the opportunity, and with the silver still on the counter he ducked through the doorway and made his way gingerly up the stairs.

Guy locked the door behind him and put his kit down to lie on the cot. It may only have been a week since he left, but he had missed the comfort of something to sleep in. It was too small, he could not lie flat aback. Two coppers for a bed that he would not be able to sleep in. He would soon come to realise that this was a curse of a big man who travelled the lands.

His body screamed out for rest, but he was full of excitement. He wanted to go and explore, the place seemed so full of life. Guy could not deny himself his first experience of a city. He sorted his kit and hid his weapons, keeping only his dagger. He tucked his coin purse into his smallclothes keeping just a few coppers in different pockets, and a silver in his neck pouch. He did not want to spend any money, or have any more kit to carry, but it was inevitable that he would see something that he had to have.

'I'm watching you,' the woman called as Guy left the inn. He stood outside looking around for a moment, seeking a landmark that could bring him back. The bearings from the afternoon sun told him he was in the south of the city. No buildings stood out immediately, but scanning the skyline he appeared to be midway between two pointed towers. He assumed that he would be able to find the towers from some distance. The Leatherback Tavern was on the first corner he came to, after that there were more shops than he had seen in his lifetime. Street vendors shouted their wares, people swarmed around him, paying him no particular mind. He felt himself smiling. Sure he looked like a man, but inside he had the excitement of a child, a restless child who needed stimulation. As he meandered through the streets he looked at stalls and in shops, he saw and smelled foods he had never seen or smelled before. Shops sold herbs and potions, weapons and books, clothes and pots. He imagined that you could find anything you wanted in Varen. All kinds of wonderful things called out to him, but he fought the urge to waste his coin.

After turning one corner he found himself faced with the market of Varen. It was an immense affair, permanent and temporary stalls filled the entire square, which itself was vast in both size and grandeur. Great statues lined the walls of the market, he was unable to make out those on the far wall such was the size of the place. To his left, sitting high, atop cliffs of volcanic rock, sat the castle of Varen. He guessed it would take more than an hour to cross the square given the amount of people, and that would be if he did not stop to look at anything on the way. People moved about him as if he was not there, as he stood dumbfounded. He had never seen so many people, there must be thousands in the market alone. With it being afternoon, he noticed that many of the fresh produce stalls were closing up, so he skirted the edge of the market for a while, glancing as he moved. Ceramics of many shapes and colours, leather work, and stalls selling a peculiar mix of items that made no sense all, called out to him to look, to buy. He vowed to return the next day to explore properly and after buying some meat on a stick he removed himself from the market and back into the city streets.

He lost himself for hours in some shops, but by the time he entered the Leatherback Tavern he had only bought two books, which together had cost him less than a copper. They were old books, one on herbs and plants for medicine that Della had recommended, the other by a previous Lord Knight on the chivalric profession itself. They were tucked safely in his waistband as he called for a horn of ale. He spoke to strangers as he supped, some merchants, some farmers, and others who were just passing through. The more he supped the more he talked of becoming a knight, and the more he saw people laughing at him. A part of him realised that it was the ale talking more than him, but he also knew that if he didn't talk about becoming a knight, then he would not become one, perhaps a tavern though, was not the ideal location.

The laughing faces started to blur and spin together and he realised that he had supped more than he should. Things were starting to close in on him, so he drained his horn of ale and made to leave. As he passed a table a man called out to him. 'Young knight.'

Guy turned, half expecting another joke at his expense, but the hooded man who had called him did not look the sort to make jokes. The hood covered his face, as the mysterious stranger sat in darkness. 'Come to my stall tomorrow, it may be I know how a man may become a knight. You'll find me as you head the market. I always have a crowd, you cannot miss me.'

Guy wanted to be told then and there, but instead simply nodded and headed out of the tavern, the cool fresh air of the night lifted him out of his stupor, if only for a second. It was enough for him to gather his wits and, in his mind, appear normal when he entered the inn. 'You missed your meal,' the old woman called out, as he ducked under the doorway and headed for the stairs. He saw from the corner of his eye that she had spoken without looking up.

As he settled in his room though he discovered a roast duck with a loaf and some leaves, and devoured the lot in minutes. He placed his kit on the bed, covered it ablanket and lay on the floor beside the bed away from the door. He thought about reading, but before he had decided between the books he was asleep. Ale aided sleep, it was as it should be.

When morning came it arrived without the birdsong and first light that he had become accustomed to, morning at the inn was a different affair entirely. Noise from the street and the inn itself reminded him that he was in a city. Even the centre of Waering was quiet in comparison. Guy lay listening for a while, imagining what it must be like for that to be normal. He didn't think that he would like it. His head was a little foggy from the ale, but as he drained a skin of the fruit water and stretched the aches from his body it soon cleared. He bent his legs, turned his waist and rolled his shoulders to wake his body. He was to head to the market, so he secured his coin to his thigh, keeping all but two silvers and a few coppers to spend. He hid these about his body aware of cutpurses and thieves. He strapped his dagger inside his linen jerkin, and had nothing of value on show. He may be new to the city, but he had heard stories, and no matter how great a warrior, when faced with a thief's deception, or a gang of thugs, it counted for little. The city was their world, and he was just visiting.

He started down the stairs in optimistic mind. He didn't know why, perhaps the invigoration the city held. There, everyone seemed to be moving forward, perhaps he too could move towards his target. He ducked under the door and saw the woman with her attention still on something behind the counter.

'A bath costs a copper,' she called out, 'If you want some assistance, that's another copper.'

'I think I can bathe myself,' Guy replied.

'I have no doubt,' the old woman agreed, 'Some people like a little company though.'

Guy headed to the door, a vague memory of Phylissa in the caves gave him understanding. He turned and thanked the woman for the meal, and stepped out into the street. Before heading to the market he made his way to the stables to see Charger, it was busy with several young boys tending to, and feeding the horses in the stalls. He wandered through until he found his horse being brushed by a stable hand. After rubbing Charger's nose and telling him to enjoy the rest and the fuss he slipped a copper into the boys hand and encouraged him to take good care of his horse. A knight knew that respect had to be earned, and not simply expected. The boy smiled widely and he knew Charger would be in good hands.

As he made his way towards the market he was so taken by his surroundings that he was not thinking of anything other than what he saw. Despite walking the same path the day before everything seemed so vibrant and new. People swarmed around him, concerned only with their business. He drifted along peering at the stalls and shop displays. As he approached the market he saw a gathering around a stall, and remembering the man from the night before, he approached. The hooded man was at the stall, behind him an eclectic mix of items from weapons to food, ceramics and linen, a mix of items that made no sense. The hooded man was moving three wooden cups quickly around a small table. When they came to a halt someone called a cup. There was nothing beneath it. The man lifted another and Guy saw a black seed. There was a murmur from the crowd as the man handed over a silver ring. Someone else stepped up to play, then another, none of them finding the seed at the first attempt.

'Young Knight,' called the man, 'step up and see if you can win what you desire to know. With what do you play?'

Guy patted around his body, cursing himself that he had nothing to play with. He finally withdrew a pot that the farmer's wife had given him.

'This healing balm.'

'Does it work?' asked the man from beneath his hood.

'It does.'

'Fair enough. I will accept your healing balm. All you have to do is follow the seed.'

He covered the seed with one of the cups and moved the three of them round, slowly at first. Guy was confident that he knew where the seed was, but then as the speed increased, he had no idea which cup it was under. When the hooded man bought the cups to a halt Guy could do nothing but guess. He guessed wrong, and handed over the pot of balm. 'Come and see me tomorrow and try again.'

'I leave tomorrow,' Guy replied.

'No you don't.'

Someone else stepped up to play and Guy's time was up. He stepped back and watched the hooded stranger for a while. Five more played, and five more lost. Guy continued towards the market confused by what had just happened, and annoyed that the hooded man was playing with him. If there was something to tell him, to aid his journey, why not simply tell him? Why play games? By the time he reached the market it niggled only at a small part of his mind, he went straight past the fresh produce section that had been closing yesterday, and headed deeper into the market. All sorts of goods passed him by, baskets, clothes, flasks and skins. Finally he heard what he had been looking for, the shrill ring of a hammer on steel, he followed the sound until he entered the blacksmith's quarter.

The smell of hot fire and smouldering steel triggered memories of solace and familiarity. As a boy of twelve he had bested those of 16 in climbing, fighting, running, archery, everything really. He thought this had made him popular, but when his father died, he saw the world through different eyes and realised that he had no connection to any of them, he had no friends, he was an outsider. That was a stark reality for a twelve year old to consider. When he was not learning or training, instead of playing and showing off to the other kids, he started spending time at the furnaces at the castle. For hours a day he would loiter, watching, until eventually they started putting him to use. Carrying at first, then the bellows, then striking. Guy had enjoyed the physical work, the exertion helped hide the pain and sorrow at losing his father. For four years he had eased his pain with fire and steel. It was good to be around it again, the memories made him stronger.

Most of the stalls that lined the market streets were selling wares, some had workshops attached and repaired armour and weapons. It was not until he explored beyond these that he found the real heart of the district. Behind the stalls the space opened out, each smith had their own area, most with covered workshops and space for horses to deliver goods. He had never seen anything like it. The area spread for what he considered to be the entire courtyard of Wearing's castle. There were so many furnaces and so much activity, the bodies of men shone with exertion and the air filled with the power of struck steel. In another life, he imagined himself as a blacksmith. He wandered through the area with a look of wonder on his face. He drifted towards a quiet workshop towards the edge where a smith was feeding a blade to the fire. He was a big man, early 40's Guy estimated, his greying hair was tied back. His grey eyes shone as he looked up.

'You're a big lad, did you ever strike the steel before?'

'I have.'

'Are you looking for work?'

'Thank you but I can't. I am looking to become a knight so that I may marry my love.' The words felt so stupid when he said them aloud.

The blacksmith let out an experienced chuckle, not enough to be insulting, but enough to show what he thought.

'Do you have any advice that could help me?'

'Aye, come and work for me, and find a less demanding love.'

'You cannot choose who you love.'

'Aye, but you can. You are young and the world is bright. It will not stay that way forever, but good luck to you. If you need work, come and find me, I could make good use of someone like you.'

8

By the time Guy returned to the Inn, he was feeling the benefit of his time in the blacksmith's quarter, his mind seemed clear, and focussed, more in tune with the world. There was no better leveller than fire and steel. It had been good for him to be around it. As he entered, the woman behind the counter informed him that there was someone to see him, and without looking up motioned him to the next room. When Guy looked in he saw Della sat at a table waiting.

'Sir Guy!' she exclaimed.

'You know I am no knight.'

'Maybe so, but you will always be Sir Guy to me, and Little Ash. He is quite taken with you.'

'He is a good boy. You have raised him well. What can I do for you?'

'Two things. One, I promised we would introduce you to our cobbler friend, to get you some boots, if you would still like to meet him.'

Guy looked at his feet, he still wore the linen wraps and crude leather that she had given him. 'That might be a good idea, thank you. The second thing?'

Della pulled a pot of balm from one of her pockets and placed it on the table. 'It looks like you lost this.'

'I did, and I am sorry. I did not have anything else.' Guy felt himself flush.

'This pot was for you Guy, I want you to have it back, and look after it this time, it will really help you on your travels. How are your feet by the way?'

Guy looked down again, he had not considered his feet at all since arriving in the city. 'They are good, thank you,' he said, as if realising it for the first time himself.

'On bad wounds be generous, let it form a barrier, on minor wounds and bruises, just a little will help a lot.'

'How did you get it back?'

'Not everyone loses to the man of cups. I won and I traded for it. Come, let's get you some boots.'

Guy left Della with the cobbler, they were indeed friends, and his shoes did look of quality. The farmer's wife knew exactly what she wanted for the shoes that he could run in, and was jubilant when Jethro had completely agreed with her. He offered to make a pair of boots that he could fight in, two pairs for three silver coins. Della wanted to use the coin that they had taken from the bandits bodies to pay, but Guy insisted on paying himself. They would be ready in two days.

The following morning after breaking his fast on fried pork, eggs and bread, Guy went to see Charger at the stable house. He was being brushed again and seemed to be enjoying the fuss that was being made of him.

'I like your horse mister,' said the stable boy, 'Are you a knight? This is a knight's horse.'

'I am not a knight, poor Charger here is the only horse that can carry me comfortably,' he replied as he handed the boy a copper. 'Keep up the good work.'

Guy rubbed Charger's nose and departed for the man of cups, stopping briefly at a pottery shop. He had three things to accomplish that day, to beat the man of cups and find out what he knew, to go and see the blacksmith, and not to spend any more coin. When he reached the man of cups there was the usual gathering of people around his stall, he watched seven games before it was his turn, the man of cups won every one.

'What do you play for today?' the hooded figure asked.

'The same as yesterday.'

'And with what do you play?' Guy placed the elegant piece of pottery on the counter, he felt the man of cups look up at him from beneath his hood. 'I will take this today, but tomorrow when you play you must offer something of value to you.'

Guy watched as the man of cups hands became a blur, he felt that he had kept track of the seed for longer than the day before, but by the end of it he had no idea where it was. He guessed the middle, he was wrong. The seed was under the left cup.

'You do not win. Perhaps tomorrow will bring better luck.'

Guy left silently, trying to figure out the man of cups. It was strange indeed, every day he was at his stall, every day people went to play. The first game of the day was a hotly contested affair, for the prize, if won, was the services of the man of cups until sundown. Guy had heard many wild stories as he waited, about what people had him do for them, but questioned the truth in them all. Would a man really go to all that effort to have him build a staircase? Would he really assassinate people if commanded? Guy was starting to learn that words in a city were not as full of truth as those in the country, perhaps not by intent, but stories passed through many lips in the city, and each time they came out a little different. Guy considered what he would have the man of cups do for him should he win the first game of the day. Get him knighted perhaps, could he do that?

Guy approached the blacksmith's quarter, the ringing of hammers filled the air, soot and heat enveloped him. The blacksmith that he had met the day before was not there when he arrived. Things were not going well, he had not beaten the man of cups, and now the blacksmith was not at his workshop. It was still early, Guy's hopeful mind reassured him, and so he passed some time looking at other stalls. The variety of weapons and armour made his head spin. He had seen some fine armour in the castle at Waering, but some of the things he saw eclipsed even those. Ornate metalwork like he had never seen, helms that looked like animals, or had faces, spiked gauntlets and other brutal weapons that could cause untold damage. There were so many swords, in so many styles, both of blade and handle. He could imagine wielding so many of them, but fortunately none called out to him as a weapon that he must own. His sword would suffice, it was castle forged and strong. When he returned to the blacksmith's workshop, Guy was happy to see that the blacksmith was there. He worked alone beating a blade with powerful expertise. Guy passed beyond the stall and approached him, announcing his arrival so as not to startle him.

'Have you reconsidered my offer young knight?'

'No, I'm afraid not, but I was hoping you may be able to help me.' The blacksmith nodded for him to continue. 'If I am to be a Knight, I shall need armour, and good armour at that. What price should someone my size realistically pay?'

'You have no armour?'

'I had to leave it behind, it was too heavy, and besides it was no armour for a knight.'

The blacksmith stopped hammering and looked Guy up and down before plunging the blade in a bucket of water.

'A knight without armour is no knight at all. Three gold should see you with a set of armour for the knight you want to be.'

'How do you mean?'

'A nice fancy set like, some enamel, perhaps your sigil on it. You would look the part for your prancing and your strutting. They call you peacock knights.'

'Should a knight not look good?'

'Aye, he should inspire awe and respect. It depends whose it is you are after. You want to impress a woman, high born at a guess. You want pomp and splendour, and you may well find it, but a real knight would rip your insides out, big as you are.'

'I'm looking to be a real knight,' said Guy through a slightly clenched jaw.

'Aye, of course you are. Three gold for a fancy suit.'

'What about a suit that wasn't fancy?'

'Three gold for a man of your size.'

'The same price?'

'Aye, but the coin here buys strength, better, lighter steel, it moves better, it protects more. But it is more than a set of armour that makes a knight.' Guy, was feeling less angry, but more like a dumb country boy, looked at the blacksmith to continue. 'Did you sharpen a blade on a wheel before?'

'Yes.'

'Well take a seat and put the first edge on these and I will finish them off later, all this talk is making me fall behind. Keep the edge even.'

Guy sat and took the raw blade that the blacksmith handed him. It had been a while, but he had spent many weeks putting the first edge on swords back in Waering, and after a few acustomary strokes he was soon working the edge. The blacksmith began polishing edges on another wheel and talked into the afternoon, Guy listened more intently than he hoped his demeanour indicated. The blacksmith gave an education on what someone should look for in a set of armour, how he should care for it and use it well. The blacksmith had many stories to tell, some that he had heard, others that he had been a part of. Each one of them contained their own lesson as to why good armour and weaponry could be the difference in battle. The blacksmith had been a soldier, but had taken an arrow to the knee. When he could no longer fight, he had learnt to make armour and weapons. One thing his former life had taught him was that there would always be a demand for what he made. Guy was on the last raw blade from the stack and was making it last, enjoying the conversation. He reminded himself that training did not have to be physical, the day had been a prime example of that.

'You'd best hand me that blade before you grind it away,' the blacksmith joked. Guy stopped the wheel and handed it over. 'Are you sure you do not want a job?' Guy laughed, and the blacksmith joined him. 'Do you want to sharpen any blades of your own?'

'I have only my dagger with me.'

'Let us have a look.' Guy withdrew the dagger from beneath his linen shirt. 'Hmm, polish her up' he said, 'and tomorrow trade her to the man of cups on your way to see me, and bring a silver. Thanks for your help today.'

The blacksmith tended to the blades, packing them away in a hessian bundle. Guy polished his dagger and looked at it. He had had it for years, never really using it for anything. It was really just something that he carried around with him. It wasn't even of high quality. Some knight. A wave of disappointment washed over him as he held the dagger to the light looking for the glint of sunlight. Even this blacksmith knew more of being a knight than he did. He knew more of battles and strategies, he knew more of everything. It made Guy feel inadequate, and he did

45

not like that. He probably appeared like some kind of wide eyed country boy to the blacksmith, happy to hear stories of knights and their deeds. He sheathed his dagger, thanked the blacksmith and wandered off into the market. He was enjoying the anonymity the swarm of people gave, not taking in his surroundings, as he made his way back to the inn. He was absorbing everything he had learnt from the day, he could feel the knowledge make him stronger, yet he was also more aware of his weaknesses than he had ever been. The foreign environment of the city reminded him that he was no one, and while he remained a nobody he could not marry Phylissa. He had started his journey though, he would become someone, someone who in the grand scheme of things would not matter, but someone enough to realise his dreams. He had to get back on the road, he had to escape the city. It was too easy to spend coin there.

He was still dreaming of his future when he entered the inn. The old woman behind the counter did not look up.

'Your bath is ready,' her steady voice unnerved him a little. He had not requested a bath, and was about to claim as such, but instead simply thanked the woman and ducked under the doorway to the stairs.

As soon as he entered the room the heat and humidity invited him to the tub and less than a minute later water splashed over the side as he lowered himself into it. He carefully removed the roll of gold coins, and for the first time in days was able to fully relax. It was rare to find a bath that accommodated a man of his size, but with tucked knees he could soak most of his body, it felt good to wash away the grime of the day with hot perfumed water and a rough washcloth. He scrubbed himself raw. Not knowing when his next bath might be, meant that he intended to make the most of that one.

Guy let the air dry him as his clothes soaked in the tub, he padded around his room, he was looking for something he knew he did not have. He felt a need to write some thoughts down, ones that he could come back to later, but he had no parchment, and he had no quill. He had almost bought some at the market earlier, but had accomplished two of his three goals. He had met with the blacksmith and spent no coin beyond the vase. He paced, trying to keep the thoughts in his mind. If he made his mind repeat them enough times, it might remember. He had never felt the urge to write before, perhaps it was reading the Lord Knight's *History of Knighthood* that had inspired him, or maybe he simply did not want to forget what he had learned.

He supped but one ale with his meal, and as he lay on the floor searching for sleep, his mind was making the most of it. The day had been intense, and he had a lot to process. He lay focusing on his breathing, on the ball of energy deep inside him. He was using his thoughts to make him stronger. When sleep did find him it was restless, as was the city. How he longed for the countryside again.

9

Guy approached the stall belonging to the man of cups, he had been telling himself that he was going to win, he had to. He had to get out of the city. The stall was busy, and there were a dozen players before him, Guy watched as one by one they lost and handed over their stake.

'Young Knight, for what do you play?' The hooded man asked.

'The same as yesterday, and the day before that. I seek information.'

The hooded man let out a laugh. 'Young knight, I have people come and see me every day for weeks at a time, I do hope you will not recount the days each time you visit. With what do you play?' Guy withdrew his sheathed dagger from inside his jerkin and placed it on the counter. The hooded man nodded 'I will accept this today. Good luck to you.'

The hooded man's hands glided slowly over the counter caressing the wooden cups as he switched them around. The smooth movements increased and within seconds Guy had lost the seed. Instead as the hooded man's hands blurred with motion his mind calculated. For the past two days he had chosen the middle cup, and both times it had been on the left. He had watched dozens of games over the last few days, suddenly he knew. As the man of cups set the three cups in place, Guy called the middle. As he lifted the cup the crowd gasped as the seed sat beneath it. Guy caught a smile, but could not hide his happiness.

'Congratulations, you win. You may trade your dagger for anything behind the counter.' Guy glanced at his dagger, he had not expected to lose it if he won, but the information would be worth more to him.

'I trade it for the information I require.'

The hooded man held his hands open. 'I cannot do that I am afraid. I am an honest man, and it would not be fair to tell you what you almost know yourself. Choose an item from behind the counter.'

Guy worked hard to control his breathing, and with it his voice. A sudden anger had risen in him, but he had seen how the man of cups dealt with unhappy customers, and heard stories of far more drastic actions.

'I would rather trade it for the information I require.'

He could feel the man of cups looking at him from beneath the hood. There was a mix of righteousness and fear swarming through him.

'If I told you to give a blacksmith a silver, would you know what I meant?' The shocked expression on Guys face told him that he did. 'Ask the blacksmith, but remember, the answer he gives is simply one solution to your problem. Now choose an item.'

Despite the fact that his mind was humming, his eyes scanned the shelves behind the counter. There was an eclectic selection, from fine horns, to linen, a brace of rabbits to jewellery. There was even a gold coin, but then on the periphery of his vision something called out to him, a carved wooden cup with the same design as the ones the farmer had used.

'I'll take the wooden cup.'

The crowd murmured as the man of cups handed it over, he leaned in close and whispered into Guy's ear that the woman who traded the cup was coming to play for his dagger, and she had won every time she played.

Guy tucked the cup under his jerkin and headed towards the market. He had a genuine fear that his mind was playing its tricks on him again. Things like that didn't happen to him, or anyone else. He kept his head down as he entered the market. He was going to see the blacksmith regardless, he had to try, just on the off chance that there was some truth in the man of cups' words. *Ask the blacksmith.*

A multitude of emotions coursed through him as he strode through the blacksmiths quarter, rage, elation and fear. He did not fight them. He was angry at the blacksmith, and at the man of cups, but at the same time overjoyed to be heading towards the first positive step of his journey, yet he was scared of what was to come. One thing he had accepted since arriving in Varen, was that he knew little of the world. That would have to change, and he knew many of the lessons would not be a positive experience. Guy realised he was breathing hard as he approached the workshop, anxiety had constricted his chest. He paused for a moment to calm himself, for his mind was racing uncontrollably. It took him a few minutes to control it. Since his experience in Waering and the cave, he was more aware of the signs, and more able to intervene when his mind ran away with itself. He did not want to approach the blacksmith with anger.

Taking a deep breath he continued towards the blacksmiths workshop. It was quiet, the blacksmith sat, resting his feet on a barrel.

'Hoy Young Knight, do you have my silver?' Guy's body did not wait for his mind, and he was reaching for his coinpurse before he realised. He removed the silver, leaving two coppers. 'I hope you have more than that if you want to become a knight.' Guy simply nodded and passed him the silver. 'Come inside.'

Guy settled onto a stool. The blacksmith was a big man, not as big as Guy, but big enough for the furniture to be sturdy and the space big. The blacksmith was gathering some items from a wooden chest.

'Did you see the man of cups? And did you trade him your dagger?'

'I did.'

'Did you win?'

'I did.' Guy was surprised by his calm manner, it certainly did not reflect how he was feeling.

'Good for you. So what did you choose?'

'I asked for some information about becoming a knight.'

'And what did he tell you?'

'He told me to ask you.'

'Did he now?'

'And he let me choose an item too. I took a cup.'

'Ha. A cup from the man of cups. It is as it was meant to be.'

'What do you mean?'

'The fullness of life is like a fine blade, it is not for us to ask how it was made, but simply to enjoy its beauty. Did you have something that you wanted to ask me?'

'I did. Can you help me to become a knight?'

'Can I? No. A man must become a knight on his own. But I can offer you an option.' The blacksmith looked at Guy. He looked as if here fit to burst. 'First to business though, and after I will tell you what I know.'

Guy relaxed someway and let out a breath, releasing some of the fear and anxiety he had been holding.

'Now you gave me a silver, and gave away your dagger. It was a piece of shit anyway, not sharp enough to be useful, nor strong enough. It was yours though, and for now that is all that really matters. Now a silver piece buys a good dagger, but daggers are what rich men and vagrants carry, not a knight.' He pulled a large knife from beneath a sheet of leather, the limped step bought him close enough for Guy to take it. 'This is a knife, and much more useful to a knight.'

He handed it to Guy. It fit his hand perfectly, its silver steel blade imposing, a long edge that started straight and slowly curved to a solid point. 'It is good strong steel that will keep an edge if you look after it.' Guy examined the knife, it felt right in his hand. 'That might have a good blade, but is no good for piercing armour and flesh in the way a dagger does, so I have something else for you.' The blacksmith pulled another item from beneath the leather sheet. It looked like a dagger, the handle matched his knife, but where the blade should be there was an 8 inch long square spike of steel tapering to a very robust point. 'This is something I read about in an old book. This is good strong steel, a man of your strength should be able to puncture any armour with it.'

Guy took the spike with his free hand and looked at the menacing point. It reminded him of the point of an arrow, a bodkin, but much bigger. It seemed sharper and smoother, and way more deadly. The more he looked at it the more he saw its strength and beauty.

'Thank you,' offered Guy, 'These are an improvement indeed.'

'Really it should be a silver a piece for the steel alone, let alone the craft, but you did help me yesterday, good work too by the way. You should reconsider, a good smith can be a rich man. Just because I appear to live a simple life, does not mean I am short on coin.'

The look Guy shot him made the blacksmith laugh, and Guy could not help but join him. 'I have one more thing for you, a gift to remember me by.' He pulled out a sheath for the knife and a weapon belt. 'If you are to be a real knight, you must have a belt that will not break, that will always be with you. This is a good belt, I give it you with my blessings.'

Guy took the belt, and admired the work. It was strong, and it was big enough to fit him, there were places for his knife and spike, his sword. There were also little pouches made in the same leather, and he saw later, two slots on the inside of the belt.

'I don't know what to say,' Guy mumbled as he searched for words, 'Thank you.'

'Just promise me that if all this does not work, you'll come and work for me.'

'It will work out,' Guy replied, a small smile of reassurance.

'Aye, of course.'

The blacksmith offered Guy a bowl of boiled grains for noonshine and told him of a man he knew. He was a knight who used to train soldiers for the king's own army, now he trained knights. Not in the traditional way, but for gold. If a man could pay his way, and survive the training, he would be knighted. A knight without lands or titles, but a knight that would be able to enter tournaments. Guy felt the elation surge within him as he realised his dream could be achieved. One gold a month saw bed and board and training. A man could leave any time he liked but would sacrifice his gold. It was a sacrifice that many had been happy to make. The blacksmith told him there was no doubt that it would be harder than he could ever imagine, that sometimes he would rather die than continue training. If he made it though, he would understand what it was to be a real knight. Guy nodded, as if he understood the blacksmith's words, but they both knew that he had no idea what he was in for.

They talked into the afternoon, a learning experience far greater than the previous day, until Guy had to leave to collect his boots. He would leave the city in the morning, now that he finally had somewhere to go. The Blacksmith clapped him on the shoulder.

'The man of cups thinks you are ready, I myself do not. I think you would be better off a blacksmith, but perhaps I am biased. You will have feelings of hatred toward me for telling you about this, but remember it was you who asked. I only gave you an option. It is you who took it. Good tidings on your path Guy of Waering.'

Guy thanked the blacksmith, the most sincere thanks of his life, and as he walked away, he felt for the first time that he was actually making progress. On his way to collect his boots he spent a copper on a message to Phylissa, it read simply '*Do not forget about me, my love, for I will not forget about you.*'

10

When he reached Jethro the cobbler's, the farmer and his entire family were there. They were saying their goodbyes over a meal, for they returned to Monkspath the following day. It seemed like too much of a coincidence to Guy, but he could not deny he was happy to see them, even the old woman. They were excited to hear that he too would be leaving, but while they were heading back towards a life that they knew, he would be heading in the opposite direction towards the unknown. Guy joined them at the table talking with them as they finished their meal, and enjoying a light wine. He was as happy and relaxed as he could remember, perhaps since Boarton, though he had supped much less. Guy and the farmer exchanged a look that said that life does go on, the horror does fade. The farmer looked genuinely happy, not the happy people show in public, a more contemplated happiness, appreciating the moment. Guy sat enchanted, *'This was how a family should be,'* he thought, and for once allowed himself to dream a little, picturing his own family with Phylissa, as happy and loving as those he shared a table with, even the cobbler and his wife were lovely people. Not for the first time since leaving Waering, he considered that he might be more suited to a simple life, with people who despite everything else, were happy. To them it seemed that life itself was a celebration and the colour of cloth a person wore mattered not. Deep down though, he knew that was destined for more. He was destined for knighthood, and Phylissa's hand.

Jethro motioned for Della and Guy to go into the workshop. 'I have your shoes,' said the cobbler. 'First the boots.' He handed them over to Guy. They seemed huge in his hands. 'The soles are half a dozen layers of pressed leather, the heels a dozen more. You could step on a blade without harming your foot. I wouldn't recommend trying it though.' The cobbler showed him a compartment in the heel. 'Open it up, put a special something inside, pack it with mud if required and close over the heel. It is very secure, and only opens when you slide it like this.' He showed him again, before having Guy do it. 'Ok, put them on while I get your running boots.'

Guy was astonished at how comfortable the boots were, even before he wore them in. Boots were hard to find in Waering for a man of his size. He often made do with what was close enough, but these boots… Yes, they were strong and heavy, but for the first time he understood what it was to have something fit him as it should. They offered support and protection. They felt good.

'Didn't I tell you they would be the best boots ever?' asked Della smiling at him as he stared at the boots on his feet. 'It will be the best three silvers you ever spent.' Guy nodded, perhaps a little ashamed, knowing that the best coin he would ever spend would see him knighted.

'Worth every iron farthing,' Guy offered still in awe of his boots.

'Don't forget, you still have these to try,' the cobbler called out as he returned to Guy. 'How are the boots?' He knelt down and felt the boots on Guys feet, squeezing and pressing. 'Do they feel ok?'

'They feel magnificent.'

Finally satisfied, the cobbler stopped assessing the fit and told him to remove the boots while he showed him the others.

'You needed boots to run in. Quite a challenge for a man of your size, not many of them run. But I like a challenge. First we bind the foot.' The cobbler whirled a linen wrap around Guy's foot, his hands blurring like the man of cups'. The binding was secure but not tight. 'Then we have these undershoes made from doe's leather, soft and flexible. Put these on.'

Guy did without hesitation. Their soft leather made his whole foot feel fluffy and light. 'This is the boot itself, he held it up. It was made of the same soft leather and appeared to reach half way up his calf. 'Inside here we have lamb's wool and rawhide to give comfort and strength. The soles are three layers of goat leather with rawhide in between. It should provide protection from thorns and stones on the highway. They will need repairing often, it shouldn't cost more than a copper for a new layer of leather, always find the toughest you can.' He slid the boot over the undershoe and laced it up tight, 'This gives you support,' he said tapping the ankle. ' Come try, walk around, tell me.'

Immediately he was struck by two things, one was that this was the most comfortable his feet had ever been, and two, he knew it would only get better when the rawhide was loosened. He stretched on his toes, jumped and bounced on the spot. 'It's like I am wearing no boots at all. These are incredible.'

Della shared a smile with the cobbler as Guy danced around like a child. 'Now please,' said Jethro, 'Give me your old boots. They want for burning.' Guy laughed and handed them over without hesitation.

'They are yours.' He looked over to the cobbler, 'Thank you so much Jethro, these are beyond expectation. I can't thank you enough.'

'They were Della here's design, all I did was make them. May they help you walk a good path.'

Della smiled and left the workshop while Jethro told him how to care for the boots. Guy looked after her, and while he was listening to the cobbler, his mind went to the wooden cup inside his jerkin and the man of cups. He had felt it when he saw it, the wooden cup had come from Della.

When he returned to the table the smiles were still present, the cobbler's wife entertaining both the old woman and Little Ash with her stories. Guy left them to it, and whispered over to the farmer and his wife. 'I went to see the man of cups today,' it was only right of him to whisper. 'I won.' He pulled the cup from his jerkin. 'I won this.' The farmer and his wife shared a smile.

'It is as it should be,' said Della, 'Now you have something to remember us by.'

'If you wanted something from me, you should have just asked,' said Guy, 'I am not gifted at social pleasantries in this way.'

'We have our lives,' said the farmer, 'We won't forget.'

'Tomorrow, we shall have your dagger too, for Little Ash,' Della proclaimed, 'To keep him true, a knights dagger no less. You will come and see us if you are passing when you have been knighted. Little Ash would love to see you as a knight, he has never met one before.'

'We would all love to see you as a knight,' added the farmer. Guy promised he would, and enjoyed a final cup of light wine with them, consciously hoping to store the memories as a reminder of what love looked like.

11

Guy had not taken the main route out of Varen, as nice as it had been to meet the farmer and his wife, it had been a distraction, and had caused him delay. He led Charger through wilderness, forests and farming land, he occasionally stumbled across villages, but passed them by. He had a destination and he was on his way to become a knight. He could let himself be distracted no more.

He was five days into his journey, was enjoying making camp, hunting, exercising and running again. He was getting stronger, and feeling more comfortable in his surroundings. Solitude did not bother him, it only made him stronger. He fought his mind's mischief in the dark of night, and he won, because what he was doing was right. He had no need to justify it to anyone, not even himself.

It was a further two days until Guy stood before the gates of Eastfield Manor. He did not carry any anxiety, he was just relieved to have found it. Inconspicuous on a road out of the village, the stone gateway was unkempt and slightly overgrown. The gates were closed, and no one manned them. He tried calling, and hammering on the wooden gates with his pommel, but no one came. It had been over two hours and the sun was starting to set, Guy was sat leaning against the wooden gates when they started to open.

Guy sprung to his feet, as well as a man of his size could, and peered through the gates. He saw a man as unkempt as the gatehouse. A scraggled beard framed a dirty worn face, clothes that were beyond needing a wash. The man looked at him.

'Ah, hoy. Yes I am looking to become a knight.'

'Wait here,' was the gruff reply.

'I am in the right place though?'

'Wait here.'

With that he pulled the gate closed, locked it and headed off towards the village. Guy watched the dishevelled fellow stagger off into the distance. What else could he do?

As he waited, evening turned to night and beyond. His patience was being tested, but so far he was controlling his anger. But with the night came his mind's mischief, he could not avoid it that night, he would be awake when the man returned, if he ever did. Every doubt and insecurity that bubbled to the surface of his mind, he accepted. He did not deny or fear it, but absorbed it as part of him. For most of the night he kept his mind's mischief at bay. Every breath he took, every time his heart beat, he was making himself stronger. He was getting closer to his goal, to his dream. Guy was fairly sure that the bedraggled man he had met was not the Knightmaker, but yet he did not think that he would be surprised if it turned out to be him after all. The whole experience since leaving Waering had been peculiar to say the least. What mattered was the path he was on. He may not have been progressing far at the moment, but he was at least on the path. The false dawn bought a purple and golden hue to the sky, he took a moment to perch on a rock and savour the sun's ascendance. It was something he saw often, but rarely appreciated as he should.

Guy was able to be aware of, and enjoy the moment of serene calm. His breathing was easy, his mind clear. It reminded him of something sailors talked of, but it was in the old language which made it hard to remember. It didn't matter, nothing did, not even Phylissa, he was truly at peace with the world. Everything seemed to fit together to bring him this beautiful moment.

He was surprised to find it almost mid-morning when movement bought him back to reality. He took a deep breath and turned to see the gate opening. The man from the night before shuffled through the gate closing it behind him. Guy raised a hand in salute, the man's body jerking in surprise.

'Wait here.'

Guy watched the man shuffle off towards the village. He rolled his neck and stretched his back and despite the hunger in his belly he decided to exercise. He climbed off the rock and stretched a little movement into his body. He started bending his knees, then added a jump. Flowing from one exercise to the next, he soon worked a sweat, and in his mind anticipated exercising until the man's return. Imagining the long workout, he was surprised as he twisted his hips to see the man returning with three loaves. He saw the man look at him, he gathered his kit, untethered Charger and followed the man through the gate. Once the gate was closed the man turned to him.

'Wait here.'

He did not wait for a response but headed off across the courtyard. It was a big courtyard, probably very grand in its day, but like the gatehouse was unkempt and overgrown. Neglected, but someway he knew that he was in the right place.

His stomach growled as he stood with Charger, surveying the house and grounds. He would have a courtyard in his house, not as big as the one he found himself in, but ornate, beautiful, and home to flowers and plants that would bring delight to Phylissa. It would be her special place, and they would take walks there together, laughing, sharing their day's events, they would romance there. He dreamed until he could see his courtyard before him, a delicate fountain at the centre, full of gentle life. Arches of roses, beautifully trimmed bushes and immaculate paths. These things did not matter to him, but a place of beauty for Phylissa would need to be exquisite.

Charger nuzzled his face to bring him back to the courtyard he was in. Looking at the sun he figured he had missed noonshine. He was hungry, and Charger probably was too. He drank from a water skin, emptying the rest into his leather hat and let Charger drink from it. Within seconds the water was gone, drunk or splashed away. He looked around the courtyard, there was an overgrown stone trough near some broken hitching posts. His initial reaction was to investigate, but he already knew what he would find. He cast his eyes further until he noticed a stream running through the courtyard alongside one of the walls. Frustrated that he had not properly surveyed the area when he was bought in, he led Charger over to the water and let him drink. Guy washed his face in the water to refresh himself. It was a nice area, shaded and overgrown but there was a distinct path that showed continued use. His mind could not fathom his location, his surroundings, his existence. Perhaps that was why he had not sought out this Knightmaker, perhaps he wasn't ready after all. He had had such a lovely day, first with the sunrise, and then dreaming of his courtyard. If he were not so hungry he would be content. As Charger started to rummage through the undergrowth Guy took some of his provisions, he had food, but it was really his emergency ration, he had been hunting well so far and it was the first time he had broken into it. There was food in the house, he knew, a part of him was expecting to be eating some of that. He chewed on some dried meat and hard cheese starting his last water skin to wash it down. He let Charger finish, enjoying the cool of the shade before leading him back towards the gate. Not even looking toward the house it was his turn to have his body jerk in surprise as a voice boomed out across the courtyard.

'Who the fuck are you and what the fuck are you doing in my courtyard?'

Guy turned towards the voice, it came from the Knightmaker himself, of that there was no doubt. He was a powerful, bad looking man, a man who commanded respect with a single glance, someone who was not to be fucked with.

'Well met Sir, I am Guy of Waering. Someone let me in.'

'Who?' The Knightmaker interrupted. 'Who let you in to my courtyard?'

'I don't know Sir, one of your men?' Guy hoped that the quiver in his voice did not carry. It was hard for Guy to estimate his age, he was different from the older men he knew at Waering. This man looked as if life itself had chewed on him, but spat him out when he fought back. He could be anywhere from forty to sixty. No matter how old he was, he put the fear of the gods in Guy.

'Hawkins!' He boomed, within the minute the bedraggled man stumbled from the house. 'Who the fuck is this, and why is he in my courtyard?'

'He wants to be a knight. I forgot about him. He comes seeking the Knightmaker,' he laughed as he finished speaking, looking towards Guy without a hint of apology.

'I don't know what you heard boy, but you don't have it in you to be a knight. Go and live life first.'

'I have to be a knight to live my life,' replied Guy, 'Besides I have coin.'

'Fuck your coin, and fuck you. Remove yourself from my land before I cut you open.'

Guys felt a fear like he had never felt before. His feet were someway rooted to the ground, his frantic mind was not in control of his words. In desperation he blurted out that Smith had sent him. 'He said he served under you.'

'Smith in Varen? He did, he was a good man. What did he think of you?'

'He said that I should be a blacksmith.'

The Knightmaker laughed. Guy felt he should be able to relax, but the bad looking fucker was just as terrifying when he laughed, if not more so.

'Yet he still sent you here? You have coin you say?'

'I do. Three gold.'

'Hand it over.'

Guy fished the coinpurse from his belt and tossed it to the Knightmaker, grateful that he had prepared it earlier, a hand snapped it from the air. 'This is my gold now. If you choose to leave you do so without the coin. Understood?' Guy nodded. 'Wait here, we start tomorrow.'

Guy's heart was pounding in his chest as he watched them go back into the house. He had seen knights before, but not one had been anywhere near as intimidating as the Knightmaker. That man looked as if he had seen and done the lot, and lived through all that life could throw at him. If he was a real knight then in Smith's words the finest knights he had seen were nothing but peacock knights. Guy was terrified, but elated at the same time. If he could walk back into Waering a knight, with a fraction of the intimidation of the Knightmaker, people would look at him in awe. The knights he had seen had been excellent fighters and tournament knights. This man was a warrior, and he scared the shit out of Guy.

Guy spent the night at peace, not able to sleep for considering his new master. Every knight had to be a squire, he assumed he was to be the Knightmaker's new squire. He should find out his name. He didn't know what the next few months would involve, but his peace with the world gave him the strength to know that he would do whatever it took. Horrors flashed in his mind, the past, the future imagined. He let them flow through him, and make him stronger. *Whatever it takes.* He was prepared to die, and that gave him the most strength of all.

12

Guy awoke with the world again, as the first dappled light penetrated the foliage overhead, he exercised, refilled his water skins direct from the stream and dipped further into his provisions. He was ready to face the day with optimism in his heart. His training was about to begin.

As the sun started its rise over the courtyard the Knightmaker and two companions walked from the house. Guy stood in the courtyard to meet them, the three of them stopping in a line before him.

The Knightmaker walked up to him. 'First of all you are too pretty to be a knight' and he slammed his head into Guy's face splitting the skin on his cheekbone. 'That's a start. A knight's face should show the pain he has gone through, it shows the lengths they will go to. Better to wear it on your face than in the eyes.'

The Knightmaker rained a dozen or so punches on Guys face until he dropped, then calmly turned away and started to the house. 'Draw me a bath.'

Hawkins and the other man carried a bathtub from near the house. In it was a bucket and a big pan.

'Knock yourself out big boy. You have an hour,' Hawkins asserted with a condescending grin, taking a moment to look at the bloodied face of a dazed Guy before he and the other man returned to the house.

The first thing he had to do was wash his face. The bastard's head had caused his face to split, and the punches, his vision to blur. His entire head throbbed with pain. He took the bucket and pan with him. The cool water numbed the pain slightly as it turned red. He reached in his pouch for the farmer's wife's balm, putting some inside the head butt wound, even though the pain screamed through his body. Guy coated the wound with the balm which seemed to pause the bleeding. He cleaned his hands and his face once more before he filled the bucket and began one of three dozen trips to the tub. It was optimistic to say that the tub was approaching half full when the three of them came out of the house. Ordinarily the thought of a man like the Knightmaker in a bathing robe would cause mirth, but as Guy stood beside the tub, panting and sweating, nothing about it was funny.

'What the fuck is this?' He boomed as he approached it. 'When I have a bath, that bath is full. When I get in, water gets out. Clear?' Guy found himself nodding. 'Fuck me. You can't even draw a fucking bath. You've pissed me off. Your defence training will be tough today. One hour, take him.'

'Come here' Hawkins said as he and the other man led him away. Hawkins was chuckling and muttering as they half dragged him to an area of the courtyard that not so long ago was clear. 'Can't even draw a fucking bath this one.' The other man did not speak. 'He's not happy with you. You see normally in defence training you defend. When he doesn't get his bath, you don't get to defend.'

Hawkins nodded and the other man bound his hands to a long rope, which he then threw over thick branch above him and tied it securely to another tree. Guy's arms were above his head, and Hawkins was twirling a sword length stick. 'Are you ready?'

For the next hour Hawkins and the other man started his education. They showed him any number of moves, all of them had names, and all of them ended with the sword sticks slamming into his body. All of them hurt like fuck, but at the same time he sensed the control. He could tell already that the man whose name he did not know was the better swordsman. Hawkins was inconsistent, some of his blows hurt more than others, some on the verge of being too much. The other man, all his blows hurt just as much, whether it be a wild swing or an elaborate turn. Each slammed into his body with an equal force, and each one he felt in his core. He felt it make him stronger.

When the hour was over Guy's vision was blurred with pain, his breathing was rapid and shallow, his body showed the signs of the beating. He felt the pain most of all where his bruise from the boar had been. That beast had almost killed him, and he still felt it.

'Every day I don't get my bath, you will learn defence this way,' he heard the Knightmaker say as he walked over to Guy. He stood in front of him looking into his eyes, seeing the pain and slammed his head into him, this time with a horrifying crunch as Guys nose took the blow. 'Still too pretty to be my squire. Leave him here an hour, then feed him. Take his horse to the stables.'

They turned and left leaving Guy in the sun, blood spittling as he tried to cope with the pain shooting through his head.

Guy half stood, half hung from his hands tied above his head, his entire experience was that of pain. If it was not for the agony in his face, he felt the pain would have made him stronger, instead he was conscious of every breath. Surviving with every breath, and it was only the first day. Through his blurred vision he saw a figure emerge from the house. It was the quiet one, the one his mind had started calling the stranger. When he approached he did not make to untie him, instead he looked at Guy's face. The stranger placed a hand running alongside his nose. Guy tried to mask the pain, but when the stranger administered a sharp crack with his other hand to the side of his nose, he could mask it no more, and let out a scream as agony once again shot through his head. As the initial pain wore off, Guy realised that it was different, less severe, and he could breathe through his nose again, blood spattering as he exhaled. The stranger untied him, and once loose he fell to the floor having used all his strength to fight the pain. The stranger walked off without saying a word.

Guy crawled over the courtyard to the stream and continued on into it letting the cool water wash over him as he rolled onto his back. After a few minutes he started dabbing at his face with wet fingers gently cleaning off the blood. There was so much he had to put his face in the water to wash it away. The cool water soothed, and as he rubbed at his face beneath the water, the pain was almost distant.

Guy was applying some balm to his nose when Hawkins approached. He put down a bowl of broth and some bread, spilling some as it sloshed in the bowl.

'Eat this, then clean the yard. The master says it is a fucking disgrace.'

Guy's vision was still blurred as he watched Hawkins return to the house. He had spilt his broth on purpose, of that he was sure. He crawled over, and soon found himself devouring the food, despite the pain eating it caused. It seemed to be gone in an instant. Guy pulled on a linen shirt, put on his fighting boots and went to look at the courtyard. Had he sat any longer he would not have got up again, and the repercussions of such a lack of action were not something he wanted to experience. If he worked it well, by clearing the overgrown areas closest to the house, he could make it look like he had accomplished more than he had, and spend some time making his camp more comfortable.

Guy awoke before the sun, and despite feeling groggy and thick in the head found himself ferrying buckets of water to the bath tub. His hands stinging every time he filled the bucket, shredded, as were his forearms, from the thorns on the undergrowth that he had cleared. He had filled the bath above a quarter the night before, it would be full that morning. When Hawkins bought some bread and fruit to break his fast on and announced that it was one hour to bath time Guy had filled it a good way, and should easily be able to fill the rest in an hour.

It took ten dozen buckets of water to brim the bath. It was so full that water would escape when the Knightmaker dipped in a toe, and Guy stood proud as the three of them stood before him, the Knightmaker again in a robe.

'What the fuck is this?' the Knightmaker bellowed. Not waiting for an answer, he continued. 'Do you think me to have a bath that is cold? There is no steam in the morning chill.' Though the words were calm, the fury in his eyes shook Guy to his core. He absorbed it, and made himself stronger. 'Defence training. One hour. Then clean the fucking yard.' He pulled up the sluice on the tub and turned away as the water flooded from the tub. Guy physically deflated.

As the Knightmaker left, Hawkins harried him towards the training area laughing, 'Did you see how angry he was? You're going to pay for that. I'm going to fuck you up.'

Guy tensed, just for a second, he should know better than to let Hawkins anger him. Hawkins could fuck him up all he liked, it would only make him stronger. His mind thought it, but as the stranger strapped his wrists together, he didn't really believe it. As the rope was thrown over the branch and his arms pulled uncomfortably high Guy tried to prepare himself for the hour of pain that was to follow. He tried to someway retreat into himself, into his core, to remove his awareness of the situation.

Guy's body was wracked with pain, through his blurred vision he watched attack after attack land wood on his skin. Hawkins had lost a lot of control and technique as he went for force, but the stranger followed such precise flowing movements that it barely caused any pain when the blow was struck, yet they made a more defined crack on contact. He was coping with the pain better, it still hurt like fuck, but by finding his core it seemed a little more distant, it was just something that was happening.

There was a pause in the assault and the Knightmaker approached. Guy feared the worst, no matter how far into his core he was, he would be unable to deny the agony of the Knightmaker's head slamming into his face. Though no blows to the face were allowed in training, his face throbbed with the pain of the previous day. The Knightmaker looked into his swollen purple eyes. 'How can you be my squire if you cannot defend yourself, and consequently me?' Guy offered a steely look as his answer. In itself that took all his resolve, the Knightmaker was an intimidating man. It took courage to even meet his gaze, let alone hold it. The Knightmaker turned to the stranger, 'You fixed his nose?' The stranger nodded, 'Fair enough.' He returned his gaze to Guy and with a flash of the fist punched Guy squarely in the mouth. The copper taste of blood filled his mouth, and his split bottom lip bought a new sensation of pain, that he could not use to make him stronger. 'Another half an hour.' called the Knightmaker as he returned to the house.

13

As dawn broke the following morning Guy had not slept. He had been boiling pots of water all night and made a big fire to heat rocks that he would put in the tub later. In the cool of the spring night he could see the steam, he just had to maintain it until the morning, and fill the tub. He was not going to have another defenceless day. The Knightmaker would have a full, hot bath that morning.

He was not given anything to break his fast on, and he had not been fed the day before, but that was far from his mind as the three of them approached, standing in a line, as they always did, Hawkins on the left of the Knightmaker, the stranger on the right. Steam was visible, the tub was full. The Knightmaker walked towards it.

'What the fuck is this?' he bellowed. 'Do you think me to share my bath with rocks?' He pulled up the sluice and the water flooded out. 'Defence training. Two Hours.'

When Hawkins and the stranger had left him tied to absorb his beating, it was the Knightmaker himself who came to untie him, standing before him. Guy barely had the strength to look up, his purple hands were testament to him passing out during his training. Guy could feel the eyes boring into him, and he had not the strength to stop them. He let the Knightmaker look, expecting another blow to the face, he feared that might break him. He had not been expecting to be defenceless and the days of beatings had taken their toll.

Instead he fell to the floor as the Knightmaker untied him, his hands tingling with fire as the leather straps were removed. 'There is a lump of rock over there that I do not like,' he gestured over his shoulder with his head. 'I have left you some tools with which to remove it. Start today.'

Guy was unable to talk or even acknowledge the order, and it was some time after he watched the Knightmaker's boots walk away that he started his crawl to the stream to try and ease his pain.

It was past noon before he emerged, and even though his body ached and his face still throbbed, he walked as a man should as he commenced cleaning the yard. He would not let them see that he suffered. Whilst clearing an area that he had not explored before he discovered a kind of dumping ground of the house, old tools and bits of metal, tree roots, rope, broken furniture, a bounty. In keeping with his approach to clearing the yard, he did quick superficial work to make it appear that progress was being achieved. Clearing away the overgrown plants made a big difference, he left the pile of junk undisturbed, taking only as much rope as he could find. He made three large nets with the thickest rope he had, and set them to soak in the stream while he examined the rock that the Knightmaker had spoken of. There was an outcrop of rock to the right of the gate, it did look out of place, but it was huge, probably ten feet high, over three feet wide and cropping at least 6 feet from the cliff that made up the wall there. He searched for the tools that he had been told he was to use, finding only a five foot long, heavy metal bar. It was heavier than the greatest greatsword he had held, it took much of his strength and caused pain in his body to even pick it up. He could not understand how it would break the rock. There was no hammer, no points, and no wedges. How could he be expected to break the rock with a heavy metal bar? It was not even pointed so he could not try to pry the rock apart at its crevices. Seeing no other option he swung the metal bar at the rock. The impact jolted through his wrists, and his entire body, but a few tiny chips of rock were removed. He swung again, harder. The shock hurt him again, pain coursing through him, but he swung again, and again. His anger at his situation was fuelling the strikes. Grunting, almost screaming with each strike, he watched at each blow reduced the outcrop a pebble at a time. *It would take forever,* he realised and swung the bar in frustration. A chip of the rock flew up and imbedded itself in his face just below his cheek. The bar fell from his hand and Guy fell to his knees, his hands instinctively reaching for the pain. He rolled on the floor as the pain exploded in his face. Breathing heavily he forced himself to sit and pulled the two inch wide piece of stone from his face with a scream. Blood flowed from the wound as he looked at the piece of stone he had removed. Shaped like half an arrowhead it was pointed and flat, and he saw from the blood how far it had been in his face. In agony he crawled again to the stream to clean his latest wound and then curled aball to let sleep take away the pain.

Guy awoke as something hit him sharply in the back. Seconds later something whizzed over his head and into the fire sending sparks into the air. Instinctively he rolled taking cover behind a nearby tree, his mind whirring. *Was he being attacked?* He would have to take them on without weapon since he was separated from his sword, he did not even have his belt. Seconds passed and there were no other noises. After a minute or so of silence in the night he started to relax. His sleeping mind woken by panic was starting to assess. It was dark, and cloudy, so he could not tell the hour. The fire was burning low. Panic gripped him again. He had not started on the bath. Listening intently, slack jawed, to open his ears, his mind formulated a plan. He waited a while until he was calm, focussed. He did not know the hour, but no matter, he knew he was behind schedule. Not knowing how long he had caused him anxiety that he could not accept, it was the overriding emotion. He did not want another day like the one that had just passed, he did not know if he could take it. They were trying to break him, he knew, and they had come close, but in his mind he was driven by love, and love was stronger than anything. As his rush of blood started to wane, the pain returned. His entire face was subject to a deep sharp pain that seemed to radiate from behind his face, his body was little more than a dull throb. It was fair to say that he had never known pain like it, but he knew that it was just the beginning.

He forced his aching body into action, first rebuilding the fire, extending it as he had the night before. When it was well ablaze he would add the rocks to absorb heat. He used the large pan to boil water as he filled the tub with the first half dozen buckets. He had discovered the previous night that a ratio of six buckets to one pan of hot water kept the chill off enough to be able to add heat more quickly. While he waited for the pan to boil he checked the rope nets he had left soaking in the stream. He would have to adapt his strategy since he did not know whether he had the time to boil a dozen pans of water. He collected more rocks from the stream and added another dozen buckets of water before the first pan boiled. He added that and refilled it. He was working quickly and efficiently, but he did not allow his mind's mischief to let him relax. There was still no indication as to the hour, and he was still far behind schedule. He would have to continue to work as he was, and even then, it may not be enough to see the tub full. Another two dozen buckets and the tub was over a third full. He added a boiled pan and set another before arranging his rope nets near the rocks in the fire. Using bits of old metal and a broken shovel he positioned three rocks in each of the two nets. They sizzled as the rocks made contact, but the rope held. He tied both nets to contain the rocks, and carried them one at a time to the tub. Holding the nets straight armed out in front of him, he waddled to the tub, and then defying his knotted shoulders lifted the nets and gently lowered them into the tub. The water sizzled as the stones, he hoped, transferred their heat.

After seeing to the fire and adding more rocks from the stream he went about filling the tub. Efficient, focussed determined, he was finding strength from somewhere in his broken body. Bucket after bucket, pan after pan. He swapped the rocks, almost pausing to congratulate himself on his nets, instead he continued. Always moving, driving himself forward, always forward. When the false dawn turned the cloudy night sky a dark shade of purple, the tub was over three quarters full and he felt that he was back on schedule. The change in light gladdened his soul as it revealed the vapour rising from the tub. Still he drove himself forward, every step an effort, every bucket an achievement. If he thought he was in pain before, he had a whole new understanding of it at that moment. Occasionally he caught himself grunting with effort, He was sweating in the chill morning air and driving himself harder than he could remember. It was a process that was working, and would only work if he maintained the rhythm. Buckets, pan, rocks.

He used the light of the morning to scavenge some fragrant and healing leaves from the bank of the stream, and put them to steep in the tub, as he set the last pan of water to boil. He had just replaced the rocks in the nets and would use the pan and another bucket to top up the tub when he removed them. There was little he could do until it boiled except squeeze and collect the leaves, to extract all that he could from them. The sun had ridden the sky for an hour when he removed the nets, topping the tub with the last pan. After dropping them back at his camp he collapsed to the floor in exhaustion, his chest heaving as he finally allowed his body to relax. The tub was steaming well when he heard them come from the house. He staggered over to meet them, too exhausted to have the ignorant sense of achievement he had held the previous couple of mornings. He was too tired for hope that morning, and Guy did not take that to be a good thing.

The Knightmaker stepped forward in his robe, inspecting the tub and wafting the steam into his face. 'Finally, a fucking bath.' Guy looked up, too tired to be pleased, too tired to be anything, not even intimidated as the Knightmaker approached him. 'You have a new scratch.'

'A chip of rock from the outcrop.'

'You are almost ugly enough to be my squire. You have made me a bath, so I know you are determined and inventive. But can you fight? Today I will see for myself. Defence training. Three hours.' He turned away and headed back to the house, pausing at the tub. 'Clean yourself up first though, the bath is yours.'

As Guy immersed himself in the fragrant water he was pleased that the Knightmaker had not tested the temperature with his hand, for he would have surely found it too hot and opened the sluice. It was the hottest tub that he had ever been in, and more than a little uncomfortable. He felt like an apple that was poaching. He cleaned himself first, enjoying the cool morning air as his feet and legs suffered from the heat. His body, covered in welts and bruises from the beatings he had taken, screamed in protest as the water almost scolded him, but other than dips in streams this was the first bath he had had since Varen and he was going to make the most of it. For the briefest of moments he wondered what he would be doing had he never met the man of cups. He had to remind himself that he could not change what was. In three months, if he could see it through, he would be a knight. Perhaps not the most honourable approach, but a knight nonetheless. Once he was a knight he could be honourable, if indeed he still had it in him. A moment of dread spread through him, as he imagined the effect the training would have on him. Would he even be Guy of Waering at the end of it? Sir Guy? He washed away the dread as he submersed his head in the steaming waters, changing the world he was in. It was too hot and it hurt his facial wounds, in fact his whole face hurt. He felt like sobbing, he should have been pleased at his progress, instead he feared for his future.

By the time he approached the training area after applying some of Della's balm, and dressing in his last fresh shirt, he had pulled himself together, the three of them were waiting.

'Come,' the Knightmaker beckoned him over. He tossed over a wooden stick like the ones he had been beaten with for the last few days. 'You have earned the right to defend yourself. If you are smart you would have watched previously and learned the attacks. They all have names, and you will learn them all, but more importantly you will learn to defend yourself against them all. These moves are from the styles taught in castles to noblemen, the people, as a knight, you are most likely to meet in combat. Before anything else, you must learn to defend yourself, and you are only permitted defensive moves. If you attack, you will lose your right to defend yourself the following day. Is that clear?'

The Knightmaker had a look about him that said things were serious now. Guy nodded, believing that he had proven himself worthy.

'Then let's begin.'

He called out a word and Hawkins came at him with a diagonal downward attack. Guy had learned the sword in a castle, and this was a move he knew, he raised his stick to block and deflect the blow. Hawkins used the momentum to spin and land a blow on Guys exposed ribs. It put Guy on one knee.

'We're not fucking around anymore,' called out the Knightmaker. 'You must learn to defend, or you will be hurt.'

He called out another name and the stranger stepped forward, Guy parried three of the stranger's thrusts before the stranger slammed his stick into Guys hand causing him to drop the stick. 'You must be more aware. Quicker. A man cannot defend himself if he cannot hold a sword. We go again.' Guy picked up his stick and stood to face the stranger. Three parries again then the stranger pivoted and slammed his stick into Guys side. He winced, but did not go down. 'You are not a tree, you need to be lighter on your feet. You need to move.'

For three hours this continued, no matter how many moves he blocked or parried, there was always another one in the sequence that clobbered him. After each blow the Knightmaker spoke. Towards the end Guy was barely able to hold his stick. His arms had taken a battering and he struggled to maintain his grip, such was the extent of the pain.

'A knight without armour is no knight at all,' the Knightmaker said at the end of the session. 'This is just sticks, what will you do when we get to the training swords?' The Knightmaker turned away, 'After noonshine, clean the yard and get rid of that fucking rock.'

He arrived back at his camp as the Knightmaker and Hawkins were passing through the gate. The stranger was returning to the house, after leaving what looked like bread, cheese and fruit near his camp. *How long had he been?* After they left, he remembered embracing the pain as he forced his hands to move, to regain movement. He had absorbed the pain and used it to make him stronger, and it had hurt like hells. His food went in a flash, a man of his size needed more. A quick and focussed effort saw further superficial clearing of the yard, and then he was in the pile of rubble rummaging through. He was sure that he had seen some bits that could be useful when he took the rope previously. He took a few things back to his camp, a pair of old boots odd bits of metal and leather cord from an old doublet that had been left to rot. Back at his camp he rummaged through his things until he found a large leather pouch. Using his knife and some of the leather cord he fashioned a simple mask of leather to protect his face. He wondered over to the rock and secured it, leaving just a slit for his eyes. The iron bar was heavy in his beaten arms, it hurt just to hold it. He was dreading the shock of the first impact.

Sensing something, he turned round to see he stranger silently approaching. He held his hands open for the iron bar, then waved Guy away as he took it. The stranger held the iron bar as a sword, and showed a move from earlier, slamming the pole into the rock. He repeated it before moving onto another move, joining two together, pausing occasionally to make sure Guy could see what he was doing. He was performing the moves that had been used against him earlier with the iron bar. He did not break anything significant off, but he did not seem to be trying to, he was concentrating on the moves. He ended with a flurry of moves, spinning, pivoting, dancing, striking the rock at great speed from all angles, ending with an overhead downward strike that looked as if it could cut a man in half, lengthways. Then he simply handed the bar back to Guy and walked back to the house.

'Thank you,' Guy called after him. There was no acknowledgment. Guy held up the bar and had a few tentative strikes, imitating the stranger. The shock hurt his arms down to his bones, but he pushed through it, as he had everything that day. He pushed himself to strike it again and again, simple strikes, as he repeated the moves over and over. By the time he was grunting in exhaustion, and the metal bar fell from his hands for the last time, there was little of the rock gone, but he had learnt some offence that day, and that was progress.

14

Twenty one days had passed, twenty one days that had required everything that Guy had to give to get through them, and he had given it. Every day of the three weeks had brought its own fresh hell for him to endure, but no matter how bad a day had been, he awoke each morning willing to give everything he had to get through the next one. He was getting better, and that was all that mattered.

Guy was deftly parrying blows coming in from both the stranger and Hawkins, he was moving swiftly, and confidently. He had trained against two swords in the castle, but nowhere near the calibre of warrior as the sticks that attacked him. He had quickly come to realise that the stranger was as skilled a warrior as he could imagine, and while Hawkins was little more than an educated rogue, he had been well educated. He struck with the occasional low blow, but these were no longer admonished by the Knightmaker, for he had to learn to defend himself against any style, against any man. Not every sword he faced would be castle trained. Hawkins took advantage of this whenever he could, but the leather he wore under his linen shirt prevented too great a harm coming to him.

Later the same day Guy danced around the outcrop of rock landing blows with the iron bar. He was nowhere close to the display the stranger had performed, but he was getting faster, stronger, he was starting to move without thought which led to the fluidity with which he performed the moves. Unaware he was being watched Guy was actually enjoying himself.

'He reminds me of you,' said the Knightmaker to the stranger, under his breath, 'always training, always improving, never complaining. He pushes himself.' The stranger watched on in silence. 'I think he is ready to move on. Or he would be if he had any fucking armour.'

The Knightmaker walked over to Guy, who was wearing his leather mask. Beneath it his face had healed leaving angry looking scars, the worst of which was from the stone chip that flew into his cheek, which still brought him pain. Guy stopped swinging when he noticed the Knightmaker's approach.

'A knight without armour is no knight at all,' he said looking Guy squarely in the eye. It was still by far the most intimidating experience of Guy's life. 'You have paid for me to train you, but I cannot train you further if you do not have armour. Take some time, go and see Smith, return with armour and training can continue. Take the cart, you can bring back provisions.'

It did not seem right for Guy to be going on a journey without Charger, but Charger would never pull a cart, and the Knightmaker said that it was to make sure he came back. There were two horses pulling the cart, and with it empty he made good time. There were no diversions, he travelled long days and made camp beside the road. He exercised every morning, but that was the only luxury he allowed himself. It was late on the fourth day when he arrived in Varen, and instead of trying to negotiate his way through the closing market with the cart he made his way to the *Four Kin Inn*, hitching the cart outside.

'Have you come for the night we owe you?' the old woman asked from behind the counter without looking up.

'No, I am happy to pay,' Guy replied. Some of the smile was gone from his voice.

'Three coppers for a meal room and your horses. You can leave the cart in the yard.'

Guy placed four coppers on the counter having noticed the improved prices.

'One for the stable boys.'

'I'll see that they get it. Up the stairs, last door on the left, the key is inside.' Never once lifting her eyes from behind the counter, she continued, 'Cause any trouble and you will have to answer to me.'

'Of course,' Guy replied. They seemed to be the words of the city. He made his way up the stairs, wondering what it was that occupied the old woman behind the counter. Her money perhaps, or maybe she was an artist. He entered the room, thinking it strange that he had the same one. He had hardly any kit, just enough to see him through a couple of nights on the road. He lay on the floor and sleep found him swiftly.

He awoke to the smell of food, real food, when he opened his door there was a meal of a duck, some boiled roots and a small bread with a horn of ale. It was among the best food that he had ever tasted, the Knightmaker may be training him, but the food was poor and scarce. The meal was divine in comparison. He sucked the bones clean savouring every morsel. The meal had made him feel so much better, he would have fuel for the next day. For too long he had been running on empty. He read a while from the Lord Knight's book, he would get some more books while he was in Varen, but sleep soon found him, a content and well-earned sleep.

Guy moved on foot through the market, letting nothing catch his eye. He would have time to shop later, first the blacksmith. It was as if the great swarm of people in the market organically parted for him and he found himself approaching the workshop in no time.

'Hoy! Have you finally seen sense and come to work for me?'

'Alas, not yet. I am seeking armour.'

'Do you have the coin?'

Guy nodded, 'Three gold,' he said holding out his hand.

'Ah, good for you. Come, sit, tell me of your training.' The Blacksmith took one gold coin from Guys hand. 'I will take this now, the rest on completion.'

'I would rather you take it all now, while I have the coin.'

The blacksmith shrugged and took the rest. They talked until Noonshine, the blacksmith reminiscing of his time with the Knightmaker. It comforted Guy to some degree to hear of the tales, and that his treatment was not as unduly harsh as he occasionally felt. The Knightmaker was a cold and distant man, but the blacksmith assured him that if he was not liked, he would not be there.

Guy talked of his timescale and the provisions he had been told to get, the blacksmith said that he would be able to help him. 'You can stay here in the workshop, bring your cart. You can help out around the forge to pay your way. I cannot make your armour in the time you have. It takes time to source and work such steel. I can however make you a set of training armour, one that can take the battering you are in for, and when your proper set is ready I will send for you.' He gestured to a pile of old armour in a corner of the yard. 'We will use that. Do you know how to use a smelter?'

'I have seen it,' he replied.

'I will show you. Before I can start you will have to melt that down into bars.'

He guided Guy through the first run, and supervised the second, leaving him to it after that to continue his own work. Guy worked the bellows and fed the fire into the afternoon and a dozen of the bar moulds were full. He went off through the market covered in sweat and soot to collect the cart. He would stop at a few shops on the way so that he could navigate the market with the cart in the evening when it would be quieter.

Once he had hitched the horses in Smith's yard, Guy started sifting through the pile of discarded armour. A thought had occurred to him. Instead of mixing different types of armour together, he could select those closest to each other and have cleaner, more defined bars to work with. He was aware it was just a practice suit, but training did not just have to be physical. If he was going to learn a new skill, he would learn it as well as he could. He sifted through and cursed the occasional pieces of good steel that had been melted down with cheap metal, thinking how useful it could be for him now. Spreading the pile across the yard into various types did not take long. Of course, the larger the size of the pile the poorer quality the metal was, but there was more than enough decent metal for a training suit, even for a man of his size.

After emptying and stacking the dozen bars he had smelted earlier, he set about refilling the moulds. He would get the blacksmith to use the new ones first, for he needed over a dozen. There was less slag to remove with the better metal, but doing smaller batches meant that it was late by the time he had filled the dozen moulds and retired. The cot was big, and he enjoyed not sleeping on the floor.

The noise of the market woke him at dawn, other people's activity soon guilted him into getting up. It had been so long since he had slept abed that he did not want it to end. He exercised and broke his fast. He worked folding steel through until dusk, stopping only for noonshine, and so the blacksmith could take his measurements. The steel had to be folded at least twice. Smith had explained that folding was the greatest skill of a blacksmith. A folded steel is a stronger steel, and in weapons, a sharper steel. He had been folding for over two days, every strike of the hammer resonating through his body, every one made him stronger. Fire and steel were all that existed.

When the steel had been folded, over a week had passed since Guy had left Eastfield Manor. He had aimed to be back in less than two. He knew that he was not going to make it, he would do well to be back inside three weeks. He told the blacksmith he had to go away for a few days, Smith had replied that Guy was not a prisoner, he could do as he wished. Smith suggested that he leave the cart and borrow his horse. The blacksmith was a big man, not as big as Guy, but he was confident the horse would be able to carry him swiftly to wherever he was heading.

The horse was indeed swift and unlike Charger was able to maintain a solid pace. Guy eased into the village of Monkspath mid-afternoon on the second day of his travel. He had covered the ground so much quicker than the leisurely pace in the opposite direction with Ash and his family. Only fifteen minutes later he tethered the horse outside the farmhouse. The village had been quiet with most people out in the fields, but an old man had pointed him in the right direction. Once he had arrived though he did not know what to do. He hovered for a moment before announcing his arrival by calling out.

'Farmer Ash,' he shouted. Four times he called until the old woman emerged from the side of the building announcing he was out, and looking bothered by the intrusion. This melted away the second she recognised Guy.

'Ash. Come, we have a visitor.'

The two of them stood looking at each other, the old woman knew pain, and recognised it in Guy. There was a sorrow, but also the resilience, the inner strength to go on. He inhaled, stood taller, stronger. Little Ash came running from the side of the house, stopping beside his grandmother and looking to Guy. Possibly the brightest smile Guy had ever seen beamed at him, and Little Ash ran towards Guy, hugging his waist. Guy ruffled his hair, unsure what else to do. When Little Ash finally released the hug, Guy crouched down to look at him.

'You have grown,' he said smiling at the boy.

'I have. Are you a knight now?'

'No little man, I am not. I have come to see your parents.'

'What happened to your face?' He moved his little hands to the scars. Guy did not stop him.

'I am training to be a Knight though. Training is tough, but soon I will visit you as a Knight. I'll bring Charger and my armour. Where are your parents?'

'Da is out in the fields. Ma is out collecting herbs.'

'Can you take me to your father?'

Little Ash looked to the old woman for approval before leading Guy past her. She nodded at him, he nodded back fighting a smile.

Little Ash led Guy through the hedges of two fields before he spotted the farmer on the far side of a large field filled with young oats. The fields at Monkspath were big, far larger than those in Waering, even those on the outskirts of Varen. He could not begin to imagine the amount of oats from this one field alone. It looked as if it would feed the whole of Waering through an entire winter. Little Ash called out to his father, but with the sun behind them he knew the farmer would not be able to see who it was. He gestured that he was coming, his body showing a little frustration at having to stop what he was doing, as he set off around the field. He approached shielding his eyes from the sun, not recognising Guy until he was about two dozen feet away. Ash approached silently, smiling and they clasped hands, hugging with it.

'Guy. What a surprise. What brings you to Monkspath?'

'You and your wife, and Little Ash of course,' he replied, ruffling the boy's hair again. 'I am hoping to buy some more of her balm. I am running low.'

'She is out collecting. She will not be back until the evening meal. She will be so happy to see you. Let's go back to the house and get you something to drink.'

'Do not let me disrupt your day. You were busy.'

'It is nothing that cannot wait. Come.'

'Well, perhaps you can show me your fields first. I have never seen one so big. How does it work?' The farmer looked to Guy, questioning whether the inquiry was genuine or polite, in the end he decided that he did not care. He loved to talk of his farming. He sent Little Ash back to the house to help his Grandmother prepare the meal. Reluctant though he was he set off without question. 'He's a good boy that you have there.'

'Aye, he is. For now.'

They watched him scurry through the hedgerow, the farmer's words resonating in his mind. 'For now.'

That was all that they could really hope for, that things are good for now. The future was impossible to determine, now was all they had.

Guy and the farmer walked the fields and talked until the sun was low in the sky.

'We should get back. They will be angry at me for keeping you to myself.'

'They should be angry at me, this is really the greatest farming I have ever seen.'

'Seen many farms have you?'

'No,' Guy replied and they both laughed.

As they approached the back of the house the rest of them were outside, around a table next to a large fire. Della had returned and waved as they approached. When Little Ash spotted them he ran over to greet them.

'Da,' he started excitedly. 'I helped Gran with the fire. She let me light it.'

'Well done Ash, for that is a great fire wouldn't you say Guy.'

'Very good indeed.'

They approached and they made a fuss of Guy, chastised Ash for keeping him so long and ate a happy meal. At the farmer's request Guy did not mention the balm in front of the old woman. It made Guy's heart sing with joy as he imagined just such meals with Phylissa and their family.

It was late and the waning moon was high on its arc when Little Ash fell asleep in his grandmother's lap. It had been such a wonderful evening of laughter and smiles. Guy could not remember the last time he laughed so freely. The old woman scooped Little Ash up in her arms and took him off to bed. It was not long after they had entered the house when Della Spoke.

'Ash says you have come for more balm. You can't have got through two pots already. That lasts most people, active people, a year, not a month.'

'Training can be brutal on the body.'

'So I see,' said Della, tracing out the location of Guys scars on her own face. 'You must let me examine you in the morning so that I may find the best balm for your needs.'

'There's no need,' Guy replied. 'More of the same is all I need.'

'You'll have none at all if you do not let me examine you. Ash can be there if that is what you are worried about.'

Guy looked to her husband, who simply shrugged. Della had the same sharp tongue as her mother, only she hid it better. It was late, he did not want to argue, he simply did not want them to worry about what he knew to be beneath his shirt.

'Alright,' he conceded.

They finished the skin of wine between them. It was the first time he had seen Della drink. Her natural happiness was exacerbated and it made Guy smile.

'It is late, let's get you a cot set up in the house.'

'Do not bother on my account, I am happy to sleep by the fire.'

'You are our guest, and I will not have a guest of ours sleep outside.' The tone was back, but Guy let it wash over him.

'I like to sleep beneath the stars from time to time, it helps me connect with the earth.'

This time it was Della who looked to Ash, he repeated his shrug of the shoulders and they laughed.

'Next time you sleep in the house,' Della offered in a self-mocking tone, knowing that she would not win. Ash felt it was important to connect with the earth, as did she. She could not argue.

'Of course.'

15

Guy awoke with a dry mouth and a dry mind. He had not drunk wine since he had started training and was reminded of the price that must be paid. It was worth it though. He smiled at the previous night's happiness, nothing specific, just the general demeanour of the evening with Ash and his family. It was Della who was responsible for his smile though. She was blessed with the gift of happiness and she was very generous in how she shared it with others. Ash was a lucky man, but perhaps, it was he who kept her smiling. Guy hoped that he would keep Phylissa smiling. He lay a while listening to the morning sounds. He had not had the chance to dream of Phylissa, or anything else, for a long time. Training was so brutal that at the end of each day he was simply happy to have survived. Work with the fire and steel was hard, and the body was so tired it slept whether the mind wished it or not. For the briefest of moments he glimpsed a night like the one before, but at his estate, with Phylissa and his own son. As he grasped for a few seconds more, he was bought back to his real existence by movement from the house. It was Della with Ash, she had a jug, and Ash carried three cups. He sat up as they approached, his body stiff and cracking.

They greeted each other and shared pleasantries as they drank the water. So impressed had they been with Guys fruit water, it was something they had adopted and used in their own lives, this water was steeped in fresh fruit, and early summer berries, and was crisp and refreshing. Before long his mind was clear of the wine of the previous night wine.

'Right,' announced Della, 'Remove your shirt and let's see what we are dealing with.'

With silent reluctance Guy reached down to remove his linen shirt. They both gasped as he pulled it up, his body covered as it was with bruises, welts and occasional splits of the skin. He figured it probably looked worse than it was. The few days with the blacksmith had allowed them to colour and start to heal.

'Gods, you have bruises upon bruises. What are they doing to you?' She didn't wait for an answer as she moved in to inspect the wounds. 'No wonder you are nearly out of balm. Guy, you cannot keep doing this, it will kill you.'

'I know. I am visiting Varen to buy armour, so I shall be protected when I return.'

Della continued making exclamations as she poked at him, ignoring his winces. Ash had a look on his face that was hard to read, shock, yes, maybe a little disgust, some sadness, but somehow a look of defiance, of pride? Ash was a man who put all his energy into his life, his work, perhaps it was a look of respect towards another who was doing the same, from a man further down the path.

Guy had drifted with his thoughts, and did not hear as Della continued to talk, but was aware of the silence, as if they were awaiting an answer. Returning to reality Guy stood and followed Della and Ash to an outbuilding near the house. Ash went inside the house while Guy followed Della into the building and she closed and locked the door behind them. It was dark, only filtered light penetrated the hessian sacks that covered the window. The first thing that hit him was the smell of fresh herbs that hung all around the room. Underneath this was a musty smell, of damp moss and something familiar that he could not place. There were Jars of liquid of various colours, grinding pots, mixing pots and a host of other tools. Della was expertly rummaging and collecting, Guy simply stood awkwardly, feeling as if his size filled the entire room.

She ground some seeds and put them in a mixing pot before finely slicing some fresh herbs and adding them. She gently pounded them together with a stone, cleaning it with her finger before placing it down.

'We must let them mingle a while,' she said as he watched her get to work on some bark, bashing it and grinding until it became a rough powder. 'There are seven jars by the window. I want you to smell them all and bring me the one that does not smell.'

Guy looked to her, unsure of the request, but she was already on to grinding a tough root. He looked to the window. There were seven jars of liquid, all plugged with what looked like live moss, ranging from almost clear, through golden to a thick dark amber looking liquid. As he approached the jars he looked around again, unsure whether to disturb the moss. Picking up the first jar he gently lifted the moss from the side of the jar and tentatively sniffed the jar. Give her the one that does not smell. That one smelled. It smelled of piss. He recoiled slightly at the realisation.

'What is this?' he asked already knowing the answer.

'It is my water,' she replied as if it was perfectly normal. 'Ash found a book about three years ago, *Healing Practices of the Old World*. It is strange, but it works. I use the book and the knowledge of my Mother's ancestors to make my own medicines. Find the one that does not smell and bring it to me.'

Guy did not quite know what to do. He wanted to appear mature about it, but there was something about smelling a woman's water in front of her that did not seem normal. As he peeled back the moss on the second jar, all he could think was that he was about to smell her piss, it did not seem right. That kind of smell was usually met with disgust, especially in Waering where any waste room was well adorned with bunches of lavender. Waste room smells were something that was never spoken of in Waering, yet he found himself actively smelling the waste of a woman. He smelled them all until he got to the fifth one. That one did not have the smell of the others, someway this one smelled almost sweet, and gentle on the nose. He went to turn and tell Della.

'Smell them all,' she said before he had begun to turn his head. He moved onto the next jar, taking a more confident sniff. He almost retched, and hoped he managed to hide it from Della, though he felt his eyes watering. Simply wafting the moss on the last jar was enough to confirm what he thought and he went back to the fifth jar peeling back the moss again. He did not want his last memory of smelling Della's water to be unpleasant. Every time he saw her, he knew he would remember this, so he inhaled slowly and deeply trying to savour the gentle sweet aroma that he could associate this experience with in the future. He turned and offered the jar to Della.

'This one.'

She took the jar and nodded, covering the seeds and leaf mixture with a splash of the liquid from it. Guy watched amazed as the mixture fizzed and bubbled in the mixing pot.

'I have work to do. Can you let yourself out? I will lock the door when you have gone.'

She was busy, adding some of the jars contents to the root she was grinding down, making it into a thick paste.

'Of course.'

Guy closed the door behind him, waited a moment as he found himself unable to see in the bright of the day, and headed back to the fire to dress properly, his mind thinking, but not judging. There was still some fruit water in the jug which he enjoyed before heading up to the house. The old woman and the two Ashes were about to finish breaking their fast, but as Guy entered the old woman shot to her feet and retrieved Guy's plate. Beaten eggs, sliced pork and two breads adorned it.

'Let's get some of that weight back on you,' the old woman said gesturing him to sit. 'They are not feeding you properly wherever you are. Look at you, you are just skin and bones.'

Guy had looked at himself, and while he could not deny that he had lost weight, he was far from skin and bone. He imagined himself to be well chiselled beneath the bruises and swellings.

He spent the day with Ash in the fields while his son and mother by law prepared a meal and a bath. Guy had protested initially at the thought of them having to make him a bath, the memories of his own ordeal all too prevalent in his mind, but when Little Ash had shown him their method of making a bath he agreed. A big metal vat sat above a fire pit, the sluice flooded water directly into the tub. So clever, yet so simple. If only he'd had such a set up at Eastfield Manor. It would have saved him much pain.

Guy and the farmer talked throughout the morning as they weeded a field. Guy harassed them from the ground with a hoe, the farmer swept them up behind him. Ash had shown him that a delicate touch was more likely to remove the whole root. Guy, as ever, used it as training and became fascinated by the hoe, he could turn that into a weapon. As if on cue Ash told him a story of an earl who had ruled through fear. He did not allow the farmers weapons and claimed ten to the dozen of their crop. The farmers, not to be outdone, learned to fight with the tools that they used in the fields. One autumn when the earl came to collect his bounty the farmers dispatched him and his men meaning that they could feed their families that winter.

It was not until they stopped for noonshine when the farmer asked him about his time with Della.

'So how was it with Della this morning?'

Guy a little flushed searched for words. 'It was… educational.'

'You know she lets no one into her workshop, not even her mother. I have only been in once, when I was struck down with fever and close to death. She saved my life, and that was the only time I have ever been in there.'

Guy had nothing to say. He was becoming more overwhelmed with the family's kindness with every minute he spent with them. 'To Della, healing is a very spiritual thing, very personal, when I found a book, something really connected with her. The power of healing in a person's water can be phenomenal. Sometimes the old ways are the best.'

Guy listened intently, as he did whenever anyone told him anything of value, subduing a little frustration at how little he knew of the world. There was so much to learn of it, and he was reminded of his insignificance. They talked into the afternoon. It was rare that Ash had such attentive ears as he explained how plants grow and what they need, about the seasons and anything else that floated through his mind. Ash sent him back to the house in the mid-afternoon to have his bath.

Guy relaxed in the tub that had been scented with oils, no doubt more for their healing properties than superficial scent. The whole sensation he described in his mind as zingy. Zing. His mind was about to chastise itself again for his lack of knowledge, his lack of words, but as it attempted, it was met with no resistance, found no purchase, and soon faded away. The warm water relaxed him, taking him back to the hot springs near Waering where he would make his home. He remembered how he would lie in those springs and let his mind wander for hours, dreaming of the life he wanted, and for a moment allowed himself a vision of Phylissa and their son on the manicured lawns by the river. A beautiful image was forming and his mind was ready to embrace it when he heard a lock turn that snatched his attention away. Guy opened his eyes, and when his vision cleared he saw Della starting towards him from her workshop. Her focussed and determined demeanour said that she was still very much working. For a moment he wondered how he must appear to people when he too was working towards something. How that when someone is focussed on the future, they neglect the now, a sacrifice almost, for the want of a better life.

Della arrived as he considered whether he was neglecting now, and he never got to his answer.

'Let me have another look at your wounds.'

Guy found it strange to hear them referred to as wounds for he did not consider them as such, just the result of training without armour. A wound was something picked up in battle. He imagined a Knight was seldom without bruises and cuts. Guy used each one to make him stronger. He sat up and put his hands behind his head as she instructed. 'You must be careful where the skin is broken,' she said prodding and poking at him. 'These can easily get infected, and the area is already traumatised. I have a balm for these areas which you must apply little and often. It will not improve performance if you apply more, so use a gentle amount.'

She started prodding at his bruises until he reacted to the pain. 'These are just as serious. You are bleeding inside, and the blood cannot flow as it should. I have a lotion for this, but you must not get it on open wounds. Am I clear?' Guy nodded knowing not what else he could do. 'This lotion contains fire berries and must be applied with a cloth. You do not want it on your fingers as it will be rubbed on your eyes, your mouth and other parts,' she said motioning beneath the water, 'Believe me, you do not want that.' Guy took her word for it. 'You shall have a paste that sets hard for deep cuts, and another two pots like you had before. It should last you a dozen months, and I shall give you nothing else for half a year. You must not put your body through such trauma.'

Guy did not really know what to say. He was not going to stop; he would become a knight and have Phylissa's hand, or die trying. Instead he thanked her.

'Thank you Della. It means a lot, what you are doing for me. How much do I owe you?'

'I will take no coin for this,' Della replied sharply.

'But you have wasted the day to make these, when you could have used it for something else. Besides I came here to buy some more balm.'

'You can buy my balm in Varen, you know this. I will be insulted if you offer me coin again.' For a second the stern business-like demeanour faded. 'Your friendship is more than payment enough.'

She smiled briefly, Della's smile, her gift of happiness. 'I will see you in the morning. I have much work to do.' As she left to return to her workshop, a strange wave of happy sadness washed over Guy that he did not understand.

16

It was early afternoon when he arrived back at Varen. He had left later than anticipated and had taken a day longer than expected but he did not allow it to cause him distress. Guy walked the blacksmith's horse through the city gates without anyone paying him particular mind. He passed the Four Kin Inn and wondered what the old woman was doing behind the counter; passed the man of cups with his usual crowd around him, and felt that he was acknowledged with a nod. Guy thought about playing again before he left, though he had nothing to play with. He joined the flow of the market easing his way to the blacksmith's quarter, from there to Smith's workshop. It was shut up, and the blacksmith was not there. Neither was the Knightmaker's cart. He tethered and tended to the horse, started a fire from the furnace embers and headed into the market to buy food.

It was late evening when the blacksmith returned and he was grateful of the goat leg roasting over the fire. They washed it down with Ale before the blacksmith asked Guy to unload the cart while he tended to the horses. The cart was laden with bars of steel which Guy began stacking neatly by the workshop.

'This steel is from the stone press forge, it's one of the strongest steels in Rodina,' Smith told him as they finished their meal.' They have a huge stone press that they use to work it. Many men raise the slab and drop it on the metal. It is a sight to behold for any blacksmith. It all needs folding at least once more though, and hammered to remove the last of any impurities. You will be busy tomorrow.'

The blacksmith seemed to give Guy a once over with his eyes. 'I have your training armour ready for fitting, but that can wait until morning. Rest well tonight.'

The blacksmith departed, leaving Guy alone with his thoughts and a big pile of steel. He gathered the bones and remaining scraps of the goat meat, and put them in a big pot with water to boil down. He did it almost without thought, for something else occupied his mind, it had done since the journey back from the farm. Della had spoken of friendship, and on reflection Ash was perhaps the person he spoke to with freedom more than any other. They had a bond. He had never really had friends before. Growing up he had always on the outside because of his size and ability. That, and the fact that he was a steward's son. Not born of a family of status, yet afforded too many privileges to be seen as common. He had ended up floating somewhere between the two, and accepted by neither. Aside from Phylissa there was no one he really cared about. He hoped that he could be a good friend, but questioned how he could, if he did not know what friendship was. Ash would put him at ease with some simple, yet wise words, but Ash was not there, and it did not sit well with him. It made him feel vulnerable.

Guy had been folding steel for hours, he could no longer feel his arm, yet it still worked as sparks flew with each blow. His body poured with sweat from the heat and effort, but still, he continued on, without letting the quality of his work slip. This was going to be his armour and his contribution would be the best that he could offer. He had been folding all morning and he was little more than halfway through the pile, there were still over a dozen bars left. The blacksmith had left in the morning with the list of provisions. Time was running out, and thanks to his trip to see Della, he was going to be later back to Eastfield Manor than he planned. There had been no time limit set, but occasionally thoughts of repercussions for taking too long entered his mind. He did not let that which he did not know concern him, so he let the thoughts pass through him. Concern was rising though, he had so much yet to do. He had planned on a day getting his own provisions. There was no way that he would be able to fold the rest of the bars. He drained the wooden cup of water and was set to attack another bar when the blacksmith returned. He was not carrying any provisions.

'Have you done folding already?' He called seeing Guy not hammering.

'I am just over half way.'

'Leave the rest. I only need about 15 bars for your armour. There will be more folding for you tomorrow. Come eat. I have fresh bread.'

While they ate they talked of what needed doing. Guy folding the steel would take the whole of the next day. The blacksmith had not sourced all of the provisions and suggested Guy finished getting them with what was left of the afternoon, before returning to have his training armour fitted. The blacksmith would work on that the following day while Guy folded the steel. Then he could return to Eastfield Manor.

After enjoying his noonshine Guy headed straight out into the market, still covered in sweat and soot as he was. People paid him as much attention as ever, none. Looking as he did he found it easier to trade for better prices, perhaps being taken as one of their own. He made arrangements with three vendors to deliver goods to the blacksmith the next day and moved out of the market towards the street with the bookshops. He would look at those later. There was one item on the list that he had not obtained. He searched through the streets and back alleys until he found what he had been looking for. He had seen the place last time he was in Varen, an apothecary. He had never seen one before and had not gone in last time. Now that he had a purpose, he would have preferred to have more time to explore it, for thanks to his time with Della, he felt that he would have a better understanding of what was there. He closed the door behind him, suddenly feeling enclosed. He had to duck and a smell crept up his nose that made him want to sneeze. He paused for a moment, allowing his eyes to adjust to the dim lighting. *What was it about these places that made him feel so out of place?*

'What might you be after?' called an old woman from behind the counter. She was small, seemed calm and someway part of the room.

'I am looking for white mist,' Guy replied, trying in some way to make it sound like he knew what he was talking about.

'White mist?' the old woman replied, 'and what might a young man like you be needing white mist for. Are your dreams so bad?'

'My dreams? No, my dreams are good. This is for my master.'

The old woman opened a drawer and placed a small glass vial on the counter. Its contents were white, and seemed to glow in the dimness of the room.

'I need four if you have them.'

The old woman looked up at him.

'Four? I don't have four, but he does not need four. Everyone must dream sometime.'

'I have been instructed to buy four, if you will not sell me them, perhaps I should find somewhere that will.'

Guy was bluffing. He did not have the time to find another apothecary. You either knew where they were or you did not. He sensed the woman knew he was bluffing, but he felt justified. He needed all the time he could get right now, and was not in the mood for wasting it.

The old woman opened the drawer and removed one further vial. 'You can take the two that I have, they are a silver each, but they are the purest white mist you will find. Your master will wake refreshed and without a bad head. White mist will replace his dreams.'

Guy handed over two silvers and the woman wrapped each vial in cloth before placing them in a small box and handing it to Guy. He thanked her and turned to leave. As his hand reached for the door, he paused.

'Do you have a copy of Healing Practices of the old world?'

'Does this look like a bookshop?' Guy flicked his eyes to a small pile of books about herbs. 'No I do not.'

'If you happen to come across one, do you think that you could keep it for me?'

'If I happen to come across a copy I shall be keeping it for myself.'

She sighed as Guy maintained his expectant look. 'If your master needs four vials of the white mist, you will be back soon enough, you can ask me again then. Tell him though, two drops is all he needs, no more, or he may not wake from his dreamless sleep.'

Guy shielded his eyes from the sun which spread a bright light, in contrast to the apothecary hut. They had not fully adjusted before he ducked into a bookshop. Neither they, nor any of the other bookshops, had the book he was after. Having learnt from his last experience he browsed each of the shops before making his purchases. This bought with it new problems because he saw so many books he could not decide what to buy. In the end he bought a book that Della had told him he should get, and an old book on smithing weapons and armour. He had wanted a book related to knights, but nothing jumped out at him except a copy of 'Legendary Weapons', but at six silvers he could not justify the cost. When he had his house though, he would have a room just for books and he would have a copy then.

Guy took the chance to dream of his future life as he walked back towards the market, he almost passed the messenger's office, as his dreams consumed him. He seldom had the time to dream as he used to, and other than being with Phylissa it was his favourite thing to do. He paid a copper for a message to be sent to her. It stated simply 'I am on the path that will bring me to your hand.' Somehow that simple act had him lighter on his feet and bought a smile to his face as he approached the market.

'Young Knight!' a voice called out. He looked round to see the man of cups closing up his stall. Guy brightened in recognition. 'You have not come to play this visit.'

'There is nothing else I need,' Guy smiled.

'You will always find something you need at my stall.'

'Then I have nothing to play with.'

'You will always find something to play with. You should come and play before you leave.'

'I will,' Guy nodded. The man of cups nodded back and continued his business. Guy meandered through the market wondering what he could play with, the thoughts of Phylissa long since faded.

By the time he returned to the blacksmith's it was empty, and while there was much he could be doing, his body commanded that he sleep, and before he knew, without even eating, he was laid out on the cot, submitted to his body's demands.

He did not awake with the sun, not until noises in the blacksmiths yard ended his sleep did the panic of the new day hit him. He had much to do and hoped only little of the day had been wasted. When he left the workshop he saw the blacksmith laying out the armour and a doublet for him to wear.

17

The armour felt big, heavy and cumbersome. Even the mismatched set that he had left in Boarton had fitted better. It had not been as strong, he was sure, but he would much rather be wearing that than the set he currently wore.

'It takes twice as much effort to walk when you are wearing armour. It takes twice the effort to do anything. Whilst armour is designed to protect a man, it can also be a weakness. You must learn to move in your armour as if you are not wearing it. Do you understand?' Guy mumbled inside his helm, unsure how he would ever feel comfortable in such a big and heavy suit. 'A man who lets his armour slow him down, is not long for this world. You need to be strong and fast. Let's take it off, I know what needs to be done. Besides you have work to do.'

Guy was relieved to be out of his armour, his body felt free again. Smith took him over to the fire and told him to break open a three foot long clay brick while he fed the furnace. He cracked the clay with a rock and pulled brittle chunks off. It was hot and his hands moved quickly, and it was not long until he wore thick smithing gloves and pulled what looked like two bars of steel from inside the clay brick. The steel was hot as he brushed off the remnants of the clay. The fire seemed to have burned the top of the bar, the soot would not come off.

'You need to forge these together and fold them a dozen times.'

Guy looked to the blacksmith, not protesting, but not simply accepting. 'A dozen times, for two reasons. One, it will make the steel strong, number two will reveal itself as time passes. *A dozen times!* Guy realised that it would take the entire day. He did not mind, it was for his armour. If he had to fold it a thousand times he would.

Guy had folded deep into the night, stopping only to eat, and have his training armour fitted twice more. The second time it had felt much better, but was still way too heavy. Instead of sleeping he had wrapped and packed his armour on the cart, along with the provisions that had been delivered throughout the day by various merchants. He had packed his things separately, pleased to be taking some luxuries with him. He knew that he would not fare so well for food once back at Eastfield Manor. When he had packed the cart he filled his skins and left a jug of the fruit water for the blacksmith. He had broth and a day old loaf to break his fast, and prepared to leave. It felt strange indeed to leave without Smith being there, but they had said their goodbyes the previous night. Guy allowed himself a look back when he nudged the horses through the workshop's gate, as dawn was only thinking about breaking, and offered a quiet thanks. The city was mostly sleeping. People cleaned the streets and the earliest of starters were making their way to begin their days. It was strange to see the city so quiet as the cart trundled quietly through it.

'Blessed indeed young knight, you will be my first game of the day. Do you know what that means?' Guy looked up surprised, the man of cups, who was setting up his stall, called from beneath his hood. Three men were sleeping nearby.

'That I have your services for the day if I win?' he replied in the kind of hushed voice pre-dawn demanded of decent men.

'Indeed, though rare is it that I do not win the first game.'

'Let one of them have it,' Guy said waving his hand towards the sleeping men, 'I have no need of your services today for I must leave.'

'A noble act, but you cannot change what is meant to be. You are the first game. Should you win, you shall have my services for a day. It does not have to be today, I can man my stall as usual.'

The man of cups looked towards the men who slept beside his stall. 'You snooze, you lose. With what do you play?' Guy looked around the cart, for a moment panicking that he was wasting the man of cup's time.

'I have nothing to play with.'

The man of cups spread his hands, 'You have a whole cart full of things, but nothing to play with?'

'Alas much of it is not mine, and what is, is carefully selected and needed.'

'You will always find something to play with.'

Guy rummaged through a bag, not really knowing what he was looking for, he needed everything. His hands paused for a moment on his book of healing herbs that he had bought on his first visit. He had a new one suggested by Della, and he had read much of the old book several times. The man of cups gestured with his head. Guy removed the book hesitantly. He had paid less than a copper for it and did not want to insult the man of cups. From what he had heard, that was one thing he definitely wanted to avoid.

'I have a book on healing herbs that I have read and could part with.'

'I will take your book. Come, play. Follow the seed.'

Guy dismounted tied the horses and made his way over to the man of cups, one of the sleepers stirred, but did not wake. Guy had considered playing from the cart, for he had played often enough to know that no matter how close he was he would not be able to follow the seed. Guy looked into the man of cup's eyes, with a nod the cups started moving. He ignored the cups, instead levelling an unthreatening gaze into the man of cups focussed, yet smiling eyes. He certainly seemed to enjoy what he did. The man of cups' hands settled.

'Where is the seed?'

'Left,' Guy called. He imagined that it sounded like it came with confidence, but he had decided before he had dismounted the cart that he was going to choose the left cup.

The man of cups lifted the left cup to reveal the seed. Guy glanced down to glimpse the dark bean. He was surprised, but not, at the same time, a confusing combination.

'You win. You have my services for a day. Congratulations.'

'But I have no need for your services.'

'Maybe not today, maybe never, but you have them anyway. You know how to find me if the time comes?'

Guy nodded with an intrinsic knowledge that he did. He didn't know how he knew, but he was slowly starting to trust himself.

'You cannot win and leave empty handed. I will take your book, and give you another in its place. A book for a book, it is as it should be.'

Guy took the book from the man of cups. It was simply titled *The Battle of Ashford*.

'This is from the scribe's college, an accurate account of a recent battle of note. You should learn from it. A knight should know what he is letting himself in for.'

Guy thanked the man of cups and retreated to untie the horses not entirely sure what had just taken place. He put the book safely into his bag, and tucked that beneath his feet. Rippling the reigns he got the horses on their way. As the cart pulled off he saw one of the sleepers awaken, angry at himself for sleeping and missing the all-important first game of the day. Guy imagined the man of cups telling him that there was always tomorrow.

As the cart was being drawn through the city gates, Guy's mind was swarming with events from the whole trip, but especially of that morning. It was such a strange turn of events that it would take him the rest of the day to process, and even then, he would not feel like he understood. But that was the enigma that was the man of cups.

18

The two weeks since he had returned to Eastfield manor had been even more brutal that before. There had been a time when Guy thought that things could not get any worse. He no longer had those thoughts. He had his armour, and for the most part was able to defend, but when he failed they were not holding back with their blows, which brought with it a whole new sensation of pain as the blows reverberated around the armour. The Knightmaker was supervising the training more, shouting commands at him, calling him a lump of clay and much worse besides. It had taken Guy several days to get accustomed to his armour, and even then was not as light on his feet as he should have been. Each and every movement in the armour made him stronger. He wore it when he cleared the courtyard, he wore it when beating the rock with his iron bar, no longer fearing the shards of rock that occasionally bounced off him. He was training his eyes too, getting them used to seeing the world through the slit in the helm. It was dark, hot and heavy inside the armour and his lungs screamed for air, but he knew the importance of being able to move as if he was not wearing it, to be able to function well in his metal suit, to keep his speed and power. It was taking all his effort to get through the days, but it was effort he was willing to give.

Guy sat beside his fire gnawing on a rabbit, it was perhaps an unusual meal with which to break his fast, but since his return he was free to come and go from Eastfield manor, as long as he was present for training. He had taken advantage of this to set traps and take his food into his own hands. A man of his size needed more than he was being provided. He had also collected plants and had replanted them around the courtyard, he had made quite a camp for himself. Guy enjoyed the mornings most of all, it was the only time that he had to himself. He was waking with the sun, and with summer arriving that was getting earlier by the day, but that gave him more time to exercise and get the blood flowing around his beaten body to prepare him for what lay ahead. He drank some fruit water before filling the bucket from the stream and giving it to the plants. Ash would be proud of him, he was nurturing the plants, Della too, for he nurtured plants that she had told him about. His body had become accustomed to the sheer exhaustion and pain that training bought, and his inner strength was growing every day. He was making himself stronger as the Knightmaker and especially Hawkins were trying to break him. He would have Phylissa as his wife, no matter what he had to endure, he would show her that he was worthy.

With his mind focussed entirely on the plants and their connection to the world, Guy did not notice the arrival of the Knightmaker. He stood flanked by Hawkins and the Stranger. It was early for them and Guy felt the all too familiar dread surge through him.

'Training goes up another notch this week. At the end of it you shall take part in your first tournament, a squire's tournament. You must be ready. I take it you know how to bend a bow?'

'I do,' Guy replied as excitement joined the dread coursing through his veins. *His first tournament!*

'I don't give a fuck about bows and fucking arrows, there is seldom a knight who uses them, and in a battle it is the weapon of the coward. In a blood and guts fight the bow has no place. For squires though, it seems that it does. You must come in the top dozen archers to get to the melee. So this week we fight for real, for though they may only be squires, they will fight to win, do not doubt that.'

The Knightmaker turned to Hawkins. 'Control yourself this week, he should be in good shape.'

Hawkins nodded, but Guy knew enough to know that Hawkins could not control himself if he tried, not like the stranger, he was controlled in everything that he did. Returning his attention to Guy, the Knightmaker continued. 'Train yourself with the bow, it is not worth my time. We do double defence training from now on.'

They left a bow, a dozen tournament arrows and two straw targets which Guy set up facing each other in opposite corners of the courtyard, one in the shade and one that would be in the sun later in the day. He took time to finish watering his plants before refreshing his mouth with a fragrant leaf and testing the bow for the first time. He used a bow for hunting, a smaller bow, not like the longbows used at tournaments. It had been years since he had used one of those, it felt alien in his hands, and not refined at all. These bows were made for power and distance, not accuracy. At least, not in terms of the targets. He had been gifted at long range, closest to the flag games in his youth, but that kind of bow for straw targets seemed alien to him. He notched the first arrow and loosed it at the target, satisfied as it thrumped into it. Target archery seemed easy and pointless. He fired a dozen arrows, familiarising himself with the bow. It soon came back to him, and not one missed the target, but then he stood only a dozen paces away and no one should miss from there.

Defence training had intensified, instead of the choreographed moves of taught swordsmanship it was now mock combat. Guy was still only allowed to defend, but the attacks were more of a freeform variety. They often performed the taught moves, but did not follow the taught sequences, and threw in moves that were not taught. The first two sessions saw him receive a battering unlike any he had taken so far. When he picked up the iron bar to strike the rock later in the day, it was heavier and more cumbersome than even the first time he had tried it. Hawkins, for all his control had cracked him on the elbow with a blow that found a weakness in his armour. Instead of striking the rock he found himself nursing his elbow, his mind whirring through scenarios of if it did not improve, not one of them was good. It hurt to grip anything and he could not even fire his bow, his arm shook so much that the arrows flew wildly. For the first time since his training had begun he gave up and returned to his camp, anger rising inside him. Hawkins was no more than a horses arse, but he was angry at himself too. He let Hawkins get to him, something about him caused upset to Guy, but he knew, he would likely face more devious or clumsy foes than he, and he should be prepared to deal with anything. It was all well and good learning defence against fighting styles, but it was the ability to defend against different people that Guy would need to learn. Perhaps that was what was intended for the week, it was a painful lesson with which to start.

Guy was sat by the stream holding a cloth with Della's fire berry balm against his swollen elbow as the stranger approached. His arm felt paralysed, so tense was it, as fire burned through his veins, his breathing was quick and shallow. The stranger gestured to see his arm. Guy raised his swollen arm to show him. The stranger tilted his head before taking his hand. In an instant Guy found himself pinned to the floor, the strangers boot in his armpit. He looked up at the stranger with panic and fear in his eyes as the pain sent jolts down his arm. With his free hand the stranger made an exaggerated exhaling gesture. Guy tried to calm himself, tried to exhale. The stranger repeated his long slow deep exhale. As Guy tried to mimic the breath, the stranger pulled and twisted his arm, it cracked sending a pain he could not control. He screamed, but within seconds through the pain he could feel an improvement. It hurt like hells, a pain both deep inside and all over his elbow, he could feel everything, his whole being seemed focussed on that part of his body. The stranger sat him up and gently folded his arm across him gesturing at the cloth and nodding. Guy tried to accept the pain as the stranger headed back to the house. He really tried, but it was a pain unlike any other he had known. By the same token, his mind was relishing the experience of having such a singular focus. He could feel the blood pumping through his elbow, he could feel every muscle and sinew, and he could feel his bones. He could see it in his mind's eye, inside his own body. Never had he known his elbow so well. He used his inner core to make himself stronger, moving the strength to the only part of his body he was aware of, the bones, stronger. The muscles, stronger; his arm, stronger. Instead of spreading the inner strength from his core, this time it spread from his elbow, spreading the strength of pain throughout his body. He could move his fingers without the intense pain of before. It just hurt like fuck, and he could deal with that.

The following morning he was still unable to hold his sword, not even two handed, but the Knightmaker was not going to go easy on him. 'In war, in battle, injuries happen. Do you think an opponent will take it easy on you because you cannot hold a sword? Fuck no, he's going to kill you. It is your job to stop him. Use your other hand.'

Hawkins came at him with a wooden stick, the stranger still had a training sword. Hawkins battered him time after time with anger and joyful arrogance. Guy knew he was being made to look a fool, but he learned from it. While his left hand was not doing what he asked of it quickly enough, he could feel it starting to. If Hawkins wasn't being so much of a prick and attacking him with all the ferocity he could muster, he felt sure that he would be able to block some of them. Whilst the sticks impact did not penetrate the armour at all, it made the sound of a broken bell inside his helm with each strike.

'Enough,' called the Knightmaker, flicking his head at the stranger, 'You're up.'

The stranger stepped up and performed a formal salute. Guy knew what moves were coming, and while he did not block the first few attempts, before long he had joined the Strangers pace and parried a few strikes in a row. He knew how to defend against the taught techniques, and while he knew that the stranger was taking it easy, he felt elated that he was able to match him, he no longer felt like such a fool.

It was a further two days before he was able to fire his bow more than half a dozen times in a row, but the accuracy was still lacking. His elbow was improving though, and he was getting stronger by the day, by the heartbeat. He trained, he read, he tended to his plants.

Hawkins fired spite at him the whole time, belittling, insulting, but not once did Guy rise to the provocation. A knight should have control, he knew this, he considered it training, yet in his mind he had decimated Hawkins in any number of ways, which gave his eyes the smile that made Hawkins' anger burn stronger.

Hawkins was still seething as they started their journey to the tournament. Acting as his squire, Guy was spending more time with the Knightmaker than he had before. The Knightmaker spoke for the duration of the journey, explaining how tournaments worked, what was expected of a squire and the normal protocol for becoming a knight. Guy listened intently, his ears wide open. He knew that he would not be able to recall all of the words, but he was concerned with the essence of what the Knightmaker was telling him. He felt that the Knightmaker was perhaps trying to curtail the excitement that was building inside him, but Guy did not have control of that, he could feel it rising like some tremendous swell of the ocean inside him. He was going to his first tournament. How could a man not be excited?

19

It was only a three hour ride to Rowansbrook Castle where the tournament was being held. The journey passed quickly, yet at the same time took forever. It was a sensation that was becoming all too familiar to Guy the more he explored knighthood. How something can be its two opposites at the same time, and both reside within him? He could feel his heart pounding in his chest as they approached the castle walls. They were directed to the Eastern gate and the tournament fields to register. Excitement pumped through his body. Where he kept his core had been replaced by a feeling not dissimilar to the one the cloudy ale at Boarton had caused. He wondered how he appeared on the outside, because on the inside he felt like an over excited child. Nothing he could think of calmed him, if anything, he made it worse. He was going to his first tournament. Dread and excitement flowed freely through him.

As they approached the Eastern gate, it was not as he had imagined it, none of the pomp and splendour, no crowds to welcome them at what felt very much like a worker's entrance. There was a wooden table, the tournament master and his clerks raised their gaze to meet them.

'As my Squire you should announce me,' the Knightmaker told Guy. In an instant it was dread that took over his being, and words failed to reach his mouth.

Hawkins stepped up and looked at them in the cart. 'He can't announce you, he doesn't even know who you are.' The scorn was without disguise. Guy felt himself flush.

'Is that right?' Guy simply nodded ashamed. 'You do it Hawkins.'

Hawkins stepped forward. 'My lords, may I present to you Sir Edrick Parcifal of Eastfield.' There was an intake of breath from those behind the desk, and gasps from those nearby, who all seemed to have stopped what they were doing. Guy through his shame, heard the words, but they took time to register.

'An honour to meet you Sir Parcifal, in which events will you be competing?' A small crowd was gathering and Guy could not understand what all the fuss was about.

The Knightmaker let out a laugh. 'Alas my days on the field are behind me.' Ignoring the catcalls and accusations of being a drunk from the crowd, he continued, 'I wish to enter my squire in the squire's tournament.'

'Alas Sir Parcifal, only squires whose masters compete can enter the tournament. I cannot change what is, even for you.'

The Knightmaker nodded towards the jousting emblem. In a hushed tone the tournament master added 'May I remind you sir that if a knight withdraws from the tournament their squire is disqualified.'

The Knightmaker gave the tournament master a stare that would wither most people, but he simply shrugged. 'Rules are rules.'

Sir Parcifal straightened oblivious to the crowd's catcalls. 'The melee. I shall enter the melee.' The jeers turned again to gasps.

'Very good, Sir Parcifal. There is a pavilion available for you in the knight's quarters to use as your own. Fourth on the left.'

The Knightmaker nodded his thanks and set off in the direction the tournament master had indicated. Guy was trying to pick out words from the crowd, but realised that Hawkins and the stranger were following the Knightmaker, so he led the horses and cart through the yard to catch up with them. So panicked was he, to avoid falling too far behind the others, that he did not take the time to appreciate the moment. He was entering the knight's quarters as a competitor for the first time, but Guy just marched on in, keeping up with his master. He would have to wait to hear the murmurs of the crowd.

Guy had neither gained on them, nor fallen behind as they entered the wide avenue that held the knight's quarters. In his peripheral vision Guy saw tents adorned with arms and bustling with activity, he felt the activity stop as they passed, but all his focus was on keeping up.

He slowed the horses when he noticed the others stop ahead of him, bringing the back of the cart to a stop just past the pavilion where the others stood. The Knightmaker pulled his shield from the back of the cart and placed it by the entrance of the tent before sitting on one of the provided chairs. Guy was already unloading the cart, quickly and efficiently as Hawkins was sent to see to the horses. Guy was proficient at setting camp, and before long had hauled their belongings inside, separated each person's equipment and seen to the Knightmaker's cot. He had the fire going and a pot of water on to boil before Hawkins had returned.

'Bring me wine,' the Knightmaker called as Hawkins approached. For a second Guy's instinct almost made him start to move, but while he was Sir Parcifal's squire, Hawkins was his cup bearer. He emerged from the tent a moment later with a skin of wine and three wooden cups. Inside Guy smiled knowing that Hawkins was only able to do that because of how he had set up camp. Guy was busy preparing rabbits as the kingmaker raised his cup. 'Now that was quite an entrance.'

Guy heard the words, but he did not allow himself to be pleased. It had taken all his efforts to keep up with them, and to be a squire required all his attention now. To those who looked on, Guy had to be seen as the Knightmaker's Squire. It was part of being a knight, and Guy was going to do it to the best of his ability. His master would recognise the efforts. Guy did not stop moving, cooking, improving the camp. Even after cooking he set some dried fruit in freshly boiled water and set the bones to stew before heading to the stream to clean the dishes.

He still felt the throb of pain in his elbow as he scoured the dishes in a nearby stream. He was not the only one there, other squires fulfilled their duties. He paid them no real mind, he knew they were there and what they were doing, but he saw no threat, instead he let his mind whir. He wished that he had spent more time as Sir Parcifal's Squire. It felt unnatural to him, and he wanted it to feel better. Yes he could fulfil all the functions of a squire, but there was not the relationship between them that a knight and a squire would have. He would regret missing out on all that training, but time was important and he had none to spare. For all he knew the earl could be arranging a more favourable match at that very moment. While Guy cleaned dishes, his life could be being decided elsewhere.

'Hoy!' Guy's attention snapped back and he looked to see another squire nearby on the lake. 'Hoy, big man, are you Sir Parcifal's squire?'

'I am,' Guy replied.

'Is it true what they say about him?'

'What do they say about him?'

'The things that he has done, that he survived the battle of Ashford?'

'Who told you that?'

'Some of the other squires, but I never know to believe them. I don't think they like me.'

'Why not?'

'They have all known each other for years. I am not one of their group, so…'

'It is no reason not to like someone.'

'Ay, but it's true. So is it right, about Sir Parcifal?'

Guys mind whirled searching for an answer. Was that why the man of cups had given him the book? He was angry at himself for not reading it before now. He would though, and soon.

'He doesn't like to talk about it,' was all Guy could offer. 'I should get back,' he continued as he collected the plates, 'He is not a man who likes to be kept waiting.'

'I'm Johnny by the way. Sir Chandley's Squire.'

'Guy.'

'Well met Guy, until tomorrow.' There was a glint in his eyes as he nodded his goodbye. Guy could not decide whether Johnny was pleased to meet him and the same would apply next time they met, or whether he was pleased to meet him, but it would be a different story when they met again. It was gone from his mind by the time he had returned to the tent. Sir Parcifal's shield, battered and worn, was in contrast to the bright newly painted displays of the other tents. It was robust, simple black and white arms adorned it, two white chevrons on a black background. The Knightmaker's shield told a story that was yet to be written for the others.

As he returned to the pavilion night was falling and all but one of the tents was occupied. The Pavilions he knew, were for the more prominent knights. Landless knights and free lances made their camp outside of the castle walls. Braziers and lanterns lit the way, past the shields that marked occupancy. He did not know any of them, and he chastised himself, hells he had not known who the Knightmaker was until that day. Had it been the arms under Waering, he would have known them all. *He was just a young boy from a small town, he had no place here.* His minds mischief started, but he reminded himself that he was no more or less significant than any man or boy here. In a hundred years no one would remember anything that would happen there, or most likely anyone who was there. Even the Knightmaker himself, Sir Parcifal, and all his great deeds, would have faded from people's memory.

When he returned to the tent the Knightmaker did not appear to have moved, still sat achair drinking wine. He looked as if he had supped plenty, but as he approached, Guy heard him sending Hawkins to find some strongwyne.

'My squire,' he called out as Guy returned the dishes to their spot. 'Tell me, did you see the shields on the way back?'

'I did.'

'Did you recognise any?'

'No,' was Guys sheepish response.

'That is some relief I suppose. Tell me, did you really not know who I was?'

'No.'

'Did no one tell you where they were sending you?'

'No.'

'Did you not think to ask?'

'No.'

Sir Parcifal looked to the stranger muttering something to him, he got no response, but chuckled at his own words.

'So Squire, how did you come to be here without knowing who I am?'

'I need to become a knight, and I need to become one quickly. I must be a knight to marry my love.'

'You are doing all this for a woman?'

'I am.'

The Knightmaker laughed, but Guy did not mind, the blacksmith had done the same. It was not a mocking laugh, he noticed, and he had said it with enough conviction that his belief would not be questioned.

'You know over the years I have had dozens, maybe hundreds of men come and try to get famous off my name. Most do not make it past the first week. You who did not know my name have made it this far. Let me tell you something, three gold would have bought you a knighthood from any of the knights here today, and you end up with me.'

'I must be a tournament winning knight.'

'For another three gold you could buy a tournament win. The champion of this tournament only receives a couple of gold, a nice statue and a white cloak.'

'I don't have the time to do it properly, or else I would, but I need to do it right.'

'No peacock knight for you.'

'No sir. If I am to be a knight, I shall be a real knight.'

'There are no real knights any more. It is all pomp for the king's fancy.' Guy had nothing to say, so let the Knightmaker's words hang in the air. 'What is your name boy?'

'Guy, Guy of Waering.'

'Guy of Waering, I am Edrick Parcifal, your knight and master. You fight in my name tomorrow. If you succeed in your training exercise I will train you for what you need. Now go and sleep, you are keeping watch tonight. Where there are knights, there are thieves.'

20

Hawkins woke Guy with a kick to the elbow. 'Hoy fucker, get up, the men want to sleep.'

Guy had known it was Hawkins, he had heard him come into the tent. He imagined that had it been the stranger he would not have heard him, and if the stranger was even half as malicious as Hawkins he would have kicked his injured elbow. A smile crept over Guys face as he cleared away his rollmat and grabbed his bag before heading out to keep watch as the others entered the tent. Hawkins headed for Guys spot on the floor, the stranger and the Knightmaker took the cots.

As Guy sat achair and acclimatised to his surroundings he realised that they must have been the last ones to sleep. The other tents were quiet, a few fires loaded with overnight logs. There did not seem to be anyone else keeping watch, other than the few guards positioned where the knight's quarter began. He refreshed his mouth with a cup of his fruit water, checked on the pot and the fire and pulled a book from his bag before lighting a candle to read by. He knew he should be more focussed on keeping watch, but he had to find out about his master. He flipped the book open to the point he had last read. It was about the most boring account he had ever read. It may be from the squire's college, but the political details that led to the battle went on and on. As ever Guy had every intention of reading the book properly, from start to finish, but as was becoming more common, he did not have the time. He flicked through the book looking for some reference that may indicate the battle was underway. It was over two thirds of the way through the book before he stopped skimming. Guy was pleased to see that the level of detail remained. The battle itself, which was what Guy was interested in was an incredible story. The book mapped out the repercussions of each event which gave Guy his first real understanding of battle strategy, and its importance. Even the greatest army could be defeated with the right strategy.

When he returned the book to his bag it was still some hours until the sun would rise. Guy simply sat, almost a statue, focusing on his breathing and his inner core while his mind processed what it had learnt about Sir Edrick Parcifal.

When movement began in other tents Guy's morning began. He collected bread, pork and eggs from the station before they had started work, and had the sliced pork cooking gently over a low fire before any other squire had passed on the way to the station. Despite his lack of sleep he felt fresh, alive. The stranger was the first out of the tent, nodding a silent greeting and heading off through the quarters towards the stream. The Knightmaker soon followed, surprising Guy with how normal he seemed. He had supped substantially the night before, yet he seemed the same as ever, and it was early. He commented on the smell of the pork and sat in his chair.

'Last night when I asked if you recognised the shields, I never got to finish what I was saying,' the Knightmaker began, 'It doesn't matter whose shields you saw. It doesn't change anything, you still need to beat them. In war a stable boy can kill a king. Whoever it is, they are just a man, and they have strengths and weaknesses like anyone. You must learn to judge a man for who they are, not what name they carry, because when the time comes none of that matters. You have a big day today, so why don't you go and do whatever it is that gets that big body of yours ready, perhaps freshen up a little. I will see to the pork. You are relieved of watch duty Guy of Waering.'

As Guy stood and left the tent area he heard the Knightmaker's booming voice commanding Hawkins to see to the food. He started his run slowly, cumbersome as ever, through the middle of the path that ran through the knight's quarters. It was still early and people were only just emerging from the tents, he felt their eyes on him as he lumbered through. It did not take him long to get into his stride, and by the time he passed the last tent he was starting to move more comfortably. He arrived at the stream all too soon, so crossed it and continued his run through a castle gate and around an adjoining meadow. When he was far enough away from the castle he bent his knees, rolled his shoulders and exercised. He had much on his mind, so exercised well, before returning at a steady run to the stream area to bathe. Despite him walking the last quarter mile, he was still panting and sweating when he got to the bridge. The stream area was busy with others bathing and collecting water further upstream. He bathed himself by the bridge, away from the others in the castle, and those further downstream who were not fortunate enough to be staying in the castle grounds.

When he returned to the tent, the others had long since finished their meal. He had wanted to serve the food. He had planned a good meal with which to start the day, and selfishly wanted the credit for providing it. As it was they would remember Hawkins as the one who prepared the meal. It was still a wonderful fuelling meal. The bread and broth, the pork and eggs, the fruit water, or wine for the others. Guy felt good after eating.

As he cleared the dishes, the Knightmaker told him to stop and told Hawkins to do it instead, instructing Guy to sit beside him.

'Today, all you need to do is qualify for the melee. If you are in the top dozen by the end of the day you will continue. I have no time for archery, though I appreciate its uses. Qualify today, and when I get through the qualifying bouts we shall both take part in the melee tomorrow. The jousting is all well and good, but that is for the peacock knights who desire fame and adoration. If you want to know how good you are, you find that out in the melee. Get yourself ready, we go to see the tournament master soon.'

Inside the tent as Guy rummaged through his bag, all the nerves and excitement that he had rid himself of through exercise returned and consumed him. He could not quite believe it was happening. He reminded himself that it was only a squire's tournament, but a tourney nonetheless. He had a long way to go until he won one, but he was taking a significant step. In his heart Guy knew that returning a knight would probably be enough to claim Phylissa's hand, but she always wanted more, and he would do his best to give it her. He found his clean linen shirt, well as clean as he could get it, and the bracer he had fashioned from leather. He held his leather chest plate that he had been using before he got his armour. It was crude, far from beautiful and it showed the signs of heavy use. He knew there would be squires with fancy outfits showing the highest colours they could wear, but that did not matter to Guy. He wore no green, or even burgundy, his colours were of any man. He made a small daysack up, putting in his chest plate, bracer, some rations and filled two skins of his fruit water. He did not know what the day would bring, but he had the essentials.

As he left the tent the Knightmaker stood, seeming to have made the same effort as Guy with his outfit, and beckoned to leave. When they approached the table, they did so with purpose. There was a small gathering watching the affair and three knights in front of them. Guy watched as each squire presented their knight to the tournament master and were informed of the schedule. Johnny winked as he passed him having presented Sir Chandley. Guy listened intently as the squire in front of him presented his knight. He would be next. His insides boiled with nerves, but Ash's words comforted him. *You always look so confident, so sure of who you are.* Guy had laughed, informing Ash that he had no idea what he was doing half the time, and was about as far from confident as a man could be. But as the time arrived Ash's words gave him strength. He stepped forward.

'Sirs, may I present Sir Edrick Parcifal for the melee,' he found himself performing a small bow, as he had seen others do.

'Step forward Sir Parcifal.'

The Knightmaker stepped up and stood beside Guy. 'Sir Parcifal, it is an honour to have a knight of your stature take part in our tourney. It has been unanimously decided, and at Earl Rowans insistence, that you be given a place in the melee. No qualifying for you Sir Parcifal.'

The Knightmaker nodded.

'That is kind indeed. I am honoured.'

'The honour is ours. Your squire must register with the marshals within ten minutes of the sounding horn, or they cannot take part.' The tournament master motioned with his head towards the far side of the yard, and they were dismissed.

Within Earshot of the table Sir Parcifal told Guy that he had no need of him today, and to come back to the tent when he had qualified, before walking off leaving Guy in the yard as the presentation of knights continued behind him. Guy watched a while at how the squires presented their Knights. It was all very formal, and he had played his part quite well. He had certainly not let anyone down. Perhaps coming from Waering had its uses after all.

He moved himself closer to the wall and out of the immediate bubble of activity, controlled his breathing and focussed on the strength inside him. He tried to take in as much as possible of what was going on around him. He was not trying to process it, he could do that later, more, he wanted to absorb his first real experience of a tourney.

'Have you seen to Sir Chandley?' asked Guy as he saw a smiling Johnny approach.

'Pah, he does not need me fussing around him,' Johnny started, 'He only comes to these things to let me compete, and to drink. He'll be out in the qualifying round. Get him in around a table and he would outdrink anyone, and take their gold with it. Except maybe Sir Parcifal, he looks like a bad fucker.'

Guy allowed himself to laugh a little, 'He does,' he agreed.

'Is he though?' Johnny mistook Guys pause for thought as lack of understanding. 'Is he a bad fucker?'

'He is.' Guy sighed.

'I shall look forward to seeing that tomorrow. Hopefully he'll put a few of these fuckers on their arses,' Johnny said softly as the first of the other squires started collecting at the muster.

'Might have known he'd be here first. That's Jefferson Strawson, Son of Sir Joshua Strawson and squire to Sir Robert Young, one of Lord Batsford of Maybury's knights.'

It meant nothing to Guy, but he nodded as if he knew. 'He won every squires tournament in the region last year, they say that he will be knighted before the end of the summer. An actual knight. I'm going after him tomorrow. I know a way to beat him. He thinks he's invincible, but he's not. I can't wait to see the look of surprise on his face when I knock him on his arse. Pompous prick.'

'Aye,' said Guy not really knowing what else to say. Johnny certainly did not lack confidence. A group of four squires arrived at the same time. 'Who are they?' he found himself asking, despite the Knightmaker's words. Guy was intrigued, feeling like a child in a new village. He realised that he should pull himself together as Johnny answered.

'They call themselves the Adler's. Their masters all serve Earl Adler of Helmingford. Sir Chandley once served him too. I think that is why they gang up on me.'

They were the best dressed of the squires so far with fine linen and very well equipped. A vessel of their master's vanity, their master's master. 'Every fucking time...'

'Hey Johnny, who's your friend?'

Johnny looked up unable, and perhaps unwilling, to hide the venom in his eyes.

'This is Guy of Waering.'

'Where the fuck is Waering?'

Guy did not flinch, did not react, instead he simply looked at all four of them at once, not focussing on any particular one of them, but hoped that it appeared that he was looking directly at all of them. 'Well new boy, you should be careful who you have as your friends. See you on the field... if you make it.'

The Adler squire turned away and laughed with the others as they headed over to the muster station which was now attended. There was a huddle of squires already around it. Guy was not sure where they had come from.

'Fuckers,' muttered Johnny. His next words were drowned out at they sounded the calling horn for the squires. 'We should head over.'

At the desk Guy was given a wooden token with the number 23 on it, and they collected out of the way to hear the tournament master's instructions. It was not the tournament master that he had presented Sir Parcifal to, one of his deputies Guy presumed. It was all very efficient, organised. Guy was beginning to realise the amount of effort required to run a tourney. He would do his part to keep it running smoothly. He would listen well, and follow instructions. Guy hoped in his mind that he did not appear like some young, over eager country boy. They were to hand in their disc to the quartermaster and they would receive a bow and a quiver of arrows, each distinctly marked. There would be a dozen range arrows, three practice, and four long arrows for the afternoon.

Three events, points from 24 down to one, for the position in each event. Top twelve qualify for the melee.

'Numbers 1 to 12 to the quartermasters, the rest of you follow when they have finished. May your arrows fly true.'

The first dozen squires made their way to the quartermaster, including Jefferson and the four Adler representatives.

'Hey big man, what's your number?' Guy looked at the token, though he knew the number it bore.

'23.'

'Hey not bad first time out, I got 24 my first tourney. They say it doesn't mean anything but we know better.'

Guy gazed at his token, it meant nothing to him, but continued the conversation, more out of politeness than interest.

'What number did you get?'

'14.' said Johnny. 'I should be top six really but…'

Guy watched the other squires collect their equipment as Johnny talked to him about all of them, who they were, what they were good at, their weaknesses. Guy was not really interested. He was listening, just as he was watching, trying to take it all in to process later. He heard Johnny's words just as he saw some of the other squires glance at them disapprovingly. None of them said anything, at number 14 Johnny was one of the big dogs of those that were left. They were a strange mix, the squires. Some were young, and yet to grow into their body, others were older, more seasoned, and further down the path towards knighthood. All of them were further down the road than Guy, but at least he could now say that he was on the road. He just needed to travel it quickly. The Squires were finally having their moment. They spent their lives in servitude to pay for their training. This was it for them, their chance for a moment of glory. Guy almost pitied them, but deep down still wanted to be one of them, to do it properly, to get training in all aspects of knighthood, not just combat.

As the numbers around the quartermaster's hut dwindled it was Johnny with Guy beside him who led the rest of them over. Johnny handed over his token and was given a quiver from the stack.

'Number 14. Black feathers, red band,' one of the assistants called out. His words were written by a scribe. The quartermaster swapped the token for a bow from the rack and handed it to Johnny.

'I'm stronger than I look,' said Johnny and handed it back to the quartermaster who bought back a longer thicker bow. 'My thanks to you, sir,' he turned to Guy and winked. 'For the long arrow events.'

Guy stepped up and handed over his token, He was sure the custom would be that lower numbers than he should go first, but no one seemed to be complaining, at least not out loud.

'Number 23. One white feather, green band,' the assistant called out. Guy watched as someone filled in the space next to number 23 with the details. No name, just a number.

'Are you good with a bow?' the quartermaster asked.

'I make do.'

'The long arrow?'

'Better.'

'Are you as strong as you look?' he asked in reference to Johnny's boldness.

'How strong do I look?' asked Guy. The quartermaster huffed at him and swapped his token for a bow towards the biggest and thickest of them all. He handed it over.

'If you break my bow it will cost your master a silver, and you a thrashing. Next.'

'Thank you,' Guy replied, 'I shall try not to break it.' Guy thought that he should not be fucking with the man as he wandered over to Johnny. The first dozen squires were finishing their practice arrows. There were not straw targets like he was used to, instead two stuffed sacks were nailed to a post, a smaller one above a larger to resemble a head and torso. Three points for the small sack, one for the large.

Guy watched enthralled, trying to keep points on all those who shot their arrows He could not make out some of the more distant targets, but he had a fair idea. He knew inside that it did not matter what the others scored. It was what he scored that was important, but still his mind was whirring with all the excitement. He watched and took in as much of he could of what was happening around him, the arrows flying, the crowd's cheers of encouragement, and occasionally, derision. Johnny looked like he was coming alive, there was a fire in his eyes, the lust of competition perhaps.

Guy's attention was drawn back to the tournament. The first dozen archers had finished and their scores were being called and recorded. Most seemed to be in the high teens and low twenties, with a smatter of scores in the mid-twenties. One had scored thirty. Guy questioned whether ten arrows would even fit on the smaller sack.

The first group of archers were led off in procession, and returned to ready their masters for the qualifying rounds, those that remained were called up to their position and introduced to the crowd. The crowd was thinning as many left with the first group of archers, but each squire got a cheer. When Guy's name was read out there was no punctuation to his cheer, there was no one to support him. He had to rely on the crowd's politeness. At 23 he was positioned away from the view of most of the crowd, but that did not matter. Getting through to the melee, that mattered.

Guy fitted his hand-made bracer and focussed his attention on the sacks, his target, and notched his first practice arrow. The bow was big, and had a heavy draw. He hadn't used a bow like this since… it was no time for memories. He had used a bow like this. It took more effort than he expected to draw it and doing so caused a deep throb of pain in his elbow. He released the arrow too early and it thrumped into the ground before the target. He looked around in embarrassment, but no one was looking. He pulled out a second practice arrow, centred himself, controlled his breathing and drew. He pulled further than before, but the pain in his elbow was greater, when he loosed the arrow flew past the target. It did at least fly as an arrow should. The pain in his elbow concerned him. The draw on the bow was so heavy. It was the right bow for him, if his elbow was not injured, but he could not draw it enough to do himself justice.

After declining the third practice arrow, the competition began. Guy stood for a moment. This was it, his first step, his first tournament. He calmed himself with controlled breaths and notched his first arrow. Focussing only on the targets he drew back the bow until his elbow throbbed and released, missed. He missed with the next arrow, but managed to score with six of his remaining ten arrows, three in each sack. The pain in his arm was so intense he felt close to tears with each arrow he fired. It was taking all his effort to keep his injured arm from shaking. He dreaded how it would be with the long arrow.

The scores were called and recorded, Johnny had scored 27, which to Guys reckoning has him second. Guy had scored 12, and wherever that put him, it was not good enough. As he followed the rest in procession his mind was in turmoil. He had not done well, and his arm hurt like hells. He did not think that he would even be able to attempt the long arrow events. Johnny was waiting as they passed through a gate into the preparation of the main arena.

'Eyes up big man, it's not so bad.'

'Is it not?'

'No, you said you were better at the long arrow to the quartermaster, and you have the bow for it.'

'Aye.' was all Guy could say.

'I must go and tend to Sir Chandley for his qualifying. You should come and watch.'

'I will, later.'

'By the way, bows have a habit of going missing, if you know what I mean. Keep yours with you.'

He nodded, still distracted by his elbow, and watched Johnny work his way through the activity. In that moment Guy felt separate from everything, still, while the world busied itself around him. He did not belong there, he was just a dreamer from the country.

21

As Guy aimlessly walked back towards the tent he tried not to be despondent, for even at his young age, he knew it to be the downfall of many a man. There was too much for his mind to process. How could he fare so badly at the archery when he knew himself to be so much better than the twelve points he had scored? He had taken a hare at full tilt, yet he could not hit a stuffed sack. It was, he knew, his elbow that caused his errors. Whether the pain inhibited him to the extent that he scored so poorly he could not be sure. His arm had not been strong enough to hold the bow sufficiently, that was true, but he wondered how much his minds mischief had played a part. Was he sabotaging his own chances?

They were not pleasant thoughts to be having, he would have rather spent the time thinking about the best remedy for his problem, but he was too tired and deflated to fight the mischief. He let his mind roam free, not even bothering to take in the activity around him until he reached the tent. Once there all his focus moved to finding a remedy. He gathered his pouch of herbs, his ointments, some leather strapping and his book on herbs and evaluated his options. The balance had to be correct. He could make a tincture that would ease his pain, but make him lethargic. He could numb his pain completely, but then ran the risk of causing permanent damage to his arm. There was no point in qualifying for the melee if he would be unable to wield a sword. In his mind when he focussed on the pain, he was sure that it was the result of trauma, and not anything that would injure more. It was just pain, and he could fight pain. But with trauma comes unpredictability. What if something more swollen than usual snapped, what if his arm sprung back to its form before the stranger fixed it? He was doubting himself, but he used the doubt to make him stronger. It would ensure the decisions he made would be the right ones.

In the end the answer that came to him was threefold. He made a gentle tincture to soften pain through his entire being, he wished he could add a stimulative root to ensure a sharp mind, but he had none. The second stage was to apply some of Della's fire berry balm to his elbow which he did with a soft cloth that was then itself bound around his elbow, secured with the leather straps, the third stage. The strapping would give some support to the elbow. It took him three attempts to get the binding right, he had to be able to bend his arm, but it had to be tight enough to provide the support. Pleased with his efforts he flexed his arm a few times before clearing away his things. He changed into the tightest long sleeved shirt he had. It was not particularly smart, or even clean, but it was the most practical for the long arrow. He would wear his leather chestplate over it. He fitted it at the tent where he would have less of an audience, refilled his skins, collected his bow and returned to the tournament grounds to watch what was left of the qualifying bouts.

All the other knights and squires watched on from the wings out of sight of the large crowd that looked on the arena. The dignitaries and important people sat in a raised stand giving a decent view to everyone. The normal people watched from the public area, which whilst on a slight bank, did not afford the view or the comfort of the stands. Without the constant throb of pain from his elbow Guy was finally able to start taking in the events of the tourney again, the crowds, the banners, and the people. He imagined Johnny watching on, looking for faults, weaknesses, things to avoid. Not that he would be facing the knights, but it was something Johnny would do. He scanned the area, expecting to see Sir Parcifal somewhere looking to see against whom he would battle, but did not spot him. He did not see any of them. They must have been somewhere else, most probably where there was wine. The sound of steel on steel did something to Guy. He knew it was not real combat, but some of the knights did not look as if they were holding back. Guy found himself imagining he were one of the knights. What would he do, how would he counter, how he would win?

The horn sounded soon after the final bout and once assembled, the archers were led through the castle gate and out into the cleared lands that formed some of the grounds. They gathered around a marshal as he read out the standings from the first round. 23rd for number 23, and two points. He looked for the squire who had finished below him, a slip of a boy, no more than fourteen, and Guy had only outscored him by one point. They would be called up in order and fire one arrow at a flag around 500 feet away. They had three arrows in total, closest to the flag wins and gets 24 points. Jefferson, by virtue of his thirty points, was the first squire called, and he loosed an arrow that looked to be good. Johnny was up next and seemed to be better. It was hard to tell at that distance when he was so far back in the queue. After that there was a mixed bag of performance, some were good, some terrible, none seemed as accurate as the first two arrows.

When he was finally called forward his focus zeroed in on the flag. That was all there was, he ignored calls from the Adler's, even from Johnny. The long arrow was all about focus, see the flag, see the arrows course to it, draw smoothly until the bow lets you know to loose, and watch the arrow fly. He had always bested his peers at Waering, always. He had the strength to control the power of the bow and get a truer flight than those who strained.

Guy needed a good long arrow. Five hundred feet was a distance, but he had tested himself beyond that in his youth. He took a breath as he pulled back the string, there was a gentle breeze from the left as his hand slid over the leather chestplate in his sideways stance, he raised the bow, saw the arrow as he continued drawing. A sudden sharp reminder of pain meant he loosed the arrow before the bow was ready. The arrow flew wildly, falling short and significantly left. Guy lowered his bow, and headed to the back of the queue flexing his elbow and fighting despair.

'Eyes up big man,' Johnny called as he passed him in the queue. Guy stood angry at himself, at his arrogance of believing he had the herbal skills to heal such an injury, angry at himself for not being able to shoot his bow, angry at many things.

When Johnny passed him on the way to the rear of the queue after firing his second arrow, he stopped beside him, planting his bow next to Guys. 'You ok big man? I saw you flexing your arm.'

'Aye, it's my elbow. It shouldn't affect me, but it is.'

'With a bow like that it will. Fuck me, that's the biggest fattest bow I have seen. It looks like you need a winch to draw it.' Despite it all Guy found himself offering a small smile. 'Take my bow for this round, and give it maybe eight out of ten. See if you can get one in.'

Guy felt Johnny's hands take away his own larger bow in a subtle swap. Guy knew it was wrong. Once you had been assigned a bow, that was your bow. He could be kicked out of the tournament if he was caught, and Johnny too, come to that. He was lucky that Johnny's bow was larger than most of the others, perhaps it would not be noticed. He felt his heart pounding in his chest as his turn approached, but what he was doing was not wrong. He had a genuine injury, and he should have gone to see the quartermaster himself to petition for a change of bow. As he was called, he hoped that any nerves that might be showing about the deception would be read as tourney nerves. He was not pulled up as he approached the rope. Sliding an arrow from the quiver, he notched it with the white feather to his right, saw the arrow fly in his mind, exhaled sharply and drew the string as he inhaled. The string bent the bow as his hand slid across the battered leather he wore on his chest, he raised the bow and released his breath with the arrow as it sang through the sky. It fell a little short, but on target. It was a good arrow, top ten at least. It was a more positive Guy who was smiled at and was waved on to the back by Johnny, who with only two before him would have to loose this third arrow with Guy's Bow. That was potentially as dangerous a time for discovery as when Guy approached. There was a little apprehension which allowed him to ignore the comments of it being a lucky shot, and Guy watched intently as Johnny loosed his arrow. It was not as good as his previous two, but matched Guys, and there was certainly no suspicion aroused. Guy was relieved to have his own bow back in his hand when Johnny stopped on his way to the back of the queue. The exchange was as slick as before, even the young lad behind Guy did not seem to notice.

When Guy's third arrow came about, he fluffed it into the ground fifty feet away. There was mock disgust at himself on his face as the other squires laughed and some, still bitter, continued their chides of a lucky arrow from the turn before. Guy did not care. He had scored well and saved his arm. Once the young lad had loosed after him there was a pause in proceedings as the marshals scored the contest and awarded positions. Johnny approached Guy.

'Good job big man. That should keep you in it, just the longest arrow to go.' The young squire, number 24 approached, seemingly happy with himself. 'Good job wee man. That is a great effort for a first tourney,'

Guy smiled to himself as he looked at the young squire's bow. He would certainly not have been able to swap with him. The bow fitted the man, it was small and slender, but he had made it work for him. By the bow alone though, Guy knew that he would struggle in the longest arrow, no matter how well he made it work. Guy just hoped he could get his beast of a bow to work well enough to see him through.

The three of them talked like three young squires at a tournament might, full of youthful enthusiasm and ignorance, but they shared laughs and soon those around them did not matter.

A marshal called them over to announce the scores. Johnny had won, 24 points, Jefferson second. Guy had just made the top ten and got 14 points for tenth, the little lad had come fifteenth and happily received a pat on the back from Johnny. Once they had announced the scores for the two events combined Guy was only in 18th place, the young lad a couple of places behind him. It was still not a qualifying spot.

For the longest arrow the rules were simple. They would shoot one at a time in reverse order. The arrow that flew the furthest won 24 points. They filed into position. With only half a dozen squires in front of him Guys mind had turned to the event. He had saved his elbow in the last round, but he had also felt great pain when he had drawn his bow. Guy had always used big bows, and it frustrated him that he could not get the best out of that one.

His mind reminded him of when he was about ten, a man of the west visited Waering and Guy's father had asked him to teach Guy how to shoot a bow. He thought back to the training, the westerner had taught him in a strange way. Because he was young the strain of a longbow could be too much and affect growth. He had made Guy take some steps as he drew the bow, using his whole body instead of just his arms to pull the string. He had always felt strange doing it, that it just was not right, but it had enabled him to shoot with bigger bows, and realise just how much power he was able to generate. The memory gladdened him, a happy cringe as he replayed the movement he was forced to do it. It just looked ridiculous, and he had told his father as much, his father had told him to listen well because men of the west were the best archers in all of Rodina. The Westerner had left after a fortnight, but in Guy's memory it appeared as if it was a week ago. He had not thought of the westerner for years, perhaps the situation had bought it back.

Guy was trying to think how to fire a decent long arrow without damaging his arm. He had the bow, if only he could draw it to its effective range. He could not return to the Knightmaker having been eliminated, it simply could not happen.

A smile started to creep across Guy's face as the first archer loosed their arrow. He was smiling at the absurd, he was actually considering trying the westerner's strange dance. If it took the emphasis off his arm, he might be able to access the effective range of the bow.

He was seeking reasons not to as the second archer loosed their arrow, and the third. Guy did not even watch their arrows. It was the ones after his that would have the winning distances. As the squire in front of him stepped up, Guy realised that he was next, and he could not discount it. In fact it seemed like the only solution. Guy watched as the squire squeezed every morsel of power from his bow until he began to tremble, and loosed a good arrow. He seemed pleased as he took his place to the side of the firing line. Guy was called forward.

With no other option, he stepped forward, rolled his neck and stretched his back to snickers behind him. He saw in his mind what he was supposed to do. The reality of it though was that he not tried this technique for half a dozen years, and had never been great at it then. He took a breath, took four paces back ignoring the blurred voices as he saw again the arrow, the motion. Inhaling he took three steps forward planting his foot, using his body to generate power which reached the torso, through his arm as the string slid past his chest plate, the bow rose, arm straightened. A jolt of pain shot through him, but the arrow was loosed before it registered. A scream chased the arrow into the sky to whoops and gasps from the other squires. As he screamed the pain subsided in his arm, and the arrow flew. Breathing heavily, pain burning his arm, he turned and took his spot beside the young squire before his arrow had landed.

He was bursting inside, from elation, from pain, he tried to control it, but that was all he could do. The young squire had congratulated him as he passed, but he needed a moment. He watched in a daze as squire after squire stepped up to the line, none of them beat his arrow, or even got close. As the numbers beside the line increased he knew that he had made it to the melee before Johnny and Jefferson took their turns. Johnny, perhaps by virtue of the bigger bow finished second behind Guy and therefore won the Archery event. It was not a popular win with the Adler's, and those supporting Jefferson, showed their disgust by jeering and scowling at them.

Sharp looks were thrown their way as the marshals declared the arrows and recorded the score. Of course they had to wait, but Guy knew he had won, and therefore earned enough points to qualify. Johnny was certain that he had beaten Jefferson, and won the entire event. Plots were being made to rectify the situation in the melee. The trouble was that they still did not know for sure who would be taking part.

Guy accepted the congratulations from Johnny and some of the other squires. Johnny looked genuinely pleased for him, and not bitter at the defeat. He found himself smiling, getting drawn in a little to their strange world, if for no other reason, he told himself, than to maintain the reality of their moment. He could tell himself many things, but deep down he was pleased, it would mean denying what it was to be a person to be otherwise. He controlled it, watching the nervous chatter from the small group around them. He had done as the Knightmaker had demanded, he had qualified, he was certain. The next day he would be in the melee.

It was close to an hour later before the squires were called forward. Johnny had indeed won the archery to muted cheers from the small group. Jefferson was second, then an Adler, the names kept on coming with scores over 40. Anxiety was starting to spread within Guy, his calculations… Eventually his name was called in 11th place, 40 points, number 23. That was closer than he had estimated. He had made it though, the young squire congratulated him, Johnny clapped him on the back.

'It will be nice to have a friendly face in the melee,' he said, just loud enough to be heard by the group. He drew glances from the Adler's, Jefferson, and a few others too. The young squire came in 18th overall.

'For a first tourney that is pretty good,' Johnny offered. 'You were not far from making the melee.'

'I wasn't supposed to make the melee. I'd get destroyed out there. Look at me. If I had wanted to be in the melee I would have used a bigger bow. The melee is not for me. Not yet.'

'Well in that case, mission accomplished. You should be pleased, both of you.'

After returning the bow to the quartermaster and bidding the others farewell as they rushed back to their masters, Guy returned to the tent at a more leisurely pace, once again able to take in all that went on around him.

22

The Knightmaker and the stranger were sat in the two chairs on his return. The day was drawing out to evening and the heat of the sun had passed. The Knightmaker looked up as he approached, Guy nodded.

'Good. Get some food.' Guy saw a duck and a bread ready on a plate. The stranger stood and went into the tent. 'Come, sit.' Guy sat beside the Knightmaker and started on the duck. 'Your elbow still bothers you?' Guy nodded. 'Then you should have asked for a bow more suited to your condition. The wrong equipment can be the downfall of any knight. You almost fucked it up. Had you not switched bows in the long arrow, you would not be in the melee tomorrow, even with your longest arrow. You must learn from this.' Guy nodded. *How did he know about that?* 'Tomorrow we both battle in the melee. You get to watch me first. Suit me up, hand me my sword and then stay the fuck away, even if it looks as if I am hurt. You do not enter the field of battle. Am I clear?'

'Yes Sir,' replied Guy through the ducks carcass.

'When your turn comes you are to show me that you have learnt defence, and with it restraint. You may only defend. Should you make an offensive move, you shall not be able to defend yourself for a week. Am I clear?' Guy looked at him over the duck that he was now picking scraps from. *Defence! He could never win with just defence.* The look on the Knightmaker's face said that he was not fucking around. He nodded, not knowing what else he could do. 'If you make it to the last three I will consider defence training complete, and we can move onto offence. Make an offensive move, and we go back to the start until you learn it properly. A knight should always be able to show restraint. This is your chance. Leave your dish and get some sleep, for you keep watch again tonight.'

Any elation that Guy had felt in qualifying for the melee had gone, instead there was confusion, frustration and a little anger. How could he get to the last three simply by defence alone? It looked as if Johnny would not get the help he hoped for.

Guy reflected on the day, a thousand images flashed through his mind that he had stored to process later. He was glad that the Knightmaker was not like other masters, he pictured the other squires feverishly working away to fulfil their duties alongside their own tourney, and felt pity for them. It was short lived though, as he was sure none of them would be keeping watch that night.

Guy was awake, his bedroll, packed away, and his bag beside him as he sat afloor. It was late, he had slept. He had been awoken by their drunken laughing. The Knightmaker was recounting stories of old, but Guy found it hard to hear the words. He seemed to be speaking to the stranger, he could hear the familiarity with which the words were shared, and he could only hear Sir Parcifal's voice. He and the stranger had a history, unlike Hawkins, who he had not seen since the morning. The Knightmaker was entering the tent as he left.

'Keep good watch. Where there are knights there are thieves.'

He kept the fire burning bright that night, and was busy around camp, making fruit water, and boiling oats in the leftovers. If there were thieves in the night, there would be no question about avoiding that tent. Not even the night's mischief visited that night.

The stranger silently relieved him as the sun began to rise in earnest. Guy collected the provisions, dropping them at the tent before beginning his run to the stream. It was still early, and there were only the beginnings of movement in the occasional tent. He did not run as far as the previous day, taking advantage of the early hour to exercise in solitude. As he bent his knees, his mind drifted to the melee, and how he was going to survive using only defensive manoeuvres. His mind gave him no answers, but gave him focus while he exercised, pumping up his body for the day ahead like bellows pumped the furnace. That day there would be steel on steel.

As he cooled and cleansed himself in a pool in the stream he heard a familiar voice.

'Hoy Big man. What the fuck is wrong with you?' It was Johnny he knew without turning, but he turned anyway. 'You have the melee later. Why train now? You'll need all your energy for later.'

'I train every day.'

'We all do big man, but a day like today, the melee is training enough. You need to be fresh.'

'I do this for myself. I'll be fresher than without.'

'Fair enough, so big man, about the melee…'

Johnny sat on the bank of the stream shaking his head after hearing of Guys instructions.

'Your master really is a bad fucker. Who sends their squire into a melee without permission to attack? I find offence is often the best form of defence.'

'I must do as I am bid. I'm sorry, I cannot help you.'

'Hey, perhaps you can keep them busy while I pick them off.' Johnny offered, quickly revising his plan of the two of them fighting together. 'Just standing near me will help me out a lot to be honest.'

'Well that I can do,' Guy said as he dried himself with his linen shirt before pulling it over his huge frame.

'Are you any good with a sword?'

'I guess we will find out later,' Guy offered honestly. He had thought himself good with a bow, and only just scraped through to the melee. Compared to the others he had not had the training or the experience. He was hoping that he would be good enough to make the final three.

Those thoughts continued in Guy's mind as he made his way back to the tent. There was a chance that he could be humiliated, especially if he was unable to use offence. He was used to battering people into submission with intimidation and use of his size. He did not have that option any more. He remembered the training he had received and even still, the stranger and Hawkins battered all kinds of hells out of him, every session. Guy had not yielded throughout his training, to have to yield to a squire was not a prospect he enjoyed considering. On his return to the tent nerves had consumed him, but he gained comfort in preparing the food as Hawkins emerged briefly before disappearing again.

'Fuck me. These are the best boiled oats I have ever tasted,' boomed the Knightmaker, who turned to the stranger. 'Just think if we'd have had oats like this on the South Eastern front…' The stranger cracked a smile, the first Guy had seen, and gave a nod. 'Fuck me this is good. Fuck the pork this morning. I'm going to have more boiled oats, and these are not words I ever thought would pass my lips. I almost wish it were winter.'

It pleased Guy that the Knightmaker enjoyed his oats, and enjoyed the moment that he had been denied the day before. His fear of humiliating himself was fading. He had done something good, something simple and it had made everyone's day better.

Guy approached the stream to clean the dishes, Johnny was hurrying in the other direction, as were most of the squires. 'Hoy Big man, are you ready to play?' Guy nodded that he was. He wasn't, he knew, but he would be, something would come to him. 'I must hurry, Sir Chandley wants to get a good seat, apparently the whole town is coming to see your master in action.'

With that he scurried away. As he cleaned the dishes, Guy could feel eyes on him, and words of him, and Sir Parcifal. He could not hear what was said, and every time he looked up gazes were averted and silence fell. He freely admitted that he could not wait to see the Knightmaker in action himself, and he hoped, that after the years of drinking and white mist, that he still had it in him. The fear of a realisation shuddered through his big body. He had been so concerned about humiliating himself, but perhaps it would not be he who was humiliated. He shook the thought away, but it gripped a distant part of his mind.

As he approached the tent the stranger was fitting Sir Parcifal's armour. It was practical more than elegant, some chipped black enamel on the pauldron and placart the only decoration. It appeared to be a familiar situation, the stranger silently going about his work, which only served to make the Knightmaker look more menacing. Guy found himself stood, simply watching as the stranger adjusted the strappings until he was happy. The Knightmaker simply stared at Guy, a fire so deep and so dark burned within his eyes. Guy held his gaze, feeling the same fire ignite within him. For a moment he felt connected to the Knightmaker as the intensity grew. The Knightmaker gave a single shake of his entire body with a deep *hyu*. Guy felt himself flinch, not from fear, but flinch nonetheless. He knew the Knightmaker would have spotted it, but that did not matter. He had just looked into the eyes of perhaps the most intimidating man in all of Rodina. He suspected there would be few men who would not flinch at such a move. He knew for sure that Hawkins would, the stranger though…

The stranger fitted Sir Parcifal's sword and belt. He would not be able to use it in the arena, but whatever weapon he took, he would receive a more tournament friendly version from the quartermaster. Sir Parcifal looked at Guy.

'When we go we go with purpose. All that matters is us. The other people do not exist. Learn from it for later. There is no right or wrong thing to do, just follow our lead, but do it with purpose.' Their eyes met again and they nodded to each other without moving their heads. The stranger handed Sir Parcifal his Barbute which he pulled over his head. The helmet put that which was exposed of his face into darkness, save for the dark fire that burned in his eyes and the occasional glimpse of teeth. The Barbute was not the most protective of helms, but gave good vision and would not impede the breathing, not only that, but it made him look like a very bad fucker indeed. Guy found himself handing him his shield without prompt.

'We go now.'

The Knightmaker strode from the tent with the kind of purpose that tells you a knight is approaching. Guy fell in two steps behind and one to the left. The people that did not exist had stopped to watch, but Guy did not see them. Hawkins appeared from nowhere and scurried past to lead the procession as they passed from the knight's quarters into the yard, ready to announce him to the tournament master. He soon settled in, and the four of them approached with purpose. Lord Rowan himself was sat beside him, flanked by guards and tournament officials.

'May I present Sir Parcifal, for the melee,' Hawkins announced louder than necessary.

'Check in with the quartermaster, and prepare to be announced,' the tournament master said as one of his assistants marked some paper.

'Sir Parcifal, if I may…,' Lord Rowan said quietly. Sir Parcifal stepped forward, the rest of them remained still, and they did it with purpose. 'I wanted to welcome you personally, and thank you for attending my tournament.'

'I am here only for my squire, but I thank you, my lord.'

'Having you here brings honour to my tournament. Never before have so many attended. You have my thanks.' Sir Parcifal bowed respectfully, but with purpose.

'My lord.'

He turned towards the quartermaster, Guy joined him, with purpose, two steps behind, and one to the left.

The quartermaster asked to examine the Knightmaker's sword so that he could find the closest match. He asked for Sir Parcifal's sword to be left in exchange.

'I do not give my sword to anyone,' he gestured over his shoulder at the stranger. 'He shall have my sword, and will not enter the arena.'

'I need to take the sword please Sir Parcifal.'

'Do you?'

The words hung in the air. Guy felt intimidated standing behind him such was the purpose behind the words. He could imagine the Knightmaker's stare boring into the quartermaster.

'I can make an exception this time.'

'You do that.'

Sir Parcifal handed his sword to the stranger, and took the tournament sword from the quartermaster. They left towards the holding area together, with purpose and the next participant stepped up, brandishing a longaxe.

Though the holding area was not large, Sir Parcifal and his party were afforded plenty of space as the knight familiarised himself with the sword. Short sharp tiny movements that made his armour snap like it had back in the tent. Guy was transfixed at the power the Knightmaker managed to generate with such minimal movement. It was, he realised, the first time that he had seen the Knightmaker with a sword in his hands. This took his level of intimidation to beyond anything Guy had imagined. He was just glad that he was with him. He could not imagine facing such a foe. It was a squire's duty, he felt, to survey the opposition, and Guy cast his casual glance around. A knight should always be aware of his surroundings. Eleven other knights and their parties prepared, bright and shiny armours of locally distinguished knights with a variety of weapons, the longaxe of course, but there were battle axes, hammers, a morning star and a selection of swords. The crowd was big, his casual glance could not fathom how big, but he suspected it would be bigger than any he had seen. There was no laughing or joking, these knights meant it. Guy wondered if the presence of Sir Parcifal had caused it, knights were often seen drinking and laughing before a melee. Not this time. As he surveyed, his situation flashed in his mind, he was actually doing it, he was about to see what it takes to win a tournament first hand, and then take part in one himself. He controlled it quickly, or as best he could, it was not about him, it was about Sir Parcifal.

In his peripheral vision he saw Lord Rowan taking his seat, which meant the announcements were about to begin, and as instructed he let his eyes see, but there were no other people there.

The Knightmaker beckoned Guy over with a nod of the head. Guy stepped up before him, and even though he towered over him, still felt like he was looking up at him. 'You will walk me out, and you will bring my shield back, you will not go back into the arena unless I beckon you. Am I clear?' Guy nodded.

In his mind Guy was picturing how he looked. There he was, about to squire for one of the most famous knights in the kingdom, and he was dressed like a farm boy in his linen. For a moment he considered the uproar this would cause back in Waering, perhaps it would cause uproar in Rowansbrook too.

The knights were called to formation to be led out, as others made their way to the tournament master, Sir Parcifal remained still, with purpose, and Guy did the same. They remained this way for some small while, for it was sought after to be the last knight announced, they often received the greatest cheer. But Sir Parcifal, he knew, did not care about such things, he was just doing it to piss someone off. He was beating them before they even got out there. Only after the other eleven knights were lined up did the Knightmaker mutter 'We go now.'

Before they had joined the back of the procession the other knights were being led to the arena. A huge cheer came from the crowd as they entered. Guy followed Sir Parcifal out to join the line before the Lords and heralds, two steps behind, one to the left. Though he walked with purpose the atmosphere of the arena and the size of the crowd hit him like an invisible sack of hay. His breathing shortened, it was simply too much. He remembered the Knightmaker's words, *use it as practice for later*. He could use it as training. He focussed on the ball of strength inside him, calmed his breathing, as the horns commenced the announcements. Time had someway stopped for him again, he was aware that the announcements were happening, but he felt distant from the arena, distant from himself, focussing on his breathing and what he had to do.

When Sir Parcifal was called the biggest cheer of the day erupted. He stepped forward, standing a moment. Then as earlier that day, he gave his body a small jolt that reverberated through his armour, only this time the '*Hyu*' was punctuated with the crack of the pommel on his shield, and made those around him flinch, even some of the crowd. It was as if a wave of energy had spread from the Knightmaker slightly repelling those in its path. Guy did not flinch. A huge cheer erupted, Sir Parcifal raised his sword before turning and giving Guy his shield. He took it, and despite everything, walked back to the holding area with purpose and gave the shield to the stranger. He had done it. He had done what was asked. He found his breathing heavy, but the sound of the horn bought his attention back to the arena. The melee had begun. Sir Parcifal stood where Guy had left him. He was in the ready position, sword pointing exactly north east from his body. He was motionless, but Guy knew he would be surveying what was before him. It was quite a few seconds before the sound of steel on steel raised a cheer from the crowd as the first blows were struck. For many of the knights though, it was yet to begin as they continued to stalk and observe each other. Whilst the knights started circling and moving for position, the Knightmaker was motionless, but motionless with purpose.

It was the longaxe that came for him first, the knight whirling it around his head as he strode towards Sir Parcifal, building up the momentum for an overhead strike that looked as if it would fell the mightiest tree. The Knightmaker remained still, for too long, Guy thought. The longaxe and knight approached him swiftly. It was not until the offensive manoeuvre had begun that the Knightmaker moved, too late for the attacking knight to adjust the axe. Sir Parcifal spun inside the axes arc, slamming the flat of his blade against his attackers back. The contact, combined with the momentum of the striding swing saw the knight off balance and he found himself sprawled on the floor, less than an instant later the Knightmaker's boot was on his back and he felt the cold tickle of steel under the back of his helm. The yield was immediate.

Before the Knightmaker could even take a breath a morning star was being swung towards his head, he stood as the knight approached, before turning into him and slamming the pommel of his sword into the knight's guts. The knight bent double, but before he was able to gasp for air, Sir Parcifal's blade was at his throat. Upon the yield, Sir Parcifal removed his sword and moved away as the knight fell to the floor, clutching his mid. The Knightmaker returned to a ready position, this time his sword pointed exactly North West of his body. All other fighting had ceased as the knights looked at their two fallen comrades. Sir Neville of the longaxe was a tournament regular, occasional champion, and Sir Dedryk Ternant, a fine, yet rash knight. Both lay, almost atop each other, yielded.

Two sworded knights, who had previously been fighting each other, through unspoken communication, attacked Sir Parcifal at the same time. The Knightmaker remained still, again for what Guy considered too long, but he parried both their strikes with one move, and had turned ready before them. As they turned, both had the horrifying vision of the Knightmaker leaping towards them, landing acrouch between and before them. They both moved to strike at the same time as two gauntleted fists powered at them as Sir Parcifal drove his body upwards, connecting at the front base of their helm, and knocking them both off their feet. Sir Parcifal picked up his sword and placed it through each eye slot of the helm until a yield was given.

The Knightmaker took one of the fallen knight's swords as the crowd roared and turned to the remaining knights. He snapped into a fighting stance with a north facing sword in each hand. The clatter of his armour and the deep '*Hyu*' brought a cheer of excitement from the crowd. Guy's skin was prickling as he watched open mouthed at the happenings.

He was not the only one, the remaining seven knights he imagined were agape beneath their helms. They no longer seemed concerned about each other, sharing looks between them, confusion. To a cheer Sir Parcifal strode towards them with purpose. Those on the periphery outskirted, the three remaining met the Knightmaker's approach with mace and swords. Steel clashed with steel, and all four made it through unscathed, the Knightmaker with his slower pace was able to pivot and engage the others as they turned, both swords flashed through the air. One knight countered and rolled away, ready to come again. The Knightmaker exchanged parried blows with the other knight, as the knight with the mace leapt at him aiming an overhead blow with both hands. The Knightmaker span away slicing a sword across the knight's gut. The mace missed Sir Parcifal but dented the helm of the other knight leaving him flat on the floor. There was no yield required from him. The Knightmaker had struck the maced knight several times before parrying a blow from the other sworded knight. Sensing weakness other knights moved to join the fight, having eyes only for Sir Parcifal, but the Knightmaker danced among their numbers delivering blows, putting them on their arses, whilst they could not seem to land a clean blow. A knight crawled from the battle, dragging a limp leg behind him, another seeing stars was helped from the arena by his brave squire, yet another lay flat aback his helm having been introduced to the pommel of Sir Parcifal's sword. Seconds later the Knightmaker had secured enough time for another to yield with his swords crossed theatrically at the neck of a shocked knight. The remaining three Knights realising perhaps that a group ambush was not working, spread themselves across the arena looking to find time to recover and reassess. The Knightmaker moved towards the nearest knight raining blow after blow in a fast flurry of violence. The knight to his credit parried or blocked many of them, but the Knightmaker never stopped moving forward, and had soon driven the knight from the arena. He looked up from the seat of his armour in anger and frustration. The crowd in that section cheered madly and the Knightmaker beat his chest with a sworded hand for them.

The Knightmaker turned to face the last two Knights. 'You can yield now, and save yourself some pain.' His voice boomed across the arena. Cheers from the crowd as they hooted their derision at the remaining knights. Neither yielded and Sir Parcifal strode towards them, clashing with a sword and shielded knight in shiny silver armour. The knight was a gifted swordsman and they danced a short while, until a blow to the shield sent a splinter as it cracked. Sir Parcifal struck again, and again, meeting no resistance. Sir Parcifal rained blow after blow to the shield as the knight was forced to his knees, cowering behind his shield as it began to break apart. Guy knew Sir Parcifal could have ended it much sooner by aiming blows elsewhere than the shield, but as almost half the shield fell away, the yield came soon enough. Turning to the last knight he stood a moment looking on as the dark armoured knight held a greatsword pointed at him. Sir Parcifal tossed away the other knights sword, and twirled his own in fast practiced motions, ending with a snap in a ready position. For a moment there was stillness, even among the crowd as the two knights faced each other, both waiting for the other to move. What was probably only seconds felt like all time to Guy. A shout from the crowd inspired motion and it was the dark armoured knight who moved. It was clear he was a practiced knight, the blows he aimed were neither tentative, nor over committed and they shared several exploratory clashes where blows were exchanged and parried before separating. The greatsword came in, Sir Parcifal slipped to the side, tapping his sword on the dark helm. He did it again on the next pass, from then on the crowd cheered every time Sir Parcifal's sword tapped the Helm of the dark armoured knight, and it happened pass after pass, clash after clash. Sometimes there would be a substantial trade of blows before it came, but it came every time. The dark armoured knight unable to hide his growing frustration was making more mistakes. On one exchange Sir Parcifal tapped both sides of the helm. The crowd were laughing and something in the knight changed. He attacked the next pass with more aggression and speed, the greatsword unopposed. Guy's heart lurched as it appeared inevitable that the blow would land, instead there was a huge crash of armour as the Knightmaker had gone to ground, catching the knight's feet between his own, sending him slamming face first into the ground, the greatsword bounced from his hand.

Sir Parcifal stood and walked away before turning and seeing the knight try to raise himself. 'You should yield now and save yourself some pain.' Instead the knight crawled to his sword and used it to right himself, slowly climbing to hold his sword ready. The Knightmaker moved to a true north ready position. The knight composed himself before striding towards the Knightmaker, the greatsword in both hands behind his head, he leapt into the air, the blade coming down with him looking to cut Sir Parcifal in two. The Knightmaker had stayed still too long this time Guy was certain, though ways of blocking it flashed through his mind. He had gotten caught up in the Knightmaker's games. If Guy could imagine ways to block it… The Knightmaker barely moved, but his sword flashed, catching the wrists of the arms wielding the sword as it sped towards him. With a scream the greatsword left his hands just before making contact with the Knightmaker. It spun twice in the air before landing and sliding in the dried mud. Sir Parcifal spun connecting the flat of the blade with the dark armour chest plate, then in a flurry of blows he slapped every piece of armour the knight wore. A heel to the back of the knee had the swordless knight on his knees. The Knightmaker stood before him, sword held horizontal in line with the dark helm visor, staring down at him until he raised his two fingers in silent yield.

The crowd erupted, Sir Parcifal removed his sword and strode with purpose to stand before Lord Rowan who declared him the victor. The melee was over in less than ten minutes. Sir Parcifal bowed to Lord Rowan before turning and striding out of the arena to where Guy and the others watched in the holding area. Despite everything Guy composed himself, and watched the calm purposeful stride as the Knightmaker walked towards him. As he approached he showed no signs of slowing, and almost without realising Guy had fallen in behind him, two steps behind, one to the left. He looked only at the Knightmaker, hoping no expression was on his face. There were no other people, though he felt them stare. The crowds parted as the Knightmaker passed. Once out of the holding area it was quiet and Guy felt a lot more comfortable. They continued their march in silence though through the knight's quarters to their tent. Back at the tent nothing was said as the stranger removed Sir Parcifal's armour while Guy prepared noonshine. Cold pork and eggs.

23

For all that had happened that day, Guy knew better than to try and process any of it. What occupied his mind was how he was to survive the melee using only defence. If that were not enough to consider he could not help but feel that Sir Parcifal's display earlier would make him a target. He could imagine the glee with which the tale would be told. 'I was at the melee of Rowansbrook, I saw Sir Parcifal with my own eyes, then later on that day I made his squire yield.'

As he passed one of the last tents before the stream a familiar voice called out to him.

'Hoy big man,' Johnny came running from Sir Chandley's tent. 'Fuck me. I knew he was a bad fucker. I just knew it. That was incredible.' Guy could not help but smile in agreement, his own concerns prevented him from joining Johnny's level of excitement. 'I've been going to tournaments all my life, and never seen a thing like that. Listen I must get ready. But I have a plan for the melee,' Guy looked up, 'You defend, I'll attack.' Guy smiled, and Johnny returned to his tent.

Guy sat outside drinking his fill and preparing a skin to take with him. The sun was hot and high in the sky, he could feel his sweat already, before he even wore his armour. He liked to drink before training. He would rather take a piss in his armour than be unable to continue because he needed water, he was focussed, but without having a plan formulated. It was to be his first real melee after all, and it was hard to plan for something that he knew nothing about. The Knightmaker emerged from the tent and approached him. 'Hawkins and I are going to get a good spot. Remember what I said, if you survive until the last three using only defence, you defence training is complete.' Guy nodded, but without conviction. 'When you are out there, there is no one else, there is only your opponent.' Guy met his eyes, and nodded.

'I'll try.'

'You cannot try to survive. You either do or you don't. It is the same for everything. HAWKINS!'

Hawkins hurried from the tent and they set off towards the arena. Guy went into the tent to fit his armour. The stranger sat within, Guys armour was laid out. The stranger beckoned him over helping with the doublet and chain before fitting the armour. He was swift and precise, and did it so much better than Guy had ever managed. He felt free to move, everywhere. Usually there would be some area where he had not fitted the armour correctly and movement was restricted, but it felt good, probably what wearing a suit of armour should feel like. The stranger handed him his helm, nodded to him, and left the tent leaving Guy alone. He rolled his shoulders, twisted hips and even bent his knees a few times, enjoying the freedom of movement whilst wearing armour. Guy punched the air a few times and tried to mimic Sir Parcifal by making his armour clatter with just small movements. It felt clumsy, he was moving too much, it needed more practice. He was already sweating in his suit, and his heart was pounding in his chest.

The horn sounded giving the squires ten minutes to report to the muster. Fighting the urge to follow convention and leave immediately Guy sat awhile controlling his breathing and focussed on the ball of energy deep within him, hoping that answers would come to him. He took a dozen slow deep breaths. 'We go now,' he muttered to himself.

He stood, stretched his body a little, drained two cups of fruit water, and pulled the helm over his head. When the helm slid down, his vision was restricted to the reinforced eye slit. He envied the Knightmaker's barbute helm with the vision and ventilation that offered. The holes punched in Guy's visor to aid ventilation seemed to stifle the air. He rolled his head to ensure it was fitted properly, attached a skin of water to his belt and picked up his sword. It was a greatsword to any man, but on him it appeared more like a three quarter or bastard sword, he slipped it through a loop on his belt, took one more breath and stepped from the tent, with purpose. He walked straight out and towards the tournament area. There were no other people he told himself as he felt eyes turn towards him. He walked alone through the Knight's quarters, reporting at the muster desk with only a minute or two to spare. He was the last one, and was instructed to head straight to the quartermaster. Guy handed over his sword, he did not have quite the attachment to his sword as Sir Parcifal did to his, nor the authority.

'Number eleven, Greatsword,' called out the Quartermaster, and handed over a blunted greatblade. Its simple leather strapping and solid brass pommel seemed secure enough, and while heavier than the training swords he had used at Eastfield Manor, it was significantly lighter than the iron bar. It felt good in his hands, a few short practice swings reaffirmed. He had no complaints about the sword, any shortcomings would be his alone. Making it look like he was examining his sword, he took the opportunity to look beyond the blade and cast an eye over the other squires. Most of them were beautifully adorned in expensive shiny armour, all the colours of a summer meadow punctuated the steel outfits. Guys armour had dinks and imperfections all over it, but it was strong. He could tell just by looking, that the same could not be said for some of the other armour on display.

He struggled to recognise most of them from earlier as they formed a line, much like the knights had done earlier. They were to enter in the position they had finished in the archery, so Johnny would be affront the line. He wore relatively simple armour, punctuated with claret, Jefferson's behind him was much more elaborate, shiny black enamelled armour trimmed with gold. The three Adler's who had qualified were almost as fancy.

'Number eleven,' a voice called. Guy moved his head in an exaggerated fashion towards the sound. He was being called to take his position, and while there were no other people there he paused a moment before beginning his purposeful walk to the back of the line, the eyes of no one on him. The last squire fell in behind Guy and the tournament master addressed the squires.

'There are three ways you can be eliminated. You can yield, if someone yields you cease immediately. If you leave the arena for any reason, you are out, and finally if you are incapacitated. Let's try not to make it the last one eh?'

There was polite laughter from some of the more experienced squires. Guy was not laughing. Guy did not know what the fuck he was doing. He was about to enter an arena with no idea what to expect, and no plan to counter his defence only instructions. All he had was his heart, and his desire. He reminded himself briefly of Phylissa and the reason he had begun this journey in the first place, as the tournament master continued talking. Nerves and excitement had dried his mouth. He closed one eye before lifting his helm, drained his skin of water, then returned to the darkness before opening it again. He readjusted quickly to the light and vision of the slits in his helm, and this time he felt that there was a new element of focus. All his training so far had led him to this point.

The squires were led out to stand before Lord Rowan and the heralds. When it was Guy's turn to step into the arena, the power and energy of the crowd surged through him. The crowd though smaller than earlier was still much larger than he would have expected a squire's melee to achieve. He reminded himself that the crowd did not matter, there was no one there, no one but his opponents. Each squire stepped forward and received a cheer when announced, some bigger than others. When Guy stepped forward he was surprised by the cheers that he heard. Considering nobody knew of him, it was loud indeed. Much of it for Sir Parcifal rather than Guy, but he enjoyed it all the same. Guy bowed to Lord Rowan and stepped back again, all with purpose, all with focus. He hoped that he looked composed to the people that were not there. Once the last squire had been announced they scattered throughout the arena, finding space and allies. Someway Guy found himself on the opposite side of the arena to Johnny who seemed to be surrounded by the Adler's and Jefferson. Guy stood facing the centre of the arena, able to see all the other squires, in a ready position, his sword, he hoped, pointed north east from his body.

When the horn sounded everyone but Guy moved into action. Guy fought the urge to join in. He could not defend until someone attacked him, and no one approached him. Other battles erupted throughout the arena, some battled each other alone, others in groups. The Adler's were heading towards Johnny, who seemed as skilled with a sword as he was with a bow, he could fend the Adler's off, but when Jefferson joined them Guy could see him start to struggle. Guy had to show that he had learnt restraint, and he remained motionless as they seemed intent on removing the archery champion first. Guy knew that there was a history with Johnny and the others, but there was no doubt that he was also a threat. What did that say of Guy who was still waiting for an attack? All the other squires were engaged, but he could not until someone engaged him. Whilst he was aware of the crowd, the Knightmaker had been right, all that existed were his opponents and the threats that could come from all sides. He was coiled, ready to react, but there was nothing to react to.

Johnny had managed to turn his attackers and now backed away from them towards the centre of the arena as they came at him. He was no longer surrounded. Two squires fighting each other nearby attacked the group as they passed causing a moment of mayhem, where swords flashed in all directions and the sounds of landed blows and groans of pain punctuated the crowd's cheers. From the madness Johnny emerged and made his way over to Guy.

'Alright big man?' He shouted through panted breaths, as Jefferson and an Adler came towards them. 'You defend, I'll attack.'

Guy moved from north east to north west in his ready position and blocked an awkward swipe at him. He could hear grunts and laboured breathing all around him. He was finally in it. The blows aimed at him were easily blocked, and easily predicted. These squires were all castle trained, and not yet old enough, or good enough, to add their own interpretation and improvisations. The more skilled ones were precise he noticed, but focussed on the movement itself rather than the intent. The less skilled were oft times clumsy and prone to reverting to more natural attacks. Guy moved slowly and with purpose, deflecting blows, and moving people away from Johnny. The urge to attack was burning him inside, he could see openings that would enable his greatsword to gain quick yields, and there was something inside him that just wanted to damage all the fancy armour that danced around him. Guy moved smoothly, but well within his limits. He did not spin, or need to move at his optimum. Let them think that was it, he was big after all, and big often meant cumbersome. His mind was focussed, and he deflected any blade that came too close, but compared to the stranger, and even

Hawkins the swords were no threat to Guy. His armour had not been rung once yet, and he was used to being battered by now. More swords there may be, but less skill with them.

Guy had worked his way to the outskirts of the battle, and saw Jefferson with his boot on a young squire's chest, sword pointing at the helm for the first yield, and a roar from the crowd. The roar seemed to fill him with confidence, and as he turned to re-join he looked at Guy and went after him. Jefferson was more skilled there was no doubt, but his attacks were not hard to deflect as he moved into space. An Adler and another squire had joined him and they were pressing Guy. Their attacks were easy to defend and escape. They were meant to be, Guy realised. They had separated him from the pack and were penning him back towards the edge of the arena. He accepted his realisation and let them continue pushing him toward the boundary. A dozen feet from the rope Guy stopped retreating and prepared for an onslaught. He imagined they would rush him and try to force him from the arena. The blows soon started, he could not parry them all and he heard his armour sing its protective song a few times. He did not feel it though. When Hawkins and the stranger rang his armour he felt it, often through his whole body. He could take a beating like this all day. The squires attacking Guy stepped back, five of them, surrounded him, penning him against the boundary. Behind them he could see other fights and Johnny was heading in their direction after gaining a yield.

A squire stepped forward and engaged Guy, He parried two blows before another stepped forward slamming his sword into Guys side. He felt it, but it did not rattle him as much as he made out, stepping back closer to the line, parrying another blow as he staggered, The two squires stepped up and another joined them charging in with a wild overhead swing. Guy pivoted, causing the attacker to lose balance, but in the space it gave him Guy raised his sword and much like the Knightmaker had done earlier blocked the incoming blow by connecting sword with wrist. The sword fell outside the arena. As it landed there was a crash as Johnny joined the battle and planted a boot to the chest of the squire who had momentarily lost balance. He lay flat aback outside of the arena, Johnny used the surprise to engage the other squires. Guy turned to the squire who had lost his sword, and was trying to nurse his wrists, and made ready with his sword in the true north position. The squire looked up through his visor, and stepped backwards from the arena. A sword clapped his shoulder and he turned ready, just in time to see a squire charging at him. He was looking to remove Guy from the arena, even if it meant leaving it himself. The fancy armour told Guy that it was an Adler. As he launched Guy span away with breath-taking speed for a man of his size. Where he once was, he was no longer, and the crowd gasped as the squire succeeded only in launching himself from the arena, beating the ground in frustration as the crowd jeered.

The spin had taken Guy closer to the others where Johnny was on the receiving end of a three on one beating. He continued the movement to block a blow about to be delivered to Johnny, and, once Johnny had recovered they soon reversed the position, and it was they with their backs to the centre. For a moment they stood ready, but no attack came. Guy and Johnny retreated slowly towards the centre, where two squires who had just teamed up to gain a yield turned on each other. There were seven left. Another four yields and he would have made the final three. Guy himself was panting now. A melee in the late afternoon sun was not a good thing for any man, sweat was pouring off him, and he was not being exerted. Not really, not compared to his training. He took the chance to catch his breath, to control his breathing and gorge on as much air as he could suck in. Everyone seemed to be taking the opportunity to recover, a temporary lull in the battle, the two squires fighting separately still wary of each other made their way closer.

'Hey big man. You are quick. Want to have some fun?' Johnny did not wait for a response. 'Let's turn our backs on the fuckers, that will bring them in. You keep them busy, I'll take them out.'

Guy nodded, and turned to face Lord Rowan with his sword held ready in the north east position. The crowd cheered, but he blocked that out, focusing his ears instead on the sounds of any approaching steps. Guy's mind flashed back to the Knightmaker in his melee, how he had waited so long to move that Guy had feared he had left it too late. He hoped he would not leave it too late. He opened his ears as wide as he could, cursing once again that his helm was not more open. There was only silence in terms of advancing steps, and that was all he heard despite the crowds jeers. He imagined the others looking at each other, all they would be able to hear was the crowd, it would prompt them into action.

Either time had someway paused for him or there was a continued stillness in the arena, finally though, he heard the first steps towards them, quickly joined by others. In his mind he pictured their approach as the steps picked up pace, he imagined them charging, swords high. His heart pounded in his chest as he held out, until he could fight it no more as the footsteps thundered towards them, he turned with a high block to the shrill ring of steel on steel. The crowd cheered and life someway returned to full speed, he blocked, parried and spun. Johnny had been taken out, one of the squires had dived shoulder first into his legs, sending him on his arse. Jefferson had followed up, with a boot on his chestplate and a blade at his visor. Johnny had no option but to yield. At the same time, the two other squires had joined and together had earned a yield from the diving squire while Guy battled with the last remaining Adler. The two other squires, buoyed from their success went after Jefferson. They traded blows as they danced around the arena in their two combatant groups. With Guy only defending, and the two squires working together, the exchanges continued with none getting the better of others. The Adler squire kept on coming at Guy, raining blows from all directions, Guy blocked, parried or avoided most of them, but by the way he was attacking, Guy considered that the squire had not realised that he was not fighting back, and probably thought that he was overpowering him. He blocked and moved with comfort, for he was not being tested, unlike Jefferson who was skilfully holding off the other two squires, but it was testing his limits to do so.

Jefferson was clearly a skilled and experienced combatant for a squire, able to maintain his form while the two squires he fought began to tire, he kept inviting them on, and then driving them back, draining their resources as the afternoon sun beat down on them. Once fatigue began, with it came the realisation that they would not beat Jefferson and from that point on it was only a matter of time. When the first yield came, the second soon followed, the exhausted squires had to be helped from the arena, as Jefferson joined the assault of Guy.

He had made the final three, he realised as a blow caught him on the shoulder while he parried a blow from the Adler. He had completed his defence training. He had done as the Knightmaker asked. Whilst relief washed over him for a moment, something stronger replaced it. He was not going to yield easily to these fuckers, and he blocked and span into space with a new resolve, and with purpose.

'Fight back,' called Jefferson, 'Fight back you dumb fuck.' They came at him again, and again. More often than not Guy deflected the blows and moved into space, he was dragging them all over the arena. 'You will not beat me if you do not fight me.'

The words kept coming as frustration started to rise. Guy was starting to tire, was getting slower, but so were his attackers. They were, after all, expending more energy in attacking him than he was using to defend, and while there were two of them, he felt himself slightly ahead in terms of endurance. He could see their movement starting to labour as they approached him. He continued to move them around the arena as the sun started sliding down the sky. He had been caught on the helm by a blow after the low sun momentarily blinded him. *How long had they been out there?* Guy reversed their position at the next attack, forcing them to see the sun behind him. He had no option but to outlast them, and fighting the sun would cost them energy and concentration. He dragged them up and down the arena as they continued to attack and shout abuse. If he could attack he knew he could take them both in minutes. They would be too tired to withstand an attack from Guy. He would just batter them into submission. Instead of simply parrying or blocking the blows, he had begun to continue his movement, dragging their sword away and causing them to lose balance, it was all causing them to use energy that Guy did not have to, and it made them look clumsy. When Guy disarmed Jefferson, a cheer penetrated his concentration, then a scream of frustration as the embarrassed squire collected his sword while Guy let the Adler attack.

Guy disarmed them both several times, but took more joy in causing Jefferson's sword to leave his hand. Anger and frustration were building in him so much that on one occasion he punched Guy's chestplate before scurrying to collect his sword. The Adler squire was spent, he barely seemed to have enough energy to swing his sword, eventually resting aknee to try and recover. Jefferson ceased his attack on Guy to plant a boot in the Adler Squires chest, and standing over him taking the yield.

'I will finish you myself, and I swear to you that you will fight back. I swear it.'

Jefferson went at Guy with a new intensity, a new ferocity, as Guy let himself be driven back, the sight of Jefferson coming at him, with the colours of an incredible sunset behind him, burned into his memory forever. His opponent was grunting and screaming with every blow in a continuous attack that drove Guy back the length of the area, unveiling the entire blazing vista. He paused his retreat as he approached the rope boundary of the arena and considered whether he may be able to cause Jefferson to stumble out of it. A better idea came to him, and he took a few blows to set it in motion. Four uncontested blows rang Guys armour, and it appeared as if he may be struggling, Jefferson remained cautious, but continued the attack. Guy bought his sword up to parry a blow, hoping to spin Jefferson's sword out of the arena. It flew toward the rope, but at the wrong angle, and it landed on the dirt safely in the arena. He glared at Guy with pure hatred in his eyes.

'I'm going to fuck you up.'

Guy stood ready in North East and allowed the sword to be collected and followed as his opponent headed back to the centre of the arena. Suddenly Jefferson turned and charged at Guy looking as if he were to deliver a leaping downward strike. As Guy readied himself the squire changed his position in the air, and before he could do anything about it Jefferson's armoured knee connected with his chest plate. The force of it knocked Guy aback, but he did not lose his sword, and the two of them rolled a while, until, after overpowering Jefferson, he stood and returned to his ready position.

'Fight me,' he roared coming at Guy once again. They battled around the arena. Jefferson was giving all he could just to swing his sword, but he kept swinging. Guy kept defending, tired himself, his arms had lost feeling some time ago, it was only instinct that kept the sword in his hand as he blocked blow after blow.

Another idea was forming in his head, but it was a dangerous one, dangerous for two reasons, it would be easy to take it too far, and let what began as pretence become a harsh reality, and also because it may contravene the Knightmaker's defence only condition.

Jefferson kept coming at him, demanding he fight back. Guy's armour was being rung more often, and his hands were a little softer in the sword. He was driven around the arena, occasionally Guy had to step back for some respite. He was panting inside his suit, and he knew Jefferson would hear it, as through the battle cries he could hear gasps for air that were not his.

Jefferson was driving Guy past Lord Rowan and connected a heavy blow to the helm that caused Guy to stagger back a few paces, and those that remained of the crowd to gasp. As Guy stumbled time seemed to someway slow, it all depended on what move Jefferson did next. Finding balance and connecting with the earth, Guy snapped out of his lethargy as Jefferson came at him as he had hoped. Sensing weakness, Jefferson's intentions were on the finish, and he was ready to ring Guy's helm again. As the attack was launched, Guy span, moving quickly into a crossbody ready stance, and in the process slamming the brass pommel into the onrushing Jefferson's chest. A loud crack reverberated and through the eye slits Guy saw shock register as the impact sent Jefferson reeling backwards trying to absorb the impact. Five steps he staggered, on the sixth he fell, slamming dead weight into the hard dirt ground, the sword bounced from his hand as he landed. Guy remained in the ready position, primarily to emphasise to the Knightmaker that it was a defensive stance as the crowd roared. He could hear the rattle of his opponent's armour as he tried to get up. Guy had been dragging him all over the arena, exhausting him, and he was yet to find the energy to rise. Guy turned and walked with purpose toward him, planted a boot squarely in the chest of his armour and ground his foot as if Jefferson was a stubborn ember, scratching the beautifully polished enamel. He pinned Jefferson to the ground and purposefully aimed the tip of his sword at eye slits in the helm, whilst adopting the south ready position. Jefferson glared at him for some time with eyes of burning hatred, but also exhaustion. He knew he was beaten, and finally offered the two fingered silent yield. Guy kept the sword aimed at Jefferson and this time it was he who stared. For as long as it had taken him to yield, Guy made him suffer his dominance. He removed the sword, and his boot, turning to Lord Rowan, who had the Knightmaker and one of the knights he had beaten earlier, sat in his box with him. Guy looked to them and bowed, taking a moment to enjoy the cheers of the small crowd that had stayed for the duration of the bout. Lord Rowan announced Guy the winner. Guy bowed again, turned, and walked with purpose to the holding area, and from there through the knight's quarters to the tent. Only once he was inside did he let the façade fade, and collapsed on his arse afloor. His mind drove itself like a wild horse as he sat panting trying to remove his helm. His mind was trying to process what the fuck had just happened, and he did not have a clue. He knew one thing though, his defence training was complete.

24

The Knightmaker himself entered the tent to wake Guy for watch duty that night. The smell of wine on his breath woke Guy before he nudged him.

'For a first time that was not bad, even if it took you all day, but you got cocky, and it could have cost you. It certainly cost your friend. Come, keep watch. Where there are knights there are thieves.'

As Guy exited the tent Hawkins was sent to prepare the cots. Guy stood letting his eyes adjust to the firelight, as the Knightmaker turned to the stranger. 'I wager there are few knights in the kingdom who can lay claim to having won a melee without landing a blow.' The stranger said nothing, as the Knightmaker mumbled a continuation of the conversation to himself as he stood to retire. The stranger looked at Guy as he stood. There was no smile on his face, but in his eyes there was something unusual. He was saying that he had done well, Guy someway knew. He nodded to him and took his seat by the fire and, once the stranger had entered the tent, allowed himself to smile. He was still far from where he needed to be, but he was getting there, and the entire day had been more incredible than he could ever have imagined. Seeing the Knightmaker in action before his own victory, he felt good on the inside. He had calculated in his mind, but still failed to believe that the melee had lasted almost three hours. That could not be.

A little after an hour into his watch, movement and supped voices snatched Guy from his thoughts. Potentially a knight returning after revelry, Guy sat forwards quickly wakening his senses. He could not make out the words, but they were not the words of a night of enjoyment.

They were coming his way, but their tent was early on the quarters, and those based further down would have to pass. As the sounds got closer though Guy knew they were heading for the tent. Still unable to see who approached he heard a voice directing them towards him. Guy dipped a torch in the fire and once lit took it with him to stand beside Sir Parcifal's shield on the perimeter of their tent area.

It was Sir Robert Young, the knight Sir Parcifal had beaten earlier. Jefferson stood beside him and Guy fought a smile. The guards whose duty was to prevent such trouble hung back at the entrance to the quarters, presumably on the orders of those stood before him.

'I have come for your master.' Sir Young slurred loudly.

'My master is sleeping.'

'Then go and wake him, or I shall cut you down and wake him myself.'

'I don't think that is a good idea.' replied Guy hoping the surprise in his own confident manner did not show.

'I should cut you down anyway you impudent little prick. Because of you we must travel to the north for Jefferson's silver token.'

'I do not think the fault is mine.'

He had taken it too far, he knew it before the words left him, but still he could not stop them. Sir Lane drew his sword.

'Step aside.'

'You will not enter this tent.'

As Sir Lane stepped forward he was met with the substantial fist of Guy, cracking his jaw and knocking him out cold before he fell on his arse beside Jefferson.

'I suggest that if he does not remember what happened here, you tell your master that he tripped and fell.' There was defiance, in Jefferson's eyes, and a sense that he would not back down. 'We are in no arena here, there are no restrictions. Get him out of here now, or suffer the same fate, and when you wake in the morning you will both be tied naked to a tree.'

Guy lurched at him, just a tiny movement, but it was enough to have Jefferson flinch and hurriedly try to lift the dead weight of his master. Sir Parcifal stepped from the tent.

'What the fuck is going on out here?'

'Sir Lane had just come to congratulate you on your tournament win, but he tripped and did himself some harm. Jeff here was just taking him back to their pavilion.'

'Is that so?' Jefferson nodded, so keen was he to escape the situation, he lifted Sir Lane under the shoulder and dragged him away.

'Do you think that was wise?' the Knightmaker asked as he ducked back inside the tent.

The night passed without further event and Guy was grateful when movement began in other tents. He had been on high alert, with the Knightmaker's words and the night's mischief, he had been waiting to hear the sound of an arrow loosed in his direction all night. It had not been a good night, but a price always had to be paid for reckless acts, and he had paid it. He should not have struck Sir Lane, he could lose his hand for it. Worse still, they could make Sir Parcifal take it, the knight's code was very specific, and outside of battle it was unheard of for a squire to strike a knight. The knight's code was sure to have provisions for drunken challenges in the night, but that was really beside the point. Among the first to move were the Knightmaker and the stranger.

'Load the cart. We go now.'

Within ten minutes Hawkins led the cart through the knight's quarters, their possessions, hastily but thoroughly wrapped, piled within. Guy sat aback the cart packing away armour more securely. The guards called them to a halt.

'You may not leave until after the presentation.'

'I have been called away on an urgent matter that requires my attention now,' the Knightmaker replied, in a calm but forceful manner.

'You must at least bid Lord Rowan goodbye. He takes his tournaments very seriously and your appearance here has honoured him.'

The Knightmaker relented and nodded, gesturing for Guy to follow as a guard led them to Lord Rowan's chambers. They waited in an adjoining room as Sir Rowan was roused. Guy had never seen a Lord's private chambers and it was opulent beyond his imaginings. Everything looked so old and beautiful, everything had a story through generations of the Rowans. Guy was not really able to take it in for what it was, he was anxious. The night's mischief had won its battle in the night, and everything had a terrible foreboding about it.

Lord Rowan entered the room, not fully dressed, and though flustered, not upset. 'Sir Parcifal, I am told you must leave before the presentation.'

'Indeed my lord, a matter of some urgency. If you need a presentation, give it to Sir Lane. You can always disqualify me.'

'Nonsense. You are my champion and I mean to present you. You have made my tournament into something special, both of you. Let me thank you before you leave. They will be here in just a moment.'

Guy's heart pounded in his chest, his mind showing him images of guards and knights on their way to accost them. He had assaulted a Lord's knight.

Sir Parcifal nodded.

'May I ask what it is that takes you away from us so soon?'

'Someone I know is in trouble, my assistance is needed.' He leaned in and whispered details that Guy could not hear.

'Say no more Sir Parcifal, if you aid a brother, you leave with my blessing. Is there anything you need from me that could help?'

'Thank you my lord, but no. This requires my attention.' The door between the rooms opened, and to Guy's immense relief, the only person on the other side other than Lord Rowan's wards was a Steward, carrying a golden sword on a plaque.

'Ah, here we go.' Lord Rowan took the plaque from the steward. 'Sir Parcifal, melee champion of Rowansbrook, I thank you for your efforts.' The Knightmaker bowed as he received the plaque. 'And for you…' Lord Rowan looked to Guy expectantly.

'Guy. Guy of Waering'

'For you, Guy of Waering, champion of squires.' He held out his hand and presented Guy with a silver token. It was twice as big as a regular silver and had gold inlay of a sword on one side, and spurs on the other. 'Congratulations and good luck. Please, come again next year.'

Guy bowed, took the silver token, placed it safely in a neck pouch and tucked it away.

'Thank you Lord Rowan, you hospitality is appreciated.'

The Knightmaker made to leave, and Guy did not hesitate in following, sending only a brief glance towards Lord Rowan. He was polite, and nodded. Not the sign of someone who was about to have you arrested. Or was it? One thing Guy knew, was that despite growing up around the earl of Waering, he had no idea how the rich and powerful operated. Guy followed as they were led through corridors back to the cart. The Knightmaker took his seat on the bench while Guy climbed in the back.

'We go now.' The Knightmaker called and Hawkins encouraged the horses. Eyes watched as they left. The Knightmaker made sure that they did not hurry, but they left with purpose. It was only two hundred yards from the castle walls that Guy allowed himself to think that they had made it. The horses drove with urgency away from the town, so much so that he could not package up the armour, instead it clanged with every bump in the road. Hawkins drove the horses hard for a good hour before letting them relax. Guy was convinced that if there were going to be any immediate consequences, they would have happened by then. The journey continued in silence at a more leisurely, but brisk pace. Guy examined the token as he considered how close he had come to failure. He could not be a knight without a hand, nor Phylissa's husband. He had to avoid getting drawn into situations that detracted from his mission. He had nearly fucked it right up, and the anxiety still refused to leave his body.

The token was a thing of such workmanship that Guy had never seen its equal. Intricate, but simple, incredible. He spun it carefully between his fingers and admired it for some time, it had a calming effect on him, he wondered what he would do with it. Perhaps it could be displayed in his home, and be the start of a collection like he saw at Lord Rowan's. For the first time in a long time, his mind dreamed of his future with Phylissa, his house, his legacy. It was good for him to remember why he was taking his path, it gave him strength.

25

When they pulled through the gates at Eastfield Manor, the anxiety had been replaced by strength, Guy was feeling good, and he was happy to be back. The Knightmaker gave him two days to rest and recover, and disappeared into the house without saying anything about the tournament, Sir Lane, his passing defence training, nothing. Guy was left helping Hawkins unload the cart, separating his possessions and loading the other's equipment on the balcony. Guy realised that he had never set foot in the house in the whole time that he had been there. He spent the rest of the day organising his camp, going through and checking his equipment. He tended to the plants in the courtyard, letting them drink freely, and went to see Charger, taking him back to the stream so they could spend some time together. Guy had missed Charger, but Hawkins, despite his faults, was good with Horses and had looked after Charger well.

A little after noonshine, about the time when he had been preparing to enter the arena the day before, Guy set out following the stream, there was a certain plant he was after, and it was found on the edge of woodland, often near water. It was hot like the day before, but this world was completely different, wide, open and bright, clean and natural. Wildlife enjoyed the summer around him. Dragonflies skirmished among the reeds, and he remembered the first dragonfly of the year, when he was with Little Ash on the rock. How far that world was away from the one he lived in now. He was no more than a boy then. Now he was a boy who could take a beating. Guy paused his walk, and took a big lungful of the country air awakening the ball of energy inside him and feeling its pulse radiate as a realisation sunk in. He could take a beating. He was proud, and it made him stronger as he continued his walk. Only this time, he was walking like a man. Knowing that he could take a beating beyond all beatings somehow made him stand up within himself. Certainly there were good feelings for winning the tourney, but this was beyond that. For the first time in his life he realised that he could keep the company of men, and not be intimidated, for he was a man himself.

Guy cracked his head on a branch, his eyes quickly darting to look if anyone had seen. He was alone and he knew it. After rubbing away the pain he caught a smile. He could not remember the last time he had bumped his head. He was always so careful, because it hurt like fuck. Being a man would take some getting used to. He thanked the world for the reminder of his insignificance.

He followed the stream for around an hour, until it pooled into a pond. It was too small to be a lake, almost too big to be a pond, beyond it woodland began. The sun was high and hot, so he sat by the pond, drained a skin of water and ate some rations. The loaf was dry and hard, so he flicked crumbs to the ducks that swam nearby. Soon there were a dozen around him and Guy was smiling as they fought and squabbled over the bread. He dropped a crumb by his foot, and a brave duck nipped in to take it, before running off to the side. Guy paused a moment and dropped another by his feet. Again a bold duck nipped in to snatch it. A third duck tentatively approached, as its beak snapped for the crumb. Guy's hand was equally as fast, grabbing the duck by the throat, wringing his neck and placing it quickly behind him. Most of the ducks flew off in a panic, landing in the middle of the pond. Two remained, perhaps oblivious to their flock mate's demise, and enjoyed feasting on the crumbs unchallenged as Guy tempted them closer, until he grabbed another by the throat and the other took off.

Guy sat enjoying the view and enjoying the calm. He was able to relax, despite his minds frantic processing. Nature serves as a good reminder to our intended path, and for a moment, his mind drifted to Phylissa. She had been right to send him off. He was just a boy back then, and if she was to become the earl's heir, she would need to marry a man.

In less than half an hour the ducks had returned to the pond's edge, and were soon gobbling the remains of his stale loaf. Guy smiled at their stupidity as he teased them closer, taking two more. He removed their innards and tossed them in the pond noticing that there were fish within, some looked of a decent size, as they flashed their silvery backs whist feasting.

Guy left the ducks on a rock and headed off towards the woods where he thought he may have spotted some hazel growing. He was pleased to find that he was right, it made him stronger. There was quite the stretch of hazel bushes with their long straight upright branches. He harvested over two dozen from around the patch, never taking too many from one spot. He tied them in bundles of around a dozen with bark from a nearby willow, collected the ducks and returned upstream to Eastfield Manor, enjoying the walk, the freedom, the nature.

By the time Guy had removed the wings and tail feathers from the ducks, he decided he may as well finish the preparation and plucked all four clean. He had plucked many birds in his time, he had always been a good hunter. He placed three of them on the balcony and returned to his camp to make a fire to cook his own. While the bird cooked he read. He had a puzzle in his mind that he could not solve. The Knightmaker, Sir Parcifal, and two of his knights had survived the battle of Ashford. He had been able to identify Smith, but the other was more difficult. It made sense for it to be the stranger, he had a bond with the Knightmaker, they had shared time together, but it did not seem to fit. The stranger was not the man described in the book. He could not shake the man of cups from his mind, but he could not figure out why. His mind continued mulling as he ate the duck, placing the carcass in a pot for some morning broth.

He stripped the bark from the hazel branches, and straightened out any imperfections with the heat of the fire. As he scraped and shaped each branch to look and feel as close to each other as possible, he let his mind wonder, scouring his memories of what he had read, hoping somehow an answer would come to him.

By the time he had shaped all 26 branches the sun had long set, and stars winked through the clear night sky. He heard an owl off in the distance and momentarily yearned for its feathers, but night birds were not to be killed, such magnificent beasts as they were. He lay aback looking at the sky waiting to see a star flash across his vision, it was always something that caused wonder in him. Sleep found him first however, relaxed and content as he was.

Guy woke naturally with the world. It was summer, he knew it would be early and that he really should sleep more, but the birds were awake, and so was he. The cool morning breeze was someway refreshing. He drank some fruit water as he examined his work from the night before, the branches had firmed well and they were all of similar shape. One or two were thinner than the others, but that was nature, not everything was the same. He pulled on his running boots and before long was comfortably following the stream, lightly leaping over ditches and obstacles in his path. He was just starting to work his body when he reached the pond, and took a few minutes to recover. Stretching himself on the bank, he tried formulating a plan, but got absorbed in his exercises, and the strength within him.

When his breathing had returned to normal and his body felt alive he concentrated his mind. When he had been harvesting the Hazel, the previous day he was sure he had seen some odcha. He had been pleased to recognise it, it was good for cleaning the teeth. When he had read up on it the night before, he had found it had other properties, similar to the obovate, that he had not seen in these parts. Della had told him that *no matter where you are, if you know what to look for, you will find what you need.* He smiled at her words.

Guy located the odcha quickly enough, but he hunted around deeper into the woods for the ones he was looking for. He wanted the tender young shoots of the plant and was careful not to take too many from a single plant, unsure as to how much he would need, he harvested a good handful in his leather pouch before returning to the pond. He found a flat surface of rock and piled the shoots on it. He was to crush them with water to a paste, which he did using a rock and some water scooped from the lake, not much, just enough to wet them. Della had shown him to look, to see when it changes. *When it stops being mashed up roots and becomes a paste, you will see the change.* It did not take much crushing for the paste to start, the consistency changed and it became a bright white. He worked the shoots until they were all incorporated into the paste before scooping it into a pile on the rock.

He collected a few good sized pebbles and a handful of gravel, and surveyed the pond in front of him as he mixed the paste and gravel together and made a plan. Guy flung the stone he had mixed the paste with over arm, with enough purchase to see it towards the middle of the pond. It came down from a good height with a deep plop. As it landed he tossed the paste and gravel into the water a dozen feet from the shore and watched as the water turned white. As it spread he launched the pebbles into the air, one after another in rapid succession. In a half circle they splashed into the middle of the pond, hopefully directing some fish towards him. He collected another handful of gravel and scattered that towards the middle of the pond. As it landed it looked and sounded as if he had taken an enormous lash to the pond, the slap of entry moving from right to left. He waited, hoping that it had worked. Fish were unpredictable creatures, but he hoped that he had driven at least some of them his way.

He was just starting to entertain the idea that it had not worked when a tiddler rose to the surface and lay on its side. A shiver of excitement ran through him, and made him stronger. Within minutes there were several fish floating on the surface, but as Guy congratulated himself he realised that he had not thought of how to retrieve them. He removed his running boots and waded into the lake, trying to collect the slippery silver objects with his hands. He managed only to throw one to the banks before removing his shirt and using that to scoop up some others. There were two reasonable sized fish that would serve for noonshine, which he collected and left the rest to recover. The Odcha only stunned the fish. They should all recover in a few minutes, probably with a headache of the hells, if indeed fish could have a headache. It was strange, thought Guy to himself, the differences between the animals, though they all have the same intention, to see tomorrow. These fish, as the ducks before them, would not see tomorrow, and someway that touched Guy. They had died for a good cause though, and that was all anyone could really ask for.

When he was dry, Guy put his running boots back on, tied the fish in his shirt and started the walk back to Eastfield Manor. He was starting to think that things were going his way, and despite knowing it was a dangerous path for the mind, he did not stop himself. In fact he enjoyed it, there was some positivity about him. For the first time he thought that he may actually be able to fulfil Phylissa's desires. For once it seemed real, and he was not about to prevent himself from having that experience. He pulled himself together before he crawled under the bridge with more care than usual, and within a minute he was back in the familiar surroundings of his camp. The mind-set of his quest returned, and just like that the romantic notions of him having completed the quest vanished from his mind.

He gutted the fish, disposing of the waste over the wall, perhaps a fox would enjoy them later, they ate anything. He sharpened some skewers and set them to soak in the stream while he cleaned the two larger fish putting the heads and trimmings in a pot. He skinned and filleted the smaller fish, the skin and bones going in one pot, the flesh in another for a broth. He added water to both and set them over the fire as he harvested leaves to flavour the fish, and larger ones to bake it in. He wrapped the fish in a parcel with the leaf and secured it with the dampened skewers. You had to work quickly with fish, it could spoil quickly.

It was only once everything was set that he looked towards the house. There was no one around, the courtyard was still and he could see the ducks were still sat atop the steps. They would have been spoiled by the sun, but while he considered the waste, he also thought about why they were still there. *Had they gone?* While he waited for the fish to cook and the pots to boil he split and trimmed the larger feathers from the ducks.

After eating he rummaged through the pile of scrap looking for any thin bits of metal, from buckles and harnesses to odd bits of flat metal, and used pieces of roughly equal size as the arrowheads, using the iron bar to bash and bend the metal onto the shafts. The pot of fish skin and bones had boiled away to a thick sticky mass, and he set the pot to cool on a flat stone. He ripped the sleeves off one of his linen shirts, and picked out threads from one of them, forming a pile beside him. Guy picked up a shaft and dipped a thread in the sticky mixture before dipping each feathers stalk into it and holding three onto the shaft. He took the thread and carefully wrapped it around the base, then through the spines, and secured it firmly at the other end. In two hours he had done the lot, and was pleased with the quality of his work. He had not made arrows in some years, but was happy with what he had produced. Now he could practice the long arrow.

26

It was four mornings later when the Knightmaker approached his camp as he sat down to a bowl of boiled oats. Without a word Guy offered him the bowl.

'Fuck that, I'll take the pot,' and he did, using the stirring spoon to shovel the oats in his mouth to satisfied grunts. Guy ate his own in silence, the Knightmaker was not for talking. He placed his bowl down as the Knightmaker scraped the pot clean. 'You make good fucking oats Guy of Waering.' Guy just nodded, hoping the smile he felt inside was not on his face. 'My business took longer than anticipated, I trust you are well rested.'

'Your business?'

'I had an urgent matter to attend. What, did you think we ran from Ashford because you punched Robert Young?' He laughed. Even when he laughed he scared the shit out of Guy. 'If that little prick had said anything I would have ripped his fucking head off before I took your hand. And Lord Rowan would applaud me for doing it. You are young, I know, but the world does not revolve around you.' The Knightmaker stood to leave, 'Offence training. Two hours. Wear your armour.'

With that he returned to the house leaving Guy a little confused. *What was the urgent matter?* He put it from his mind as he drank some fruit water and put his armour on. He had been practicing over the last few days. Now that he knew how the armour should feel, he was better able to fit it. He had not done it as well as the stranger, but he was improving. When he walked around to the training area Hawkins was heading into the house favouring his blood stained side. Guy knew he could help, but a distant throb in his elbow made him keep his silence. The stranger and the Knightmaker stepped forward standing on a step before him, the stranger in his armour, holding his helm under his arm. For the first time, he stood before the Knightmaker knowing who he was and ready to learn from one of the baddest fuckers who ever lived. The truth was Guy did feel refreshed. He had allowed his body to recover, yet kept his training ticking over. The six days of solitude had revealed much to him about the workings of his body, and he had absorbed the transformation from boy to man. He stood before the Knightmaker for the first time as a man, and any man is worthy of respect.

His heart beat firm in his chest, his breathing controlled, inside he felt as if a spring coiled, waiting to release. Release the doors to learning, to training, to making himself stronger. For the first time he stood before the Knightmaker, and he wanted it.

'I trust you were paying attention during your training. The moves used against you are moves taught in castles throughout the kingdom. Show me what you have learnt.' The stranger pulled on his helm, stepped down to join Guy in the yard, tapped his sword to his helmet and was ready in North East.

Guy nodded, and readied himself, moving cautiously towards the stranger. Guy Struck, the stranger parried, and Guy continued a sequence he had been on the reverse of many times, stepping, swinging high and low. At the end of each sequence they returned to the centre of the training yard and the Knightmaker offered instruction. The moves came easily to him, he had seen them often enough, knew how to counter them, and had performed them many times with the iron bar. With a sword in hand it felt right. The Knightmaker ironed out any learned imperfections at a casual pace, Guy was feeling good, confident in his progress.

'A notch further' called the Knightmaker. The stranger tapped his sword against his helm, harder this time. Guy realised that they had been going at a slow pace because the stranger had told him to. Guy nodded, and stepped in, with more purpose, with more speed. They danced a few sequences, and while Guy's breath was heavy, he was smiling inside his helm.

'Now let us see how to turn defence into attack.'

Guy did not understand the difference, and stepped in as before. The swords sang steel on steel as he pushed the stranger back with each parried attack. As he went for a low strike to the thigh, the stranger stepped in and rang Guys helm with his sword.

'Just because you attack, do not forget your defence. We go again.'

Guy stepped in, blow parried, as he moved seamlessly in to the second move, the strangers sword moved his off course before slapping his ribs. 'We go again.' Called the Knightmaker and time after time Guy stepped in, and time after time the stranger made his armour sing. Unpredictable, coming at different times in the sequences, but Guy soon realised that each time the counter for a certain attack came, it was always the same move. Guy stepped forward, someway slowed in pace, the stranger matched him, and a more precise, more intimate dance began. The stranger always got him, but on occasion he had begun to block or had seen it coming, and that pleased Guy.

The Knightmaker called halt to the training and told Guy to get rid of the fucking rock, and clear the fucking courtyard as if it were his second day there. Guy had never heard him talk so much, giving direction and encouragement. 'We go again.' was a common shout, and for the first time Guy felt like he was a part of the 'we'.

The following morning as Guy was about to break his fast on boiled oats, the Knightmaker appeared and cleaned the pot again, the only sounds coming from him the grunts of satisfaction as he ate. As he placed the pot on the floor he turned to Guy.

'Yesterday, I wanted to tell you that you did well at the tournament, you showed restraint. And if you restrain, you should also release. I want to show you something.' Without word Guy stood and followed the Knightmaker over to the outcrop of rock and watched him pick up the iron bar with excitement building. The strangers display was burned into his memory. Was he about to get one from Sir Parcifal himself? The Knightmaker gently swung the bar a few times to feel its weight, then as the stranger had done commenced the moves as if the bar was a sword. The Knightmaker was only warming up, merely tickling the rock with the iron bar. Guy watched as he stopped the high velocity bar as it approached the rock, with enough control to barely touch the rock itself. He was being precise in his movement, he wanted Guy to see as he began to draw the iron bar across the rock as he made contact. At first Guy thought that it was to demonstrate the superb control he had with the bar in his hands, but as the Knightmaker picked up the pace he saw there was a further message. The Knightmaker was slicing rather than striking the rock. The Knightmaker ended with a flurry, showing incredible speed and agility. The bar moved so fast he could barely see it, but it moved with control, with purpose.

Guy watched, hoping he was not open mouthed in awe as the Knightmaker stepped up to the rock, the iron bar out in front only a few inches from the rock. A loud crack came from the rock as the iron bar met it with incredible force. As he had seen at the tournament, the Knightmaker had raised immense power with such little movement. He repositioned the bar and repeated the show.

'Release.' he said as again the bar made the rock sing with deep resonance from its impact. Three further times the Knightmaker shook the rock with his blows before spinning, tickling the rock with controlled slices before, combining the grace and fluidity of movement with the power of the last few inches, the final blow was landed with a crack that shook the morning air, and caused nearby brownspots to take to the wing. A chunk of rock fell from the outcrop, landing with a thud and rolling away. The Knightmaker laid the iron bar afloor. 'Offense training, two hours. Wear your armour.' The Knightmaker walked back to the house, but Guy just looked at the chunk of rock that had been removed in absolute awe.

After training, clearing the courtyard, and failing to recreate the Knightmaker's power with the iron bar, Guy sat gazing afire as he cooked a rabbit. His mind was constantly working, assessing, training, surviving. The moment's peace gained from staring afire was a moment to cherish. It was disturbed as the stranger opened the main gate and walked into the courtyard followed by an old woman. The sun was setting and shadows teased, but it was the figure of an old woman that followed the stranger. A memory of Della's mother flashed with fondness in his mind. A short time later as Guy was gnawing at the rabbit's hind the old woman left the house, followed by the stranger and the Knightmaker. They talked awhile, though Guy could not hear, and the stranger escorted her home while the Knightmaker returned to the house. In his entire time at Eastfield manor, that was the longest he had ever seen the gate open for. It was closed again once she had left, but it had been open for the duration of the old woman's stay. Someway Guy was more comfortable when the gates were closed.

The following morning after removing his own bowl of oats Guy placed the pot on the balcony. There were enough oats for everyone. No sooner had the first spoonful passed his lips he saw the Knightmaker walking across the courtyard towards him. Guy stopped eating and looked up at him. 'I have been told that you are good with plants, and have some knowledge.'

'I have barely taken a step along that path of learning.'

'Yet you keep yourself healthy where others have festered. I want you to have a look at Hawkins.'

'The old woman?'

'Would not help him. She says it is beyond her current ability.'

'Then it will most certainly be beyond mine.'

'You will see him anyway, maybe give him something for the pain.'

'I don't have anything ready.'

The Knightmaker turned and began walking back to the house. Guy stood and followed, two steps behind, one to the left. It was not have the moment that he thought it would be when he entered the house for the first time. He had thought that it would have more significance. *To live in expectation is to deny true experience.* Who had told him that? He tried to remember as he followed the Knightmaker down an unremarkable corridor before entering a room. It was sparse, baron of any personality, or even furniture, just a cot and a chair. Guy had more possessions in his camp than were in this room. There was a smell of blood, and disease in the air, Hawkins lay on the cot, fevered.

'A morning star cracked his armour and pushed it into him.' The Knightmaker told him as the stranger pulled back a damp bloodstained cloth that covered the midriff of Hawkins. Guy winced, happy someway that he had not been able to break his fast. Regurgitated oats would not help the situation. A big angry red gash met his eyes and the smell of rotting flesh burned his nose. Along with the gash was an area that looked as if the chain mail had been embedded in the flesh. Where the skin was broken the flesh was starting to discolour, and the area around the wound a dark red was spreading. Guy had never seen such a wound, and any resentment that he may have held towards Hawkins melted away.

'Do you have any strongwyne?'

'Aye.'

'Can you boil some?'

'No. The old woman says the wound is too close to the guts to treat with boiled wine or fire. It would most likely kill him.' Guys mind whirred, what would Della do?

'I can make something for the fever. Get the strongwyne, it can clean the wound. We must remove the rotting flesh, so tie him securely to the cot. He must not move.'

Guy scurried out of the house and back to his camp. After checking his book and wondering what the fuck he was doing, he collected some herbs and leaves from the courtyard, some from his pouch, and set about crushing them in a bowl and stone. He waited for the sweet smell to emerge before scraping the rough paste into half a skin of fruit water which the then shook vigorously as he returned to the house.

The stranger was tying Hawkins uncontested to the cots wooden frame. Guy gave the skin to the Knightmaker 'Have him drink this, it will help calm the fever. I will be back as soon as I can. Wrap his legs and bind him to the cot, his chest too.'

Guy rushed back to the camp, gathered Della's potions and other equipment and left it on his rollmat. He ducked under the bridge and followed the stream a short while until he saw the Arnica patch, the daisy like flowers were known for their wound healing properties. He harvested a handful of fresh flowers, some yarrow, wild garlic and elderberry leaves. After slicing the leaves and flowers with his knife on a flat stone he combined some herbs from his pouch and ground them into a thick paste with a clean rock, scooping it onto a plate when he was done. He thrust the Spike that smith had given him into the fire, gathered his knife and the plate along with his healing pouch and returned to the house with hurry.

As he entered the room he saw Hawkins had been secured to the cot, the stranger held the strongwyne.

'I think it is starting to take effect.' the Knightmaker said, though to Guy it appeared there was still much effect to be had. Guy walked over and looked at Hawkins eyes. Through the fever there was fear, delirium.

'This is going to hurt I am afraid.' Guy held the gaze for a few seconds before moving to examine the wound. He turned to the Knightmaker, 'We need to remove the infected flesh.' Guy poured some strongwyne into the wound and a scream came from Hawkins, though with the secure strapping he barely moved. The wound was deep and open, Guy hoped he had prepared enough paste. Guy pulled his knife from its sheath. 'It is the sharpest blade I have,' he explained.

Holding the dead flesh in his fingers he slowly pulled the knife through cutting a sliver of flesh from Hawkins as he screamed. 'There is a metal spike in my fire, I need it.' The stranger disappeared returning quickly as Guy poured more strongwyne into Hawkins. Guy scooped out some of Della's balm with two fingers and applied it inside the wound, the squishy softness unnerved him. If Hawkins had not passed out from the pain before, Guy was certain that he would with his fingers inside him. He remembered the pain when it had been applied to his arm. He took the spike from the stranger gently and carefully pressing it where he had cut, stemming the flow of blood. He only held it long enough to stop the bleeding, it would be important that the blood could flow again soon to help the healing. Guy worked quickly, yet it was with a gentle touch that he packed the wound with his paste of leaves and flowers. The mixture healed wounds and helped fight infection. He packed until the cavity was full, and then applied more, covering much of Hawkins' midriff with the paste.

'It should set hard where it touches the air, the rest should help it heal. He must remain tied and still until it has healed else it will rip open again. I can look again in a few days. If I may be excused I need to gather more herbs to fight the fever.' The Knightmaker nodded.

'Aye, but after noonshine we train until sunset.'

27

Guy's life was busy for the following days, not only did he train with the Knightmaker and stranger twice a day, but he maintained his own training, and provided the food, along with the tinctures to fight Hawkins' fever. He had carefully been drying rabbit skins for a couple of days and ground them in his pot and stone, it took several hours to achieve the fine powder that he was after.

After preparing the oats and setting a pot of boiled water to cool, Guy meticulously prepared his equipment. It had been a week since Guy had packed the wound, and whilst Hawkins had not died he was still in the grip of a strong fever. Guy controlled his breathing, he had never done anything like this before, and no matter how much he had read and considered and even practiced on a small boar, he was struggling to comprehend what he was about to attempt. When the Knightmaker approached he was double checking that he had everything he needed.

'Are you ready?'

'I will be. Could you give him this to drink,' said Guy handing over a tiny bottle, 'It will make him sleep. Please fetch me when he is.' Guy returned to his equipment. He scooped out a little of Della's balm into his pot, added just a few drops of water and combined with the rabbit skin to make a paste. He would add more water when he needed it later. There was a pot steeping herbs wrapped in linen, Guy squeezed as much as he could from the mulch, making the water in the pot a darker more vibrant shade of green. He coated some thread with Della's balm and threaded it through the thickest of his needles. He had spares, made of bone, but hoped that if the needle could deal with boar skin, that it would handle Hawkins. When the Knightmaker returned a few minutes later, Guy was ready and rehearsing in his mind what was to follow. Gods he hoped he did not fuck it up.

Trying to appear composed, he followed the Knightmaker across the courtyard, two steps behind, one to the left. His appearance was for himself as much as anyone else. There was a purpose about him as he stepped inside the house for only the second time. It smelled stale in the room, which pleased Guy, for whilst not a pleasant aroma, it was better than the one of rotting flesh. Guy packed rolls of cloth beside Hawkins and pressed at the pack that filled the wound. It had solidified on the surface, Guy broke away pieces from the edge placing them in a pot. He wet the edges of the pack to bring it away from the skin and gently worked the pack, hoping it would not break as he removed it.

He was calm, and worked with a careful mind, unlike before where it had been instinct. He was well prepared this time, he had to be. He worked the pack loose and finally it broke free from one side of the wound, then, with a little persuasion, the other. With one gentle, smooth movement he lifted the pack from the wound as a wet sound squelched their ears and the smell of raw flesh stung their nostrils. He only released his breath when the bulk of the pack was safely in the bowl, the stranger removed it immediately, replacing it with an empty one. Looking inside the wound there were remnants of the pack, flecks of black dead blood that he would wash out, but no clots, no real mess to clear out. He emptied a ladle of the gently warm water into the wound and wiped away residue from the side. The angry redness had not spread, it had in fact subsided. Guy flushed the wound several times, the excess water flooding into the rolls of cloth. He gently pushed the two inch wide wound closed, pushing out more water and enabling him to see inside. He could see the sack that held Hawkins' guts, intact but exposed. It could have been so much worse for him. A part of Guy wanted to look, and learn from seeing the inside of a man, but another part, a greater part, was unnerved by it. Instead he examined both sides of the wound ensuring he knew where to place the stitches. It was good clean flesh and he could sew at the depth required without any obvious problems. He flushed the wound again, this time with the bright green herbal liquid. It would keep it clean and help it heal. Gathering his needle and balm soaked thread, he flushed the wound one more time and turned to the Knightmaker.

'I need his wound pushed together, but from far away to give me room to sew. Like this.' He placed his hands on Hawkins body, one around the side, under his ribs, the other on his abdomen. Gently he pushed and the green liquid escaped as the wound was pushed together. Guy poured more green liquid into the wound as the Knightmaker nodded to the stranger who stepped up. He kept out of Guy's way and copied his hand positions before slowly and gently pushing Hawkins' body back together. Guy trembled as the needle penetrated Hawkins flesh for the first time. It was not easy to get a deep thread to hold him together, it was even harder when Guy considered that this was a real person, whose life depended on his actions, and not just the corpse of a boar. Guy controlled his breathing, found the strength inside him and focussed only on the sewing of the wound. Blood trickled from the holes of the needle which pleased Guy, as only when blood flowed would the body heal. Despite his best efforts the stitching was not particularly neat, certainly nowhere close to those that Della had sewn on his arm. But they were secure, and did not seem to pull the flesh into unnatural shapes. He did not let himself relax as he tied and cut the thread, he still had work to do. He emptied a ladle of green liquid over the wound, and added a quarter ladle to the rabbit skin mixture in his pot, working the thick gelatinous paste into something more workable. He would have preferred to apply it before sewing the wound, but in practice, it had made it more difficult to work with the needle and the area could get more slippery. He applied it directly to the wound, covering the length of the stitches, leaving a little built up between them. This would set and bind the flesh together, or so the book told him, and he had no reason to doubt the book. The book had kept Hawkins alive so far. He cleaned the area, and removed the rolls of cloth.

'Keep him tied for a few days, let the wound breathe. It needs air to heal. Don't let him move, and keep an eye on the fever.'

The Knightmaker nodded as Guy gathered his equipment and returned to his camp, finally able to collapse onto his bedroll, emotionally exhausted. It had taken more out of him to sew the wound than an entire day of training. He found himself wanting Hawkins to recover, which confused him as he had no love for the man. It was the human conundrum of knighthood.

It was a day without the need for training, but Guy trained anyway, it helped him to re-centre after the events of the morning, it helped him remember why he was there. He had been on a good driving run. It was a beautiful thing to run in the summer, he had the energy to go on forever. He had worked hard on his exercises in the courtyard, and had enjoyed over an hour stretching his body in the sun. As he was stretching the stranger returned with the old woman and took her to the house. Guy felt concern arise within him. *Had something gone wrong with Hawkins?*

After his stretches he idled around his camp, drank some fruit water, fiddled with his arrows, all the time awaiting the old woman's exit. She had been in there for half an hour when the stranger escorted her from the building. The stranger turned and left her on the balcony where she waited a moment before turning and walking towards Guy's camp. Anxiety biled in his throat as she approached. *Was it bad news that she was bringing?* Being old she remained silent until she stood before Guy and was sure that she had his attention.

'That was good work on the boy.'

'How is he?' he asked, though his mind amused itself at Hawkins being referred to as 'the boy'.

'It does not matter how he is. It was good word regardless. You should acknowledge my words when I speak them. They are not said for naught.' Guy stopped in his tracks, the words cutting him, not the severity of the tone.

'I'm sorry. Thank you. It was my first time.'

'Then a good start has been made. Tell me, where did a man like you learn this?' *A man like him?*

'I have a friend who has helped me in the past, and I have a book that helps me now.'

'Show me your book.' Without a single thought of questioning the old woman he reached immediately for his book, it was easy to hand. He passed it over.

'My friend recommended it.'

'Natural Remedies of Rodina, a fine book, I owned it as a child. Beautiful pictures if I recall.'

'It certainly helps to identify the plants.'

'Indeed, Now this friend of your gave you a balm. Give it to me.' This time Guy did hesitate for a moment, but retrieved the near empty pot of Della's balm, the one she sold in Varen. The old woman opened the pot and sniffed it. 'This is old world healing.' She gave the pot back to Guy, seemingly satisfied with what she had found out.

'So the boy has woken up, they wanted me to see him, so that he thinks it is I who healed him. Why is this?'

'I would rather he not know I helped.'

'Helped? You saved his life. I told them to make him comfortable and let him pass in peace. But you, with your patient ways... Well I will not do it. I will see to his healing from now on, but when he is capable I will tell him exactly who saved his life.' Guy started to protest, but the old woman was having none of it. 'He should know and I will tell him. I am not sure he will thank you for that stitching though. It is messy, but not bad for a first attempt, though you needed a curved needle for that work. I have some old needles you can have in my hut, if you walk me home you can have them. Bone... pah, we have developed some since the old world. You should at least use a proper needle.'

'I had...' Guy started, but he was not about to defend himself to someone who knew much more than he. She must have seen his spare bone needles. Fortunately he had not needed them.

'Come on, I have things to do,' she said as she headed to the gate. He scurried after the old woman, and again after he had closed the gate. For an old woman she had some speed, it made Guy smile. Her hut was the most westerly building in the village. Once inside there was a large sparse room, dominated by a straw mat on the floor. He stood by the entrance as she went to a cupboard by a chair on the other side of the room and rummaged through removing small metal box which she brought over. She had not been lying when she said she had some old needles. The tin was full of them, different thicknesses, some curved, some straight. As she sorted through them her nimble fingers deftly removed half a dozen and she held them out for Guy to take.

'Take these and learn how to use them. Let's hope you never have to.'

'Thank you.'

'Since you are here, there is something else I can give you. Your friend has paid this time, the quiet one, he used to visit me often. If you come again it will be a copper. Take off your shirt while I get ready.'

Guy sat a moment as the old woman vanished through a curtain into another room. Absurd thoughts were running through his head, and a lack of explanation of what was about to happen did not help him dampen them. *Was this to be the stranger's way of thanking him?* He could not banish the notion, and it continued developing as the old woman returned from her room wearing tight trousers and shirt. *Not like this!* A mischievous part of his mind called out. He was preparing to extrapolate himself from the awkward situation as she told him to stand still so that she could get a good look at him. Nerves and anxiety made him obey, he was sure the old woman could see it on his face, she could see his innocence. She stood looking at him in a manner not dissimilar to the way the blacksmith had looked at him. She was sizing him up for something, he could see her mind working, calculating. As she looked at him from behind she prodded at his back and shoulders, sometimes finding sore spots that sent a silent jolt of pain through him.

'It is important for you to be relaxed. I want you to relax with your breathing. Lie on your front with your arms to the sides.' Guy was trying to relax his breathing, but it would not slow his mind. There was no idea in his mind what this old woman was about to do to him, but someway he found himself lying down. 'Relax.' Guy exhaled, relaxing as much as he could. In a flash the woman's arms looped under his armpits and she jerked his body backwards. Bones cracked, some kind of sublime agony shot through him, his scream never reached his throat, being absorbed into his body instead. It made him stronger. The old woman pulled his body using knees and elbows to give purchase to her movements. They were very precise, very quick and she handled his bulk with impressive ease. She cracked near every bone in his body, even his toes. She dug her elbows into his back, as she stood on his hips, the deepest crack he had heard resonated from within him. He felt it. Sharp agonising pain, but distant. He knew it should hurt, he could feel the wave of pain, but it was a pain that did not hurt. She had him sit before her and relax, her hands on his head, one on his jaw, the other on the opposite crown. He breathed out, she twisted his head and a blinding white light shot through him. There was no pain, only ecstasy as she repeated the manoeuvre on the opposite side. It cracked from between his shoulders to the very base of his skull, and energy flowed uninhibited through his body. He wanted to use it to make him stronger, but it moved with such intensity that he had no control whatsoever. He let it flow though him until it exhausted itself leaving a white void inside him that was bigger than Rodina itself. His body had just experienced the biggest release of energy he had known, and he had found bliss in the void.

Through the bliss be became aware of a burning warmth coming from his elbow. The old woman's hands were not even touching him. It took a few moments for his brain to register and react. Whilst it burned, it was not hot, the pain, if it were indeed pain, was different to the pains he had experienced before, this somehow went deeper and had no menace. Still, he found that he pulled his arm away from the old woman, his eyes meeting hers. There was no malice, no anger, no frustration, nothing at all really. She moved Guy to the edge of the mat having him sit so that his bare feet touched the earth. She placed her hands on his feet.

'I am going to reconnect you to the ground, for you may feel a little like the sky. Think of the roots of a great tree reaching into the ground, think of yourself connecting with the world.' Guy breathed and for a while could feel the void absorbing into him as his spirit reached into the ground. He needed to do nothing for it to make him stronger. His mind had been bombarded with energy and blown apart, connecting with the world bought it back together again, with a new awareness. All those times when he had felt connected to nature and to the world, no matter how profound they had been at the time, they all paled in significance to what Guy had just felt, and continued to feel. A deep connection with the world, and he allowed himself to absorb his awareness of it.

He inhaled sharply involuntarily, it snapped him out of his dream and the old woman sat before him in her tight clothing. It did not seem absurd any more. There was so much that he wanted to say, but words were not making their way out of him. She instructed him to dress and made herself busy in the corner as he did.

He found it difficult composing himself, a memory of leaving the earl's feast flashed through his memory, a touching point. He focussed on keeping steady breaths, pulling on his final boot, and collecting the needles.

'Thank you for the needles,' he said as he stood.

'They need a clean, but should serve you well.' Guy met the old woman's eyes.

'How did your hands get hot?' he asked. There were no other words in his mind.

'My hands did not get hot,' she replied to the direct question as people often did.

'How did you make my arm get hot?'

'I did not, your arm got hot because it had to.'

'How?'

'Ahhh,' she sighed, 'Who are we to question the way things are? Next time you come, bring a copper.'

Guy took it as his cue to leave, he wanted to know a lot about what she had done to him that day. He would bring her a copper next time and find out more.

'Thank you,' he offered. The old woman nodded, an unreadable smile on her lips.

'Your friend is not the only one who knows old world healing,' she said quietly with a wink as Guy pulled the door to. Guy expected his mind to be whirring with unanswered questions, but as he straightened in the sun, he stood taller and straighter than he ever had before. The energy still flowed through him. Something he wanted to explore back in camp.

28

For three days he trained, then had one day of rest. Every other rest day he went to see the old woman, but by the end of his fourth visit to her, he knew little more than he did after the first. There were many things occupying his mind in between training, but training always came first, and he was able to dance with the stranger better than he ever imagined. The Knightmaker always found fault, and always saw place for improvement, and in the end the stranger always rang his helm, but he was quick of both sword and feet. The iron bar was proving more difficult, he could wield it well, but struggled with the Knightmaker's 'release' blows. His archery was of a good standard, and his long arrows had been well used. Stretching was now done with a new emphasis, and he tried to keep his spine well cracked. He began to look forward to visiting the old woman, the feeling it gave him was better than anything, even winning the tournament. Every time he left he wanted to walk back in and give her another copper. She seldom showed him the burning hands, but Guy was happy to have his body in full working order. He never felt more alive that when he left the old woman's hut. They were the best coppers that he had ever spent in his life.

At training the following morning the Knightmaker stood beside the armour clad stranger, and Hawkins was sat achair beside them. He wore no shirt, and Guy tried to see wound. He saw no angry redness of infection, which was good, but saw not the wound properly. As he nodded to Hawkins he wondered if the old woman had told him. Judging by Hawkins lack of response, he guessed not. He walked up and stood before them.

'Let's show Hawkins how far you have come.' declared the Knightmaker. 'Today we freestyle, anything goes.'

The stranger tapped his helm with his sword, then again harder. They would start steady and work towards Guys limit. *Freestyle.* Guy nodded to the stranger and pulled on his helm to stand ready in north east. The stranger walked towards him casually spinning the sword in his hand. The spinning tuned into a blow as the stranger stepped in. Guy managed to parry it, but at the expense of having to retreat. This happened again and again as Guy struggled to stop the casual blows. They came in from different angles, from new angles, but he parried and stepped out from each one. Guy imagined the smirk on Hawkins face. He was struggling to get to the strangers pace. The stranger stepped in again, casually aiming at Guys thigh. He parried it, but the stranger used the momentum of the parry to sweep into another move as Guy stepped back. It was a move that Guy knew, and he spun the stranger's blade away before cutting back to his midriff. The stranger dodged before meeting the blade, but Guy was ready, and the dance began.

When Guy was getting lost, the stranger offered him a familiar move to counter. They danced around the training ground, the Knightmaker offering his usual critique and encouragement. Guy had his helm rung many times, but he too was landing blows, and he knew, one or two that caught the stranger by surprise. It was hot in the suit, but Guy was enjoying the training so much that he was disappointed when the Knightmaker called halt for the morning.

'Yes. You are getting somewhere.'

He turned to the stranger, 'You are taking it easy on him, inviting him in, but I think on this occasion it was to his benefit.' The Knightmaker returned his attention to Guy who had pulled off his helm and lowered his coif revealing sweat matted hair and the redness of exertion. 'This afternoons training requires no armour. Go to the village and get loaves for noonshine, and some meat.' Guy nodded and returned to his camp, his body was buzzing, despite the exertion. That had been the best training session by far. Freestyle. *Wasn't that what it was all about anyway?* Even the most disciplined of swordsmen must have their own interpretation. In the heat of battle technique faded, there were things of more importance to occupy the mind, like survival.

Guy removed his armour, freshened himself in the stream and dressed in his armless linen shirt. It has smelt of fish for some time, but had quickly become his favourite thing to wear. After pulling on his boots, he removed a few coppers from his coinpurse and slipped them into a pouch on his belt. He had started spending again and would soon need to break another gold. He returned with four loaves, some cold boiled pork and soft cheese, which he left on the balcony once he had taken some for himself. He left a serving jug of fruited water with it.

After his noonshine meal Guy removed his belt and examined it. He had become obsessed with organising his kit and was starting to make the most of the belt that had been given to him. He was able to incorporate some of his kit into the belt. He had two golds hidden in slits between the layers of leather, his tournament token received the same treatment in a pouch that was attached. Needles and thread were hidden within it, a pot of balm secured in its own pouch. It held his knife and spike, had places for a sword and water skins. It had a large leather pouch that more often than not was empty. There were still loops that he had not used, and set his mind to seeing how he could further improve it.

When he reported for training the Knightmaker was stood with the stranger. He did not wear armour, he wore a cloak, a dark, medium heavy cloak.

'There is more to being a knight than combat. There is the knight's code, there is chivalry. There is surviving when no man should, there is doing whatever it takes to get to safety. We are not here to fuck about. You can swing a sword pretty well, and I have seen you forage and hunt. That is a good start. Battles are not always fought on the battlefield. There is much a knight should know of the land they live in. It is time you started to learn. You are going on a little camping trip. When you come back we will finish your training.'

The Knightmaker turned toward the house, but not before a final glance toward Guy. He did not know what it meant, but he was glad it had happened. They stood for a moment, the stranger motionless seemingly waiting for Guy.

'I must get some things,' said Guy before rushing over to his camp, quickly grabbing his sword, spear, bow and arrows, his herb pouch, a bag for spare clothes, water skins. He was silently cursing himself for not having a day sack ready. A knight should always be ready. He spotted the stranger approaching his camp. He was quite pleased that he had managed to ready himself so quickly. But when he looked up, the stranger shook his head and nodded at the pile of kit on the rollmat. Guy looked at it, it was excessive, but he did not know what to expect. He picked up the spear and held it up for the stranger. He shook his head. Guy stored the spear away. The stranger looked on. His sword, a shake of the head. He stored it away, thinking perhaps of asking to put it in the house. It was his sword, it had a story to tell. The stranger looked on. The bag, the clothes, a shake of the head, he stored them away. On it went until Guy stood before him with no kit whatsoever. Exasperated Guy lifted his shirt to show the stranger his belt. The stranger nodded, but as he lowered the shirt, the stranger motioned with his finger to stop. He motioned at Guys waist. He fumbled around with the pouches, until hand his hand rested on his coinpurse the stranger shook his head. Accepting that they may have no need for coin Guy stored his it away, conscious that the stranger was watching him. For an unexplained reason Guy found that he did not distrust the stranger. Had it been Hawkins watching he would have moved the coin at the earliest opportunity. The stranger, he felt, supported him, they danced well together. The stranger motioned for them to leave, but Guy bid him pause, pulling up a blanket. The stranger wore a cloak. Guy did not have one. *How could he not have a cloak?* He chastised himself but for a moment, shaking the blanket open, pulling out his knife and cutting a slit in the middle. He pushed his head through and let the blanket sit around his shoulders. He probably looked as ridiculous as the old woman in her tight trousers, but he cared not. A cloak was a useful tool that he did not have. The blanket would have to do. He looked to the stranger, whose shrug Guy took as consent. The stranger motioned Guy to follow the stream, and as he emerged into the world a bright summer's day was there to greet him. He was about to find out just how big the world was.

29

Guy stepped from the cover of the woods, taking a moment to let his eyes get used to the glare of the sun. He was dirty, exhausted, dehydrated and in need of a good meal. His clothes were torn and stained with blood, his eyes were almost feral, alert to threat. Every step over the last two days had taken everything he had. He had been running on empty for too long. In the valley beneath him the many faceted emerald garden city of Varen spread out before him in full summer thrust. From his vantage point the true majesty of the garden city glimmered at him. It was an experience of green that Ash would contemplate for hours.

Whilst he saw the city before him, it took some time for his mind to register it. Starvation and exhaustion affect more than just the body. His mind had been fried, he did not even know how long it had been since he had left Eastfield manor, he estimated ten days, but would not be surprised to find out it had been a round dozen, or even a fortnight. He had eaten things no man should eat, he had survived on drinking his own piss, he had been pushed beyond limits he could not have conceived of only days before. Guy had long since discarded his concerns that his mind may have broken again, his only concern had been survival.

Survival. For the first time in days he was not on full survival mode, someway it was fading leaving a void in his being. He looked to the stranger, who despite having been through everything with him, eaten what he ate, drank what he drank, looked little different to usual. His clothes were dirty and torn, but he wore it well.

It was over.

'Ha,' Guy exclaimed. It was the only noise he made, as the realisation finally dawned within him. It was over. 'Ha.'

Guy fell to his knees as relief stole his strength for a moment. 'Ha,' his breathing was rapid and deep, and that made him laugh. Relief made him laugh. It was over. The hells were behind him. Controlling his laughter he looked to the stranger. 'Is it over?' The stranger nodded and Guy's world paused. In that moment Guy absorbed the greatest sense of achievement of his entire life. Nothing else came close. He had survived. The stranger had taken his limits of endurance, his mental limits, and shat all over them. He had forced Guy to confront everything and to leave it behind. He had taught Guy the real meaning of survival, but Guy had learnt so much beside that. One of the first things he had realised was that his previous self-congratulation of becoming a man was just the thought of a boy. He was a man now, there was no doubt. It was not a question that would ever rise in his mind again.

Guy again looked over at the vale. He had never been so pleased to see anywhere as much as he was at that moment. It meant more than the vision of the place portrayed. It meant survival, it meant freedom. There was elation building in him but still the emotion that flooded him was relief. Through his breathing an occasional chuckle escaped. He looked to the stranger, the look in his eye said that it was over, that he had done well. There was a respect. The stranger gave the slightest of nods before reaching into one of his pouches and producing a wax tablet which he handed to Guy. Guy took the tablet and looked at it nonplussed. The stranger made a motion of breaking a dry bread with his hands. Guy bent the wax tablet until it cracked, splinters of wax falling away to reveal paper inside. There were two sealed notes, one for him, one for Smith. The stranger nodded encouragingly and Guy opened his note. It simply read *'Bring back White Mist'*. Guy found himself laughing again. After everything he had just been through… He looked to the stranger, who nodded at him, tossed him one of the bandits coin purses, turned back towards the woods and disappeared into their darkness. They were dark woods to Guy, woods that would probably haunt his dreams as long as he lived.

The hunted had become the hunters, and then died.

Guy sat awhile looking down over the valley, reflecting, absorbing, and recovering. He could not simply walk into the city until he had some of himself about him again.

The sun's afternoon slide was in motion before he felt able to stir himself. He could see the garden city before him, but he would do well to make it there before sunset, long as the days were. He would do it though. One more run. He had left exhaustion behind him long ago, it was no longer relevant to his existence. Instead of running for survival though he would be running towards something. Towards food and ale, towards a room to sleep in, towards normal, or as normal as a trip to Varen could be. He was running to familiarity, and that was what he craved more than anything.

He crawled to his feet, and without looking back lurched himself down the hill. He ran at a pace that went beyond simple exercise, there was still fear in his body, though it was gone from his mind. His body ran as it had become accustomed to. It ran fast, it ran efficiently, it ran on the fumes of his survival instinct, driving him through the meadows and the orchards reaching the irrigated fields of many crops. He stopped his run to bathe in an irrigation ditch and allowed the last of the day's sun to dry him as he walked to the city wall. Touching it made it real, and he spent a moment absorbing the reality of the city, letting it ground him. He made his way along the city wall to the gate he was most familiar with, barely a glance was cast his way as he entered the city with farmworkers returning home after a day in the fields. The hot bustle of the city quickly absorbed him, the smells and sounds sending his senses on a frantic dance. He kept his head down and focussed only on getting to the Four Kin inn.

Closing the door behind him he breathed awhile letting the hecticness fade away. As he stepped forward the old woman from behind the counter called out.

'Have you come for your free night?' She never looked up from the counter.

'No, I am happy to pay.' Guy unclenched his hand revealing the pouch to himself, he rummaged through it and removed two silvers, placing them on the counter.

'How long are you thinking of staying?'

'Only a couple of days, but I will need food, lots of food, and ale, and a bath.'

'Up the stairs, last door on the left. I'm going to be keeping my eye on you.'

Guy smiled inside as he ducked under the doorframe. Keep her eye on him, she would have to actually look at him first. He stepped through the door to his room, closed and locked it and sat on the cot for a moment before flopping himself backwards as his mind switched itself off. It had reached its saturation point, there was no more it could take.

It was the growl in his belly and the smell of food that woke him. When he unlocked and opened the door, two plates of food, a small cask of ale, a serving jug of water and a horn sat before him. A better sight he could not imagine. After taking them quickly inside he set about devouring the food. The duck gave him a sense of absolute joy as he sank his teeth into the breast and duck fat dribbled down his bearded chin. He ate like a man starved, gulping ale to wash it down. Fresh evening breads fed him with a familiar comfort as he forced food into his mouth, almost unable to keep up with his body's demands. But just as quickly as it started his appetite stopped. Only half the duck and a single bread had been eaten. He was so full that no matter how much he wanted to keep eating, to refuel, his body simply could not take any more. He drank ale until he passed out, which did not take long.

When his mind's eye opened in the morning his body screamed at his stupidity. His stomach wanted to eject its contents and his head was little more than a cloudy thump. He would keep the food inside him, he would use it to make him stronger, the ale too. His body had been through much worse than having to contend with a good meal and too much ale. But the ale had allowed sleep to find him, and if he had dreamt, he did not know it. He forced his eyes open and familiarised himself with his surroundings. He found himself curled aball on the wooden floor. Two empty plates and one empty cask next to him along with one full pot. The hour did not matter. It was day, he was alive, that was all that mattered. That, and the fact that if he did not piss soon he would burst. The pot was full, but in seconds he had removed the bung from the cask and imagined himself half filling it as relief swept through him. When there was finally no more to pass he crawled onto the cot and curled aball.

The next time he awoke it was with more purpose, he readied himself to go out into the city and find some clothes, but as he opened the door to the room he was faced with a noonshine of fruit and sweetbread with a wooden cup of red berry juice. He took the plate inside and ate at a more sedentary pace, confirming in his mind that it was the right thing to do, the sweet fruits brought vibrant freshness to his body. As he left the inn he sheepishly placed a silver on the counter.

'For the cask.'

As he stepped out into Varen he realised it was early evening, but even that light assaulted his eyes. He blinked and shuffled off towards the market. Only minutes away, doors down from the leatherback tavern a shop sold farmers clothes. Inside Guy easily found good robust clothes for a good price. It did not matter to Guy how much they cost, he would have bought them anyway. All he wanted was to crawl back in the cot and let sleep find him again.

He paused outside the Leatherback tavern, for a moment considering a horn or two of ale, but it was loud and busy. He did not feel like busy.

'Young Knight.' A voice called. Guy did not need to turn to know that it was the man of cups, he turned anyway. The man of cups met his eye. Guy let him look, he no longer cared enough to stop him. There was something in the man of cups eyes, an understanding, and something else. Something that told Guy that no matter how much he thought he had been through, the man of cups had been through more, much more. He had seen something similar in a man's eyes before. A realisation, a reaffirmation began to form in his mind, slowly like the blooming of a jungle flower, the petals slowly opened to reveal an understanding that needed pollinating.

'You should come and play tomorrow.' Guy opened his arms, in his mind asking the question *with what?* 'Tomorrow you can play with your blanket. I would be happy to take that.' Guy looked down, realising the mud and blood and gods know what else stained blanket still adorned his shoulders.

'My blanket?' The man of cups nodded beneath his hood.

'Tomorrow then,' and he ducked inside the Leatherback tavern leaving Guy to head back to the inn with his head down, and his mind spinning like a drunk in a cesspit.

'Your bath is ready,' called the old woman from behind the counter. That was it, no other words, not a glance. No reprimand for pissing in the cask.

'Thank you,' relied Guy as he ducked under the doorway to head up the stairs.

'I shall have another prepared for you in the morning.'

Guy ate his meal before climbing into the tub. The water still steamed, even in the summer heat as Guy enjoyed feeling it engulf him. Even though he knew he could not wash away the events of the last few days it did not stop him trying as he scrubbed himself raw with the bathing brush. He soaked awhile before climbing out of the tub and onto the cot. Sleep found him before his naked body had dried.

He woke with a start, the night's mischief turning to terror. He was cold, yet he sheened with sweat, he was panicked, yet calm, knowing it was a dream, his heart pounded, though he was relaxed. Sleep would not find him again soon. He could hear the sounds of the city waking on the other side of the shutter and someway he felt more able to be a part of it. Climbing from the cot he refreshed his face in the cold water in the tub before dressing in his farmers clothes. The trousers were just trousers, but the linen shirt fit like it was made for him, hanging on his frame like a tapestry on a castle wall. He rolled his shoulders enjoying the fit, he stretched his back feeling the effect of the last few days with pain and tightness. He spread his coin throughout his body in pouches and pockets. Farmers clothes were, it would appear, well equipped. He gathered his blanket and headed out.

He was not surprised to see the old woman behind the counter, he imagined she would be there whatever time of day or night he passed. He approached the counter, she did not look up.

'When I was here before, you said that if I needed help with a bath it would be a copper?'

'That's right.'

'I know a woman where I stay. She cracks bones and put the body right. Is there someone who could do that here?' He placed two coppers on the counter.

'I will have someone here this evening.'

'Thank you.'

Guy turned and left the inn, knowing that she had not looked up at him as he left. The morning air was cool, the sun not yet heating the sky. The streets were quiet, the city was only just starting it's day. If it could only remain like that, he wished to himself, it was almost serene. After breaking his fast on sweetbuns and fermented milk, whilst sitting achair on the side of street, he watched the carts and people bustle by. He approached the man of cups' stall with fuel for the morning. There were a good dozen people gathered around his stall, and more watching from a distance. What a spectacle it was, despite the man of cups seemingly having won his first game of the day. It amazed Guy that a man could make a living from a game. He joined the crowd watching from the outskirts. It would appear that the man of cups did not always require an item to play with. Some offered silver, sometimes he accepted coppers. The potential to turn a copper into gold at the turn of a cup was too much for some with greater need to resist, some people played when they should not. Guy found it particularly amusing watching a young brash socialite make absurd announcements when he arrived, striding forward to take the man of cups' gold. The man of cups did not move, the simple announcement that there was a queue was enough to have the crowd jeering at the young man. In frustration he joined the back of the line muttering to himself. Guy slipped in behind him, partly because he had seen enough of the man of cups' show, and partly because he wanted a closer look. The man of cups won the five games before the young rich boy, who had been looking strangely at Guy, stepped up with a silver, announcing that it was time to turn silver to gold. Guy quickly looked himself over in his mind. He thought he was looking quite smart in his new clothes, he was clean, what was it about him that caused such a look of disgust? Perhaps he had simply been intimidated having someone of Guy's size standing behind him. Guy looked down at the blanket he was holding and supressed a chuckle. That was far from clean, and had been closer to the socialite's nose than Guy's.

'I am taking your gold this time.'

'With what do you play?'

'A silver piece.' he declared slapping it on the table.'

'A silver for a gold. I will take your silver. Follow the seed.' Guy watched on as the rich boy concentrated with all seriousness as the cups began their slow slide over the table. Guy had kept up with the seed for a while, but knew that there was absolutely no point in trying to follow it once the man of cups' hands got up to speed. The crowd was silent, the wooden cups sliding was the only noise Guy heard. The rich boy was still looking, giving a good impression of knowing where the seed was, perhaps he even believed it himself. The man of cups' hands came to a stop and he looked up from beneath his hood. 'Pick a cup.'

'I have you this time. You may think you are fast, but my mind is faster. I choose the right cup.'

The man of cups' hand hovered over the right cup for a moment. When he lifted, it was empty and the crowd burst to life with gasps, exclamations and occasional laughter. The young socialite seemed genuinely shocked, frustration rising within him once again. The man of cups lifted the middle cup to reveal the seed.

'Perhaps your mind is not as quick as you believe,' said the man of cups as he collected the silver. The rich boy stepped to the side, Guy could see he was considering protesting. Guy stepped forward.

'Ah, young knight, for what do you play?'

'I do not know.'

Some in the crowd laughed as the rich boy, in his frustration, had begun a commentary about the farm boy who did not know what he was playing for. Frustration must have still resided in the socialite, because Guy reckoned he could send him at least a dozen feet through the air with a single punch. That would stop the crowd from laughing at him. In truth, the crowd's laughter did not bother him, nor the little prick's commentary, he knew that he could silence him with just a look if he took liberties.

'With what do you play?' asked the man of cups after a pause for drama.

'I play with my blanket,' said Guy as he placed the many stained, tattered reminder of his time of the hells in the woods on the table.

'He plays with a blanket,' the rich boy announced, his mockery unable to hide his exasperation.

'I will take you blanket.'

'What?' blurted out the young socialite, 'A stinking blanket?' It was the man of cups who silenced him with his stare, and it was not unnoticed by the crowd.

'I always prefer to play for something with a personal connection. Follow the seed.'

Guy watched the man of cups' hands start their dance. He watched with no urgency, only curiosity, he could feel the rich boy's eyes on him. The truth was he had already decided which cup he was going to call before he joined the line. It just so happened to be the same one that the rich boy had called before him. Unable to help himself Guy turned to the socialite as the man of cups' hands picked up speed, and gave him a nod to a murmur from the crowd. When Guy's eyes returned to the table, there was no way he would have any idea where the seed was. The man of cups slowed his hands and set them to rest. 'Choose a cup.'

Guy paused a moment, hearing the crowds murmurs as they guessed which it would be, sensing the frustrated rich boy was about to explode beside him he called the right cup. The man of cups lifted the cup and Guy was not surprised to see the seed sat beneath it. The crowd were surprised though and none more so than the young socialite whose exasperation led him to storm away from the stall to jeers from a couple of those who watched. Much of the excitement remained on Guy though.

'Congratulations you win. You may trade your blanket for any item behind the counter.' Guys eyes flicked across the shelves behind the table. There was the customary gold coin, jewellery, potions, pots and skins. Such an assortment of items, but he could think of nothing he needed. He was sure there were things that he wanted, but his mind presented nothing. His eyes scoured the shelves again. His eyes rested on an ale horn, adorned with simple yet elegant pewter work. A knight should have his own horn he considered. But then, tucked away behind the horn he spied what looked to be a familiar pot.

'Can I see the pot behind the horn?' The man of cups nodded and reached for it as those watching murmured. There were much finer things, including a bejewelled dagger that would cost at least a gold, possibly up to three, Guy imagined. The man of cups presented the pot. 'The woman who traded this, did she win?'

'She did.'

'When was this?'

'Yesterday.'

'Then unless you have any other suggestions I will trade my blanket for this.'

'It is as it should be.'

Guy nodded to the man of cups, popped the pot in his pouch and turned away to perplexed applause from the crowd as the next player stepped forward. As Guy merged into the flow of people, he was not concerned that it was busy. Della may be in the city, and Ash too. It would be good to see them, but he wanted to tidy himself up first. There was the hope that if he could appear normal, he would feel normal. On the outskirts of the market he found a stall where he had his first real beard removed and his face shaved clean. He even had his hair cut back. When they saw him this time they would not be concerned as to his wellbeing. He would look as if he was doing well, groomed and wearing new clothes, he could snatch a happy memory. He needed one of those.

30

Guy had been wandering around the area that he thought the miller's to be in for some time before he saw it around a corner. He had been going the right way, it was simply further than he remembered. He could already see the cart being readied for departure and saw Della pack something away atop it. Guy approached regardless, his desire to see a friendly face uppermost in his mind. When he stepped into the yard everyone turned to look at him, a man in part armour was all too eager to reach for his sword.

'Guy?' called Della, 'Guy, is that you?'

She stepped forward to meet him. 'Guy, what happened to you? You look awful.' Guy stopped in his tracks as she took his hands that still carried the grime of his horror beneath his nails and looked up at him, so much for appearing normal. 'What have they done to you?' Guy did not know what to say. *Could she tell that he had killed again just by looking at him?* His eyes flicked to Ash, who in a second understood, and that understanding was what he had been craving. A wave of emotion washed over him, sorrow for himself, sorrow for Ash. He looked back to Della and felt his eyes sting.

'I'm ok. I have just been training hard is all.'

She was not convinced, he knew, but had the grace to flash her smile and give him his happy memory. Della's smile just lifted a person, kind and gentle, yet unrestrained as it was. Guy smiled back. 'How are you? How's Little Ash, your mother?'

Della relaxed and smiled as Ash joined her, clasping his arm with a brotherly solidarity. It was good to see Ash, it was good to see them both. It reminded him of his dreams, of what he aspired to.

'We are good thank you, they are good too. We decided not to bring them with us this time.'

The man in part armour stepped forward, and whispered into Ash's ear that they should be leaving before returning to ready the cart. Ash looked to Guy.

'We decided to be safe and hire a marshal to escort us. He thinks is best we leave now, to get some distance from Varen before making camp.'

'He is right. It was good to see you. I wanted to ask about the book you got for Della, but I will come and visit when my training is done.'

'Healing practices of the old world? What of it?' asked Della, seemingly willing to delay departure.

'I was wondering if it had anything about… I don't really know how to describe it, burning hands perhaps?'

'Burning hands? Not that I have seen, but if I am honest I have not read much beyond the herbs and potions. Have you?' she asked Ash.

'I have flicked through, but I bought the book for you. Nothing about burning hands as I recall.'

'It was just a thought. It is hard to describe what I mean.'

'We will have a look though, for when you visit. Little Ash will be so pleased to see you. Will you be a knight then?'

'All being well, I will. I'll bring something for him. Be safe on your journey.'

'And you on yours.' Della smiled a smile he had seen before, it did not hide her concern for him, as she returned to say farewell to the millers. Ash clasped his arm in a silent farewell of unity. Guy sighed as he left, nodded to the miller's family and the marshal and headed back to the market. It was not the happy memory he had thought of. There were so many things he had wanted to say to them, but instead he found himself wondering what it was that had Della concerned for him. His eyes, he guessed, were still to recover from the horrors they had seen.

He headed through the market, after stopping for a noonshine of boiled barley and meat, towards the blacksmiths quarter. He would deliver the note to Smith and perhaps beat some steel. Fire and steel always helped him quiet his mind.

As he approached the blacksmiths yard, there was no ringing of steel on steel, instead Smith was polishing some fine detail work that Guy could not make out.

'Hoy, have you finally seen the way of things and come to work with me?'

'Not this time I am afraid.'

'Then you must have got my message.'

'I do,' said Guy wondering how he would have known. He reached into his pouch and pulled the sealed note out. Smith laughed.

'I guess you never got my message. Your armour is ready for fitting. I thought you would have been here by now.' Guy felt momentarily stupid, misled, but these people seemed to thrive in intrigue and misdirection. 'What do you have there?'

'A note from Sir Parcifal.'

Guy handed it over. Smith took it, and tucked it in his apron for later.

'So, let me have a look at you. You have scrubbed up well.' Their eyes met, Guy let Smith look. Time passed between them. 'You look like you are doing well. There are seldom few who make it this far. You must be almost done. How long has it been?' Guy thought back, his life before training seemed so long ago. Hells, a fortnight ago seemed like another lifetime.

'A long time,' Guy replied.

'But not yet long enough.' Guy looked to his eyes again, he felt his own displaying a fear, a doubt that he could take any more, but behind that, and deeper, he knew, there was a resolve, a determination harder than any steel. Smith's eyes held a history of pain behind a show of content. The blacksmith's eyes were different to the others. He had found a peace that they had not. Guy felt a swell of emotion build. It made him stronger. 'Come, let us see your armour.' Guy paused a moment.

'Can it wait until tomorrow? I have an appointment to keep, and need another night of rest.'

'Tomorrow then, you can bring your things and stay here. I have work for you while I fit your armour.' Guy smiled, nodded.

'Thank you. It is good to see you.'

Guy turned and left Smith's Yard, thinking to himself that it would not be difficult to bring his things. He did not have any. During the walk through the market back to the Four Kin Inn, his mind was confused, concerned. He had made efforts to make himself presentable, but those who knew him saw right through the deception. He was broken inside, not his mind this time, but something of him was broken. He had betrayed his better nature and it caused conflict within.

'Head to your room, I shall see you attended,' the old woman said from behind the counter. 'I am glad you have made yourself more presentable. I have had your old clothes burned.'

'Thank you.' Said Guy, he did not know what else to say. He ducked under the doorframe and headed up the stairs, thinking that the old woman was just fucking with his mind. He would catch her looking at him one day.

Within moments there was a tap on the door, Guy opened it to see another old woman wearing a long coat.

'It is a silver, and you pay me first.'

'It costs but a copper where I stay'

'Ay, but this is the city, and this is my time. A silver, or I go.' Guy reached into a pocket inside his shirt and removed a silver, handing it over without reservation, the woman's bony hand curled gratefully around it. 'Remove your shirt, and let me have a look at you.'

Guy removed his top, no longer feeling the discomfort he felt before, and watched as she looked him over, prodding first at his face, then at his elbow. 'Your wounds heal well, but you are young. You will not be young forever. I want you to sit on the floor.'

Guy sat without question and waited for her to correct his position, instead she stepped in to him, somehow bending him with a sideways twist over her hip. Deep cracks resonated from his spine. Within seconds she had swivelled and repeated the move on the other side, the cracks released trapped energy inside him, energy which flowed with the intensity of a soft lightning. She grabbed his head and cracked his neck before throwing him around the room, cracking everything from his toes to his hips. Guy let the energy flow and the silent pain make him stronger. His eyes saw white, and he felt ecstasy, his horrors far from his mind. She left him lying on his front. He did not move, and before long he felt her hands on either end of his spine. He felt the heat of the burning hands and in his mind saw thin strands of steel interweave themselves through and around his spine, spreading from each hand until they met in the middle. The strands continued though each other, travelling the full length of his spine.

He felt hands on his shoulders and the energy spread to the pathway created down his spine. As he inhaled the energy flowed into him, as he exhaled it compressed and became a part of him; soon to be swelled again when he took another breath. Her hands moved to his hips and a surge of energy swept through his entire body, solid, yet free flowing. Guy tried to remain calm and open, but also aware of what was happening. She turned him to lie aback, her hands found his lungs, his heart and the energy became a part of his very being, pumped around him as he breathed steadily.

'It is not just your body that requires healing.' She said and placed her hands over Guys eyes. The energy poured into him unabated, there was no resistance, his world went white, so calm, so peaceful, so safe.

He became aware of himself sometime later, and he did feel refreshed and calm, it was to be expected, but it took nothing away from the reality of it. Without opening his eyes he realised that the old woman had gone. He lay at peace a while longer, his world quiet and serene. He had not yet fully returned, and he enjoyed his partial existence. He simply was. He was not Guy of Waering trying to gain Phylissa's hand, he was not the pseudo squire of Sir Edrick Parcifal. For that moment in time he was no one. In realising this though, it bought about its end, his mind's mischief denying him the freedom to float. Gradually he returned to himself and opened his eyes to let life continue.

It took a moment for him to see the tub steaming beside him. *How could he have not noticed that being brought in and filled?* He found himself trying to remember the details, she had used the burning hands on him, but no matter how much he tried to understand, his mind would not come up with an explanation. He stood and stretched a little before stripping and sinking into the tub. It was a glorious moment in his life. His body felt beyond good, and his mind was still calm and with peace. He absorbed what he could before climbing out, laying aback on the rug and letting a peaceful sleep find him without even wanting his evening meal.

31

Guy awoke, not with the world, but not far behind it, the streets were coming to life below him. After allowing the day to gently rouse him it was with a freshness of body and a quietness of mind, that he had feared he would never find again. He dressed and caught himself preparing to gather his equipment. It felt peculiar leaving the room with nothing to take, but he took comfort from a quick check of his belt. It had served him well this past fortnight, he would have been dead without it, of that he had no doubt. He covered it with his linen shirt and stood, looking once more around the room before he closed the door behind him.

'I am leaving today, but I thank you.' He said to the woman behind the counter.

'I trust the services offered were well received.' She said without looking up.

'It was just what I needed.' The old woman grunted some kind of acknowledgment and continued with whatever occupied her. Guy smiled, turned, and walked out of the Four Kin Inn. It was early and some of the shops that he wanted to visit were not yet open. He broke his fast at a street side table on fruit wrapped in flat oatcakes. The summer fruits gave some zip to his body.

Guy had spent an unsuccessful start to the day in the many bookshops in this area of the city, he had found nothing on either burning hands or old world healing. He did pick himself up another copy of 'The battle of Ashford'. There were still questions in his mind. Four into three did not fit.

He ducked into the apothecary, thinking it best that he pay for the white mist before spending all the coin from the bandit's purse. As his eyes adjusted to the dark room he scanned the shelves. There were some things that he knew, others that he had read about, and some that were dangerous. There were many more that he did not recognise, he looked forward to the time when he would know them all. The smell of the room, he imagined, was a mix of all the aromatics, his mind described it as medicinal. It was the smell that he would associate with healing. Overriding the delicacies of the aromatic experience were the bunches of white sage that hung from a beam.

The old woman looked up as he approached. Guy had already begun to bid her a good morning when he recognised something in the woman. She had cracked his bones the night before. He could not hide the surprise in his voice.

'What might you be after?

'I am after some more white mist for my master.'

'Ah yes. I knew you would be back. How many do you want?'

'How many do you have?'

'I have the four that you asked for last time, but might I suggest you take only two, so that you may return sooner, you have not yet finished healing.' Guy pulled two silver coins from his pouch and placed them on the counter. 'Is there anything else you might be after?' Guy looked around. There was much he would like to buy.

'Not just now. Thank you.' Guy watched as the old woman wrapped the vials of white mist in cloth and packed them in a small wooden box. He wanted to ask her so many questions, but it did not seem appropriate. Nonetheless the questions made their way to his voice. 'What did you mean by not yet finished healing?'

'I meant that you have not yet finished healing.' Guy shook his head at himself.

'Yesterday, when you put your hands on my back, it was a strange sensation. I was hoping that you might tell me what it is called, so that I may learn more about it.'

'Were you now?' asked the old woman with a smile. It was a kind smile, but a smile that told him something else. She was not going to tell him. He assumed only her apprentices benefitted from her teaching. Guy chastised himself for his question.

'But your hands…'

'My hands did nothing, everything that happened you did, perhaps you should give it a name.'

Guy was about to ask another question, but as he opened his mouth to speak, the door opened and an old man walked in making the small room feel very full. Guy nodded thankfully to the old woman, picked up the wooden box, thanked her, and squeezed past the old man to leave the hut. He felt that he had been so close. For a moment he considered waiting for the man to leave and ask her again, but he had a feeling that he had learnt all he would for that day, which was nothing.

He stopped to buy more dried fruit on the way to the blacksmiths. He bought all kinds of dried grapes, berries and other fruits, even some dried lemon skin. His mind danced as he imagined the waters and oats that he could make. Even though the summer berries were fresh and vibrant, he bought a small sack of dried berries. Perhaps they would remind him of the summer when it had passed. He bought the hind half of a suckling lamb to share with the blacksmith and two fresh loaves. He was looking forward to seeing his armour.

When Guy approached, the blacksmith was unloading a large cart that was piled high with used armour and weapons. Most of it he tossed into a large pile in his yard, some bits he kept to one side.

'Hoy, young apprentice! Come and help an old man unload the cart.' Guy put his purchases in the workshop area. 'Just make a big pile over there' he said, nodding his head away from his own pile, 'We can go through it later. If there is anything particularly nice, put it here.' He said nodding to the pile by his feet. 'Let's go. Owin here wants to get home.' As Guy approached the cart, he wondered why Owin was not helping if he wanted to get home so badly. Guy unloaded with pace and care. He had split his pile in two, one half was for damaged items which he tossed, the other was made up of intact pieces and weapons which he placed. Much of it was standard quality armour worn by those that did not often fight. There were sometimes better pieces. Nothing that he put by Smith's feet, but the perhaps he did not have the eye of the blacksmith. Some of the pieces were badly damaged and stained with blood and more. 'There was some trouble on the Eastern border,' was all the blacksmith offered. With Guy's help it did not take long until the cart was empty, its contents filling much of the yard. The blacksmith paid two gold for the cartload, and pressed a silver into Owin's hand. 'Come see me again soon.'

Owin packed away the blankets that had covered the bounty and led the horse off, bidding farewell to Smith, who nodded before turning to peruse his latest purchase.

'We have a lot of work to do, but I have worked up a hunger. Did you stop for noonshine yet?' Guy shook his head. 'Wait here, I will get us some.'

Smith departed, heading toward the main market area, leaving Guy with a yard full of used weapons and armour, the people it belonged to were most likely dead and been stripped on the battlefield. He had never been surrounded by so much death.

By the time the blacksmith returned with a barrel of ale under his arm, two roasted birds and a sack of rollbreads Guy was scanning the piles, looking for the better quality pieces, remembering from his time at the workshop before. Had the armour he had trained in been made from the armour of dead men too he wondered. *Was it a good thing to wear the armour of someone who had died in battle?* At least his real suit was being made with virgin stonepress steel. It would bring him comfort, if he ever wore it in battle, knowing that no one had died in it before him.

They ate and drank ale as Smith explained the many ways that a blacksmith could benefit from war. Tensions increased demand, battles were a good source of materials. A lucky blacksmith could make enough from a single battle to never have to work again. The blacksmith described the encounter that led to this haul as nothing more than a skirmish. 'A skirmish?' thought Guy to himself as he looked over the piles of metal before him.

They worked through the afternoon sorting the piles. The main focus was of course on the finer items, some of which looked to be worth a gold on their own. The blacksmith showed him what to look for in the items, surprising Guy with the simplicity of some of the finer metals. There were some ornate pieces, a couple of fine swords. Guy had never seen so much metal in his life. Not even the Great hall at Waering had that much armour and weaponry. Guy covered a large pile of damaged and standard metal pieces with a large hessian sheet, and helped the blacksmith move pieces of better quality to the workshop area, the rest was piled up against the far side of the workshop.

'I almost forgot. I need a gold from you.'

'A gold? Was the armour more expensive than anticipated?'

'No, the armour is good. This is for something else.' Guy removed his left boot, opened the heel compartment and prised a gold coin from the mud inside it. He wiped it on his hands before handing it over to the blacksmith. 'You give me your gold so quickly?'

'I remember what I got for a silver.' said guy tapping his belt. 'Even if there is nothing in return, it is still worth every iron farthing.'

'Take a look.' The blacksmith nodded his head to the corner where a white cloth covered something. 'I have taken the liberty of doing some of the work for you.' Guy pulled the sheet away and saw two large bars of metal. 'Tell me, what do you see?'

'Two bars of metal.'

'Aye. Do you know what I see? Potential. Do you remember before you left I had you fold some steel a dozen times? 'Guy nodded. 'It was good steel, and I used more in your armour than I anticipated. Tell me, aside from a horse and armour, what does a knight need?' Guy looked up at him.

'A sword.'

'A sword. That's what you should see when you look at the bars now. You will have serious work to do over the coming days, as will I with your armour. Come, we have much to do. There is a small river ten minutes north of the city walls. Follow it until you find a willow tree, a large one. I need five dozen slender branches, the freshest growth if possible. Bring them to me while I start the firepit.' Guy drank a ladle of water and set off towards the Northern gate.

When he returned dusk was well established, it was a warm early summer's evening, even hotter in the blacksmith's yard. A six foot firepit was becoming well established. A large set of bellows sat at one end, pipes split from it, feeding into the fire at six different points. The suckling lamb had been butchered and the legs sat high above the fire roasting gently.

'Hoy. Come, it is late in the day and there is much we must do. Bring the branches.' Guy followed the blacksmith to a small building towards the back of the yard that he had not noticed before. He was usually keen to be aware of his surroundings, but whenever he was there he was always kept busy. The blacksmith opened the door. 'Tomorrow you will replace these with the branches you gathered today. You must strip the bark. He gathered slender black stems of charcoal in his large hands with a delicacy that saw not one of them snap. He closed the door with his foot and returned to the firepit. He laid them gently on a cloth. As the blacksmith crouched Guy noticed a large slab of clay laid out on hessian aside the firepit, it looked to be two inches thick. 'Fetch the bars, and bring them here.' Guy fetched them and positioned them on the clay as instructed.

'You did not get to see this last time, but it is important you know how to make this steel. It will be what identifies you as a Knight. You never got to see the effect of folding the steel so many times, but you will, and then you will understand. This is a type of steel that originates from the south. It is rarely seen these days, but aside from legendary steel, this is the finest technique there is. We have two different steels, one is stone pressed steel, the other an ancient steel, the best I could find.' The blacksmith caught Guys eye. 'First we must prepare the steel, and then bake it in clay until tomorrow. Most knights inherit their swords, some buy them. The bond between a knight and his sword is a hallowed thing. You are lucky enough to be assisting in the making of yours, which means the bond can be even stronger here. I need you to grind the charcoal down into a fine dust and cover the top of each bar with it. Should you wish you can add something of yourself to the steel. Some knights have covered them with blood, some have spilled their seed, and others shed tears. For some the creation of a blade is a spiritual thing. I do not know if it will be so with you, but I shall leave you for an hour to prepare your steel. When you have covered the steel, cut the clay and wrap it tightly. Use wet fingers to seal it. There should be no gaps. It must be fully sealed. 'The blacksmith turned the meat over the fire and went into his hut, closing the door behind him.

Guy looked to the two large bars of metal sat in the slab of clay for a moment. They were going to become his sword. It was difficult to see the potential in the bars, but he did not let it concern him, there was work to do. He ground the charcoal in three batches in a large pot and stone. The charcoal turned quickly to a fine black dust as long as he did not compress it too much. He had more to stroke it with the stone. He had quickly filled a large pouch with the powder and moved over to the bars. It was hot by the firepit and Guy removed his shirt. It somehow felt like the right thing to do. He knelt before the two bars of steel looking at them, contemplating, opening himself to see the potential and what it meant to him. He wanted the sword to be bound to him, wanted it to be his sword, and almost without thinking he drew his knife, and held its silvery steel blade to the firelight. It gleamed in the orange glow as if it were brand new. He drew it across his forearm. The blood flowed quicker than he anticipated, and did not take long to splatter a pool big enough to spread the length of the bars. He bound the wound with the white cloth that the charcoal had sat on, which quickly reddened. He caressed his own blood into the steel, trying to equally distribute it. There were a couple of dark spots where the drops had fallen, but he had covered the surface. The blood, his sacrifice, to ease the pain of the lives the sword would take, at least in his mind. His arm throbbed and he found himself instinctively reaching for his pot of Della's balm. It was over half empty, he had used a lot on Hawkins, but he had acquired one from the man of cups. He put some on his still bleeding wound, spilling blood onto his trousers, and retied the wound, tighter this time. He wiped the remainder of the balm onto the steel. If he could somehow imbue some of Della's inherent goodness into the blade… he spent the rest of the pot applying some along the top edges of both bars before coating with a generous sprinkle of charcoal dust until the surface was black. Guy sliced the clay across the middle and carefully enclosed the bars in it. As soon as he was satisfied with the two long bricks before him, the blacksmith emerged from the building, as if he had been waiting.

'Good, you are finished. Give me a hand with these.' He picked up half a dozen pieces of metal that looked as if they could be supports for a low table. Guy held them in place while the blacksmith embedded them with a hammer, spreading them so that they spanned the firepit. Together, carefully, they placed the two long clay bricks on the metal supports, so that they sat a little over a foot above the embering flames.

'We are lucky indeed, the required heat for this process is exactly the same as that needed to roast a lamb.' Said the blacksmith with a chuckle, 'Come, let's eat.'

They ate, and shared a skin of lightwyne as the blacksmith talked of the history of the process that they were using for the steel. He talked of the steel itself, harder and sharper than ordinary steel. The blacksmith explained that the fire needed maintaining through the night, and that during this time, Guy should further consider his association with the weapon, for inside the clay brick the steel was slowly absorbing the charcoal, and anything else that may be in there. It would change the metal inside. Guy should be a part of that process. It was well into the short night when the blacksmith departed, leaving Guy alone with his steel. None of the questions that usually bothered his mind arose, and the night's mischief was nowhere to be found, as Guy sat, feeling connected to the world and letting it feed the strength within him.

He remained with his steel as the sun rose higher in the sky, pushing fresh embers in as required to maintain an even burn. He had cleansed and sewn his wound, it had been deeper than intended. He looked fondly at the stitches, they meant something to him, and most of all it had given him some kind of release from the things he carried within him.

32

It was after noonshine before Smith returned, carrying fresh loaves and humming a content tune.

'Hoy, young apprentice, how was your night?'

'Good. Thank you.'

'How is the lamb broth doing? Making money always gets me hungry?'

'It should be good,' Guy offered, his eyes spying liquid steaming from the edge of the firepit. The blacksmith sat down, and told Guy how he had been selling some of the undamaged items they had sorted yesterday.

'I got two gold for one blade alone.' He said as he jangled his heavy coin purse. 'There might well be more good stuff in there.'

The blacksmith inhaled as he stirred the pot with a ladle. 'Smells good.' He poured some into a wooden bowl and handed it to Guy, filling his own before sitting and telling him of the morning's sales. When the bowls were empty and the breads no more, they sat a while content. The blacksmith reached into his coinpurse and fished out two gold coins, offering them in his palm to Guy. 'For your work yesterday.'

'Emptying a cart does not deserve two gold.'

'No? I made over a dozen gold from just a few items. I reckon there is at least another dozen gold in what is left. Besides, I have no real need of coin, and a knight always needs it.'

'Why did you make me pay for the steel, if you were only going to give it back to me?'

'This is not the gold you gave me yesterday, this is an entirely different thing all together.'

Guy took the gold, gratefully, knowing the blacksmiths words to be true. Being a knight was an expensive affair. There was no question of him needing the coin. He took off his left boot, and placed them both in the compartment, packing them in with a little clay.

'Thank you.'

'No, thank you. I have no doubt that you and I could make a lot of money together, but you must first be a knight. I understand that.' Guy nodded in thanks. 'So now we leave the fire to burn out. By tomorrow it should be cool enough to break open and you can start folding.' The blacksmith reached into his apron pocket and removed the note. 'I have not read Edrick's note yet.' He cracked the wax seal and flipped it open, offering considered hums as he read. He refolded it and returned it to his pocket. 'I am to continue your training while you are here, and he wants me to tell you of Sir Winton Tardy.'

'Sir Winton Tardy?'

'Aye, he is someone who served with us in the king's own army. He was one of a dozen knights, Edrick's knights. It was one step down from being one of the king's own knights.' There was a remembered pride in his voice. 'Winton was a big man, like us. He was strong, and had speed, but with a sword in his hand he was clumsy. He could not make it sing as a knight should.' The blacksmith chuckled at a memory. 'It was early on in our training, he was getting humiliated every day on the training ground, and he was frustrated. There was talk of him being removed from the program. He had had his helm rung by every knight there, including me, and these guys did not fuck about. So pissed was he that he threw his sword to the ground, walked to the edge of the training ground and returned with a mace in each hand. He went through everyone as if they were not there, myself included. There were two that were unable to train for a week. They were upset, but they never humiliated him again.' The blacksmith's gaze lingered on the embers, reflecting on memories he had not visited in some years. 'Go and find two maces and some armour from the pile if you can. Defence training. Two hours.'

Guy stood in the yard, wearing a chestplate, gauntlets, a pauldron and guardbrace covering each shoulder, facing the blacksmith through the slits in the great helm, who wielded, what he hoped, was a blunt sword. A mace in each hand felt like a good thing to Guy, metal extensions of his own arms. The blacksmith stepped in with a swing that was easily diverted and pivoted.

'Good. Let's see what you have got.' The blacksmith attacked with castle taught moves he blocked and parried, moving quickly on his feet away from the out of practice blacksmith. But they danced well, and Guy's helm was rung but a few times. Guy was already seeing new attacks that he could make if permitted. Having a weapon in each hand was a revelation, one that he felt very comfortable with.

When the two hours was up, the blacksmith puffed heavy breaths.' I am not the man I once was when it comes to this kind of thing, but you are progressing well. See if you can find some decent pieces of armour for me to sell, and see if there is any that fits you better. Oh, and finish the broth, for tomorrow, not only do you fold steel, but we continue your training.' The blacksmith drank a ladle of water and headed off towards the market.

The next few days for Guy involved the folding of steel, he had first had to join the two steels together, then fold for the first time before drawing out the steel and folding it again. His break from folding was training, and very little else. Life was hard, and when he was not working he was asleep, but he was folding steel with more precision and purpose than ever before, for it was going to be his sword, it was of his blood. The charcoal had stained the topside of the bar, and each time the steel was folded a fine streak of darkness remained. The effect was incredible when finished. He had seen it on his armour. It looked so natural, yet so refined. He had never seen armour like it. The blacksmith had introduced a style to his armour that came from the metal itself. There was no enamel, no fancy designs. Just practical armour made elegant by the feathered design of the southern style steel. The simple beading made using it framed the rest of the suit with strength, and with purpose. It really was a fine, yet understated set of armour that, more than anything, Guy hoped that he would be able to do justice. On the initial fitting the first thing that he had noticed was that it was significantly lighter than his training armour. Guy considered for a moment whether he was intentionally given heavy armour so that it would feel light, or if it were the quality of the steel itself. A bit of both probably.

Guy's training had evolved, the blacksmith did not feel agile enough to test him, so everyday a man came and attacked him for two hours and was paid a silver. The blacksmith was very precise with his instructions to Guy during the training, and he was forced to focus on specific elements, more than he did with the Knightmaker. Smith was a big man too, and Showed Guy the importance of balance and how to move with speed and precision. A correctly planted foot could keep a man alive. With the Knightmaker it was about the essence of it, of what was behind it, about going again. With the blacksmith the details were the focus, sometimes using blacksmithing analogies to explain their importance. It was a new kind of training for Guy, and each day a different man came to face him, and everyday Guy defended. When he was not training or folding his own metal, he was smelting down the damaged armour into bars, while the blacksmith sold what he could, and worked on fitting Guys armour. They worked together on his sword, the gold seemingly not simply paying for the blade itself, but an education in how a sword was made.

Guy was exercising himself despite the physicality of his life. Every other day he had taken to running the city walls. It took him over two hours, but it gave him strength. He stretched, and bent his knees, but found himself missing the rock. He imagined that he could do some damage armed with a pair of maces rather than the iron bar.

The blacksmith had been teaching him how to best fit his armour, and when the final fitting came, Guy was overjoyed. It did not feel like he was wearing armour at all. At least no armour he had worn before.

'Now you and I have one more day of work left, but I have two days of work to do first. Why don't you head off into the city, find yourself a way back to Eastfield Manor with your armour. Hire a cart, or find a trader to escort, and earn yourself some coin. Come back after two days, and think of your arms, and we will finish our work together.'

Guy awoke with the world, and had left the blacksmiths quarter without seeing another person. The market was slowly coming to life.

He had food for the day and three freshly filled water skins. It gave him comfort to have more than one skin. The man of cups was not yet active on his stall when he passed, such was the early rise of the summer sun. He headed out of the city's southern gate and followed the road for around an hour, until he got to a fork in the road. Left, and he could leave it all behind and return to Waering, and Phylissa. Right would lead him back to Eastfield Manor and the unknown. He took the right path. Sometimes a man had to head away from his destination in order to get there. He enjoyed a casual walk along the path, he was not actually going anywhere and he enjoyed the freedom of walking without intent. A leisurely hour later, Guy arrived at a small clearing in the orchards beside the road, a resting point for travellers to Varen.

The sun was beginning to bring the heat of the summer which seemed to bring the clearing to life and invite him to stay. He could hear the trickle of a natural stream nearby, and birds plucked insects from the sky. It was an inviting spot indeed. Guy settled himself under an apple tree at what to him was the start of the clearing, ate a sweetbun and drained half a water skin. He took out his book and started to read while waiting for the carts to start passing. He flicked to the now familiar part where Sir Parcifal's involvement began. He had been summoned by the king and told of the troubles. Sending his squire to ready his kit, he set about gathering a dozen knights. There were nine of his original dozen remaining, he had not replaced the three who had passed. It did not seem right, besides it was widely acknowledged that the nine remaining knights could take on any other knight's dozen, possibly two. They were more brothers than soldier knights. He had to find three more to fill his dozen, and it was these that Guy focussed his attention on. He had identified the man of cups and Smith from members of the original group, but the stranger did not fit. Perhaps he was one of the others, perhaps there had been four knights that survived, the stranger getting lost in history. The scribe had provided a brief introduction to each of them, yet none of them sounded like the stranger he had come to know. Two of the three had put themselves forward simply to fight, to kill. It was supposed to have been a diplomatic mission, a show of force to implement the king's will. The other one had potential, there was not much known of the man, being new to the king's army, but he stepped forward with no hesitation, even given the stories of Sir Parcifal. There was something about the stranger that was different to this knight though. The bond between them, though it could have developed after the battle, seemed deeper. Plus the stranger never spoke, the young knight in question spoke aplenty.

Guy flicked through the book seeking only references to the third volunteer knight, unable to deny that it could be the stranger, until in the heat of battle the knight's head was caved in. So he wasn't the stranger.

A few carts had passed him by that morning, paying him no particular mind. He was dressed as a farmer, so probably blended in. Even a couple of marshals escorting a cart and party barely glanced at him. There was no point in asking if he could use some space in their cart when they returned. They looked like they needed neither coin nor protection. Guy knew what he was looking for, people like Della and Ash, unassuming, but who would perhaps be in possession of more coin that is safe to carry on their return. The more he waited, the more he realised that he was not going to find someone like that. He had called out to a few of the poorer looking carts, and some a little smarter. 'Hoy, I am looking for a cart to transport myself and some goods to Hopwood. I shall be in the leatherback tavern.'

He called out to maybe a dozen carts throughout the day to mixed reactions. Some looked down on him, some feared him, some pretended he was not there, they all heard him though, of that he was sure. As the sun began to slide and colour began to appear in the sky Guy made his way back to the Southern gate none the wiser as to the strangers identity, or whether he would find a cart. He might have to hire one after all.

On his return to Varen he bought some food from a stall set up so that farmers without wives could satisfy their hunger. A thick broth of beef in a hard bread bowl, good honest food thought Guy as he enjoyed it. He could see further up the street that the man of cups had quite the evening crowd, a lot of people seemingly stopping by on their way home, many just to watch the constant stream of people gambling on something special to end their day. Most of them left empty handed, but there was a cheer when a pauper gambled the copper he had earnt for a few days work, won. Guy imagined the elation he must be feeling. There was always a gold coin on the man of cups stall. Always, though where he would spend it Guy had no idea. Poor people though, were nothing if not resourceful, something he had occasionally envied, but only briefly.

After his meal Guy ducked into the Leatherback tavern. It was hot, busy and noisy. It smelled of men and ale and smoke. It was dark inside, the only light coming from candles and torches which added to the discomfort. Guy soon acclimatised and worked his way to find a position in a little space against the far wall of the tavern, and after a while a table, once those drinking on their way home had continued their journeys. Later still he took the table that he had wanted and lit a six hour candle placing it at the end of the table visible to the rest of the tavern.

He sat and observed the tavern, those that had been supping ale for a while were hitting their walls and one by one disappearing. He could see other people who would be there for the night. Candles burned at several tables. He nursed his horn of ale, its warm staleness slightly offending him. He called for a fresh one as the hooded figure of the man of cups entered and tossed a silver on the bar before taking what looked to be a familiar table. He was in a dark corner looking out over the tavern, the hood of his cloak hiding his face as it always did.

The candle got shorter as the hours passed, and aside from the occasional mouthful of ale, Guy did not move. There was very little movement in the tavern. Occasionally people approached other candles, never his own. The night's mischief brought an old acquaintance of Guys, one that he was not keen to remember. Frustration. It began in his belly, a dark ugly void that he knew would consume him soon enough. He was frustrated though, it would be wrong to deny it. He was frustrated that he did not yet have a cart. He was frustrated that the man of cups sat only a matter of feet away, but he could not talk to him. Most of all he was frustrated that he was not doing anything. The training had kept the frustration at bay these last few months. Though he did not like it, it was a familiar feeling that spread through him, constricting his chest. As his mind raced with everything that was annoying him and his breathing quickened, Guy gently accepted the frustration. He would use it to make him stronger. He could train sitting still. He could keep moving forward.

He could not fool himself for long, frustration was like the air. It was breathed in, became a part of your body, but soon enough you would have to breathe in again. Frustration rose in him many times that night, and each time it was a little stronger. Each time it required him to be a little stronger to keep it from showing. He had watched the man of cups without looking directly at him. He had questions, questions that frustration had goaded him to ask. He had framed them many ways in his mind, but none of them sounded right, and if his suspicions were confirmed regarding who the man of cups used to be, it had to sound right. He would not allow frustration to boil over. It bought him a relief of sorts when the man of cups departed. Guy was certain there was a nod beneath the hood. Guy nodded respectfully, whether the man of cups saw it or not, he did not know, but it was the right thing to do. There were around two hours left of the six hour candle, and he knew he would not find a cart that night, but still he waited, he considered it training.

33

Guy returned to his spot beneath the tree at the stopping point in the orchards. He was glad to arrive, the residue of the night's frustration had made him want to weep. He had not, of course, but it was a sensation that he did not enjoy. He refreshed himself with some fruit and pulled the book out again. From memory the man of cups had been a knight of some repute. It was through an act of his that the king's level of tolerance was shown. A lord of the east had been overthrown, a single knight vanquished the conqueror. First by slitting the throats of the new lord's entire family as he watched, then by killing the usurper. It is unknown whether he was suffocated by his own manhood, or died as a result of its removal. According to the scribes anecdote there had been so much blood on the marble floor of the audience chamber, it and the pews had all needed replacing. He found the first mention of Sir Benjamin Cooke and followed him through the book. Then he did the same for the knight he knew to be Smith calling out hopefully to selected carts as they passed.

He dozed during the afternoon letting what he had learnt absorb into his mind. He opened his eyes enough to survey the carts as they passed, occasionally calling out, but it was a restful afternoon, and he was a little reluctant to leave his spot as the sun began to slide towards the evening.

He soon reclaimed his table in the Leatherback Tavern. He had feasted on a pheasant and a bowl of leaves, and felt ready for the night ahead.

The tavern was still busy with farmers quenching their thirst after a day in the fields, the tables were mostly occupied by those with candles, something to offer, an invitation to approach. When the man of cups arrived, he went straight to his table. He had no candle.

With the man of cups arrival, frustration returned. He had resolved none of the previous night's frustration so it was able to take hold fast. This time though, frustration was not alone, it had bought its friend pessimism to share the fun. Guy composed himself ready for a long night. Within minutes though, a man approached his table. Only a little older than Guy, he was clearly well supped, small and wiry, he reminded Guy of a hungry weasel. Guy motioned for him to sit, as he had seen others do. There was more than ale on his breath, a hint of strongwyne teased his nose.

'I need to hire a man.'

'For what purpose?' asked Guy hiding his excitement. If this man had coin and an empty cart, he would benefit from some protection.

'To beat a man who beds my wife. You don't need to kill him but…' he let the lack of words hang in the air. 'I have coin, six coppers.' He looked on expectantly.

'I am afraid you are speaking to the wrong man. I am seeking a ride to Hopwood.'

'Six coppers will buy you a ride to Hopwood and beyond.'

'You are speaking to the wrong man.' Guy wished he had a cloak so that he could pull up the hood to signify the end of the conversation, instead he just stared at the man thinking that he should try to be a better husband, until he finally stood and walked off on aled legs to re-evaluate his situation. Guy let out a breath, and with it some frustration, composed himself and continued to wait, feeling the man of cups eyes on him from beneath the hood.

To occupy his mind he set to thinking of his arms. His father had not had any arms of his own. As a steward he took on the arms of the town. His father had never spoken of his life before Waering, the town had become his life, and he had given his life for it.

On the night of his death he had heard his mother's sobs. His parents had truly loved each other, which even as a child Guy knew to be a rare gift. He had seen her with the remnants of a shield, a curved three quarter length shield that could be interlocked with others to form a shield wall, a trait of the northern armies. There was a chunk missing, be he could make out the small blue and white diamonds that covered it, and a golden falcon emblazoned on its centre. It had looked to be real gold, one of its wings was missing, but it was unmistakably a falcon. Guy had never spoken to his mother of that night, and it was the one clue he had to his father's previous life. He felt that he wanted to display his family's history on his arms. He was picturing his shield in his head. It was round and solid like the Knightmaker's, and he wanted to incorporate some of the black into his own. He was Guy of Waering, so thought it only right that Waering should be represented. The turrets of the castle, in blue and white diamonds, intruding into the black half, the night sky, above it. He would not put a falcon on it, he did not know what it represented. It was a good start. It was simple, yet encapsulated his journey so far. More importantly he had never seen anything like it, but then again heraldry was not his strongpoint.

His attention was taken by movement on the edge of his vision. Someone else approached his table. They did not look as apprehensive or as supped as the previous man, though he was about the same build, thin and wiry, but older and looked less like a weasel. Guy nodded for him to sit.

'You are looking for a cart, and passage to Hopwood.'

'I am,' Guy replied, 'But forgive me, I do not recall telling you that I would be here.'

'But yet here I am, and I see no others. I have a cart going through Hopwood and a little company never did me any harm. I leave in three mornings, Early. What is it that you are looking to transport?'

'My armour.'

'Your armour?' The old man sucked his teeth, 'A knight without a horse is no knight at all.'

'I have a horse, it is just not here. Besides, I am no knight.' The man looked thoughtfully for a moment.

'I have space for a set of armour.'

Guy gave him directions to Smiths workshop and the man departed the tavern. Guy sat a moment, there were still four hours left of his candle and he knew not what to do with the remainder of the night. He thought he should have felt elated having secured passage to Eastfield Manor, but he did not. He felt tired, and frustrated.

He sat a moment waiting to feel the elation, instead frustration rose in him, and had not passed when he felt eyes on him. He looked up to meet the gaze of the man of cups, and before he realised it he was standing. He motioned to the bar for two horns of ale and approached the man of cups at his table.

'May I?' The man of cups nodded him to sit, and Guy squeezed himself under the table.

'Young knight, you have secured your ride?'

'I have, thank you.' The two horns of ale were placed on the table by a woman approaching her elderly years. Guy thanked her.

'What can I do for you young knight?'

'Why are you playing games with me?' were the words that escaped Guys mouth. He had been hoping to approach it more delicately. Flustered, he tried to diffuse his direct approach. 'All this business with Sir Parcifal and Smith…'

'Did you not meet Smith yourself?'

'Yes.' Guys mind remembered that he had met Smith before the man of cups sent him there.

'Something drew you to his stall. What was it?'

'I don't know, it just seemed real and honest.'

'And so it was. Do not think I played games with you young knight, I only told you what you almost knew yourself.'

'But you knew the same thing, why could you not have told me yourself.'

'Smith always had better judgement than I when it comes to these things.' Guy felt the frustration in him. The man of cups answers frustrated him, the fact that he was even having the conversation frustrated him. Guy managed a smile, even a chuckled breath.

'The why does it feel like you are playing with me?'

'People are not always direct with their words or behaviour, sometimes you have to work to find the truth of things. On my part, there was no malice.'

'No, I don't believe there was. I think perhaps, the real reason I came over was to offer my thanks, for you have indeed helped me.'

'I only told you what you almost knew yourself.'

'Except that you never directly told me.' Guy could not see the man of cups face, in fact he never had, but the eyes showed that he was smiling.

'Aye, but where's the fun in that? Too many people have everything given to them, when it is so much more rewarding to discover it yourself. Do you not agree?' Guy looked at the hooded face, thinking of the things he had read. He could not disagree. He shrugged.

'I suppose you have the truth of it.' Guy thought for a moment about asking of the stranger, and how he fitted into the Battle of Ashford, but knew he was unlikely to get a straight answer.

'I have seen the frustration in you these last nights. You hide it reasonably well, but I see it. You should not let frustration get the better of you. Things are as they are meant to be, and what is meant to be will always come to pass. Frustration only delays it. A frustrated knight is a knight that is easily beaten. Learn to control yourself more.' Guy sighed, the man of cups had the truth of it again. For the merest of seconds Guy almost reacted, that youthful arrogance wanting to defend itself, but when he looked at who was talking to him, he realised that whatever he thought he was controlling, the man of cups had keener eyes than he could imagine.

'I will try.'

'There is no try, you either do it or not. That is the way of a knight. They do things other people would not. You should come and play tomorrow.'

'I will,' Guy said, realising the conversation was over. He finished his horn of ale, and worked his way from behind the table. 'Thank you.' The words carried a truth, even to Guy's ears. He was thankful, and the man of cups had heard the truth of that, Guy was certain. He gave two coppers to the patron and found himself in the quiet solitude of a night in Varen. There was an eerie stillness to the city. It was too late for the night owls and too soon for the early birds. He knew there would be activity somewhere, but there was none to be seen or heard where he was. Not knowing where to go or what to do, Guy found himself wandering towards the man of cups' stall. There were three already sleeping in the queue for the first game of the day. It would not look out of place if he slept there. He sat against a wooden post and settled into a knight's sleep. One that gave him rest, but one that kept him aware of his surroundings, his eye flicked open when anyone passed too closely.

34

By the time the city started waking up Guy was feeling well rested. He wanted to stretch, but made do with rolling his neck and arching his back. There was tension at the front of the queue, one man felt wronged. When Guy joined the queue at number four, towering above those in front, they silenced, and all three of them looked at the floor. It was only a matter of minutes until the man of cups arrived, ignoring everyone as he set up his stall. He started the day with only a few items from the previous day, and the obligatory gold piece, but of course the first game would not be for an item. It would be for the day.

'Young knight,' the man if cups called out. 'Thank you for coming to play. Would you like the first game?'

'I am not the first in the queue.'

'So I should let this man play?' He said nodding his hooded head towards the man at the front.

'Maybe, though he is there through deception. Perhaps allow the man behind to play as if he were the first of the day when you have won the first game.'

'What about me?' said the man immediately in front of Guy.

'You should try again tomorrow,' Guy offered. The man grunted in disgust, and left the line, remaining nearby to watch.

'It can only be the first, you cannot change what is meant to be. Who is it to be?' Guy looked at the two men in front of him, both turning to Guy, a defiant pleading in both their eyes. Guy knew that in a just world, it would be the man second in the queue who should get to play, but the world they lived in was not always just. In reality though, Guy knew that it mattered not which man played, the man of cups would win.

'The man who was at the front of the queue,' announced Guy, and triumphantly the man stepped forward, the other man deflated. 'Worry not, for he shall not win, and neither would you have. This was so you do not build your hopes.' It was small comfort to the man, but he turned to watch along with farmers and traders that happened to be passing. The first game of the day could be quite the spectacle.

'For what do you play?' asked the man of cups from beneath his hood.

'You,' the man replied.

'With what do you play?' The man pulled a jewelled goblet from beneath his cloak, no doubt picked up when it should not have been.

'I will take your goblet.'

The man of cups showed the man, and the audience, the seed under the middle cup, and then covered it. 'Follow the seed.'

The man of cups hands started their purposeful slide over the table, slow and steady. As his hands picked up momentum the man of cups looked up from the table at the man he was playing against. He held the gaze until his opponent met it, and in doing so, lost all track of the seed. The man of cups bought his hands to a still, resting on the table behind the cups. 'Choose a cup.'

The crowd caught their breath as they waited for the man to choose, and gasped when the man of cups lifted the middle cup to reveal nothing. It was under the left cup. Anger flashed in the man's eyes as the man of cups took the goblet placing it on a shelf behind the table.

'Perhaps tomorrow,' said the man of cups, and an angry, dejected man walked away from the stall. He would not have the man of cups that day. The man of cups invited the man in front of Guy to play. He stepped forward. 'For what do you play today?'

'Nothing, I think I will try again tomorrow.' He nodded to the man of cups and walked away, turning to watch from a distance.

'Young Knight,' beckoned the man of cups. Guy stepped forward. 'For what do you play today?'

'Nothing in particular.'

'With what do you play?' Guy pulled his book from his belt and placed it on the table. The man of cups picked it up. 'The battle of Ashford,' he read, 'I will take your book, as it is not the one that I gave you.' He placed the cup over the seed. 'Follow the seed.'

Guy smiled, he had already selected a cup. He met the man of cups eyes with a smile. After the familiar blurring of the man of cups hands they came to rest. 'Choose a cup.'

Guy paused a moment, for the crowd more than anything, before calling the left cup. It was empty. Guy shrugged, he had nothing to be angry about.

'Did you learn everything you wanted from the book?' he said in a low voice that was just for Guy.

'Almost, there is a man I cannot place who I am sure was there.'

'I believe the book is very clear. Only three knights survived. You should look to yourself for the answers you seek.'

Guy smiled and nodded his thanks to the man of cups before turning away and starting his day with honeyed breads and spiced milk. He had things to buy before meeting Smith, and as much as he tried to keep a clear mind, the man of cups' words echoed in his mind. He spent upwards of an hour selecting a cloak. A mid grey medium weight hooded woollen cloak. He needed no colour, and had come to learn in the woods that a black cloak stood out at much as a white one. A grey one would not be noticed so easily. He took a yard of spare cloth for repairs with some yarn and sewing needles. It was tied abundle under his arm, bringing him a sense of satisfaction. He finally had a cloak. It was still a couple of hours before noonshine as Guy, who carried sliced pork, eggs and two fresh loaves approached Smiths Workshop.

'Hoy, young apprentice, come. We have work to do.' Smith was busy tapping detail with a small hammer. Guy smiled as he put the food safe and set some water to boil. Smith had taken to calling him his apprentice in humour, but Guy was learning all he could from the man. In another life he would have been proud to be Smith's apprentice. 'Under that cloth, he beckoned with his head, 'is your sword. See what you think. It is you who will have to maintain it, so it is only right that you should give it its edge. Come we have much to do.'

Guy lifted the cloth, beneath it his sword was much transformed. It was still in its component parts, the crossguard, oiled and polished feathered steel of the south, the same as the blade. The blade had been formed, a double fuller ran two thirds of its length, it too had been polished, or maybe oiled. It was the most excited Guy had been to see any material object. This would be his sword. He picked it up marvelling at Smiths touch, and his own folding. Even aware of his own participation in its production, Guy felt that it would be the best sword he had ever seen.

'I do not leave until the day after tomorrow. I have a man to collect me early.'

'We still have much to do, but that is good, we can take the time to do it properly. Now it is time to form the edge on your sword before we harden it. But be precise, and do not touch the wheel with any steel other than that you wish to sharpen. Take your time, do it right.'

Smith stood and left Guy to it, entering his hut and closing the door. Guy stood a moment eyeing the components of his sword, imagining it complete. He ran his hands over the steel. This was to be his sword, his knight's sword. It would become his most important possession, and one that would define him as a knight. This sword was of his blood. Within each feather of darkness on the steel was a part of him. He took the blade, feeling its balance in his hands, and took it to the wheel. He worked it to a steady, smooth pace, took a breath and pressed the steel to the stone. It felt and sounded good, and Guy examined his first touch. He repeated the same on the opposite side of the blade, and slowly, carefully, he began to stroke the steel across the stone, barely touching it, but allowing it to work the metal, allowing a good consistent edge to reveal itself. He took care not to overwork the blade and gently set the untempered steel aside when there was an even edge on both sides of the blade. It had taken every ounce of concentration and control, but he was happy to have reconnected with his sword.

'Are you done?' called Smith as he came from the hut. 'Let me see.' Guy carefully handed him the blade, and he looked down its length from all sides, inspecting some areas closely. 'This is a good edge. You should really come and work with me, you could make a lot of money.' Though Smith said the words, he knew it would not come to pass. 'We need to set the blade.' He said handing it back to Guy and seeing to the fire. 'Why don't you see to noonshine, and I'll show you how to make the fire hot.'

By the time Guy had prepared the meal Smith had built a pit of embers so hot that it resembled the sun itself. They ate as Smith explained how they would heat the blade to a very high temperature, until the very point before the metal melted. 'Then we normalise the blade and let it cool before heating it again to a point just below the previous.' A dozen times they would heat the steel, where most blades were heated only two. Smith was happy that they had an extra day as they could let the blade cool more in between heatings, a slower cooling would make the grain finer and the steel stronger, and was of most benefit on the initial heating.

Leaving the blade to heat the blacksmith took Guy into his hut.

'A knight needs a shield to bear his arms. Did you think on your arms?'

'I did.'

'Good. Under that blanket is your shield. I need you to take it to a man called Evrand, on the main blacksmith parade. Tell him of your arms. He is expecting you. I will see to the blade.'

Guy lifted the blanket, before him was a solid round shield similar in style to Sir Parcifal's, except Guys was made with the Feathered steel and had a raised studded central boss. Looking at it, his design of the previous night would not work. It looked incredible even with its naked wood which looked to be inch thick oak with no substantial grain. He picked it up. It was heavy, but it felt solid, it felt like it would protect him. He wrapped it ablanket before leaving Smith to tend to the steel. He was looking at the blade often to get it to the right point. Too far and the steel would be ruined, not far enough and the blade could be prone to brittleness. Guy set off to find Evrand whilst trying to redesign his arms to fit the shield. He knew that he could, like many knights did, have the boss painted to show off the arms, but the feathered steel looked too good to be covered, besides, Smith had said that the steel would be what identified him as a knight. He would think around it. By the time he had located Evrand he knew exactly what he wanted, and was told to collect it the next day after noonshine.

When he returned the blade sat on a stone with only the glow of a blood red heartbeat running through the spine and fullers.

'Hoy young apprentice. The setting goes well. The next heating will set it strong, the more we let it cool the better. Come sit, watch the blade. A friend of mine roasts an ox. I shall get us some.'

Guy sat cross legged on the floor by the stones upon which sat his sword. He felt an energy surge within him, the surge of potential. He quenched his own thirst with some of the fruit water which had cooled, and returned to look upon his blade. Though he tried to clear his mind and focus only on his sword, he found himself looking within for the answers he sought. The man of cups and his cryptic words denying him the peace that he thought that he should be feeling. It did not frustrate him though, you cannot change what is meant to be.

The blacksmith returned carrying a three rib section of the roast ox.

'Hoy young apprentice, fetch us some loaves, and a skin of wine for me while I see to the fire.' Guy stood and made his way out of the blacksmiths yard without question. When the smell of the roast ox crept up his nostrils he realised just how hungry he was. He walked apace and within moments had left the blacksmiths quarter heading towards an evening baker securing two large loaves that still held the heat of the oven. Their smell matched that of the ox, his mouth moistened. He was fortunate to catch a wine merchant packing up his stall, and bought a good two copper skin for the Smith. It was the most expensive skin available.

When Guy returned to Smith's yard, his blade was back in the fire, and Smith was forcing air into the embers with the bellows. When he was satisfied with the intensity of the fire he examined the blade, plunged in back into the embers and joined Guy at the fire who handed him the skin of wine.

'Come, give me your knife and let's eat.' Without hesitation Guy released his knife from its sheath and handled it to the blacksmith. He sliced through a rib portion, forcing the knife through the bone with a crack from his other hand. 'We will keep this for noonshine.' Deftly removing the remaining fillet from the bone he sliced it into thick chunks on a wooden slab that soon flooded with meat juices. Guy

229

handed Smith a loaf, and they ate, the only sounds being the satisfied grunting of men eating meat and the crackle of the firepit.

The blacksmith showed Guy what to look for in the metal, sometimes it would change, as it took on the heat of the fire, a trained blacksmith knew what to look for. He showed Guy the point at which the heating should be stopped next time round, and thrust it back into the fire for a moment more. After removing the blade with tongs he held it up allowing the glow to light up the darkening evening before setting it to rest on the stone.

'You have seen me do it,' Smith called 'Next time I shall see you do it, and then you must do it nine more times throughout the night.'

Guy sat at an angle to the blacksmith, his breathing slighty laboured after feeding more coal to the fire and working the bellows, waiting for further instruction.

'In the old world there were many gods. Many were left behind when the sky rained fire, and the great wave washed away many more. But we bought some of them with us. Some of them have faded away over the years, some we carry with us today. Hefestus was the God of the forge, it is his fire that heats the metal, and it is he that brings to form every sword, every arrowhead, every horseshoe. It is said that the legendary forge was powered by the blood of Hefestus himself.' As he spoke he opened a flue gate and air fed the fire causing it to rise and roar. 'It is said that if a blade was plunged into it, it would melt in an instant, unless of course it were a legendary weapon, forged in the blood of Hefestus himself. It is customary as a blacksmith to offer, or seek, a blessing every time steel, or any other metal is heated. Most of us do it silently in our minds, but this, this is your sword, you should offer a blessing as you see fit.'

Guy took up the blade, 'Hefestus bless this sword. May your fires make it stronger, may the steel feed your fire.' With that he plunged the blade into the coals and sparks jumped from the fire fading into the air.

The blacksmith told Guy about the heating process and showed him how to watch for an inherent change in the metal, where the blade as a whole changes properties. He made him look closely at the last couple of stages, points where on subsequent heatings he would stop and allow the blade to cool. He then told Guy to remove the blade at the next discernible change in the blade.

As Guy watched the blade a shimmer of light seemed to cascade to the point. Guy was half sure that his mind's mischief had returned, but looked to Smith anyway who nodded and he pulled the blade from the fire and held it aloft, its glow gave off heat in the night. Guy felt the heat spread through him someway. He held the blade until the glow began to fade and set it on the stone to cool. The blacksmith talked as they watched the blade. The steel had been folded a dozen times, it would be fired a dozen times, and allowed to cool a dozen times. To those who believed in the Gods it would have the status of a holy sword. But this sword was beyond that, Smith had told him. This was his sword.

The blacksmith tended to the fire before turning to Guy.

'Fire it nine more times this night, and allow it to cool as much as possible. Tomorrow we set the blade.' Guy nodded, he had been looking forward to sleeping a real sleep, but it seemed the blacksmith had other plans. 'Give me your belt for the night, remove your coinpurse if you must, but I need to make alterations for your sword.' Without hesitation, and without removing the coinpurse, Guy took off his belt and handed it to the blacksmith, who bid him good night. Guy sat a moment when he left, reflecting, not on the act of trust, but on the feeling of not having his belt. The belt that had been a part of him since he had left Eastfield Manor. He may as well have been sat naked by the fire. He missed not having it. It did not take away from a night that he would always remember though. Guy did not believe in the Gods, but he offered his blessing to Hefestus all the same, and in return experienced what could only be described as a spiritual moment where the only things that existed were, himself, his sword, and the fire.

Guy was flat aback when the blacksmith returned shortly after first light, and awoke when he entered the yard. He woke cleanly despite his lack of sleep over recent nights.

'Hoy, young apprentice. We have no time for sleep. There is much to do. While I see to the fire and food, take your blade to a stream and let the worlds water wash over it. Running water both cleanses and energises the blade. Find a quiet spot.'

35

By the time Guy had pulled on his boots, drank a ladle of water and wrapped his blade in a burlap bundle, the blacksmith was raking the fire. Guy returned to the spot where he had harvested the willow and found a place where the water ran fast and shallow setting his blade on some rocks as the water swirled over it. He watched awhile before stretching on the bank and finding his energy before mimicking the burning hands with a hand on each end of the blade, imagining his energy flowing through it as the water washed over it. A distant part of him ridiculed himself for trying to make a connection with his sword, more of him did not care that it was absurd. A knight without a sword was no knight at all. This would always be his sword.

When he returned the blacksmith was in a flurry of activity, the quenching pool was freshly filled, the fire burned as well as it ever had, there were blankets and his armour laid out, and he was cracking eggs into a pot. He called out for Guy to set the sword astone before breaking his fast. When he unwrapped the sword from the bundle, the steel was cold in his hands, and he looked down the blade a few times before gently resting it on the stone.

The blade sat astone while they ate, waiting to be fed to the fire again. The blacksmith cleared away the bowls and returned with Guy's belt. There seemed to be a few new hoops added to it. It looked like a proper belt, it looked full, though the loops remained empty. His scabbard had gone too.

'Thank you,' said Guy, not entirely certain for what he was giving thanks. The blacksmith laughed.

'Look under that blanket there,' he said with a directional nod. 'Sir Parcifal wanted you to learn of Sir Winton Tardy, perhaps one day you can show him what you have learned.' Guy revealed a pair of war maces. Good solid balls of steel with curved flanges of the feathered steel in each quadrant, and the feathered metal decorating the handle. They looked incredible, more like they should be on display in a Lord's castle than used by him.

'I don't know what to say,' said Guy picking one up and feeling the weight in his hand. Once again it fit his hand perfectly, and felt good when he flexed his wrist. The blacksmith nodded towards the blanket again. Guy put down the mace and lifted it further revealing a knife and spike, like the ones in his belt, only this time in the feathered steel. His hands reached in excitement for the knife. It felt the same as his other knife, it was as big and similarly shaped. If his sword ended up anything like the knife, then it would indeed be a sword to behold.

'If the old feathered steel is how you are recognised as a knight, it should carry through.' Guy looked at the spike.

'They are beautiful.'

'Aye, the blade will be sharper, stronger. As you make your sword, these were made the same. A dozen firings, and a dozen coolings in between.'

For a second the image of his spike puncturing a breastplate and sinking into a man passed over his being. *Stronger than that?* he thought. He could not fight the emotion that was welling up inside, he looked at the blacksmith without words to say. The blacksmith smiled an acknowledgment. 'Come, let us make ready to fire the blade again, lest you will have no sword to go with them.'

Smith became serious in his demeanour and set about preparing for the blades quenching, he slowly worked the bellows pushing air into the fire pit from six different points. The coals pulsated as the air fed their glow until the heat turned their glow yellow and bright sparks rose, crackling in the mid-morning air. Smith put a bar of steel in the coals before ensuring the tongues and gloves were close to hand.

'This is the most crucial stage in any blade's construction,' Smith began, 'The quench. This is what sets the blade hard. All the work we have done so far is to give us the best chance. If it does not work, then all we have done is for naught. We will have to start again, and I have no more ancient steel to use, so let's get it right.'

Guy saw the experienced Smith's eyes survey the area again. Guy had lost blades in the quench before, the transition from fire to water could be too much for the metal, and it could crack or warp. Suddenly he shared Smith's anxiety. After all their work, if the blade cracked in the quench… He did not even want to think about it. The steel was good, and well worked, they had given themselves every chance.

'We need to get the blade hot, almost as hot as the first time we heated it, then we quench in snake oil.'

Guy was taken from his thoughts. *Snake oil?* Smith must have seen his confusion.

'We can heat the oil a little, so as to minimise the shock to the blade. Ancient smiths used oil, they claimed that Hefestus would show himself on a successful quench. But the right oil costs, and people took their chance with the water. For Southern steel like this, oil is the best. Let's get to it, are you ready?'

Guy nodded, but took a moment to control his breathing and focus his mind. He had connected with his sword, as he took it from the stone, it was there immediately. Him and the sword were one. He admired the feathered steel, the shape, the fullers, even the initial edge. It was straight, he hoped that it would remain that way after the quench. It was a long blade, there was much that could go wrong.

He closed his eyes, breathed deeply and offered a genuine plea to the god of the forge.

Hefestus bless this sword, make this sword stronger with all that you have, may I make you stronger with all that I have. He eased the sword into the fire pit, it had a good even heat. Guy held onto the tang until the heat was in his hands. He let go, unhurried, and felt as the heat spread up his arms, across his shoulders and down his back until it found his energy making him stronger. The wave of heat passed through him and into the ground as he watched his sword in the fire.

Smith removed the bar of metal he had placed in the fire earlier and plunged it into the oil. Guy could hear the hiss and bubble as the heat transferred from the blade. He never took his eyes off his sword as the forge worked its magic. He fought the urge to fiddle with the blade to make sure it was heating evenly, but Smith had made a good hot pit. The coals glowed evenly beyond the length of his sword. It was only when the tang itself started to glow that he used the tongues to look at the blade until it reached the point he had remembered since the night before. He looked to Smith for confirmation, to realise that Smith was as engrossed in the blade as he was. There was a nod. Guy took a breath, prepared himself, and removed the blade from the fire. It was hot, yellow more than red, energy burst from it. He held the blade away from him and took the three short steps to the oil filled barrel that was the quenching pool. He steadied himself before lifting the sword high above the barrel. This was the moment. He held the blade as straight as he could and plunged it into the barrel.

A wave of energy ripped through the blacksmiths yard as he quenched the blade for the first time. The oil bubbled violently and gave off steam, but he held the blade steady. He heard no tell-tale dinks that indicated cracks to the blade, he felt nothing through the tongues. He removed the blade from the oil, eyes darting to check for warps. The blade had been out of the oil for a couple of seconds, long enough for his mind to think that it was straight, but not long enough to be sure, when suddenly a ball of flame rose from the blade. Guy, was shocked but managed to keep hold of the blade. The flames seemed to fill the entire workshop before dying down to gentle remnants on the blade. Guy eased the blade back into the oil to put out the flames. Smith whooped with delight.

'Hefestus shows himself this day.' They shared a look, Guy did not know what to feel, he felt a lot of everything, but wanted to check the blade before he allowed anything to take over. 'Come, let us check the blade.'

Guy pulled the blade from the oil. It dripped dark oil from the thick coating that had collected on it, but he swung it to the stone where Smith was waiting. It seemed straight, but his mind would still not allow certainty to win. Smith gave it a quick rub with a rag, before picking up a file and looking to Guy.

'Let us see if it is hard.' Smith ran the file along the blade, Guy's heart was in his mouth. The file slipped easily along the blade, the high pitched scrape of metal told him that the blade was hard. Inside he wanted to burst, there were no noticeable warps, and now it was hard. But Smith continued testing the blade with the file until all edges had not let the file bite. 'Hefestus has blessed us,' he confirmed, 'The blade is hard.'

Guy only nodded, though elation ran through his veins, he thanked Hefestus in his mind and shared a satisfied look with Smith before he retired to his hut, leaving Guy alone with his sword.

The blade was complete. It had been folded, edged and fired. All that remained was to polish it, assemble the sword and put the fine edge on it. It felt complete in his hands, it felt a part of him. He wanted to start cleaning and polishing the blade, but he also wanted to take it to the stream. That was what the blade was telling him, that was what he should do.

Guy lay in the stream, the blade lay down the centre of his body as the natural running water washed the soot and fire from them both. Accepting the blade as part of himself, the sounds of the water drifted Guy towards his dreaming state. There was just too much chill on the water for him to drift completely, but he was serene with his sword on his chest. He was reluctant to leave, but as the sun crested the sky, he knew the blacksmith would have returned. Thoughts of the Smith and the man of cups swam in his mind as he wandered back, sword wrapped abundle over his shoulder. Sir Parcifal, the man of cups, Smith, the stranger. He remembered the man of cups words, *look to yourself for the answers you seek*. Guy sat on a rock beside the path to contemplate.

He was a squire, a pseudo squire at that. Sir Parcifal had said that he would only ever have one squire. Suddenly thoughts and realisations flashed before his eyes. The first time the stranger had fitted his armour, the synergy he had with Sir Parcifal. If he had the book, he would read it, but in his mind he knew the passage. 'Sir Parcifal sent his squire to ready his equipment while he rounded a dozen men'. Could it be that Sir Parcifal took his squire with him? Did the other knights? It made sense in his head. It had been bothering him for weeks, but now, finally he could explain who the stranger was. Whether he was right or not, he would ask Smith later, but he was happy to finally have an explanation.

When Guy returned to the blacksmiths yard the food was ready and Smith had not long started eating.

'Hoy, young apprentice. Did you visit the stream?' Guy nodded. 'Good, good. You look as if you have had a moment of peace.' Guy nodded again. 'Come, tell me what you have realised.'

'I have been reading the battle of Ashford,' Guy began, 'I have identified Sir Parcifal and the two nights that survived.' He said with a respectful nod to Smith, 'Sir Benjamin Cook, and um… well, yourself. But there is someone else that I could not place.'

'Well that is not quite what I was expecting, but go on.'

'The man of cups told me to look to myself for the answers. The only thing I am is a squire, and not a real one at that. The book talks of Sir Parcifal's squire. Is that the other man at Eastfield Manor?'

'Come and eat. This is a story I have not thought of for a long time,' he said as Guy plated his food. 'There were many things done back then that would not make any man proud. It was a dark time of betrayal against Rodina itself.'

He ripped a mouthful of the rabbits flesh and paused while he ate, reflecting. 'We arrived at the scene of a massacre, many a families name was removed from the world that day. Caught up in a bloodlust they attacked us before a word had been spoken, perhaps not wanting any witnesses to their treachery. That was not the right thing to do. We were knights of the king's army. To attack us was to attack the king himself. A gross of men, against a dozen. It was carnage. Winton was in his element, a big man in heavy armour wielding two maces against the victors of a recent battle, he swept through them, letting the rest of us pick them off. We lost two men quickly, good men, but overwhelmed by the numbers they had little chance. I thought I was to join them when I took an arrow to my knee. Somehow it slipped between my greave and poleyn. It chopped me down like a tree.' He gnawed on the rabbit some more. 'Some opportune prick was coming to finish me off in half armour and with a shit sword. I readied myself, through the pain, wielding my sword on one knee. I was not going to die a death like that without a fight. But before the fight came a spear erupted from him and I was being dragged to safety in agony.'

'Who dragged you?'

'I could not see, such was the pain. I could see only white, and even whiter stars, but the other knights were busy battling. I knew who it was though. He dragged me and left me against a pile of bodies and dying men. From there, when I came to my senses, I managed to see the battle, and more of our men die, and many more of their men. We were Sir Parcifal's men, we did not fuck about. For a while I thought that I might be the only one to survive. But as the screams quieted and the bodies fell, two men remained, Edrick and Ben. They did not stop to marvel in their glory though, and exhausted as they were Sir Parcifal checked on all the men that had joined him. I was the only one he found alive. He and Ben threw me over a horse and led me the fuck out of there before more men arrived. Once hidden in the woods Edrick's squire found us and led us to the horses that he had led away from the battle. It was he who had dragged me to safety, who saved my life.'

Despite the horror of the story, Guy felt himself smiling. He had been right. 'What is his name?'

'No one knows. Shortly after Sir Parcifal joined the king's own knights, the king told him to take a squire. A week or so later a woman dropped off her son, who was maybe 12, and left. He did not talk and she never told us his name. He was known to us as Squire.'

Guy had a thousand questions that he wanted to ask, and of those who survived, he felt Smith would be the one more likely to share the truth with him, instead he found himself simply offering thanks as Smith cleared away the dishes and gave his knee a little rub with remembered pain.

They continued in silence as Smith showed Guy how the sword was assembled, and then sent him to collect his shield while he polished the blade. He had become so absorbed in firing the blade, that Guy had forgotten about his shield, and a new wave of excitement washed through him as he quenched his thirst with a cup of fruit water. He cast a glance to the blacksmith, as one of the most revered warriors of recent times, rubbed oil onto his blade with a cloth, and shook his head in wonderment.

Guy's mind considered his situation on his way to collect his shield from Evrand. He was certain that all the knights in the kingdom had stories of war and chivalry, and that their squires treated such stories with the awe and respect they deserved, but Guy felt different. Sir Parcifal and the others had never tried to impress him with their feats, he had found them out on his own, with a little help from the man of cups. Guy would not be parading his master's stories to other squires, as he had seen them do, he would live off his own glories, he would give Phylissa the man she wanted.

Phylissa. He altered his course and picked up his pace as he headed to the messengers station chastising himself. His mind had been so caught up in his training, in his journey that he rarely considered the reason he was on it, Phylissa. So far removed was he from the dreamer boy who left Waering, but still driven by the same cause. He would have Phylissa's hand or die trying.

At the messengers station, the scribe penned his message and sealed it while Guy paid his copper. The message he had asked for was '*We shall wed next summer so the sun can accentuate your beauty.*'

When Guy had given where it was to be sent, the man behind the counter had asked if he was Guy of Waering. When he offered a nodded reply the man scurried off returning momentarily with a sealed message.

'This was sent back with the last message that you sent, in the hope that you would return.' He handed it over.

'Thank you,' said Guy, taking the note which caused his heart to pound. He tried to appear calm as he tucked the note in his pouch, and when his business was complete, he left aiming towards the stand of Evrand. Once out of sight he ducked between two buildings and took the note from his pouch. In beautiful writing it held his name 'Guy of Waering' The wax seal was Phylissa's. He cracked the wax and opened the note.

Hurry my love. I cannot wait forever. Instead of fear or urgency, he felt something else on reading the words. Something he could not explain, a mixture of pride, selfish happiness, and love. She had called him her love and it made him feel a dozen feet tall and gave him a grin to rival that of the village idiot when the moon was full. That was why he was on his journey, and it was with renewed enthusiasm that he headed to collect his shield.

When he reached Evrand's stall the old man was not there, his daughter handed over his shield wrapped in burlap. Tempted as he was to take a look, he was starting to adapt his behaviour to that of a knight.

Instead he took the heavy bundle, offered his thanks and set of back to see Smith.

'Hoy young apprentice, did Evrand keep you talking?'

'He was not there. I had an errand to run.'

'Well come, Show me your shield before I show you your sword. Defence always comes first.' Guy sat beside the blacksmith and cut the string with his knife. There was a time when Guy would have untied the knots and kept the string. His time in the forest had seen an end to that, he could make something adequate if he needed. As he pulled back the burlap the first thing that struck him was the colour. The blue and white diamonds seemed to shine from the shield. The tower's silhouette framed the central boss perfectly and was as good a representation of Waering's great tower as he had seen. Evrand surely knew it. Guy held it up. It looked better than he could have expected. They were good arms.

The blacksmith looked and nodded. 'Tell me of your arms. A knight's arms should have a story. Tell me yours.' Guy looked up. The blacksmith had been straight with him about the battle of Ashford, he could be straight about his arms.

'When I was born my father was a steward to the earl of Waering. As such he gave up his name, and I was born Guy of Waering. The tower represents where I come from. The black comes from Sir Parcifal's Arms, for it is he who makes me a knight and should be represented. Before my father was a steward of Waering he was someone else. On his death I saw my mother sobbing over a shield, or what was left of it. It was the blue and white diamonds adorned with a falcon. I did not know what it represented, so took only the diamonds.'

'Ah, and you are sure this shield was your fathers?'

'Aye, why else would my mother hold it to her chest as she grieved her loss?'

'Indeed. You have the truth of it. Tell me, the falcon, was it golden?' Guy looked up at him unable to hide the surprise.

'It was. Do you know it? Did you know my father?' The blacksmith smiled a forlorn smile.

'I have a vague recollection, but it is lost in the past. I did not know your father though. There could have been many men who bore the arms. They could belong to an earl or lord he served. I have nothing that will help you.' There was a pause as Guy allowed the disappointment to fade. 'Come, see your sword.'

When he pulled back the burlap Guy could not help but gasp. Before him was a real sword. It already seemed to have a history, though it had just been made. The design was simple and strong, but the feathered steel pommel and quillion block gave it a sense of grandeur, of quality. Guy looked up at the blacksmith, aware of the emotions that consumed him and gave a nod that meant many things.

'How does it feel in your hands?' asked Smith. Guy looked at the almost black leather grip and slowly closed his hand around it. His hands wrapped perfectly around it, as he felt its weight for the first time. He rose to his feet and headed to the clearing they had previously used for training and slowly moved the sword with his wrists. The sword was light for a blade of its size, but it still had some weight to it. A weight that was so perfectly balanced it seemed to have no location, just a presence. He swung the sword wider, one fluid motion swinging it from one side of his body, then the other. His feet moved and the blade followed, and before long found himself performing a dance that the stranger himself would be proud of. The sword moved with precision and fluidity. He bought it to a halt in the North ready position and exhaled before returning to Smith.

'It feels perfect,' a wide eyed Guy replied, his breathing was hard, his eyes burned with ecstasy.

'We need to put the fine edge on and polish it. I am happy to do it for you.'

'I think I should do it.'

'Aye, but it requires a gentle touch, you should calm yourself. Take a drink, find your peace.'

The blacksmith talked him through the final stages of polishing the fine edge. It had been a calm learning environment for Guy. There was a peace about him. When he had polished all four sides of the blade he held it up to the sun and looked down its length. This was his sword. It was of his blood and his sweat. The blacksmith pulled back the rest of the burlap revealing the scabbard. It had a throat of the feathered steel that had an elegant simplicity to it, along with the chape and hangers. It was bound with the same dark grey polished leather that adorned the grip of his sword. Over that non polished leather of the same kind spiralled the scabbards length. He handed it to Guy who slid the blade in. It was a natural and smooth fit, Guy hoped it would draw just as well.

'Now, before you go, let us see it all together.'

Guy stood in his armour, his belt fully equipped with his knife and spike, a pair of war maces and his sword. He wore his helmet with the visor attached for full effect. Guy wished that he could see himself.

'Draw your sword.' called out the blacksmith. He did, it slid smoothly from the scabbard ready in North West. 'Again, with purpose.'

For over an hour the blacksmith drilled him, drawing his sword and maces in various ways, the blacksmith guiding his moves in fine detail. Guy realised early on that Smith was teaching him to make his armour sing as Sir Parcifal had, a ripple of shock with very little movement. The blacksmith had him stepping into it at first to generate the momentum. It was difficult, but Guy kept a clear mind and absorbed the blacksmith's words. This was something that he had tried and failed to teach himself. Already the blacksmith had him causing more of a rattle than he had managed in weeks on his own. He followed the instructions without question or hesitation, allowing his body to learn. It was hard work and he was soon sweating inside his suit and feeling his body working. When the blacksmith called a halt Guy was pleased with the progress. His efforts were still feeble in comparison to Sir Parcifal's, even Smith's who seemed to make the air pulse around him with the strength of his movement. He knew how it should be done, he could teach himself to do it well.

Once returned from cleaning himself in the stream, Guy prepared his things wrapping his armour in burlap and tying it in bundles. Before long a neat pile was prepared ready for the arrival of the old man and his cart at dawn.

He looked over at Smith who was spit roasting a young pig over the fire. This was to be his farewell. He took a moment to be aware, to give himself something to remember, to acknowledge all that he had learnt, for he had much to be thankful for.

36

It was a week later when the cart pulled up outside the gates of Eastfield Manor. The old man, a candle maker, did not believe in travelling hard, quite the opposite. It had been by far the most leisurely trip Guy had ever taken. He was all too aware that not that long ago he would have grown frustrated at the old man's lack of urgency, but he was different now. The blacksmith's words of their last night together had stayed with him. 'You cannot change what is meant to be.' He had learned a lot about making candles, and had thought how much Ash would have enjoyed the conversations. Guy had enjoyed them on his behalf, for while Phylissa had encouraged him to hurry, he had to accept things for what they were. He would have her hand in the following summer. He knew she would wait that long. Guy stacked his armour neatly by the gates, placed his weapons and a cask of wine that Smith had had delivered next to them before sharing a pleasant farewell with the candle maker and waving him off. He was back. He waited a while, attempting to focus his mind. A fear had risen inside him prompted by memories of the forest. What would the rest of his training entail?

It was with some trepidation that he hoisted himself up and over the wall. He was about to re-enter a place that had changed him, and he wasn't sure it was for the better. He opened the gate from inside and took in his things. A strange sensation swept through him. He felt like he had arrived home.

He closed and barred the gate, returning it to how it had been when he arrived. As he turned, the Knightmaker stood on the balcony. He was still as imposing a figure as Guy had ever encountered. Guy waved, happy to see him. There was no response from the Knightmaker, who simply stood, waiting. Guy approached the balcony as the stranger emerged from the house. It was the stranger's eyes he met first, the horrors of the forest flashing through his mind. The strangers face bore none of them, he was as passive as he ever was, but ever so slightly differently. The stranger nodded a greeting, Guy nodded back and switched his eyes to the Knightmaker as his voice broke the silence.

'Young Guy. We feared you had left us. What took you so long?'

'It would appear that candle makers have a very relaxed approach to their travels.' Guy smiled.

'Aye, they do. Do you have everything you need?' Guy's eyes flicked to the pile of burlap bundles over by the gate.

'I do.'

'Do you have what I asked for?'

'I do.'

'Good, go fetch it.' Guy head over the courtyard without question and collected the small wooden box and the cask of wine from Smith. He handed over the box to the Knightmaker and offered the cask.

'It is from Smith. He said you would like it.'

The Knightmaker gestured to the stranger who was already reaching for it. Guy fumbled in his pouch and retrieved the note Smith had given him. It was battered, but the seal remained intact. 'He also sent you this.' Sir Parcifal took the note giving it a once over and returning his gaze to Guy. Guy remembered how good he was getting at holding the Knightmaker's gaze before he left, but no more. His look went right through him. He was still broken from the forest, and he could not hide it when someone looked that deep.

'Two hours, settle in then I want to see you fully suited. Let me have a look at Smiths work, see if it is as I remember.'

Guy moved the pile of burlap parcels over to his camp, stacking them neatly nearby. He did not open them though, instead he set about collecting wood for a fire. There were charred half logs in the hearth, he built sticks around them and a rolled ball of dried grass. He went over to his rollmat that had been hastily packed away. Everything appeared to be where he had left it, even his coinpurse. He quickly retrieved his flint and striking stone as if he had never been away. It was an old way to light fire, but it was simple and worked well in the summer months. The dry grass would catch quickly, it had almost turned to dust in his hand when he had rolled it aball. When he turned back to the firepit he noticed a figure coming from the balcony. It was the Knightmaker and he carried a small burning log in his bare hands. He would look just as intimidating if it were a bunch of flowers that he carried. Guy stood and stepped out to meet him.

'A welcome back gift.' The Knightmaker held out the log, Guy tried to fight his natural instinct to be hesitant, but knew that it had shown itself. He took the log thanking the Knightmaker and thrust it into the centre of the balled grass. The fire took instantly. Guy paused a moment to make sure the twigs caught and turned back to the man who still intimidated him more than any other. Instead of leaving the Knightmaker nodded and sat alog. Guy sat opposite.

'Being a knight is not about tournaments and battles. Being a knight is doing what is right, what you believe in. Sometimes a knight has to do things that an ordinary man would not. That is what makes us special. It is what puts coin in your purse and food in your belly.' The Knightmaker paused letting the words sink in. 'Sometimes knights are sent to solve problems.' He tugged at his beard as he considered his words. 'You thought that we left the tournament to keep you out of trouble. Not so. Someone I used to know had their daughter taken, in itself a terrible thing. When there is a group of sadistic fucks taking women, torturing them and using them before killing them, it is far worse. The three of us went to get her back, which we did. But before we could finish the group off, Hawkins got hit and we had to retreat leaving five of them unaccounted for. I believe you met them during your training in the forest. What you did was knight's work. Mayhaps I should have told you, but a knight must adapt to any situation. It is part of being a knight. After a battle you may find yourself without possession in the woods, chased by the enemy. A knight needs the confidence to know that he will make it to safety, or a knight must face death. Those men beat, raped and murdered women. The combined Lords of the area put a bounty on their heads. A dozen gold. It is not why we went after them, but coin is coin. He fished in a pouch handing over two gold. This is your share. Six for me, and two each for the rest of you. It is as it should be.' Guy reached for the gold coins when the Knightmaker gestured for a second time and tucked them in his pouch.

'Thank you.'

'Aye, thank me now, for you will not be thanking me later. Smith said your training suffered while you were with him. So we step it up. You have to show me that you have what it takes to be a knight, and I am going to break you in the process. When you come to the training ground, I am going to break you.'

The Knightmaker stood leaving Guy with his fire. He sat awhile contemplating. Sir Parcifal could snap him like a dry twig, he knew, but he also knew that this was not the break that the Knightmaker sought.

Guy stepped from his camp, and pulled down the visor on this helm. His breathing was ragged, instantly building heat inside. He had exercised before. Whatever was to happen, he wanted to be ready. It had felt good to bend his knees and stretch again. He checked his weapons and put his arm through the shield before heading to the training ground. He paused momentarily before turning the corner. He was walking into the unknown, he was walking to his end. He set off, with purpose and strode to a halt before the Knightmaker who was waiting with Hawkins and the stranger. Guy was ready.

He stood as the Knightmaker circled him as he inspected the armour without a sound to indicate what he thought. The moment lasted as Guy tried to remain stoic. His mind was racing, his heart pounding. He had hoped that he had seen the end of the beatings. Something inside told him that it was far from the truth. He felt nervous, but perhaps that was just the warrior blood starting to boil within him. After an age the Knightmaker returned to the balcony and turned to face him.

'Draw.'

Guy pulled the sword from scabbard with the stepping motion that allowed him to get some snap in the end of the movement into the North ready position. The Knightmaker stepped down from the balcony, again walking round his as the effort of staying perfectly still caused beads of sweat to roll down his face. The Knightmaker stood in front of him looking the sword up and down. Even now, fully suited and armed, he knew that the man before him in a linen shirt could finish him in a second. It unnerved him, but gave him strength at the same time. Finally the Knightmaker returned to the balcony.

'Away,' he called and Guy, relieved at being able to move, throated his sword with one fluid movement and stood with his arms at his side. 'Draw maces,' called the Knightmaker. Guy released the maces as best he could, all too aware of slight fumbling. He stepped forward snapping into a half crouch, one mace out front for defence, the other ready to strike. Before the Knightmaker had moved from the balcony, the straining muscles in his legs were informing him of the mistake that he had made. This stance was meant to be fluid and always moving, it kept the body coiled and ready. By holding the position he was denying himself the required movement, and his body was rebelling. By the time the Knightmaker reached him it was taking all his effort to control the shaking in his legs. He did not hear the rattle of his armour betraying movement, though after inspecting the maces he heard the Knightmaker mutter that he should work on it before returning to the balcony. 'Away,' he called. Guy could not remember ever being so thankful to hear a word, he was finally able to end the agony, legs afire as he straightened. 'Draw.'

Guy lost count of the times he had been made to draw his weapons. He gave it everything, every time, and his body was hurting as a result. Such small movements were exhausting. He could feel his body become heavy and each time it required more effort. He drove himself. He wanted to learn, training was his life.

'Defence training. Two hours. You have ten minutes to remove your armour.' His tired body was slow to reach, and muscles threatened to seize as he rushed, fumbling to remove his armour, but he took the time to place it carefully on the floor. It was difficult, but he just about made it, standing before the three of them in the farmer's clothes he had bought in Varen. The linen shirt wet and clinging to his body, his face was red beneath the scruff of sweat soaked hair and he was still to catch his breath. The Stranger stepped forward in half armour, their eyes met briefly and the stranger slammed the wooden stick on his chestplate. That was not a good sign.

The stranger strode over to him, breaking into a run, coming straight at him with the wooden stick. Unarmed and without armour it was all

Guy could do to roll to the ground to evade him, when he looked up the stranger was coming at him again. The stranger was pressing him so hard that he could not stand, and could only scramble out the way as the wooden stick was wielded with menace. After several attacks Guy saw an opportunity, and after rolling away from a downward strike, his movement continued as he swept a leg, taking the stranger's from under him. It allowed him to roll away and get to his feet before putting a safer distance between the two of them. Even as he retreated the stranger started towards him, controlled in his approach the stranger launched at him. Guy regained enough of his balance to pivot and avoid the blow, but the stranger quick to react slammed the other end of the stick into Guys guts bending him double. The stranger struck the stick across Guys thigh causing him to lose balance. Suddenly Guy could not see, his shirt had been pulled over his head. The stranger span around him landing blows to Guys back, ribs and legs before a boot to the arse sent him sprawling face first on the dirt floor, his arms caught up in his linen shirt.

'Get up!' called the Knightmaker. 'We are not fucking around. We go again.'

Guy rolled to the side, the left side of his face throbbing from the impact, he could taste blood. A kick to the ribs sent him sprawling again, but he rolled into it, and rolled a further three times before bending his legs and pushing himself up, staggering for balance as he clawed at the back of his head trying to release the shirt. The stranger landed a hard blow to the ribs and Guy span away as the pain shot through him. Before he had completed the rotation, he span back the other way and took three quick steps away before sidestepping and doing the same. Hoping that he had found some space, Guy pulled the shirt over his head, the first thing his eyes saw was the stranger charging at him. He rolled forwards on the floor to escape the stranger, trying to work the shirt down his arms. They were restricted in movement as the sweat soaked shirt clung to his skin, the more he pushed at the sleeves, the more they bunched up and gained traction. He dodged a few attacks from the stranger, but he was soon caught with a blow to the hip that threw him off balance. Once two more blows had struck him he dived into a roll to escape, but the stranger learnt quickly and struck Guys thigh and caused his roll to lose all control. Guy found himself crouched, instinctively turning to face the stranger. A knight should always keep eyes on the enemy. The stranger was barely a step away, the wooden stick was beginning its movement from an overhead strike that could cave in his head. The shirt was still caught around his wrists, but survival kicked in and he thrust both his arms up towards the blow. The shirt stretched out between his hands and stopped the stick. The blow was one of such force that even with the shirt absorbing its force it would have still rang his helm had he been wearing one. His eyes briefly met the strangers, and for the first time Guy understood that they really weren't fucking about. He rolled away, putting some distance between them and finding his balance.

Guy stood ready for the first time since training had begun, feeling that he had survived the ambush. The stranger had changed his pace from unrelenting to calculating. They moved together as the stranger prowled, but Guy was also prowling, he was waiting for a moment to strike. It took time, and he got hit, His body was wet with sweat and the dirt clung to him covering most of the grazes he was picking up. He didn't feel any of them, even the blows from the stranger did not hurt him as they should. The warrior blood flowed freely through his veins. He had kept the shirt around his wrists, but had wrapped it around his hands to make it tight between them. He had blocked many blows this way, and he was keeping his feet. When the blow to his ribs came, he was ready, blocking the blow with his shirt, one hand flashed over the stick wrapping the shirt tightly around it. Before he even felt the tension in his shirt the movement had begun in his hips, and as soon as the shirt had purchase on the stick he flicked his arms away from the stranger and the weapon was ripped from his hands. Before any thought of success could form in his mind, three quick punches to his gut doubled him over, and a knee to the chest left him flat aback. He rolled away, but the Knightmaker called a halt before he had fully turned. The stranger offered a hand and pulled him up.

Guy stood before the Knightmaker who gestured to the stranger. 'Go pick up your stick.' Turning to Guy who stood panting, dirty and bloody, 'You have earned the right to a stick of your own.' Hawkins tossed one down from atop the steps. 'I suggest you get it quickly. We go again' He bellowed.

Guy's eyes flicked to the stranger who had just retrieved his stick from a dozen paces away. As their eyes met his aching body spurred itself into action. He had taken the first step, and had a lead on the stranger. After five full power steps he threw himself at the stick grabbing it mid roll, coming up just short of the steps, turning just in time to use the stick to block the first blow. He did not block the second, or the third, finding himself trapped between the steps and the stranger, who was picking him off at will, Guy's blocking moves were behind the pace. Every blow sapped energy from his bruised body, every blow drained his speed. The stranger danced around him with the space to move and soon settled into a rhythm. It was this rhythm that allowed Guy to make his escape, making the most of a glimmer of space. Once free, he put distance between himself and the stranger. As they eyed each other for a moment Guy thought that he would enjoy dancing with the stranger if he were not so battered and beaten. He would enjoy nothing about this dance as Guy learned a different kind of defence, one that was not taught in castles.

Guy did not know how long the session lasted. If it had been two hours as the Knightmaker had indicated it was quite possibly the longest two hours of his life. The warriors blood had faded and with it some of his strength and speed. Every blow hurt and his entire body ached. When the Knightmaker finally called a halt the stranger clapped him on the shoulder. Whether it was to show there were no hard feelings, or to say well done, Guy did not know, neither did he care. He appreciated the gesture, but what meant most was that it was over. The stranger moved up the stairs and the three of them returned to the house leaving Guy in the training yard, exhausted and hurting, but not broken.

37

A dull bodied Guy stirred the boiled oats, his aching muscles protesting. He was not surprised to hear footsteps approach, and he turned his head slowly.

'The oats need a couple more minutes.' he called to the Knightmaker who sat on a log near the fire.

'You look in pain'

'I'm alright, just a little stiff this morning, it's been a while.'

'Aye, it is as it should be. It will help you remember why you are here.'

They continued in silence as Guy served the boiled oats, handing a bowl to the Knightmaker. A satisfied grunt came from him as he spooned in his first mouthful. 'You do fucking good oats.' Guy smiled.

After eating, the Knightmaker did not get up and return to the house as usual. Instead he examined Guys armour and weapons.

'I can see why Smith likes you.' he said. 'You are driven and do not know when to stop, he can spot that a mile away. But you have your differences too. Smith was much more confident of his abilities, which made him better than he was. He too understood things outside of combat, which is why he is the only one of us that has moved on. For the rest of us, we don't know any different, and cannot be arsed with learning. He did the right thing sending you to me.' Guy simply looked at the Knightmaker. He had nothing to say, and was slightly overwhelmed at his words. 'There are too few knights in the kingdom with the drive and desire of the knights that forged it. If you keep true to yourself you can achieve all that you want to. A woman, is that right?'

'It is my lord.'

'I am not your lord. When a man talks to another there is no need for such references. I know my name, I know my place, you need not remind me.'

'It is a woman, yes. The earl's daughter. She told me to come back in white.' The Knightmaker laughed, not out of malice, more exasperation.

'You mean that after I have finished with you, you need to win a tournament?'

'I am hopeful that she will overlook that and that being a knight will be enough. Time is short apparently.'

'Fuck me,' the Knightmaker cursed as he shook his head. He looked at Guy and they shared a smile. He had just shared a smile with Sir Edrick Parcifal, one of the baddest fuckers in all of Rodina. Suddenly his aches did not concern him. It was only pain, it would fade. 'Let me see your shield.' Guy reached over and handed it to the Knightmaker. 'That's a good shield. Heavy, just right for a big man like you. It is good work. Tell me of your arms.' Guy looked to his shield, and then Sir Parcifal, remembering the same discussion with Smith. 'If I am to knight you, I want to know of your arms.'

'The tower is the great tower of Waering. It is where I am from. When I was born, my father was the earl's steward, so I was born Guy of Waering. It is black to represent you, your arms are black. The blue and white diamonds represent who my father was before he was a steward.'

'Is that so?'

'I found my mother weeping over a shield with them on when he died.'

'Do you know what they represent?'

'No.' Guy said, thinking that he should find out, 'Do you?'

'No.' said the Knightmaker, 'I do not know what they represent.' There was a silence between them.

'I think that there are things that you are not telling me.'

'Do you now?' The Knightmaker stood. 'Report to the training ground for defence training in one hour. Wear your training armour.'

Guy watched him walk back to the house. He was sure the Knightmaker knew more of the arms, but he had allowed the question to be phrased for him, and it had not been the right one. It was as if mystery and intrigue was as much a part of his training as anything else. No sooner had he identified who the stranger was, a new question remained unanswered. At least it kept his mind away from the pain in his body.

When he reported for training a wooden bathing tub was on the balcony and a wooden frame had been built housing a pulley beam high above his head. A large metal bucket rested on the floor beside the well. It must have been built while he was away.

'Do you know what that is?' called the Knightmaker as he appeared from the house. He did not give Guy chance to answer. 'That is pain.' He let the words hang in the air. 'It is to be hot today. I wish to be refreshed while I watch you train. Three dozen buckets of nice cold water in the tub. You must use the pulley beam. If you are able to defend yourself at the end of today's training, tomorrow you can pull the water before you put your armour on. Get on with it.' The Knightmaker returned to the house leaving Guy to explore how best to fill the tub. The rope was thick and heavy, even his great hands would not wrap all the way around it. The metal bucket was big and solid. It looked as if it easily held three dozen pints. The rope had been woven around the handle to form the securest of fittings. His mind whirred, a quick decision was not always the right one. With the equipment he had there were not many options. He took the bucket and grasped the rope that was coiled beside it. Three attempts later and the rope was hanging from the other side of the pulley beam and he was already fucked. The rope was a lot heavier than he anticipated. He kept hold of the rope while he moved the bucket into the well. The three foot of slack jolted his arm so hard he almost lost his grip on the rope, such was the weight of the bucket. That did not bode well. He carefully moved into position and passed the rope through his hands whilst looking up at the beam. It had to be at least twice his height, probably more. The rope went slack for just a second before it became heavier, as the bucket filled.

It took much of his strength to pull the bucket from the water, he hoped that it would get easier as he raised his heavy load. It didn't. His own movement, restricted by the armour, meant that he was unable to hoist the bucket to the extent that he normally would. It required lots of short little movements, feeding the rope through a hand at a time, and each time concerted effort was required. He grunted and cried out as the pain gripped his entire body, to the same extent that his hands gripped the bucket. His muscles screamed and threatened to tear, but he kept pulling the rope. Finally, he saw the handle of the bucket rise over the lip of the well. A final heave lifted it to ground level, wrapping the thick rope around his arm, he leaned to grab the other end and pulled the bucket onto land, some splashed over the side to his annoyance. He sat beside it trying to catch his breath and enjoying the relief of being able to relax and move his knotted body. The Knightmaker had been right, it was pain.

After a moment he picked up the bucket and staggered with it over to the tub. The water was hard to carry, he tried to keep his movements small lest he spill more of his precious cargo, but the heavy rope stretched out behind him and before long he had to drag the rope along with the bucket which made it feel a dozen times heavier. When Guy arrived at the tub, it took all his remaining effort to lift the bucket and empty it. He held himself bent over the tub gasping for air. In his mind he counted one, thirty five to go.

He staggered back with the empty bucket and looked up at the pulley beam. He was going to have to throw the rope over it again, to lower it into the well. He pulled off his helm and gauntlets and coiled the rope beside him. It took him four attempts to get the rope over the beam, any jubilation he felt was quickly replaced with the dread of having to do it all over again.

The sweat stung the cuts and grazes that adorned his body. He should have put some of Della's balm on the previous night, but he had been so tired that he had fallen asleep without eating. The armour exacerbated his niggles, it rubbed against him when he pulled the rope. As he lowered the bucket back into the well, blue and white diamonds were the furthest thing from his mind, all that consumed it was pain and survival. The Knightmaker was trying to break him. He would not be broken.

He had not filled the tub with even a dozen buckets when the three of them came out of the house and ate noonshine on the balcony. Guy occasionally felt their eyes, but none of them said a word to him. He carried on. He had found a system that worked. Guy was breaking the pain down into sections to make it more manageable. All the sections hurt like he was on a rack, but all the components were possible. He knew it was training, and that it made him stronger, but this was pain like he had never known before. The hardest part was getting the fucking rope over the pulley beam, or at least that was what he thought until he started pulling the full bucket to the surface.

After every dozen buckets he took a moment to stretch relief into his body, he even bent his knees a few times to work familiar muscles. By the time he hoisted the last of the three dozen buckets into the tub the sun was lowering in the sky, the three of them had already eaten their evening meal on the balcony and Hawkins and the Knightmaker were supping their evening wine. While Guy leaned on the tub, his head pounding, his body drained. Hawkins cried out in despair and both he and the Knightmaker tossed the stranger a coin. He gathered them up with a knowing nod.

'Defence training. One hour.' He looked to the stranger 'Get yourself ready.' Guy watched the stranger dressed in half armour get up and head towards his helm and sword that were nearby. Guy's mind burst into life and was making him stagger his pain wracked body to where he had left his helm. As swiftly as he could he pulled it over his head, and glanced through the eye slit, the stranger was ready and marching across the courtyard with intent, hitting the sword hard against his helm. Guy's sword was three steps away. Instinct took over and his body launched to the dulled blade, swooping to collect it, and turning to block as the strangers sword cut through the air towards him. It was instinct that made him block or escape many of the stranger's attacks. Instinct would have protected him for longer had the stranger not stuck his unprotected hand with the flat of his blade. Guy cried out in pain, his sword falling to the ground as the stranger prepared to ring his helm. The Knightmaker called halt before the sword had landed. The stranger stopped immediately holding the position, the strike a foot from Guy's helm.

'You are unprepared and unprotected. You should know better than that. We are behind with training so pull on your gauntlets and try not to get injured.'

Guy flexed his hand. Gods that had hurt, but his hand still worked. It hurt, but it worked. A new pain came to his hands when he pulled on the gauntlets over his bleeding and blistered hands. That rope had really fucked him up. His hands were numb with pain, and the only way he knew his sword was in his hands was because he could see it. As he stood, he stretched his back and rolled his shoulders, trying to ease some of the pain, and strode back towards the courtyard with as much purpose as he could muster. The stranger stood waiting. 'We go again,' called the Knightmaker. The stranger slammed the blade on his helm and came at him. Though his body denied him, instinct did not, and he was able to protect himself against most of the significant blows. The stranger had kicked him all over the courtyard, but he was still managing to escape. Though the stranger seemed relentless in his attacks, Guy knew that there was still an element of control about it. He did not have to strike his hand with the flat of the blade earlier, and though it had hurt like fuck, he was grateful. He took blows, and his helm was rung many times. He was taking a beating there was no doubt. He could barely move, his awareness consisting solely of the strangers attacks. He didn't know anything other than those that made it through. Attack after attack, until suddenly, they stopped. The world was quiet, and Guy collapsed aback and lay on the courtyard floor. He remained there for an hour until he slowly became aware of the strangers figure standing above him, the meeting of eyes snapping him out of his exhaustion. Survive. That is what he saw in the stranger's eyes. The stranger held out a hand, Guy somehow managed to reach up to it, and let the stranger guide him up. He stood awobble as his mind swirled in a high pitched chamber and vision slowly returned, along with his balance.

The stranger gestured to the table where a plate of food waited, and returned to the house. Normally Guy would have collected the plate and returned to his camp but it was all he could do to make it to the table and sit on the bench. He was happy that it was solid because a suited Guy could break many a bench and he was too weak to control the descent. He heaved off his helmet and gasped for air as the evening colours flooded his eyes. He was still breathing heavily. He forced food into his mouth and drank his fill of water not entirely aware that he was doing it. His mind was still someway detached from his body, perhaps its way of dealing with pain and exhaustion. After he had finished the meal it was some time before he moved, unable or unwilling, he found himself in the same position he had been when he first sat down. He heard movement behind him, it was Hawkins, he walked over to the tub and lifted the sluice. Guy saw it, but it did not affect him.

'Master says you can do it without armour tomorrow, but do it quicker because there is much training to be done.'

It was some time later before Guy managed to rouse himself and return to his camp, when he did he lay beside the embers of his fire and fell asleep in his armour.

He had made it through another day.

38

The three days of training followed by a day of rest seemed to have gone by the wayside. He had been training for five days straight. For five days he had filled the tub, he was learning a new kind of defence in training and even chipped away at the outcrop of rock. Only now, along with the big iron bar, he had bought back two smaller iron bars to strike it with. With these he practiced the moves he had been taught by Smith, and those that he had learnt by watching the stranger dual wield against him. It was good to have the release. The training was contracting his muscles, hitting the rock let them snap the other way and release some of the pain they carried.

On the sixth day he went to see the old woman. His body was in the worst state it had ever been in. Guy did not know how he carried on, but that was all he could do. He would carry on. *We go again.* Too exhausted to even speak to the old woman he simply held out is hand and showed her a silver piece. She took it and nodded him inside. She cracked his body and dug her fingers into his knotted muscles before she had him lay aback on the floor. She placed her hands over his eyes, not touching, simply covering. Guy felt the heat and the energy and then he faded away to a quiet place in the skies where he had no body, and hence no pain.

As Guy returned from his third visit to the old woman he did so feeling positive. He was surviving, he was learning. He knew that as soon as he slept the pains would return, and a new five days from the hells would commence, but on the slow walk back to Eastfield manor he thought of Phylissa for the first time in recent memory. The reminder of the reason for his quest made him stronger. He could do it. He would return to Waering a knight and take her hand, and all the dreams he ever dreamed could become his reality. His mind drew him back from the rewards he was yet to earn.

As he approached the manor something was not right. The gate was open, he felt his heart pump the warrior's blood through him as his mind considered scenarios. He paused a moment, but heard no disturbance, so continued his approach, peering from an angle to see inside. Two carts and half a dozen men in white and turquoise livery stood to in the courtyard. Knights of the royal order, even he knew that. The courtyard was silent as he approached, he saw Sir Parcifal atop the stairs with a knight who carried his helm underarm, and Hawkins, seated. The knight wore a cloak of black, with white chevrons, the same as Sir Parcifal's shield. He felt the two knights look at him and he stopped his approach, uncertainty froze him momentarily. He could not see the stranger, though he knew he would be nearby, watching.

'Perhaps now we can begin,' said the de-helmed Knight with a note of frustration in his voice. Sir Parcifal nodded. 'Sir Parcifal. The king has commanded us to escort you and your squire to Rodin.'

'Has he now?' the Knightmaker replied. His voice was purposefully calm, but intimidating as fuck nonetheless. He imagined how the knights of the royal order would be feeling, how the other knight would be feeling. There was no direct threat or malice in his tone, which was perhaps why it was so intimidating.

'Aye, he has.'

If the knight felt intimidated he hid it well from his men. 'The reasons are twofold.' He turned his attention to Guy. 'You won a token recently?' Guy nodded. 'Bring it to me.' Guy's eyes flicked to Sir Parcifal. He did not move.

'I'll get it,' Guy offered and headed towards his camp. None of the knights moved. The token was in his belt, but he shifted things about his camp as he pretended to look for it, buying a moment as his mind whirled. Should he take a weapon? He had his knife and spike. He was confident that he and the Knightmaker could put up a fight, especially as he was sure that the stranger would be ready wherever he was. *Was that how this was going to go down*? His mind laughed at him. Two against seven? Not a chance, no matter how good Sir Parcifal was, they were royal knights. He controlled his breath. He would be ready for whatever happened. He fished the token from his belt and looked at it. Aside from his sword it had become his favourite item, the one thing he owned that represented progress. Guy headed towards the chevroned knight and held out the token. He felt naked, dressed as he was in his farmer's clothes, surrounded by men wearing steel, he had not thought about that when he had declared himself ready. The knight took the coin, examined it and held it out for Guy to take.

'Do you know what this is?' Guy shook his head, he turned to Sir Parcifal, who shrugged. 'This token and eleven others like it permit entry into a squire's contest at the king's tournament this year.'

'That is still a month away.' Sir Parcifal stated.

'Aye sir, it is. I said my reasons were twofold. The king has summoned you both on a separate matter.' The knight's voice had become sombre. Might I suggest you prepare for the road. We leave before sunset.'

'Bollocks,' said Sir Parcifal. 'We will leave in the morning. One of my men recovers from serious wounds, I must find someone to care for him, and my squire needs to prepare his kit. You lot can stay in the yard tonight, just keep the fucking noise down.' Without waiting for a response Sir Parcifal turned and entered the house. The knight turned to his men.

'Set up camp. We leave in the morning. Early.'

Guy spent the night ill at ease. It was as if these people were intruding in his home. There was a time in the not too distant past that he would be with the knights, learning what he could, listening to their stories like the wide eyed country boy he used to be. There was no doubt these would be fearsome knights who could decimate him in a heartbeat, but Guy found himself looking down on them. Their camp was sloppy, they had too much kit. Knights of the Royal order they may be, but their skills on the road were lacking. The inns had made them soft. The other knight though, was separate, he slept affront the gate, a simple tarp marking his territory. He slept, but it was a knight's sleep. Guy knew his eyes would pop open as soon as anyone came too close. He slept by the gate to prevent their escape. If Guy were to escape he would go via the stream. Perhaps that was why there were always two knights awake. Guy too, slept a knight's sleep, his body resting, his mind considering whether he should leave via the stream anyway and arrive with fresh bread through the gate in the morning, just to fuck with them. Anything to stop him thinking about the real reason they were being taken to the king. Perhaps he was to lose his hand after all. Maybe he should just leave via the stream and keep going, and find another way to become a knight. The night's mischief ran riot in his mind, and he could not even move about thanks to the uninvited guests. The more he tried to control it, the more intense the next scenario was. In the end Guy gave in and let the mischief run amok. Just before first light, sleep finally found him.

The cart trundled in silence. Guy sat with his kit, flanked by a knight of the Royal order. Sir Parcifal was in the other cart accompanied by another. The other knight and a turquoise knight rode in front, the others in formation around them. No one spoke. They were not being escorted. They were being transported. What Guy did not understand was why he was taking his kit. He knew striking Sir Young would have consequences, even if it had been the right thing to do. Sir Parcifal would most likely of beheaded him and fucked his skull. In a way, Guy had saved his life.

He was kept away from Sir Parcifal, the two carts making camp separately. Close enough to see each other, but he was not allowed to have any contact. Guy supposed this was a tactic to cause him stress and anxiety. They were obviously not aware that he did not have a relationship with the Knightmaker outside of training. Guy got all he needed from the glimpses of Sir Parcifal. He was inconvenienced, but content. If he felt threatened, he did not show it, so Guy tried to do the same. He knew he was in trouble though. He would have to find a way out of it. He imagined the stranger watching them, waiting for a sign. He knew there would be no sign. They were safe until they got to Rodin. It was after that where the troubles would begin. He had been summoned by King Thamas himself. Three days of silence and contemplation had not stopped that fact astounding him. If only it were for better reasons, it would be talked of in Waering for a dozen years, probably more.

As the carts slowly made their way through the city gates, Guy could not enjoy the moment, he could not marvel at the greatest city in Rodina. His mind was fucked, anxiety had him wound tight. Instead he focussed on the bundles that held his kit. His knife and spike were in there. *If he could only get them...* He was fighting an urge to jump from the cart and make a run for it, but that was not the way a knight behaved. He remembered his words to himself as he left Waering. *He would return a knight or die trying.* It did not make him feel any better.

The carts came to a halt. It was relatively quiet in what looked a secure courtyard entrance to the castle of Rodin. He fought to control his breathing as fear gripped his chest. He was resigned, not defeated. He knew he would fight for his survival when he had to, and that if he had to, he would die with dignity. On the edge of his vision he saw the black cloaked knight head into the castle, people moved to let him through and he met no challenge from anyone. The knights of the royal order remained in their positions. Unskilled as they may be on the road, they were highly skilled in procedure. Guy imagined this was a carefully orchestrated formation, designed to deal with multiple threats. These knights were probably soldiers, they certainly had discipline. A glance at the other cart showed Sir Parcifal sleeping, or at least pretending to be, his head resting on his chest. Guy wished that he was asleep.

The knight returned with two others in the black chevroned cloaks, he was helped from the cart and found himself for the first time in days next to Sir Parcifal. Guy watched in panic as the carts were led away, his armour and all his kit still upon it.

'Those are knights of the Royal Order.' Sir Parcifal muttered quietly as if sensing his discomfort. 'The cart could be loaded with diamonds, ale, or fifteen year old virgins. If you get to see the cart again, it will be exactly as you left it.'

Guy nodded his thanks, but it had not helped. *If* he got to see it again? He was more assured about his possessions, less so about ever seeing them again.

39

'The king is ready for you.' The chevroned knight called out, and Guy allowed himself to be herded towards a door and through halls until they were ushered into a room. A plain room, the only furniture was a stone table adorned with wine and fruit. A stone bench by the window seemed to be the only place to sit. The walls were stone, the floor was stone, three torches on each wall provided light, even in the day. Three chevroned knights stood behind them, two more entered followed by a man. Was that King Thamas? He did not wear a crown. He looked much like a normal man, though his beard was well groomed. He stopped by the window seat and sat, a chevroned knight stood either side of him. When the king's gaze finally reached them he noticed Sir Parcifal bow. Guy followed.

'Your Grace.' Even when talking to the king Sir Parcifal still sounded as if he was in charge.

'Sir Parcifal,' the king replied. There was a pause as the two men looked at each other, both as impassive as each other, yet someway, Guy felt, they were communicating.

'I hear you won the melee at Rowansbrook.'

'I did Your Grace.'

'How did it feel.'

'It felt good you grace.'

'You used the shield of the king's own knight?'

'It is the only shield I have Your Grace.'

'It is yours to use as you see fit,' the king announced. For a moment Guy thought he saw a flash of fondness, of respect on the king's face.

It was quickly composed, a darker mask appeared. 'You eliminate all eleven other men in quite an unorthodox manner. Some good men, tournament winners.'

'I was not bred for the tournament field Your Grace.'

'No indeed, so the question remains why you were there?'

'They would not let my squire enter the tournament if I did not compete, Your Grace.'

'Your squire?'

'It was part of his training.'

'His training? Yes, I heard you won in unconventional circumstances too.' The king briefly acknowledged Guy before returning to the Knightmaker. *The king had just spoken to him.* 'From what I hear gold is all that is required to earn a knighthood from you.'

'Then you hear wrong Your Grace.'

Guy felt his Jaw drop. He quickly controlled it, expecting a reaction from the king. Instead his response was composed, but then he was the king, he should be composed.

'I hear well enough to know truth when I hear it. You take a man's gold and beat him until he leaves.'

'If he leaves, he does not become a knight. It is part of the training.'

'You take a man's gold and beat him and call it training? I call that robbery.'

'It is his choice to leave, Your Grace. The gold pays for the training, not the knighthood. Besides, there was a time when you benefited from my selection techniques. If the training is too much for them… It is blood, and sweat and tears that earns a knighthood. It is as it should be.' The king's face darkened.

'Do not dare to tell me what should be when it comes to the knights of Rodina. I decide what should be, and right now I decide that there should be a trial. You will knight no other men until the outcome is decided. But that is not why you are before me.'

The king beckoned a man who displayed Sir Parcifal's shield, and turned his attention to Guy. His face was still dark with anger. Guy supposed that he was not used to being talked to in such a way. Guy would not speak to him like that.

'Do you know what this is?' the king asked him. There was a part of Guy's mind that would not accept that he was talking to the king of all Rodina. He kept it at bay, this was important.

'Sir Parcifal's shield, Your Grace.'

'Do you know what it represents?'

'His Arms, you grace.'

'Yes, His arms. Not his families, his. Do you know it?'

'No Your Grace, heraldry is not something I excel in.'

'There are very few men in the kingdom that can bear these arms. These are the arms of my own knights. Do you understand?'

'No, Your Grace.'

The king, though obviously angered by Sir Parcifal remained composed.

'When you fought in the squire's tournament, did you use your own arms?'

'No Your Grace, I have only recently got my own arms.'

'Which arms did you fight under?'

'Sir Parcifal's' there was a pause as the realisation sank in, 'Your Grace.'

'Sir Parcifal wounded the pride of some important men, and one in particular has demanded action. Let me ask you this. Are you one of my own knights?'

'No, Your Grace.'

'Then why did you use the arms of my knights?'

The Knightmaker tried to interject, but before the first syllable had passed his lips, the king snapped at him.

'Do not dare to speak to me again. I could take both your heads right now. How could you be so stupid as to think it would not be noticed after making such a spectacle? You have broken the knight's code. Take them to the cells.'

40

The cell was cold, dark and damp, underground, Guy suspected. Wooden benches were the only furniture, but at least the straw on the floor looked fresh. The Knightmaker and he were the only occupants. Guy did not feel the need for pretence, his mind raced as he panicked, he could not help himself. They sat in silence for a while, Sir Parcifal seemed not to be concerned, but then he had lived his life. Guy had not.

'Do not worry yourself,' said the Knightmaker, 'If he was going to kill us we would be dead already.'

'Then what are we doing here?'

'Waiting.'

Waiting?' Guy exclaimed. 'For what? I don't have time to wait.'

'If the king says we wait, then we wait.'

'I should be training, at least it feels like I am doing something.'

'Aye, you should, but at least you can let your body recover. You are worried about your woman.'

'She bid me to hurry, said that she could not wait forever.'

'None of us can wait forever.'

'What do you think will happen to us?'

'We will find out soon enough.'

It was three days later when they found out. Other prisoners had shared the cell, and left again. It seemed to be a transitional cell rather than a long term cell. It was close to the guards, though they paid them no mind. Sometimes the other prisoners would bring with them attitude, or drunkenness, but one look from Sir Parcifal had them sat abench in silence. It was just the two of them in the cell on the third morning. The others having been removed during the night. For the first two nights Sir Parcifal had denied himself sleep. On the third night it found him. Guy was woken by blood curdling screams and a Knightmaker clearly taken by fear. One of the other prisoners had tried to calm him, and had been laid out by a flailing arm. It had taken close to an hour to calm Sir Parcifal down, he had been asking for white mist.

They had not spoken about the events of the previous night, they had not spoken about anything and the guards had not bought anything for them to break their fast on. It was a bleak day. For the first time Guy had seen that Sir Parcifal had vulnerabilities, like any man. It was a lot for him to take in. There was movement as a man approached the cell. Finally something to eat, or drink at least. Guy raised his head and had to compose himself. It was King Thamas Strongford himself, who approached without a guard. Guy was flapping big time.

'Good morning,' the king offered.

'Is it?' the Knightmaker asked without lifting his head, 'Your Grace.' Guy simply nodded. It was far from a good morning, but he found himself agreeing. It was the king, and he was not going to disagree. He wished he had something to say that would put a smile on the king's face, but he was all too aware that he was young and stupid. He would only fuck it up. It was best to keep quiet.

'I hear there was an incident last night. Is there anything I can get for you?'

'Some white mist if I am to stay here another night.'

'The terrors find you in your sleep?'

'Not with white mist.'

'I'm sorry.'

Guy watched the king. Regal though he was, and well versed at hiding emotion, Guy saw him battle with something in his mind. Perhaps the king felt someway responsible for the terrors. The Knightmaker, though his weakness was exposed, appeared no different. He was not desperate, he did not plead. He simply stated what was, in his own special way, a way that would lead to most people soiling themselves. Not the king though, he looked at Sir Parcifal with genuine concern on his face. 'I will have you moved to a room on the barracks, and you can have your things, your white mist.'

Sir Parcifal looked up, his expressionless face gave nothing away, not to Guy anyway. Perhaps the king saw gratitude. 'You will remain under guard until I decide what to do with you both.' The king sighed. 'You must be craving some air. I have a small hunting party heading out this afternoon. You shall join us. Have your squire attend too.' Guy looked up as the king looked at him. He had just looked into the king's eyes, and this time there was no anger. It was probably the greatest moment of his life. He could not help but smile. 'You shall be moved to your room soon, and someone will come for you later.'

'Thank you,' said the Knightmaker, 'Your Grace.' Even in that situation, Sir Parcifal was still a bad fucker, the one in charge. The king nodded and withdrew leaving the two of them to reflect in the cell.

They were collected from their new quarters just as Guy was considering whether to go for a third bowl of stew. It was simple mass produced stew and bread, but after three days of runny oats it was as if he dined with the king himself. The barracks were quite busy and noisy, but they were far better than the cells, and Sir Parcifal seemed in better spirits, despite the guards that accompanied them, the prospect of sleep perhaps. Guy too relished the idea of a decent sleep. Cells and sleep, it would appear, were not bedfellows. In the barracks they had a cot each, and Guy's was almost big enough to fit him.

They both followed the chevroned knight that had come to collect them, and the turquoise, of the royal order, were dismissed. Guy had not known what to take or wear. What was he supposed to wear when hunting with the king? For a brief moment he had imagined himself back at Waering. Such fuss would be made over what he wore. In Rodin he selected the only functional clothes he had, his farmer's clothes. He considered wearing half armour over the top, or his doublet, but they were hunting, not sparring. The Knightmaker wore half armour, but Guy was sure that was just to make sure that he looked like the baddest fucker there. Wearing half armour as he was, Guy imagined he would be the baddest fucker anywhere he decided to be. He had his cloak and his leather chestplate and greaves in his day bag, a quiver of arrows over his shoulder, his bow and two pronged spear in his hands, and his belt of course. It was fully equipped minus his sword and pair of maces.

Weapons like that had no place on a hunt, at least no hunt he had ever been on. The Knightmaker had his sword.

Guy tried to remind himself that he would be there in the role of a squire, which was why he carried extra water and a skin of wine, and that his involvement would not be significant. It mattered not, he was going hunting with the king. *If Phylissa knew of this…*

They were led through the main courtyard and under grand arches towards the rear of the castle where they were met by a man with two horses. He took one look at Guy, then to his horses and shrugged. The horse would be too small for Guy, he felt for the poor beast having to carry his weight. At least he wasn't armoured. He was offered the bigger horse and secured his bow and spear and checked the saddle. He waited until the Knightmaker was seated until he climbed on his horse, it skittered a little as it got used to the weight. It was going to be a long day for that particular horse. Seconds later the king arrived flanked by a chevroned knight in lighter more ornate armour. Hunting armour, perhaps. The king had arrived half armoured, the same as the Knightmaker. Guy suddenly felt under dressed. *What kind of hunt was this going to be?* As the king entered a gate was opened. Without breaking pace, King Thamas called out, 'Ride with me Sir Parcifal.'

The Knightmaker rib-heeled his horse and within a dozen paces had caught and matched the king's pace and they passed through the gate together. The Chevroned knight set off a small distance behind, Guy encouraged his horse to go with him. They entered a walled road. White walls stretched straight ahead as far as Guy could see. The king and the Knightmaker rode onwards, he could see them as they talked but he could not hear a word. The chevroned knight rode in silence, probably alert to threat, so did Guy. Instead of looking for threat, Guy watched the conversation in front of him. He saw a range of emotions, from the king mainly, seriousness, concern, sometimes animated anger. But then he went quiet, and listened, as one does when Sir Parcifal talks. He seemed to be asking questions, and gradually the both of them started to relax, he even saw them share laughter. They certainly had a history. Guy wanted so much to hear the words, but he was more than happy just to be there.

They had been riding the straight white road in silence for well over an hour, but Guy was not bored, he just wished he could hear the words being exchanged ahead of him, in his mind they talked of past glories. A gate began to open before them and the chevroned knight picked up speed to be the first through. Guy spared his horse further pain, and maintained the pace behind. As Guy passed through the gate he realised that men had been there to open it. They had not seen another person on the road, Guy was amazed that there were people there to open it. The power of being a king, he supposed. He rode out into the woods, the chevroned knight stayed out in front, about as far ahead as Guy was behind, and the conversation went on beyond his ears.

They came to a clearing that housed a log cabin unlike any he had seen, it was grander than most of the houses back in Waering, and he waited until the chevroned knight had nodded before entering. By the time Guy approached them they were already dismounting and tying their horses off. Guy did the same. He tried his best to act casual, but he knew his eyes were darting everywhere, trying to take it all in, and he could feel the smile on his face, no matter how much he fought it. It was a sturdy beast of a lodge house, there was a large covered seating area outside with ornate lamps and big bright cushions. The area was clear of clutter and vegetation, clean and tidy. Perhaps what one would expect from a royal hunting lodge. Two men in forest green tunics came to greet them, servants perhaps, they wore no armour or arms, two others went to the horses and led them away. The king and Sir Parcifal entered, Guy and the chevroned knight followed. They went into a large hall, a fire roared in the middle, cushions and beams were tastefully scattered around it. More traditional seating and tables were clustered in areas dotted around the outskirts of the room. Maps and trophies adorned the walls, except one, which was laden with weaponry. Some of it was decorative, historical pieces perhaps, but much of it was in racks for use. A rack of unstrung bows contained close to four dozen bows, and quivers of all kinds of arrows. He felt familiar feelings of unworthiness as he considered his quiver of home-made arrows, tipped with bits of folded scrap metal. He felt a fool, but only for a moment. At least he had a bow.

He joined them around the fire as the king and Sir Parcifal enjoyed a cup of wine, the servants disappeared into the shadows without drawing attention. The king was telling Sir Parcifal of the hunt.

'I must return to the castle for a dinner tomorrow, so we have until then. I have heard stories of a giant cow that has gone berserk. Some stories claim it to be more than twice the size of the biggest cow you can imagine. It has trampled corn, killed livestock and people. Entire villages have been deserted to escape it.'

The king looked into the fire for a moment. He looked pensive, as if considering the fate of his subjects. 'It was last seen heading towards the Kingswood. It must be stopped before it gets to Rodin. I have men out looking for it, but thought that such a beast is a rare sight that I would behold myself. The chances are we will not stumble upon it, but mayahps we can find a summer stag for the wall.' Sir Parcifal nodded. 'We leave soon. Take what supplies you need.' Guy was sure the king glanced to include him, a nod from Sir Parcifal, and Guy headed straight to the arrows leaving his feeble quiver with his day bag.

There were more kinds of arrows than he had ever seen, and more than he had imagined. From broad leaf arrowheads, to armour piercing bodkins, diamond heads, to vicious looking barbed heads that he imagined would do real damage. There were several quivers of dozens of each with a larger mixed basket beside. Guy pulled an empty quiver and set to selecting his arrows. He took a few of each except the bodkin, he doubted there would be armoured stags out there. He was tempted to tell the king of his story of the boar, but swiftly remembered he was simply a squire, who not that long ago had been in the cells, the reasons still unresolved. He felt assured though, that the Knightmaker had been right, if the king were going to kill them they would be dead already, and certainly if harm were to come their way he would not be allowed to arm himself.

Despite the plethora of weaponry available Guy was happy with his bow and spear. He had his belt with his knife and spike if it came to it. He could have selected a far superior spear, but Guy liked his two pronged one, it had set him apart in Waering, and there were none like it on the walls. As he turned to head back to the fire he saw the king looking at his bow.

'I would select another if I were you. You should find something to suit you. Big as you are, bigger have hunted here.' Guy sheepishly returned to the rack. There were plentiful bows of many sizes, some of the smaller ones were more ornate and curved. The longbows though… Guy had not seen the like before. He had been impressed by the bows at the tournament, but these just sang of quality, oiled and polished, expertly carved, fit for a king. Guy chuckled inside his mind, he had a meaning for the phrase now. He felt the weight of a few and pulled one from the rack. Before he had finished inspecting it a servant appeared. Guy gave him the bow, and within moments the servant had bent it, attaching to loose end of the string. Guy was impressed. He had always struggled to string unfamiliar bows. He had broken a few in his time, a mixture of his strength and lack of technique. The bow was handed back. Guy twanged the string before pulling the bow. It came smoothly, and just felt powerful. That was the bow he would take.

He checked his belt kit, refilled the water skins and took an extra skin of wine. He had his cloak in his bag, and a tarp. He had all he needed, and did not torture himself by rummaging through the chests of equipment that lay about the room. He found himself instead looking at a map. The lodge was marked. He did not really know a lot about maps, but looked for features like rivers, peaks or clearings. His mind was telling him that he needed to know more about maps, but for now he just had to hope that he would not get separated from the others. If he did, he would just head south until he found Rodin.

They followed a path through thick woodland, the canopy protected them from the worst of the afternoon sun. They walked at pace, in formation. The chevroned knight led the party, the king and Sir Parcifal beside each other and Guy at the rear. They each had a job to do, responsibilities and it was this that occupied Guy's mind. He was pleased that he was aware of something other than the fact that he was hunting with the king. He could reflect on that later, he had a job to do. The area was rolling hills, swathes of woodland and meadow. They did not see another person, even in open land, but Guy was alert all the same, his chest always slightly tight, coiled. *This must be what it felt like to be a knight.*

41

After a couple of hours they ventured east into some thick woodland. Their formation changed, the king in the centre of the two knights, each two dozen feet apart, Guy three dozen feet behind. They made their way carefully through the trees, moving slowly and silently as if already stalking prey. Guy had an arrow notched, ready to draw. If anything happened in front of him, he would react. Silence followed them through the woodland, for as quiet as they moved, their presence was known. Occasionally a doe leapt out from cover and bounded away, or a boar charged to freedom when they roamed too close, but they saw nothing of note, no stag, and certainly no giant cow. Guy did not mind, just being there felt unreal. Things like that did not happen to a country boy like him.

They had made camp on the edge of a clearing and feasted on a boar speared at dusk. Guy had taken first watch as the others slept, and it was not until then that Guy realised their poor choice of location. The logical point to keep watch was with his back to the fire looking out over the clearing. With the camp so close to the woodland he could not keep watch there. The fire may cause wildlife to divert course around it, but it would draw other men straight to it and give them the chance to attack with Guy's back to them. He had his ears open wide and his eyes stung from searching the darkness. Deep down he knew that nothing would bother them, but he was with the king, and any king had enemies searching for opportunities. Guy would do whatever he could to ensure there were no opportunities that night. The night's mischief and the nocturnal wildlife of the woodland kept him alert and he was relieved that his watch had passed without incident as the chevroned knight took over. Guy lay flat aback by the fire, and sleep found him swiftly, though his eyes and ears still throbbed from the effort of keeping watch.

Deep in his subconscious he felt the change from night to day, he heard the first birds celebrate the dawn, but he did not hear any other movement so he allowed himself to continue with his sleep. He had not had much of it and would grasp all he could. It was a restless sleep though, his mind was awake, though his body still slept. His mind began the day at frantic pace, the thoughts of the day before not fully resolved. Scenarios ran through his mind, some where he even got through the uncertainty unscathed. The king and Sir Parcifal had been talking and acting like old friends, yet there was still to be a trial. He did not like the lack of certainty, he had to get back to Phylissa.

A noise pulled him from his semi-conscious dreamings, he flicked his eyes open. He could hear the chevroned knight moving. He heard the noise that had roused him again, it was a snort like a spooked horse, but bigger, and further away. He lifted his head a little, the clearing was filled with a morning mist, the dawns light barely penetrated it. The knight was circling the clearing away from them, attempting to distance the king from the danger perhaps. He had not called out in alarm, and Guy did the same. He did not want to undo the knight's work by drawing attention to them. He scanned the clearing searching the mist for whatever had the knight's attention. The next time the snort came Guy fixed on the location, first seeing two red eyes glowing through the mist. Slowly the form of the beast started to reveal itself. The dun colour of grey and brown blended in with the dawn mist almost perfectly. After the eyes it was the horns that grasped his attention big and curved but with forward facing angry tips. The beast was so unnaturally big, its size could be seen from as far away as it was, but not fathomed.

The chevroned knight loosed an arrow which caused the beast to let out a roar as it commenced its snorting approach. It did not seem in any hurry, and Guy was sure that he could see clouds bursting from the nostrils as it snorted with every step. With every step it got bigger. The knight loosed more arrows which seemed to have no effect on the beast and did not deter its approach. The knight flung down his bow and drew his sword. The beast was picking up speed and starting a thunderous charge towards the knight who had made over one hundred feet of distance from the king.

Guy sprang up, grabbed his bow and quiver. 'Protect the king.' He called out and ran towards the beast. The knight had remained still as the beast approached, as knights tended to do. The cow's size was becoming more evident, Guy imagined its shoulder to be above his height. It really was huge. The Cow dropped its head to lead with its horns. *Move!* Guy's inner being screamed at the knight. At the very last second the knight spun and bought down his sword to the beasts neck, but he had either left it too late or underestimated the size of the beast for the horns caught him and he was flung to the side. The beast veered left and away from Guy as it slowed and rounded on the knight, snorting. The knight was moving, trying to crawl out of the beast's path. Guy drew an arrow, a leaf head and notched it, focussing only on the beast's head as it approached the knight. He pulled on the bow, sweetly and smoothly, he breathed and released watching the arrow sail through the air. It was right on target, but as Guy began to congratulate himself the arrow bounced harmlessly off the centre of the beasts head, unable to penetrate its hide. It had captured the beast's attention though, and Guy sprinted out into the clearing taking the beasts attention with him, taking it away from the wounded knight, but more importantly away from the king. If Sir Parcifal had any sense, he would have dragged the king deep into the trees by now. Running, Guy drew another arrow, this time one of the vicious barbed variety. He stopped, caught his breathing and took aim at the turning beasts shoulder. He drew in time with his breathing and loosed, quickly notching another. The beast's screams filled the clearing, though they were not screams of pain, more the animalistic roars of dominance. The arrows were having no effect, but he fired one more anyway, hoping for a lucky strike to the eye. He wished he had taken some of the bodkin arrows, they might have had more chance of piercing the hide. He threw his bow aside as the beast picked up pace towards him. He hoped to fare better than the chevroned knight, especially since he wore no armour. He met the frenzied red eyes of the cow as it started its charge towards him.

They froze him to the spot and panicked thoughts ran through his mind. He could try to take out one of its legs, but the damage the hooves were doing to the grassed land as it charged, told him that his skull could be crushed if he went down there. He started bouncing gently from one foot to the other, mainly so that he was rooted to the ground no more, but also to make him ready. As the cow charged him he tried to grasp a horn, but found himself flung aside as if he were a straw doll. He landed and rolled. Instead of the cow turning to the open field to slow, it turned towards the woods and the king.

It took Guy a moment to realise that he was not hurt. He looked towards the fire hoping that the king and Sir Parcifal would be long gone. Of course they were not, Sir Parcifal with this sword drawn was keeping the king behind him. The king was ready too though, or as ready as you can be to face such a beast. The Cow roared again, its blood curdling high pitched terror filled the clearing. It seemed to bounce back off the trees and hit him twice. Another roar followed it, a deeper, louder, no less terrifying scream, Sir Parcifal's war cry. The beast hesitated for a moment, perhaps not expecting to be challenged. The beast roared again and started a charge.

Guy sprinted towards the beast as it moved towards Sir Parcifal. It was about fifty feet from them when Sir Parcifal offered his reply. Again the cow hesitated, just for a moment, and that was when Guy made impact charging shoulder first into the cow's ribs with a scream of his own. He did not know what he was expecting to happen, but the cow did not go down. The surprise attack did cause it to stagger, Guy recovered quicker than the beast, locked an arm through one of its horns and tried to exert some control. The cow reared and shook its mighty head, trying to loosen his grasp, but Guy held on for dear life, aiming kicks at the beast's ribs whenever he could.

The monstrous cow soon tired of trying to toss Guy, instead, it attempted to crush him by driving its head into the ground. Guy maintained good position and with one arm locked through the horn aimed punches at the cows frenzied eye. He wrestled with the beast, not once loosening his grip, striking and kicking whenever he could, but although the cow was frenzied in its actions, he knew it was taking far more out of him than it was the cow. He would tire sooner. It felt like he had been grappling with the beast for an eternity, but would not be surprised to find if it was less than two minutes. He dug his heels into the ground to get some purchase as he pulled the cows head towards him, one hand swiftly removed the spike from his belt. He held on again as the cow tried to buck him off, waiting for an opportunity. As he levered the cows head towards him he slammed the spike behind the ear of the beast with all his might. The spike drove deep into the cow and it shrill roar sent birds from the trees. Guy pulled the spike and drove it behind the other ear as the beasts legs began to falter. As it screamed and snorted. Guy tried to position himself to strike again, but the beast was so unsteady he had to get his own balance as his feet returned to the ground. If it fell on him it would be sure to crush him. Guy wrestled with the horned beast trying to pull it down with some control, but even then it fought him. He worked himself into position with the cows legs buckled, so that he was behind the beasts head. He raised his spike one more time and drove it deep into the base of the beast's skull. It dropped like liquid and Guy rolled to safety ending flat aback panting for his breath.

He reminded himself that he was with the king, and Sir Parcifal's mantra ran through his head. *We go again.* He forced himself to his knees, and then to his feet. His warrior's blood was fading fast and already the pain surfaced. His arms, his shoulders, his chest were all wracked with agony. He pushed it to one side and staggered towards the chevroned knight as Sir Parcifal and the king approached the beast to ensure it was dead. They joined him at the knight, arriving almost at the same time. The knight was moving, gasping painful breaths. His chest plate showed the devastating effects of the beast's horns. Guy thought he was lucky indeed, had the point of the horns struck him they would have gouged a hole in him, chest plate or no. There was no blood other than from the impact of landing. Guy met his panicked eyes, as Sir Parcifal moved behind him and released the chest plate. As he did the knight gasped a hungry lungful of air. The dink in the chest plate was more significant than first appeared, it had been pushed into his chest preventing him from breathing. The armour had not split though, saving the knight from the kind of injuries Hawkins had suffered.

The knight gulped air as if he had been drowning, and once Sir Parcifal had assessed him, seemed confident that he was not in danger, both he and the king slapped Guy on the back in congratulation, but he was in too much pain to enjoy the moment.

The trip back to the lodge was long and painful, though he had little feeling in his arms, he had supported the knight every step of the way. Though his injuries would not threaten his life, they were significant, Guy imagined several ribs would be shattered, and by the way the knights arm was flopping, probably a clavicle too. As they reached the lodge the king despatched a rider to the castle to summon the butcher and half a dozen carts. He wanted the beast butchered on site to ensure the good meat was protected. He despatched half a dozen men with a cart to retrieve the beasts head.

Once they were inside and the knight had been made comfortable Guy collapsed on the cushioned floor, finally embracing the pain. The beasts curved horns and his reluctance to loosen his grip had battered his entire upper body. His arms felt as if they wanted to burst, such was the pressure of the pain.

Sir Parcifal and a servant saw to the knight, the servant strapped his arm to his chest. The knight, whilst visibly in pain, was talking to the king and the servant. Sir Parcifal had other things on his mind.

'I'm so hungry I could eat half that fucking cow right now,' he called out. He asked the servant 'Are there any oats here?' The servant nodded. 'Good.' He turned to the king, 'Guy makes the best fucking oats I have ever tasted.'

The king looked up. 'Guy, make us some oats to break our fast on.'

Without hesitation guy rolled to his side, painful though it was, and by the time the servant had returned with a sack of oats, Guy was up and selecting a pan. He had a handful of dried fruits in a pouch on his belt, enough for about a dozen. It would have to do. He set about preparing the best oats he had ever made, for despite everything that had happened, all he could think about, was that he was making oats for the king.

Guy was still feeling the pride as the led the small convoy of narrow carts down the white road towards the castle. The king rode with the chevroned knight in one cart, the other held the beasts head and heart, Sir Parcifal bought up the rear. He felt for his poor horse, but was grateful. He had felt uneasy travelling through the woods fearing his body would betray him had there been an attack. Now they were on the white road he felt safer. There would be no attack there.

The gates at the end of the white road were opened well in advance of their arrival and as they passed through and the king was seen to be safe cheers went up for his mighty deed as those who had come to greet them exclaimed over the giant beasts head in the cart. Guy was just relieved to have arrived safely. The king was obviously used to people acting the way that they were around him and gave them enough of a response to satisfy them. It was clear that concerned members of his council were present, and after whispered words the chevroned knight was escorted away while the attention was on the king and the beast. As Guy watched, suddenly exhausted, he too was taken into the castle and to the king's own physician. It was the infirmary where he remained for the next five days. The first two had seen him bled with leeches to remove the *'bad blood'* in his bruises. After complaining to the king that the leeches sucked his very life, the bleeding ceased and instead he was fed and forced to rest. He knew deep down that this was what he needed. His body had suffered during his battle with the Dun Cow, and it was not until the fourth day when he almost had full movement in his arms. The physician pestered to bleed him some more, but Guy refused, all he wanted was to get some of Della's fire berry balm on him. The leeches had left incisions in his skin that had continued to bleed once they had fallen off, and he knew he could not apply it until they had healed. He thought that once he had knocked off the scabs they would heal enough within a day or two to apply the balm.

He had been fed and watered well, the food had been among the best he had ever eaten, but Guy wondered whether this was simply because he was eating in the castle of Rodin, where the best of everything was all that was known. His mind did not rest, but instead of imagining various gruesome fates, he had re-found the urgency of his quest. He had to get back to Phylissa, he had to become a knight, he had to find Sir Parcifal and get training.

42

The king had visited him daily, sometimes just for a progress report, other times he stayed a while. It was strange for Guy to spend time with the king. Having grown up in Waering he knew about social pleasantries and was sure there would be certain etiquette when addressing the king, but in that bed he knew nothing other than to be himself. He would carry the scorn of Waering if they knew. The king spoke briefly to his physician before approaching and sitting on the cot beside Guys legs.

'Mater Guy, are we well today?'

'I am, Your Grace.' The king smiled, he had replied the same every day. 'I must get back to my training if I am to be a knight.'

'I see.' The king seemed amused, 'And what is the hurry, that you cannot allow your body to recover?' Guy stammered and felt awkward. His answer usually drew a response of mirth. He did not want the king to laugh. But the king was waiting for an answer.

'My love, Your Grace. She told me I must return in the white of a knight to ask for her hand.'

'Ah yes, fair Phylissa of Waering. She is worthy of marrying a knight?'

'She is worthy of whatever she desires.' The king smiled. He had not laughed, not a hint of it.

'If a man knighted by the king himself were to ask for her hand, would that be something she desires?' Guy's breath caught in his chest and he met the king's eye. Nothing. Was he saying what Guys optimistic mind teased him with?

'I am sure she would, Your Grace.' The king simply nodded.

'Is she worth what you have gone through? I know Sir Parcifal well enough to know it would not be easy.'

'I will return to her a knight, or die trying.' Their eyes remained locked and Guy let him see. He was the king after all, and Guy was doing some seeing of his own. How many men could say they held the gaze of the most important man in the kingdom? It was the king who looked away with a nod, perhaps he had seen enough.

'Tell me of how you have been trained. There is to be a trial, I would have your words to consider.'

'Why don't you let me out of here and see for yourself.' Guy answered. Before quickly adding 'Your Grace.'

'Do you dare spurn my hospitality Master Guy? You have been treated by my own physician, the best in all Rodina, You have eaten the same food that I have eaten, and this is how you thank me?' Panic rose in Guy's mind.

'No, Your Grace. I am grateful, truly. But I must return to my love.' The king, smiled.

'I am toying with you.' Guy could not hide his sigh of relief. 'I have spoken at length to Sir Parcifal about you, I know of your desire to be knighted. You have a problem though. Sir Parcifal cannot knight another man until there has been a trial. A good deed cannot undo the king's word. He should be grateful that sentence had not been passed. A further problem, your Phylissa told you to return in the white of a knight. You must win a tournament. This is not going to happen soon, so why the hurry?'

'I need to train, Your Grace. When I am training I am moving towards it. Sat here I am not.'

'If you were not sat here, you would be moving nowhere. Wounds like that do not heal unless the blood is let. You would be out of action for weeks.' Guy fought the urge to argue. It was the king, and you did not argue with him.

'Aye, Your Grace, and I thank you. But I am feeling well enough to train. I can move my arms now.' He said flexing and rolling his shoulders, unable to fully hide the grimace.

'You can move them indeed,' the king replied. 'You won a token. Do you have it?'

'Yes Your Grace.' Guy was already reaching for his belt which he had kept near him. The physician had not allowed him to wear it in the infirmary. He winced as pain shot through him. He pulled the token out of the slot inside his belt and handed it to the king.

'Do you know what this is?'

'My prize for winning the tournament at Rowansbrook'

'Aye, that it is, but there are eleven more of these throughout Rodina, each one granting a squire access to a tournament, my tournament. The winner of the tournament gets a set of golden spurs. Sir Parcifal did not tell you this?' Guy shook his head. His mind had so many things running through it he did not even try to stop them. 'I was going to take this token from you, for using the arms of the king's own knights.' The king looked from Guy to the token. 'But I think you have earned the right to keep it.' He handed it back with a nod.

'Thank you.' There was more relief in his words than he intended to show, but it was relief that he felt.

'The tournament is a little over three weeks away. Stay here tomorrow and rest, and I shall take you up on your offer to see Sir Parcifal's training methods for myself.'

'Yes, Your Grace, thank you, Your Grace.'

The king smiled and stood, leaving Guy with a familiar sensation. He was switched back on. He was training again. He breathed, he found that ball of energy in his belly and used it to make himself stronger.

Guy stood in the room in the barracks composing himself for a moment. The room was his alone, the Knightmaker had been moved to more comfortable accommodation. He had exercised that morning and was about to meet Sir Parcifal to continue his training. He had no idea what fresh hells the Knightmaker would have in store for him, but it did not matter. He was to be training again, that mattered. Whatever the Knightmaker threw at him, he would do to the best of his ability. Effort made him stronger. He wore his heavy training armour, but carried his helm in leather strapped hands. He took a breath and opened the door. He headed towards the main training arena, a large dirt floored area larger than the courtyard at Waering, where he had been to watch other knights in action the day before. As he approached he spotted Sir Parcifal in an area off to the side of the arena. A hooded figure stood beside him, and behind them both he could see a wooden frame over a dozen feet high. One thing ran through his mind, pain. The wooden frame meant pain. He walked towards it with purpose. Pain only made him stronger.

It was almost two hours later when he accepted that he still had much to learn of pain. All he had to do was lift the rock above his head, which was indicated by black string tied between the posts. It had taken him over ten minutes to even lift it off the ground, the rope too thick to be easily manipulated. He had tried as many methods as he could think of, but was still to lift it over his head. Sir Parcifal sat achair in front watching, ready to call when he made it. The hooded figure of the stranger stood beside him. He wore armour underneath, and a helm, but he would recognise the stranger anywhere. It had initially made him feel good to see the stranger, like things were getting back to normal, but he was far from feeling good. The muscles through his entire body screamed with pain every time he pulled on the rope. The rock was so heavy it had pulled him to the floor as he dropped it more times than he cared to count. He was grateful that he wore his armour. All that existed in Guys mind was the rock and the rope, and that cursed length of black string. He was unaware of the people who stopped to look as they passed, and those that came especially. He was tiring, he knew, the time that he was able to keep the rock off the floor was shortening. His body was giving up quicker. The point was approaching where he would have to accept that he would not be able to do it. He had been bent over panting for breath, but he straightened opening in his chest to take in more air. His big gulps feeding his hungry body as he planned his next attempt. He figured that he had three decent attempts left, if he was lucky.

There was no one way which allowed him to life the stone, but if he could combine two of the most effective... He heaved the rock off the ground, pulling the rope into his chest, his heels wedged in divots of his own making. He then wrapped the rope around his arm and pulled until he had the weight. He began shuffling his feet backwards, digging in his heels as best he could. It was hard enough to get movement started, but once it was he knew momentum was the key. Taking a dozen steps to a single regular step he breathed sharp breaths. His body screamed. It was not natural for a man to move such a weight. He had in his head, 1,2,3,4, and then again.

The numbers, the steps were all that mattered. As he approached what he knew to be his limit with this technique his mind switched to the transition. This was where he had failed last time, losing balance as he turned, the rope had put him on his arse yet again. Digging in his heel, he grasped the rope high with his free hand and levered his body into it. With a roar, he turned pulling the rope with him this time until he was facing away from the rock and drove his body forward. Each step only taking him inches further. He dug as deep as he could, his focus purely on the four tiny steps that he took. He still had the weight as his body screamed *enough*, but he drove on. 1,2,3,4. another four, and another he tasted blood that leaked from his nose as he gasped for air. He had the momentum, nothing would stop him this time.

'Clear.' The Knightmaker called out. Relief swept through Guys body, but that momentary loss in tension saw the rock fall, and with the rope wrapped around him Guy was spun through the air landing heavily with the clatter of his armour. An unnoticed cheer from onlookers was unheard as Guy assessed his body for injuries and tried to gather his bearings. He looked towards the Knightmaker, too exhausted to show his relief at lifting the rock. 'Defence training, one hour.' *Holy fuck, not now!* Through pained eyes he saw the stranger shrug off his cloak, draw his sword and step forwards, rapping it on his helm. Guy had been dreaming of this moment for days, but now that the stranger approached there was nothing he wanted less.

He tried to roll away as the strangers boot connected with him, and after a short lifetime of instinct driven avoidance, the Knightmaker called a halt and allowed Guy to pull on his helm and retrieve his sword. He turned to face the stranger again, who rapped his helm less strongly this time, and approached with castle taught moves. Guy's body was heavy and slow and he had his helm rung several times before he was able to offer much resistance. The stranger slowed his pace and stuck to the routines which allowed Guy to feel like he was making a decent job of it by the end of the session. Every time the stranger rang his helm the Knightmaker offered words of improvement and called 'We go again.'

By their last dance, the stranger had found the speed that Guy's body was able to work at, and they shared a long exchange. It helped that Guy could anticipate the moves, for it was a dance they had done many times before. Blows still struck him, but his helm was not rung until his body finally gave out, his arms too heavy to stop the downward blow that knocked him flat aback. The Knightmaker called a halt, and the stranger pulled him to his feet before he and the Knightmaker left the training yard. Guy watched them leave before falling to his knees unable to bring himself to walk back to the barracks. At least back at Eastfield Manor he did not have far to crawl back to his camp.

43

It was close to an hour that Guy remained in the square looking at the ridiculously sized rock with the rope around it and recovering. He had let his breathing recover naturally to let the air clear his body of the pain and heaviness. It still took him all his effort to stand, and make his way back to the barracks with as much purpose as he could muster.

It was late afternoon when Guy was roused by a rap at the door. He called enter, and one of the castle's servants opened the door. The light was bright and Guy could only see a silhouette of the boy, but he could see that it was late afternoon. It had been just past noonshine when he had made his way back, his armour was scattered throughout the room and he lay in his smallclothes. He must have gone out like a snuffed candle. It seemed only a matter of minutes ago. Guy squinted at the boy.

'Sir Parcifal commands that you dine with him tonight. I am to collect you in one hour.' Guy nodded, the door closed and Guy collapsed back on the cot to start his day again.

He roused himself a moment later lest sleep take him once more, he stretched, his dull body, cracking, releasing the energy within him. He did a brief stretching routine, and tried to bring some life back to his body, it felt heavy. He stretched, rolled his shoulders, and bent his knees, difficult though it was, he enjoyed it. It made him stronger. Once he had applied some of Della's fire berry balm his body was burning a rolling fire, and it felt good.

By the time the servant boy came to collect him, Guy was ready. He wore the farmer's clothes and his cleanest shirt. It was pretty much all he had. It would have to do. He had washed himself with a bucket of water before applying the balm, so at least he would not smell too foul. He followed the servant through the barracks to a block just beyond where the Knightmaker had been given residence. There were more servants inside preparing the meal.

'So how are you feeling?' asked the Knightmaker without looking up.

'I'm feeling good,' Guy replied. He did not even sound like he was trying to convince himself. The Knightmaker laughed, looked up at him and bid him sit.

'You told the king that he should see how you train.'

'I did, it was hard to explain in words.'

'Now people are watching you, and worse, watching me. I do not conduct myself in the public arena because I do not want people to know what I am capable of. The problem we now have is that during training you are supposed to find out what you are capable of, to push yourself. You do not want your opponent, your enemy to see that. So now we must train in private. There is much you must learn about being a knight. It is not all swords and lances.'

The Knightmaker talked as they ate, for longer than Guy could remember, and while his body was tired, his mind was awake and taking in everything Sir Parcifal talked of. From their training schedule and who he could talk to, through to how to conduct himself, and much more between. Guy could tell that the Knightmaker was not particularly happy having the king's eyes upon him, but he probably knew deep down that they would be on him anyway.

'Not all combat happens on the battlefield. A knight should know how to fight in any setting. Offence training. One hour.' Guy looked at the Knightmaker as the stranger stood and offered him a light wooden stick. 'Start slow, you should know the moves by now, you have seen them enough times, and try not to break anything.'

The stranger stood ready in north east. Guy stood, moved to the little space that there was available and tentatively waved the stick at the stranger. A few more times as he acclimatised, each time the stranger parried, ready for the next attack. When he finally did the first combination, the Knightmaker called halt immediately. 'Sort your feet out. Just because we are not in an arena does not mean we lose our feet. Without strong feet you will soon be on your arse.'

It was difficult for Guy, after every sequence the Knightmaker offered ways to improve, either technical or personal, and it was not until just before the end of the session that they finally completed the first dance. Just as he was getting comfortable the Knightmaker called halt and sent Guy on his way with instructions for the following day. The servant boy led him back to his room in the barracks in silence as Guy found himself a little frustrated. Everything was almost there, even his training, but he never felt like he actually got to make any progress. The tournament was in three weeks and he could not allow himself to dream. Winning the tournament back in Rowansbrook was one thing, but the best tournament squires in Rodina would be there, and he was not ready.

After a restless sleep his frustrations still niggled him as he made his preparations. He had four cabbage sized sacks full of sand on lengths of rope which he had tied and had round his neck over a strap of leather. He had four quivers of tournament arrows but took only one, and his bow. The Knightmaker had said the king wanted him to have the bow from their hunt, and hoped that while it had not served him well that day, that it would in the future. Guy was excited to try it, from memory it had pulled smoothly, even if the arrows had all but bounced off the beast. He set off at a slow run. When he was running a distance it always took him a while to find his rhythm. The Knightmaker had forbidden him from training archery in the training arena, so he went off to find somewhere else outside of the city to practice. He would head to the woods, not in the Kingswood, but close by it. There would be few who ventured there. But first he had to get out of the city.

The sun had not risen over the horizon when he made his way through the city's streets. He realised before he arrived that the place he had selected was too far away. He would not be able to run that far every day. He was concerned about the run back as it was. But he was nothing if not stubborn. He continued until he found a hidden spot and hung the four sacks from a tree that flourished within a clearing. Being more than conscious of time he started his arrows before his breathing had recovered and before he was ready and lost two arrows on his first dozen which would only make him take longer. As he felt the frustration start to rise he took some time to compose himself. Frustration rarely led to good arrows. He was training, he should do it right. He did some stretching and calmed his breathing. Fuck it, if it meant he had to run fast to get back, he would pay that price later.

His arrows got better with each dozen, as he got familiar with the bow, until the sixth and final dozen when his arm started to tire. By the time he set off back to Rodin he had only seven arrows left. He kept a steady pace, and found a quicker route on return, but he still would have to find another place the following day, one that would not see him lose so many arrows.

He had enough time to stretch out his run, drink plenty of fruit water and pull on his doublet and leather before the servant boy came to escort him to training. He was led to the main training arena and to halfway down the left hand side where he saw a familiar sight, one that bought him remembered pain. There was a well, and a bucket attached to a rope. For a moment he questioned whether it was the one from Eastfield, but he knew it was. There was a low wooden frame above the well and a log that had been spiked into the floor.

'Training is thirsty work.' The Knightmaker's voice boomed bringing the attention of those nearby. 'My squire here will pull a dozen buckets of fresh water for drinking.' In a quieter voice to Guy he added 'If you lose the bucket you are going in there to get it.' Guy nodded before looking at his hands, hoping that the leather straps would protect him, and set about arranging the rope. He picked up the bucket, a good solid weight on its own. His body remembered how heavy it had been when full. He tried to familiarise himself with, and soften the rope, as he lowered the bucket until it hit the water and was momentarily light. Holding the rope there he carefully manoeuvred himself to the log. That must have been there for a reason. He was happy that the well was not particularly deep and carefully lowered the rope allowing the bucket to sink into the water and it filled almost immediately. As prepared as Guy was, he almost lost the rope with the sudden gain in weight before he started to heave the bucket up. The log was a useful brace and after the weight of the rock, he pulled it up with relative ease. He knew it was the first of a dozen though, and that the last one would feel just as heavy as the rock had the day before.

By the time the last lift came Guy was sat afloor with his feet braced on the wooden log, pulling with his whole body, his legs first, then as he leaned back, his arms, before grabbing up the rope with speed and starting again. Eight good pulls would get the bucket up. As sweat poured off him and his groans of effort became more pronounced he finally pulled the bucket clear of the well for the last time, and the stranger set it down. Guy was offered to drink from it which he did greedily. That had taken some effort in the mid-day sun. On his third ladle he heard the dreaded words.

'Defence training. One hour.' He dropped the ladle in the bucket and turned to see the stranger approaching, wooden stick in hand. His stick was over by the spiked log. His eyes flicked to it, then back to the stranger. He was approaching, but not with his usual speed. He could make it. He drove his body into action taking the half dozen steps in a heartbeat. He had time to grab the stick and turn, continuing to back into space before the stranger met him. He met the blow, and several more. It was not until over halfway through the sequence that the stranger landed a blow. 'We go again.' called the Knightmaker. These were the only words Sir Parcifal would say for the remainder of the hour. *We go again.*

When the Knightmaker called halt, the stranger pulled him to his feet, and then retired with Sir Parcifal as they had the previous day. This time Guy did not fall to his knees, he stood, exhausted catching his breath. It took him a few moments to notice that the servant boy was standing discretely nearby. Guy looked to him.

'I am to take you into the city.'

Guy looked away and continued his recovery. All in good time, he could not go to the city at that moment.

The servant had waited quietly while Guy stretched away the pains of training, washed and changed, before leading him around the castle and towards the city. Guy was normally comfortable in silence, but was not feeling so then.

'Where are we going?' he asked the younger boy.

'I have been told to help you get some clothes.'

'Do you know where to go?'

'Of course.'

The silence returned, which made Guy more uncomfortable. But then a thought entered his mind.

'Do you know the city?'

'I do.' Guy had not spent much time around servants. They had been at Waering of course, no household could function without them, but he had never paid them any mind.

As was common in most cities, the closer to the castle, the more exclusive, and expensive the shops and stalls were, the finer the people, and their homes. Even though they entered the city from the side of the castle and he walked with a servant, people looked at Guy as if he did not belong. They were not wrong.

'If I wanted to get to the woods is there a quick way?'

'A quick way, no.'

'What is the quickest way?' The servant turned, pointing behind him but away from the castle.

'That way.'

'Can you show me?'

'No, I am instructed to help you get some clothes.'

'Afterwards?' There was a pause as the servant's mind considered. 'Yes.'

Guy asked the servant questions as they went through the city's streets, and he answered them all. He felt that he was taking advantage of the poor boy. He had probably been told to be helpful, perhaps it was simply who he had come to be, and while Guy could sense the feelings of awkwardness coming from the boy, it did not stop him from answering. He asked the boy to find an old woman to crack his bones. The boy said he would. He asked the boy if he could get him some long arrows, he said he would. Guy made the boy take him to a place that sold farmers clothes, and he bought a new set and a few other bits and pieces. Farmer's goods were always robust and rarely unnecessary. As uncomfortable as it was he decided to let the servant choose the clothes that he had been sent to buy. He figured that they had probably told him the kind of thing they were after. The choice for a man of his size was limited and they walked away with trousers and an embroidered shirt that had cost him a silver on its own. He had paid another two silvers for the clothes that the boy had requested be made for him. He had not worried about what clothes that he wore for months now, and he had not missed it. He had realised long ago that clothes do not make a man.

Guy questioned the servant all the way back to the castle. He would never initiate conversation but would always answer when addressed. He learnt as much as he could. Where the smithing quarter was, the apothecary, the food stalls and the bars. Everything he could think of he asked. The Knightmaker had not forbidden him from speaking with servants.

When they were approaching the castle, the servant hesitated a moment. Guy stopped walking.

'What is it?' he asked the boy. Again there was some hesitation.

'You asked me to show you the quickest way to the woods. It is that way,' he said pointing away from the castle. Guy could not see the woods from where they were, but he could not see much beyond the defensive walls.

'How long does it take?'

'Half an hour or so.'

'Walking, or running?' The servant paused for a fraction, and Guy realised the idiocy of his question.

'Walking,' was the polite reply.

'Can you show me?'

The servant looked up at the sun, considered a moment before answering.

'We have time if we hurry.'

By the time Guy returned to his room in the barracks the mornings training and lack of rest was catching up with him, and he realised he had not eaten anything significant. It was not long until he was to meet Sir Parcifal for the evening meal. He wore his leather under one of his old linen shirts. He would have training afterwards. He had been told to be ready.

After feasting on a chicken, potboiled with summer vegetables, and bread Guy was led to a larger room where that evening's training took place. That night his offence training took a twist. He was to attack, but the stranger was allowed to tag him in response. The sequence of the dance was not followed, but each move that the stranger countered with was one that he knew.

'You can play the same song with a different beat,' the Knightmaker called. 'We go again.'

As the stranger showed him the concept of offensive defence, Guy's mind was swarming with possibilities. What had through repetition become somewhat of a pedestrian dance suddenly sprang to life with the vibrancy of a March hare. He knew all the moves, and was amazed at the potential gained by straying from the taught course of the dance. For as Sir Parcifal had told him many times as he pulled himself off the floor, *'there are no rules on the battlefield.'* This had quickly become Guy's favourite training session so far, even above their brief foray into free style fighting. This was something he could understand. He enjoyed it when the strangers stick slammed into his ribs, or stopped just short of his head, often he would make the same attacks to see the counters. The stranger amazed him with his skill and knowledge. For the first time in a long time Guy felt as if progress had been made.

It was late when the servant escorted Guy back to the barracks, the castle was quiet and calm. Guy's mind whirred with what he had learnt that night, but still, he was distracted by the torch that the servant carried. He could not see beyond the light that it gave, though he knew they could be clearly seen by anyone who might be in the shadows. Had he been alone he would not have carried a torch.

It took all of his resolve to drag himself from the cot just a few short hours after returning, and much of his physical effort to start his run with his archery kit. The dull ache in his body was a reminder of the previous day's work, but he would get the blood pumping soon enough once outside the castle gate. Even such a small remote gateway had a guard post, and Guy was let out with only a hint of frustration. He just hoped that he would be let back in again.

Once clear of the castle he unwound a little and let his body move as freely as it could. With the new route the servant had shown him, he could afford to move with more pace, for he had much less distance to travel. He ran for what he considered half an hour. He had been running at least ten minutes through the edge of the woodland. He was looking for something specific, and he had more time to find it. He looked for where the land rose and tracked the contours of a hill until he found the embankment he was looking for. He would have preferred a larger gap to the treeline, but it would suffice for target training. The steep incline meant that he did not lose a single arrow that morning, and he would be back in time to eat before training. He was to wear his training armour from now on, at least in the public training.

He pulled a dozen of buckets for the other knights, but without the log this time. It was easier for him to use his whole body to pull the bucket, even with his armour on. Having learnt from the past he wore his helm and had his training sword in his belt, for while the helm made his life more difficult when pulling the water, he would be thankful of it when the stranger launched at him. Guy wanted to try the defence in the way the stranger had before, but was under strict instruction from the Knightmaker to follow the sequence. Even with the mid-day sun making him hot in the armour, he felt that it had been a good session. The stranger met his pace and they practiced their dance. He had his helm rung several times, but only to let him know he had fucked up. For the first time after a session he was able to walk away soon after its completion.

The servant was waiting for him to take him back to the city where an old woman would crack his bones and clothes would be collected.

When he arrived to dine with the Knightmaker that night, wearing one of his new shirts over his leather, he felt as if he were walking on the clouds. Things were finally moving in the right direction and he felt incredible. The Knightmaker talked through the meal, the training had gone too well, people would start to talk. The public sessions were to take on a new meaning. He gave guy four curved iron plates.

'Wear these on your forearms, under your armour tomorrow, and every day unless instructed.' Guy took the weights, having to tense his arms when they dropped from unexpected heaviness. 'In public I do not want you to show your full ability. Use the heavy armour and sword to bring strength to your body. You defended too well today, the arm weights should see to that.' He talked throughout their meal of venison and dark ale pie with breads, of what he wanted the public to see, of what they would do out of the public eye, and more on how to conduct himself. Guy nodded, listened, and did not question or dispute anything. He would do whatever he was told, even if that meant taking unnecessary beatings. Once they had rested into their meal he called out 'Offence training. One hour. We follow the dance.'

Inside Guy was a little disappointed. The previous nights training had been incredible, now they were going backwards. Follow the dance meant sticking to the sequence and they would dance the same dance as in the afternoon, except he was the aggressor.

They moved into space and he approached the stranger. He played along for a short while, before taking advantage of sloppy offence slammed his stick into Guy's ribs. The surprise blow knocked a little wind out of him and the stick had left a black mark on his shirt.

'When you leave yourself open he will strike. It is your job to keep his stick busy.' Guy looked at his shirt. 'This is now your training shirt, and I want it clean every night. So do yourself a favour and do not get hit too often. We go again.'

Guy only gave the stranger another half dozen opportunities to strike him, and he took every one, despite slowing his pace to match Guy's. At the end of the session Guy was pleased, he still felt like he was making progress, and was less disturbed by the servant leading the way with a torch.

The following day, instead of washing the shirt, he bought another identical one, and spent the time further exploring the city. He was managing not to spend his coin, but his shopping list was growing by the day. He had the servant escort him around the best bookshops, but none had the book he was looking for. They had many others that he had not known he had wanted until he saw them, but he was being disciplined, there was not a knight alive who carried around a library. Once his house was built, he would have an entire room just for books.

44

That evening Guy quickly realised that the Knightmaker knew of his attempted deception and the stranger had not held back. By the time he left, cursing himself, the shirt that he wore was closer to black than white. The stranger had somehow ripped it with his burnt stick. He had taken a battering that night, but he reflected that he had bought it upon himself.

Training continued the same every day for the next two weeks, while around him the castle and its grounds transformed themselves into a grand tournament arena. This was the king's own tournament, the greatest tournament of the year, the final tournament of the year. It was the one tournament that every knight wanted to compete in. To win this tournament was to become the tournament champion of Rodina, and be invited to every tournament the following year. It could be a very profitable time.

He had asked the servant the best way to clean the shirt, and had a small pail of salts that worked well. Some nights the stranger had let him escape without being struck, and some nights he did not use the burnt stick. Their training had increased in intensity and speed. Not one day passed without Guy being happy with his progress. In the mornings he fired arrows until he hit a dozen straight into the hessian sack. The servant had shown him where the longbow was to take place, but he did not practice much. It was easy to lose an arrow, and took far too long to recover them. He was happy with the bow though, more so each day. Barring any unexpected injuries, he would be able to give a much truer representation of his ability when the tournament came around.

The sorry excuse for defence training that took place in the training grounds continued to frustrate him. The weight of the armour and the iron vambraces made him slow. He tried to use it to make him stronger, but it was difficult to focus on that when the stranger was coming at him. The evening sessions were still his favourite and most productive. The Knightmaker had found a quiet courtyard where they sometimes trained in armour. He had improved so much that he was almost able to convince himself that he had the stranger in trouble most nights, as the servant led him back to the barracks.

It was a little over a week until the tournament began, and some over eager knights and lords were starting to arrive, even though preparations were not fully complete. The barracks were on the other side of the castle to the tournament fields, but his regular afternoon visits to the city had enabled him to see a small town coming together. Guy wondered to himself why something that was an annual event did not have a permanent home. Why the need for such a level of construction every year? It certainly kept people busy, and helped fuel the feeling of excitement that seemed to be all around him. He should feel excited, but someway he did not, he was just looking forward to the evenings training. He had been told to wear his white shirt, that meant that he would be busy tomorrow, and have little time for the city. Given that his offence training was really just another form of defence, it was virtually inevitable that the burned stick would strike him. The stranger was always showing him new ways to counter an attack. Even so, what excitement he did feel was for the training. Without the armour and with a wooden stick he was quick. Not as quick as the stranger, but he felt that if the stranger were as big as he was, Guy would be quicker. He was light on his feet, fluid, moving with the stick quick in his hands. He was looking forward to seeing what the stranger showed him that night.

Guys heart sank, and panic rose as he entered the room to meet Sir Parcifal, two chevroned knights were looking very officious, standing to attention as they were. Sir Parcifal did not look fussed, but then he rarely did. The Knightmaker invited him to sit.

'We are to have a guest this evening.' Guy simply nodded, his eyes flicking around the room, planning possible outcomes. He did not know what to say. He did not want to talk of his training with strangers present, and there was little else that occupied his mind.

Fortunately for Guy, within a minute of sitting down, internal doors at the back of the room were opened, and the king entered flanked by another chevroned knight. Guy felt he should stand, and was rising as the king told him to sit down. He did so quickly, a little ashamed, the Knightmaker and the stranger had not moved. The king joined them at the table and accepted a goblet of wine from Sir Parcifal.

'Sir Parcifal, Master Guy.'

He seemed to ignore the stranger, it did not seem to bother him though. 'Alas, I do not have much time. I have people arriving for the tournament that I must welcome. At this rate I shall be banqueting every night for a fortnight, but I have several reasons for my visit.' Guy found himself staring at the king, he did not think that it would ever get old. *He was with the king.* It still did not seem right in his head. He caught himself, and hoped that it just looked like he was paying attention. The king was probably used to people staring at him. Even sat casually at their table, there was something about him. He was the most important person in the whole of Rodina. 'Master Guy, I have taken your advice and watched Sir Parcifal's methods of training.'

Guy suddenly felt defensive, he knew the Knightmaker did not like the attention, and the unwelcome reminder would probably result in a shirt that took a long time to clean. 'But I have not seen much. Some good shows of strength and moderate defence drills.' Guy found himself wanting to speak, to tell of the vambraces, to inform him about his own training whilst practicing Archery. He fought it. 'It is not only my eyes that have been upon you though and I hear you are making the most of your bow.' Guy flushed.

'I am trying Your Grace. It is a good bow that I did not get the chance to thank you for.' The king waved his hand dismissively.

'I also hear that not all of your training is done in the courtyard.' Guy felt himself starting to flap, but the Knightmaker remained stoic. Returning his gaze to the king he found nothing to say. 'Show me. Let me see Sir Parcifal's methods.' Guy looked to the Knightmaker who simply nodded. The stranger stood and retrieved his burnt stick, Guy followed tentatively.

He did not know what he should do. Should he play it down or should he show the king what he had? He stood to with the stranger, and meekly struck the first attack. The stranger answered for him, parrying, spinning and slamming his burnt sick into Guys ribs knocking the wind from him and sending him aknee. Guy gasped his breath, the pain hurt, but he was more concerned about the strong black mark on his shirt. The stranger stepped back after delivering his message and invited Guy to attack him again. Their sticks clashed a dozen times filling the room with sounds of contact. The stranger stepped back. Guy stepped forward again, faster, longer, another black mark.

'We go again.' called the Knightmaker.

Guy stepped in, swivelled and controlled the dance as attacks flowed and counters were defended. The stranger was playing hard, Guy had to defend whilst attacking, but he felt that the stranger was also making him look good. A couple of rounds later and the rules changed, and they just went at it full tilt, or at least for Guy. Breathing hard, the speed of their dance was the fastest yet, and this dance was unscripted. From so many hours of dancing together Guy felt it would look impressive. He soon changed his mind as the stranger started spinning and landing blows at will. Both sides of his chest took a blow, and one to his back before the Knightmaker called out to defend himself. A further two blows before he blocked one, a further three before he hooked the strangers leg sending him flat aback. He moved to space, trying to recover and get his bearings. The stranger was up in a second, and coming for him. And this time it was Guy who ended flat on his back, the stranger marked his chest with a firm strike.

'We go again.' called the Knightmaker.

Guy rolled, spinning his leg to keep the stranger at distance while he righted himself. Another furious exchange ended with the stranger slamming the end of the stick into Guys gut, sending him aknee once again. At least it did not leave a mark.

'That will do,' called the king.

Guy returned to the table, his breathing heavy. He knew the blows would leave him sore in the morning, and that was before they had even done the training, if they were even going to do any.

'You do this for two hours or more?' the king asked. Guy was pleased that the king was talking to Sir Parcifal now. Though he tried to hide it, it would be hard for him to respond.

'Not at that speed, but aye.' The king spent a thoughtful moment.

'We shall see in the tournament. If young Guy wins then you may continue to knight men who are worthy. That is my judgement on that.' Sir Parcifal shrugged a nod. 'There is another matter that requires attention, your arms. Sir Parcifal, it is you who is at fault for this situation. You should never have allowed this to happen. I have to be seen to take action, and so I shall. You shall fight for the right to bear those arms. I shall have you defend your shield in a drawbridge challenge.'

'If you want to take the shield, take the shield. Besides I do not have my armour.'

'I do not want to take your shield. Of all men who have served, you deserve to bear those arms as much as any, maybe more so. Defend your shield, defend the drawbridge, and let's put this mess behind us.'

The Knightmaker gave the king a look that would wither most men. Not the king though. 'The knight's quarters are ready. I suggest you move in there. You are in tent one.' The king beckoned forward a servant who carried a bundle. 'Master Guy,' the king continued. 'Your bravery has earned you the right to remain in the squire's tournament. Your master's future depends on you performing well.' Guy nodded. He wanted to show the king that he was ready, but knew that he had no idea what he was facing, so he kept his face straight. 'I have something for you, to thank you for your efforts.' The servant offered the bundle, it was heavy in his arms. 'This is tanned hide from the beast that you slayed. I have some for myself, but there was plenty left, even for a man of your size.'

'Thank you, Your Grace.' He did not know what else to say.

'Thank *you* Master Guy.' He held the king's gaze for a moment, and in that moment he was just another man. An instant later he was the king. 'Alas, I must leave. I must welcome some over eager guests. Go and claim your tent.' He nodded at Sir Parcifal, who nodded back, and was gone from the room followed by the chevroned knights. Guy's eyes flicked to Sir Parcifal's, but if the Knightmaker had any thoughts, he was hiding them well. Guy's mind raced as they sat in silence. He placed the bundle on the floor, as much as he wanted to look at it, the time was not right.

Guy was relieved when their food arrived only minutes after the king's departure, at least he had something to focus on. They ate in silence. Guy had decided that he was not going to speak first. He would only end up saying something stupid. Finally after silent digestion the Knightmaker turned to the stranger.

'The king likes his tournaments. He likes the ceremony.' He turned to Guy. 'Offence training, one hour. Let's go.'

The stranger stood and Guy followed. They picked up their dance where they had left off and at the hours end Guys shirt was as dark as the night that he had been punished for his attempted deception. He did not feel like he had been punished that night. Guy was told to remove his shirt, he did without question exposing the crude battered leather that protected him, and the bruises that crept from underneath. The Knightmaker took it and threw it onto the fire.

'No more fucking around. Come let us claim out tent.' The Knightmaker grabbed his shield and headed out the door, the stranger followed. Guy grabbed his bundle and went after them, the servant following him.

It was late, and Guy felt a chill as the air cooled his sweat. The castle was quiet and only a few bewildered guards were present to see the four of them march across the castle to the tournament fields. Sir Parcifal planted his shield with purpose before the first tent. 'Get yourself back to the barracks. We move in when I am ready. When you get back, put on your vambraces and do not remove them until I tell you.' Guy nodded, not wanting to show his confusion, and allowed the servant to escort him to his room in the barracks. He wanted to speak to the servant, but that could wait until tomorrow. Now that he did not have a shirt to wash he could head to the city. There were things he needed to do.

When the servant had left, he opened his bundle to examine the leather within. Had he been wearing it for his training, he doubted his body would be quite as emblazoned with bruises as it was. Even shorn of the long hair of the beast it was still formidable. Guy wondered if an arrow would bounce off it, as it had off the beast. Then he hoped that he never got to find out. He secured his vambraces and crawled into his cot, fleeting thoughts of Phylissa shone briefly before sleep came for him.

The morning's archery session was a waste of time. His arms were knotted before he reached his archery spot, he was amazed at how much such a weight could affect him. It was all he could do to simply fire the bow, he had no control over where the arrows went. He fired a dozen and began his run back to the castle, his arms feeling as if they were on fire before he was into his stride.

When he turned up to the public session he wore his training armour, but only saw the Knightmaker present, not in armour. He did not pull water for the other knights that day, and would not again.

'It is just you and me today.' said the Knightmaker. 'Defence training, One hour.' The Knightmaker came at him. Guy only just got his sword up in time to block, it was pushed away by the power of the strike. He blocked the first few blows, but each time the power in the strike pushed his sword away. It was only a matter of time before he was unable to recover in time to continue the dance. The first time the Knightmaker rang his helm he went down. He was not fucking about. It took him a couple of moments to get to his feet, and even then he was groggy, his vision blurred through the slit of his helm, as if his head was in a bucket of frog spawn. He knew the dance well enough and seeing blurred movement he blocked the first attack, the next blow to his ribs put him down again. He could feel people watching, as the blows to his armour had cracked through the air. Those making the final preparations to the tournament arena had probably heard them. 'Take a moment.' said the Knightmaker, 'and do not go down again.' Guy took more than a moment his head still throbbed, but not as much as his side. The wind had been knocked out of him through his armour. That was not good. How the fuck was he going to stay up with this kind of assault. It was like nothing he had ever known. He took deep breaths gulping in air in the hope that it would allow him to recover and carefully got to his feet. It was another moment before he rolled his shoulders and assumed the ready position, north east. He looked on as the armourless Knightmaker moved towards him, ready to block with more purpose. The Knightmaker came at him with more power than the stranger had, and he felt anxiety rise in him. How could he not go down again when he was being hit so hard?

He had made a few steps of the dance, blocking and moving away from the Knightmaker's advance, but it was not long until the sound of sword on armour cracked through the training ground. It staggered him, but his sword met the Knightmaker's giving him a moment to escape and recover. The blow had not sent him down, but he had no time to celebrate. The Knightmaker's advance was relentless. It was not until half way through the session when he noticed that, since the first two strikes, the Knightmaker had been hitting him with the flat of the blade.

Once he realised this, he someway found more confidence, and though his arms were heavy, he settled into the dance. The Knightmaker soon put the notion to the sword, when after one exchange, he ended close to Guy, and while Guy had blocked the strike, he could not block the Knightmaker's shoulder sending him reeling backwards until he had no option but to roll. He sprang straight back to his feet and had half a second to block the Knightmaker's next attack.

'Never let your enemy get too close,' he said through smiling teeth. He was not even out of breath. The armourless old Knightmaker was kicking the shit out of him, and not appearing to tire one bit. He must look ridiculous to those who glanced over when his armour was rung, and that was often. He was relieved when the Knightmaker called a halt to the session and sent him back to the barracks. Guy did not stop to recover, instead, though it took all the effort he could muster, he made his way back to his room and it was there where he collapsed. He felt like he had just been humiliated, and whilst he appreciated touching swords with the Knightmaker for the first time, it had taken the intensity to a whole other level. He had been fucked up.

He was still trying to get his mind around his situation as he rubbed the vambraces through his shirt while he told the servant their plans for the afternoon. The servant nodded in all the right places in his non enthusiastic way that gave Guy the confidence that he knew what he wanted. There was uncertainty on his face when he nodded that they would be able to get it all done that day, especially as they had to pick up some white mist for the Knightmaker, who again had not given him any coin. Seeing this, Guy grabbed his daysack and they made a move. He would do as much as he could.

Guy kept a decent pace into the city and the servant kept up without breathing hard. Guy realised that he was, but then he had been training. Undeterred, he pushed on. He would get the white mist first, that was near the bookshop that he wanted to visit, then, they would have to head to the outskirts of the city with a diversion on the way, then get back to dine with Sir Parcifal. Fuck it. They could do it even if it meant that he had to run back to the castle.

Things got even tighter after another diversion taken after speaking with the apothecary. She did not have the book that he was looking for, did not know where he might find one, but knew someone who might be able to help him. Guy did not have time to see her that day, but went to meet her to ask if he could see her the following day. *If I am here, you can see me.* What was that supposed to mean? It played on his mind to the extent that while he was in the bookshop he forgot to ask if they had got a copy of the book he was looking for as he made his purchase. As they left the shop he admonished himself as he prepared to head through the city. He had to sort himself out.

He was happy when he heard the sound of fire and steel, but could not enjoy it like he normally would. He was happy because it meant that they were almost there. They made their way through the heat and hammering of the blacksmith quarters and approached a workshop from which no noise came. Guy barely broke stride from his brisk march as he approached a man finishing his noonshine. The man was not fazed by his approach. It was the city, people were always in a rush, and on that day Guy was one of them. After confirming that he was the man Guy was looking for, he set about explaining what he wanted, pulling up his shirt to show the leather he wore beneath.

'Something like this that I can wear beneath a shirt,' he exclaimed as if the first to ever have the idea, then slightly more sheepishly, 'but mayhaps a bit neater.' The man smiled and measured him, scribbling with chalk onto a leather square. Guy found himself having to calm his heart. He was rushing, and finding the old man's slow measuring infuriating. He tried to hide it, but the old man's smile let him know he was doing it on purpose. Guy knew that he should not begrudge the man, the measuring was the most important part. A wrong measurement could fuck everything up, not that he had measured the leather he wore, it had been battered to fit him by weeks of training. The old man continued measuring, he had Guy raise his arms in the air, and then struggled to measure his chest. Towards the end Guy was able to accept the process, and meet the old man's smile. He had the same glint in his eye that Smith had, and that filled him with hope that the servant had taken him to the right place.

When the old man started talking prices and leather Guy reminded him that he had his own leather, and wanted a cost for the workmanship alone.

'Let me see the leather,' the old man said, appearing put out that he might lose some commission. Guy pulled one of the bundles of it out of his daysack. The old man looked at it and then met Guys eye. 'What leather is this?' he asked gauging the thickness.

'It is Cowhide.' Guy replied.

'It's over a quarter of an inch thick!'

'It was a very big cow.' The old man worked the leather in his fingers, held it against Guy and measured some more. They arranged a price but he would have to wait. The leather would take a long time to work. That was fine, he had all the time in the world, except that day, he had no time at all. He tried to be civil but brief with the old man as he shared his amazement at the leather. He left with a genuine smile for him, but as soon as his head was turned it disappeared and the urgency returned. Looking at the sun, it was getting late. A part of him thought about not making the last stop. He had never been late for the Knightmaker, and did not want to know what price his tardiness would bring. He looked to the servant who had also looked at the sun. If they were quick, they could make it.

Guy wanted the servant to take him to the places that made farmers clothes, and they reached the area in good time, but Guy soon realised that the further out of the city you went, the more spread out things were. They seemed to spend as long as it had taken them to get there to work their way through the farming area to find the cobbler that the servant had found for him. As they approached Guy looked at the sun once more. He should have started his journey back by now, he could feel his heart pound in his neck as the anxiety rose. The cobbler was friendly, and let Guy thrust his running boots and two slabs of the leather at him, along with two silvers and asked him to attach them to the soles of the boots for him to collect in two days. When the cobbler had nodded, Guy thanked him, turned and set off at a run though the farming district leaving the servant behind.

He ran hard while he could, all too aware that soon there would be too many people. He still drew looks from those he passed.

He walked with urgency through the crowds taking the direct route back to the castle, glancing continuously towards the sky as the sun slid with more pace than he would have liked. It was going to be tight. The bell rang quarter past the hour as he approached the castle, and relieved, Guy slowed his march to a walk, and tried to steady his breathing. He had fifteen minutes to get there. That was fine, he would not have to find out the punishment for tardiness, not yet anyway. He passed through the castle gates and turned left where most turned right. It was definitely getting busier and the tournament buzz was starting, yet someway, still not in him. He was too busy. He weaved around buildings towards where the Knightmaker dined. As he turned into the courtyard the servant boy was stood waiting. He was calm, unruffled. The opposite of how Guy felt. He could not hide his shock.

'How did you…' He didn't even finish asking the question, he did not have time to hear the answer. It pissed him off though. He had spent real effort to bet there in time, clearly the servant had not. He chastised himself for not being aware. Of course he should have asked the servant. He had always tried not to treat him like a servant. He carried his own kit and for the most part ran his own errands. After all, he was not Guy's servant. Guy finally shook his head and cracked a smile as they approached the door. He still had a lot to learn.

'What's so funny?' asked the Knightmaker as they entered. It sounded like a menacing question, but the Knightmaker would sound menacing if he sang a lullaby.

'I had some business in town which overran. I busted my balls to get back here in time.' He did not bullshit the Knightmaker. 'Someone I had left on the other side of the city was waiting for me when I got back.'

He nodded to the servant who was yet to fade into the shadows until needed. The Knightmaker smiled, and with a nod dismissed the servant.

'Come, sit. Did you get what I asked for?'

Guy put the two bottles of white mist on the table as the Knightmaker poured a goblet of wine which he tried to refuse. He shouldn't drink before training, especially since he had not had wine or ale for some time. The Knightmaker insisted, so he drank. 'How was your training today?'

'Hard. I am glad that you took to using the flat of your blade.' The Knightmaker snorted a laugh.

'And what did you learn?'

'That until now we have just been fucking about?'

'Ha. In a way, that may be true, but you have learnt a lot. What you should have learned is that you are not ready yet. In the real world people will kick your ass, on the battlefield you will be killed. Do you know why?'

'Because I am not ready yet?'

'I just told you that. The reason they will kick your ass, is because you believe *they* are ready. The truth is no one is ever ready. That's how it is. How can you be ready to fight a man you have never met before? Not being ready is not a bad thing. It is how you deal with it in here,' he said tapping the side of his head, 'and here,' poking his heart. 'Now drink.'

They drank before the food arrived, as the Knightmaker talked to him about his training so far, and how it would change. They drank as they ate and the Knightmaker told him how they needed another three weeks to finish his training, and how he would have to learn to fight quickly. They drank as they digested their meal as the Knightmaker talked at length about what it was to be a knight. A real knight, about choosing who to work for, and how to make coin. The fact that not all of a knight's battles took place on the battlefield or tournament arena and that he needed to be ready to go at any point. He had not felt closer to the Knightmaker than at the end of the meal.

'Fighting training, one hour. Remove your vambraces.'

The Knightmaker stood, and led Guy through to a small courtyard. 'The king has allowed us to use this area for our training. Let's go.' Guy stood waiting, unsure. The Knightmaker punched him in the face. 'You and I are going to fight. You never really know a man until you have fought him man to man.' He jabbed him in the face again, Guy too slow to respond. 'I am going to make you yield tonight.' A hard punch to his gut and an elbow to the face put him aknee. The Knightmaker grabbed Guy's head and slammed a knee into his face, sending him sprawling aback. 'Fight back.' He called as he landed a boot to Guys ribs, whose knees came up and his arms shielded his head. A few more solid kicks landed and he lay curled aball protecting himself. The Knightmaker stepped back and told him to get up. 'You *will* fight me.'

45

It took Guy a moment to get to his feet. He could not tell if it was the wine that blurred his vision or the knee of the Knightmaker. He could taste blood. He could feel pain, everywhere. He could see two of the Knightmaker, and was unsteady on his feet. There was conflict within him and wine clouded his judgment. He could not fight the Knightmaker. He would get his ass kicked, besides it did not feel right.

The blurred figures of the Knightmaker stepped forward, he tried to lift his hands to block, but soon felt a fist connect with his face, then his ribs. The Knightmaker hooked his leg sending him flat aback. He saw a boot raised over his head. That was when instinct kicked in and he rolled, springing surprisingly to his feet. The Knightmaker was not fucking around, and the boot slammed into the floor where his head had been. He shared a glance with the Knightmaker who came at him again. He dodged and blocked, but soon found himself thrown to the floor again, rolling to get some distance. The Knightmaker came at him again, telegraphing the move, and Guy swivelled and landed a punch of his own to the Knightmaker's ribs, who sidestepped away from further blows.

'That's it,' called the Knightmaker as he came at him again. What followed for Guy was survival training. For a while he held his own, bloodying the Knightmaker's face, and on occasion coming out of an exchange for the better. But before long he had nothing left, he could not even lift his arms to protect himself, let alone dish out any damage in return. 'You will yield,' the Knightmaker began to say as he battered the defenceless Guy. 'You will yield.'

Somewhere in his mind Guy knew that he could submit and end it, but he could not bring himself to do it. He had not yielded through any part of his training, and he did not intend to start now. It was just another test. It was one he would pass. He could not even feel the punches that rained in as he was on his knees in front of the Knightmaker. He could not hear the Knightmaker screaming at him. He did not feel himself crumple to the floor from a punch. His world had gone black.

A long slow groan escaped as Guy woke. He could only open one eye and that gave a distorted blurred vision of a ceiling. He could not breathe through his nose, and the more aware of his body he became, the more it hurt. He took a deep breath through his mouth, trying to get some air inside him. There was no sharp pain, which he took to be a good sign. His head throbbed as he tried to remember the night before. There had been wine, he remembered and had he fought with the Knightmaker! He could remember visions of the Knightmaker's fist slamming into his body, he could remember the Knightmaker's eyes, more alive than he had seen. *Fuck.* Had he offended him in some way, was that why they had fought? He groaned again, trying to rouse himself, but his body was having none of it.

'Good morning,' came a voice from the corner, the servant. *Was he here to take him to training?* 'Sir Parcifal asked me to tell you that you have two days off to recover and sort yourself out.' Guy was unable to respond. A moment later the servant was cleaning Guy's face with a damp rag. Even the soft touch caused him to wince. The servant gave him some water to drink, Guy feebly let him hold his head as the water moistened his mouth. It tasted of blood.

'What time is it?' Guy asked.

'Daytime, still morning.'

'What happened? How did I get back here?' It pained him to even speak, and he was not sure that he would even understand the reply.

'I have come to take you to the city. You arranged to see someone, but if you do not feel up to it…' For a moment Guy's head swam with pain and the words lacked meaning. *Two days off, thank fuck.* He did not think he would be able to get out of his cot, let alone face training. He relaxed a little, but even that hurt his head. He wanted to curl aball and sleep until it did not hurt anymore.

'I can't open my eye,' he groaned. The servant did not answer and Guy felt his good eye closing. *What the fuck had happened?* He tried to move his hand to feel his face, but his arms were heavy, the vambraces were back on his arms. He gave up and let it slump back to the cot. He did not feel up to anything. He had arranged to meet someone? He took a deep breath, but it did not help, if anything it made him feel nauseous just to add to the mix. He let it out, defeated. He felt broken. He had failed Phylissa. Even that though, the one that kept him going, did not rouse him. He groaned again, it seemed the only thing to do.

He realised his mind was working through the previous day, his run back from the cobbler, the leather worker, his book, the white mist. *His book.* He had gone to see an old woman, she might help him find *'Healing practices of the old world.'* That was who he had arranged to meet.

'What time is it?' he groaned. 'How long do we have?'

'A little over two hours.' Guy flopped back onto his back. He had tried to get up, but his head had started spinning. 'Plenty of time, do you think you can make it?'

It took Guy a while to answer. He was still not able to function, everything still hurt. He needed something to get him going.

'Could you get some water please?' he groaned.

'I have water here.'

'Could you get me some food?' he groaned. He wanted just a moment to himself to absorb the pain and find his mind.

'I have food for you here.' Guy sighed.

'Pour water on my head.' The servant stood over guy with a large jug and poured. The water was cold, and made Guy involuntarily move. A sharp pain stabbed behind his eyes, and his vision blurred again, but at least he was sat up. That was a start. He slowly started to stretch and move his body, but it was a painful hour later that he was finally able to start on the bread and fruit. Every mouthful hurt his jaw, and it took entirely too much effort to swallow. Heading to the city was the last thing he wanted to do. 'In my bag over there, in the left pouch there is a pot of balm. Could you please get it for me, and a cloth?'

Guy splashed water on himself trying in vain to awaken. He applied the fire berry balm to his body, the back of his neck and his jaw. He hoped the fire that it bought would give him a sensation other than the dull ache he suffered. At the servant's suggestion he pulled on a shirt and tried to stand to put on his cloak. It took a moment for his head to settle. With every bit of determination left in him, he took slow unsteady steps to the door. He hoped that it would be worth it.

Guy had to stop and lean on a wall within 60 feet of his room. He could barely move. His body hurt, but it was the pain and cloudiness of his head that made things difficult. The servant told him that they had less than an hour, plenty of time if they kept moving. That was the problem, he was finding it hard to move, finding it hard to even think. He pulled up the hood on his cloak, and tried once again to move his feet. His existence was simply the next step, the servant was guiding him. All he could do was focus on the next step. Before long they had left the castle through a quiet gate, and the bustle of the city hurt his head even more. There were times when he could not remember where they were going, and there were times when that is what drove him. If he could get the book, if he could learn about burning hands, he would not be feeling like this. That was, if it could be even used on himself. Fuck it. One step after another and he hoped he would find out soon enough.

It took a lot of steps, more than he could care to remember, and each one of them had hurt, but they finally arrived to meet the old woman and she was nowhere to be seen. Guy did not even care, he was happy to be able to sit on a wall. He wanted to weep, not because the old woman was not there, he did not really know why. He had taken far worse beatings through his training, and they had never left him feeling like this. It must be the wine, or a combination of the two. The servant returned with a fresh skin of water. It was cool in his hands as he took it.

'How much did I drink last night?' he asked before taking a good slug from the skin.

'Eight goblets.'

His mind repeated the answer before it understood. Eight goblets was too much. It was more than a skinfull. No wonder he felt shit. Guy drank again from the skin even though it made him feel queasy. He wanted it to stop his head from feeling as if someone had planted an axe between his eyes. There was something he was trying not to think about, and was glad that his mind found it hard to think of anything.

The walk back! He would have to stall for time, it was the last thing in the world that he wanted to do. He didn't think he could. He let his head drop between his legs, someway it was the position that caused him least pain. It let him close out the world. He did not have the strength of being to pull himself together. The servant stood waiting patiently. Guy did not concern himself, he was sure that it would not be the first hangover he had attended.

'How do you expect to see me if you do not look?'

The words snapped Guy away from feeling sorry for himself. Someway he knew it was the old woman. He lifted his head and opened his eye. A searing pain stopped it from working, all he saw was light, and he felt like both his eyes were being pushed from his head. Groaning he continued to wait for his eyes to work, his whole head swam in circles and it hurt like hells. The old woman continued. 'What is so important that you had to meet me, but not important enough for yesterday?' He still could not see her, but he imagined she had her hands on her hips, the way that old people do when you bother them. In his mind Guy formed the words and spoke them well, but the only one that made it out of his mouth was the word book. 'Book? What book? I don't have a book for you.' Finally Guy's eyes snapped the world back into focus and the first thing he saw was the old woman's eyes. He met them and in that instant did not care about the book. *Help me.* He silently screamed with his whole body. He saw a change in the old woman. 'Bring him inside,' she said to the servant and disappeared. He did not have the strength to watch her. The servant would take him.

'Lay him down there,' she said pointing to the middle of the stone floor. Guy allowed the servant to lower him, had he done it he was worried he would add another bruise to his collection. Turning her attention to Guy who was happy to be lying down, she asked 'Did you know you would be in this state when you came to see me yesterday?' Guy managed to shake his head. 'Yet you want me to fix you. Do you have coin?' Guy nodded. 'Fine, you can pay afterwards.'

She hung her shawl on the door, and returned to Guy, first just looking at him, then moving her hands around him, as if feeling him without touching him. Guy wanted to ask about the book, but he did not have the energy. She put her hands over his eyes and he felt a blast of energy in his eyes and further back. He felt his body tense, then relaxed. He felt as if he were floating, and just for that moment his head was not screaming at him. For the first time that day he was without pain as he floated in a place of darkness that was someway filled with light. He was aware of himself, though he felt disconnected, as if he were attached to his body by a mere tether of being. He felt peaceful, he felt free.

He waited for the familiar feel of the burning hands, the heat coming from them absorbed and spread throughout his body. It came soon enough, but this time felt different, they were not putting the heat into his body, they were taking it out, and with it, he felt some of himself depart. It did not feel right, he had to stop it. He could not stop it, instead he accepted it. If this was to be the end, then so be it. There was nothing he could do about it.

46

The light of a single candle burned into his awareness, and with it the smell of burnt sage. Without opening his eyes he knew that the only other thing in the empty room was the servant, sat resting in the corner.

'What time is it?' he murmured.

'Night time,' was the reply. 'Keep sleeping, daylight will be here soon enough. Guy did not move, but sleep did not find all of him again. Part of his mind was awake, most of his body was not. He did not feel the pain of the day before, but he did not feel anything, not even his ball of energy that always resided in the pit of his stomach. *Had the old woman taken it*? He felt at peace, but uncomfortable. He spent the next hours breathing, collecting what feeling he had until there was a glimmer in his stomach. He nurtured it, slowly allowing it to move throughout his body, both spreading its strength and collecting it at the same time. He could feel where his body hurt, it took longer to pass the energy through, but he did not force it. His shoulders were tight, his ribs and abdomen ached and his face… his face felt much better, and there was only a hint of fogginess in his mind. By the time sunlight made it through the hessian covered windows he felt ready to actually move. He started by pointing his toes, and feeling the stretch following the tension through his body. He gently rocked the base of his spine on the stone floor releasing a deep series of cracks as he felt the energy surge up his back, he followed it, swaying his body gently to ease its passage. A crack of the neck filled his mind with white light and he instinctively took a breath. He was back.

He knew from the breathing that the servant was not sleeping, but he stayed silent in the corner while Guy stretched and took deep breaths, waiting until he sat and arched his back to a chorus of little cracks.

'How are you feeling?' the servant asked.

'I can't believe how long I slept for.'

'You must have needed it.'

Guy rolled his neck agreeing. He sipped from a water skin savouring every refreshing drop as the servant told him how the old woman had only touched him when she put her hands on his eyes, then she held her hands over him before sitting for a long time with her hands on his feet. Guy kept asking questions, but the servant seemed confused by the whole process, as indeed was Guy. The old woman had not removed any of his clothes, and not touched him. That was different to before. 'She wants to see you before we go,' the servant added. Guy wanted to see her, he had not taken the chance to ask about the book.

When the old woman returned she was still very much in business mode. It reminded him of Della when she had been making his balms. He decided not to ask about the book immediately.

'How are you feeling?' she asked looking about his body.

'Better. Thank you.'

'You must take better care of yourself.'

'I am in training to be a knight,' Guy replied proudly. He had not meant to sound so proud, but until the other night he had genuinely felt that he was making progress. He might not be a knight yet, but it was only a matter of weeks, maybe less if he won the tournament. He stopped himself, it was no time for dreaming.

'Maybe so, but this training you do does not just damage your body. You must concentrate as much on healing yourself as you do on healing your body.'

Guy did not understand what the old woman meant, and did not have chance to consider it further as she cracked his back, his neck, shoulders and hips. She even cracked his toes. She lay him aback moving her hands over him.

'Good,' she said as her hand hovered over his belly. 'Can you feel it?' The question surprised Guy, and again he did not understand. He could feel her burning hands hovering above him, he could feel it in his little ball of energy. Suddenly it felt like there was a great void inside him. Not in a bad way, for the void was full of strength and power, yet was empty at the same time. The void showed the potential capacity of his power.

'I can.'

As he said the words he felt his ball expand. It did not gain power, but grew in size, spreading throughout him. He took a breath and arched his back before collapsing back as the wave subsided. He gave his neck a final crack and relaxed feeling a calm pleasure through him.

'You had a lot of heat in you yesterday. Tell me of the balm.' Guy found himself contentedly recounting the story of Della and her fire berry balm, not intentionally missing out the use of her water. 'Do you have it here? I would see it.'

'I don't,' Guy replied. 'It is not something I use often.' He was still aback, speaking in an almost dreamy voice. 'I do have another balm she makes. It is in my belt.' The old woman had the servant retrieve it, and Guy lay considering, that as the servant held his belt, he held in it all that was important to him. He watched through closed eyes as the woman sniffed at the potion as if she were a rabbit smelling the growth of spring.

'This is old world healing,' the old woman announced. Guy suddenly felt a pang of guilt for sharing Della's potion. He did not feel that she would approve, but he had come to feel that Della undervalued herself. Guy felt the opportunity had arisen. He watched as the old woman took a tiny amount and rubbed it into the back of her hand, sniffing that. 'This is very nice, good ingredients.'

'You can buy it in Varen,' he found himself announcing, not impressed with himself. 'She learned from a book.' he paused a moment. 'Healing practices of the old world. It is the book I am looking for, and was told that you might be able to help me.' The old woman laughed.

'Were you now? Perhaps I can help. I can tell you that there are probably less than two dozen copies in the whole of Rodina, and I can tell you that no one will ever sell you one.'

'Why not?' asked Guy without thinking.

'Because you are a man. Women are the healers, men have too much self-importance.' Guy tried to hide the offence he was taking, she had said it as a matter of fact, and she was old. She probably knew more of men than he ever would. He sought something constructive to say, but she spoke first. 'There is always a part of a man that thinks of himself first. Women are less selfish.'

'Except for when it comes to books.'

The old woman laughed before Guy could scold himself.

'Maybe so, But with good reason. Leave the healing to the women, especially the old ways.' Guy wanted to ask more of the book, but he could tell that as far as the old woman was concerned the conversation was over.

'Now bend you knees, I need to ground you.' Guy did as she bid and wanted to ask what she meant. 'You have been all over the place, obsessed with your own self-importance, your own quest. You need to look after yourself better.' She put her hands on his feet, 'I want you to imagine the roots of a strong tree are coming from your feet and reaching into the ground, becoming part of the world. Strong roots are what give a tree its strength.'

In his mind Guy tried to visualise roots spreading into the ground, but soon found that it had taken on a life of its own. The roots were spreading faster and in a more complex manner than Guy could visualise. He lost track of time as he sat, feeling connected with the earth, feeling unimportant, but gaining strength. His mind was not floating as it had been, it was back as a part of him.

When he opened his eyes a few moments later he was surprised to see the old woman standing in the corner of the room. He had not noticed her remove her hands.

'Forget about the book, and concentrate your efforts on whatever it is that you are doing in this world, and make sure you stay connected to it, and to yourself.' Guy just nodded. 'Now, since you decided to stay the night that is going to be two silvers.' Guy looked to the servant. He did not feel like moving just yet, and for the first time did not feel awkward about asking.

'Could you please give her three silvers from the coin purse on the front of the belt.' Without hesitation the servant swiftly opened the pouch, fished out three silver coins and closed the pouch before handing them over. Guy had noticed the way everything was in plain view, and all the movements were smooth but deliberate. The old woman took the coins. 'Thank you for your help,' Guy said with genuine appreciation. The old woman nodded putting the coins in a pocket in her apron.

'Look after yourself,' she said and left them to it.

It was another hour until Guy had got himself together enough to leave the room. His body was stiff and throbs of pain remained. His head only hurt where it had been punched which was the greatest relief to Guy, and well worth three silvers. His mind was not as swift as usual, but he was aware. The fresh air would do him good. The servant had remained silent, though Guy could see that there were questions that he wanted to ask. He was surprised the servant had not asked him, he had always tried to converse with him. Admittedly through asking lots of questions that he probably felt obliged to answer. Guy had thought of asking him to speak freely, but did not know enough about protocol to know if he would even be allowed to. There was much to a servant's life that he did not know. As the fresh air filled his lungs for the first time Guy realised that he did not even know the boy's name. He would rectify that before the day was over.

'Are you feeling well enough to see if your boots are ready?' the servant asked. *His boots.* He had all but forgotten about them.

'Yes, but let's get some food first, something fresh.'

As they approached the cobbler Guy was starting to feel better. He had thought to talk to the servant while they broke their fast, but he was content in silence. The truth was he did not feel like talking, his mind was busy processing. He looked at his running boots when the cobbler handed them over. It was good work. Not perhaps to the standard of the cobbler in Varen who had made them in the first place, but he had not had to work with this leather. The old man was talking about his work, but Guy was not engaging. He found it strange, usually he loved to hear craft people speak, but the servant was the one holding the conversation with polite interest. The old man wanted to return a silver saying that the work did not warrant the price, but Guy dismissed him saying that he would swap it for a bag to put his boots in as he set about removing his fighting boots and replacing them with his running ones. They were still the most comfortable things he had ever worn on his feet, but now their soles were strong. He hoped that the small rocks that he occasionally stood on while running would not hurt so much anymore.

The cobbler returned with a small hessian sack. It was nicely made with a long drawstring that was looped to the bottom of the bag so that it could be worn over a shoulder. Guy popped his boots in the sack and looked to the servant.

'I think I will run back. Would you mind taking my boots?' The servant nodded. Guy thanked him, and the old man, and wandered off leaving the servant and the cobbler.

Guy was aware that he had not been as polite as usual, but he had a sudden need for some solitude, the kind of solitude a long run brings. It took him a while to get past the aches and pains of the last few days, but soon he was moving and his heart was beating, and all he concentrated on was his breathing. He headed away from the castle to the city walls and out through a gate. He would run through the countryside to the woods and back in to the castle that way. He estimated that at a steady pace it would take well over an hour, but he was in no hurry, he felt that his mind needed to wander, and he wanted to get some life back into his body.

When he got back to the castle the servant had prepared him a bath, offered to shave him. Guy was old fashioned when it came to beards. Though he could grow a full one he would not until he was a knight. He turned down the offer of a haircut though. In Waering he had always kept it tidy, but since he had left it had grown out, and he liked having to tie it back for training. He was sure that, scruffy as it was, Phylissa would like it too.

After bathing Guy was returned to his room and left alone. He took the time to stretch and sort his kit. He was grateful to have bathed, he hoped that the hot waters would ease some of his bruises, and hopefully reduce the price he would have to pay for his run. It had been longer than he had anticipated, but had been more satisfying than he could have imagined. He felt ready again.

Guy was sat on the step reading his new book on tournaments. He was amazed at the number of events that there could be. He was used to seeing only the main three, archery, melee and the joust. He had once watched a weaponless event which had amazed him as knights fought with just their fists, but some of the events in the book opened his eyes once again to how little he knew of the world. The event that he was looking for was the drawbridge challenge in which the Knightmaker was to take part. These events were usually reserved for legendary weapons. The holder would have to defend the drawbridge against up to a dozen knights, one at a time. They were often held throughout the day and drew big crowds. For many people it was as close as they would ever get to a legendary blade. Guy was reading of an unfortunate knight who once managed to best the holder of the legendary greataxe, only to lose it two fights later to the dozenth knight of the day. How tragic it must have been to have held such a magnificent weapon for such a short time.

He saw the servant approach carrying a tray. Guy realised that he would not be dining with the Knightmaker. A momentary jolt of panic swept through him, he was still unsure of the events the last time they had been together, and he still carried the reminders. Even the old woman's best had not reduced the swelling of his eye which was turning purple. As he ate he asked the servant what he knew about tournaments, and explained the drawbridge challenge that awaited the Knightmaker. Guy was all too aware that the servant only spoke when asked a question. It did not sit well with him, and he stopped talking leaving an uncomfortable silence between them. Not that he could tell by looking upon the servant, he remained calm and placid on the outside, but inside Guy knew there must be something. He left the silence just a little longer.

'Can I ask you a question?' Guy finally asked, his tone serious, yet unthreatening.

'Of course,' the servant replied.

'Why do you never engage me in conversation?' The servant did not miss a beat.

'We talk.'

'No, you answer questions and pass on instruction. We do not talk. I don't know anything about you.' The servant did not look uncomfortable.

'I am a servant.'

'I know that. There must be more to you than that.'

'Not when I am in service. It is what being a servant is.'

'When you are not in service then.'

'I am always in service.'

Guy sighed. 'Can you explain to me then why as a servant you cannot engage me in conversation?' The boy took a breath.

'As a servant I do not own anything. All that I need to be a servant is provided for me, but nothing is mine, not even my thoughts. When I am in service I am a servant, nothing more.'

'What if I said that you had to?'

'There are rules to being a servant, just as there are rules to being a knight. These must remain unbroken if a man is continue being either.'

'You must at least have a name.'

'I do.' Guy could not help but smile.

'Well what is it?'

'John.'

'John.' Mission accomplished, next he would make him smile. He would show some of himself. 'Well John, it would serve me well for you to tell me what you know of tournaments. What you have seen, what you have heard. You must have seen some tournaments? What should I expect?' Guy gave an expectant smile, and while the servant stayed within his rules, Guy considered it a small victory, as they held the closest thing to a real conversation during their time together. The servant explained that the first time he had seen anyone killed was in a tournament, a drawbridge challenge for the legendary twin swords. The knight who wielded them killed the first three knights who approached, and no others dared take up the challenge.

By the time the servant left Guy had a better understanding of tournament etiquette, and the drawbridge challenge that faced Sir Parcifal. He could not help but be concerned. The Knightmaker had not been active for years, yet he was being forced into one of the most dangerous events. Death was a common feature of the drawbridge challenge. He would hate to see the Knightmaker go out like that. It was a long and thoughtful night for Guy, the seriousness of the situation, especially for the Knightmaker weighed heavily on his mind. While his body was relaxed, it took time for sleep to find his mind, it had perhaps done enough sleeping.

He awoke naturally and well rested. A brief admonishment at waking late was soon ignored as he stretched his body into life. After taking a drink of water he pulled on his running boots. He was going to do a short run to try and bring some life back into his heavy legs. He had overdone it yesterday, but had felt so good for it. If heavy legs was the greatest consequence, it was a price he was happy to pay. He ran towards the woods, but only to the castle wall and back. It had taken time to get his legs moving freely, so he continued for a while towards the main castle. He felt good again, and it was only when he picked up the pace and his arms were pumping more, that the weight of the Vambraces became noticeable. He tried to shrug his shoulders to relax them as he ran. He was just thinking about how ridiculous he must look when he was stopped in his tracks as the tournament fields came into view. It had developed so much over the last few days. Ornately carved panels, banners and colours had appeared. There was a mixture of tournament people jockeying for the best positions, and workers adding the finishing touches. Guy stood on the periphery stunned. It really was becoming a royal tournament, the tournament fields looked more like a small city. He wanted to continue and explore the gratuitous pomp of it all, but knew he should not. They might not know who he was, but they would recognise him later for sure. There were not many men of his size in Rodina. He waited, and watched the activity as his breathing settled, then he turned and walked back to the barracks collecting some food on the way. Whilst his mind was full of the tournament, some small part of him was concerned. He was to report to training without armour. *What could that mean?* He let his mind flip through numerous options, none of them particularly good. Uncertainty remained over the last training session. He remembered being drunk and fighting the Knightmaker, but had no recollection of how it began or ended. As the time drew closer his apprehension rose and a mixture of relief and dread filled him when John the servant came to collect him.

As they approached the courtyard the only thing Guy could hear was the pounding of his heart. He slacked his jaw a little to open his ears. His eyes were waiting to survey the situation as he entered the courtyard to see what fresh hells awaited him. Instead he saw the Knightmaker and the stranger both wearing half armour sitting at a table with food and drinks, wooden sticks beside them, it did not bode well.

'Guy! Come sit. Join us.'

The Knightmaker's voice was as intimidating as ever. The stranger looked up and nodded to Guy, it was good to see him, at least the stranger showed control when dishing out the beatings. As he approached the table he saw the Knightmaker's face showed signs of their last encounter. He had a swollen eye, a split lip and a cut above the other eye that was covered by an angry looking scab. For an instant his mind flashed to an image of the Knightmaker's bloodied face screaming at him, but with eyes full of the fire of life. 'Did you rest well?'

'I did,' Guy replied as he pulled out a chair. The servant had disappeared into the shadows giving the impression that they were alone. He knew they weren't.

'Recovered well?'

There was something different about the Knightmaker. Instead of the anger he was anticipating he was seeing a different side. Was the Knightmaker trying to be friendly?

'Eventually,' Guy replied as the Knightmaker let out a belly laugh.

'And what did you learn?'

'Not to drink so much wine.' The Knightmaker laughed again, the stranger smiled. The stranger probably knew more of that night than Guy did, and he wasn't even there. The Knightmaker looked on for a proper answer. 'That not all fights are on the battlefield.'

'You must always be ready. As a knight you never know when the next fight will be. There is always someone wanting to be the big shot. Any lasting damage?'

'I don't think so.'

'Good. Now the tournament starts in five days. You have your archery in seven, the melee the day after. Your training needs to change so that you are ready. Really you could do with another three weeks, but it is what it is. For the record, I would rather finish your training before I knight you, but if you do not win my knighting you will mean nothing. If you do win, you will be knighted anyway. As you know I compete myself, on the final day, so who knows, I may not be around to knight you anyway.'

The Knightmaker seemed not to find the prospect of death unsettling, but then as a seasoned warrior, death was probably something he was well acquainted with. It was the first time the Knightmaker had spoken of knighting him, and pride swelled within him. Despite the uncertainty of everything Guy felt like he was almost there. He would soon be a knight. If he ignored the king's stipulation about Guy needing to win, he would be a knight within a matter of weeks. 'So while your training gets easier, mine must increase. It may be that I have to face a dozen men in a day, so you will help me, and it will help you to watch.'

Guy nodded. If the Knightmaker told him to stand in front of him to protect him from a volley of arrows he would. He would hope to survive long enough to be knighted for his bravery. He would become a knight for Phylissa, or die trying. He poured from a jug and watched as the Knightmaker and stranger stood, collected their wooden sticks and headed to the courtyard. They swung at each other and tasted a few exchanges before the stranger went at him with purpose. Guy knew how good the stranger was at making it look unrestrained whist maintaining control. The Knightmaker answered with equal purpose, and the stranger's skill was even more apparent. The Knightmaker did not have the same control over the stick. He fought with power. Guy watched transfixed ignoring the cold chicken and breads as the two of them danced, their different styles evident. The stranger was able to parry most of the blows, but when his helm was rung, it was rung, and likewise when the Knightmaker's defence was not as it should be, the stranger rained blows on him. It was one of the most intense experiences of Guys life, the speed, power and precision on display amazed him. Their wooden sticks whipped through the air, both of them moved smoothly across the surface. It was clear from the dazzling display of skill that Guy still had a very long way to go, and while previously this may have caused him upset, he felt so privileged to see such a display, all it did was make him stronger. It was the greatest day of Guys life.

47

Guy's day continued to improve and he learnt more about footwork in two hours watching the Knightmaker and stranger dance than he had in his life. He took it in turns with the stranger to attempt to remove the Knightmaker from a path. Perhaps to aid his own training, the Knightmaker showed Guy how to spread his weight to keep a good balance, and told him where to place his feet to generate the most power. When he was not with the Knightmaker he was practicing what he had been shown.

In the evening after eating it was his turn to dance with the stranger. It was nowhere near as impressive as the display he had seen earlier, but Guy felt that it was heading in the right direction. The Knightmaker's comments seemed more precise, it was clear what he needed to do to improve. The stranger seemed to know exactly the pace to go to bring the best out of Guy, and not a day went by when the martial ability of the stranger did not astound him. He did not know whether it was the excitement of the tournament or his training, but Guy found himself full of a positive energy. Things were good, he was finally making progress. He managed to keep from his mind the stipulations. If he lost he was fucked, and so was Sir Parcifal. He found it obscene that the destiny of one of Rodina's finest warriors was intertwined with his own. It was not right, but the Knightmaker had never shown any resentment. Guy was happy to accept that he was not ready, he could not change what was. His acceptance bought with it an inner peace that did not stop his positivity becoming optimism. It had finally come down to this. He would win this tournament or die trying. He wondered how many of the other squires would enter with that mind-set, not all of them, that was for sure. As he celebrated his small victory the realisation of the stipulation dawned on him. If he did not win he really was fucked, he would have to start his journey again, and he did not have time for that. Phylissa did not have time for that. He set about his dance with more purpose which the stranger seamlessly matched. He had to win, there was no other option.

It was this thought that kept sleep from finding him. He did not understand his emotions. He had never been the kind of man who expected things to turn out for the better, they had not so far in his life. He reminded himself of when he won the tournament whilst only defending, and that he could hold his own with the stranger. His mind stopped to laugh. He had had the shit kicked out of him by the stranger so many times, the stranger was letting him feel like he could hold his own. *Was it possible that he could win?* The best squires in the entire kingdom would no doubt be of better skill than those he had beaten before. His mind started to rush, he should have seen them, to know how they fight, how big their heart is. As his pulse raced the Knightmaker's words calmed him a little, and for the first time made sense. He could study and observe, but would that make him more ready? As it was, none of them had seen him either, and he could use his size to add to the intimidation. He settled on ignoring the uncertainty and reminded himself of the words he swore to himself when he left Waering. He would become a knight or die trying. When sleep found him he was smiling.

He carried the sentiment with him as he skipped archery practice the following morning, instead he had the servant escort him to the leather worker. In all the excitement he had forgotten about the hide, and he was looking forward to seeing what the old man had done with it. He was disappointed to see that it was not finished, but he took the opportunity to learn from the half complete garment. It had been made so that he could dress himself. What looked like loose flaps of leather surrounded a reinforced head hole. It was heavy as he pulled it over his head, and it was not until it was sat on his shoulders that it began to take shape. A large section covered his abdomen that he could wrap over his ribs, securing it in place with other larger flaps of leather that came from the back. These would be laced together up his chest. It was rough and far from finished but Guy could see the potential. It would certainly be better than his crude attempts. He let the old man measure and scribble with chalk until he was satisfied. He moved however he was asked to. He had learnt from his time with Smith that this was invaluable for a personalised piece. It would be ready the next day. He drew his arms for the old man, and left feeling positive. He was learning again, there was a purpose to his being. There was something that he had to accomplish. There was nothing beyond the tournament, his focus was simply on being the best that he could be.

He approached the training with vigour and purpose. He felt renewed in his attitude, he was keen to learn now that his efforts were not taken up by simply surviving. It was feeding him, every clashed stick made him stronger. He wished for a moment that the leather worker had moved at a quicker pace as the Knightmaker's stick slammed into his ribs while he danced with the stranger. He thought that had he been wearing it, it would not have been such a shock when his multiple opponent training began in earnest.

For the rest of the day they trained, sometimes for the Knightmaker, but mostly for Guy. He was learning so much there were times when he felt that his eyes were not taking it all in. The Knightmaker went through movements with the stranger, pausing to show specific positions, a change of balance, that he incorporated into his next exchange. When they were not training they were talking. The Knightmaker acted differently towards him since their fight, and Guy no longer feared asking questions. He wanted to know everything but let the Knightmaker tell him what was important.

The following morning Guy was disappointed again when he went to collect his leather to find that ready tomorrow meant ready for fitting. He thought that had been done the day before. His disappointment did not last long. The old man had made him take a deep breath and then bound his chest and abdomen with thick bandages. When he pulled open a big vat the smell that escaped reminded Guy of a plant. A thick sweet smelling leaf that was good against infection and bites. He could picture the leaf and the plant in his mind, but he could not remember the name of it. He had been so absorbed in reading of battles and tournaments, he would have to read his book on plants again. The old man had fished out the leather with tongues and was allowing it to drip and cool.

'The sooner we get this on the better,' the old man said. Guy simply nodded, and when they pulled it over his head was grateful for every second of every minute that the old man had waited. The heat got him immediately, the drops soon cooled, but the leather itself kept the heat, and the bandages did not absorb much for very long. It was uncomfortable immediately, and he tried to accept the pain, but in his mind he pictured having to withdraw from the tournament with scolds. The old man was working fast though. 'Take a breath.' Guy filled his chest as much as he could with the heat pressing against it as the old man wrapped the folds around him. He was taking short shallow breaths, partly because of the heat, and partly to keep his chest full. The old man pulled and prodded before he started beating the leather, and Guy, with a short, thick, round piece of wood. The heat was such that he knew it was there, there was no escaping that, but he had passed beyond his concerns of being scolded. The smell of the leather and the herbs it had been steeped in gave him strength, every tap of the stick made him stronger as he stood like a rock while the old man worked.

Finally the leather was released and relief came. He was happy to see that once the bandages had been removed there was no sign of permanent damage, and he did not feel burned, just hot. The old man sent him away and told him that it would be ready in two days.

48

Two mornings later Guy leaned against a post waiting for the old man to arrive. He stared at his boots as his mind raced, replaying the Knightmaker's instructions from the night before. It was time they arrived for the tournament. He could feel his heartbeat throughout his body. He felt that he was ready physically, and hoped that his mind would not get overawed by the event. There was a lot to contend with, a lot of distractions. He suddenly felt the pressure of the stipulation imposed by the king, not just for his own selfish needs, but for the impact on the Knightmaker's life. The Knightmaker had described how he was to behave, how they would appear to others. 'The king likes his theatre. Let's play our roles and worry not about others.' Guy was too concerned about his own role to worry about others. The moment was finally upon him. *If he fucked it up now...* He wouldn't fuck it up. He had broken everything down into small pieces, he had each stage mapped out for himself. The first thing he had to do was collect his leather. He would worry about everything else when it came to be. He had to keep his mind focussed, and he found it easier to concentrate on what was in front of him.

Guy took a deep breath and rolled his shoulders, when the servant looked over Guy told him that it would not be long. He was telling himself more than the servant, he probably did not give a shit how long he had to wait. Guy had given up trying to make him engage, but still refused to treat him like a servant. He did not feel uncomfortable in his presence any more and realised how much easier his life had been thanks to him.

Half an hour later Guy was beginning to get restless, not through frustration, they had intentionally arrived early, more to stop his mind from wandering and considering things that were not yet important. He had wanted to be there when the old man arrived so that they could meet the Knightmaker earlier rather than later. He had arranged, and left his kit as instructed, and whilst he trusted that everything would be looked after, he had more in his daysack than usual, more skins on his belt, and much of the remaining roll of leather bundled on a cord over his shoulder. It had occurred to him when he left the old man last time that his instructions were not really being followed. Whilst he admired the workmanship, it was really too complex for his needs. What he wanted was what he had made himself, but with the beasts hide. He was sure that the work the old man had done would be fantastic, but all he wanted was something to throw on when he was training.

A terrible thought occurred to him. When he thought of training it was with the Knightmaker and the stranger. He thought of all the beatings he had taken and how the hide would have helped. Except he wouldn't be training with the Knightmaker any more. If he won the tournament he would be knighted, if he did not, Sir Parcifal would not be able to knight him anyway, and that was if he survived the drawbridge challenge. One way or another it was going to end.

It was at that moment when the old man arrived. It brought Guy relief, it meant he stopped thinking about things that were not yet important. First, collect the leather. That was all that mattered, and he could do that now.

'Good morning,' said the old man as he and his sons removed the shutters from the windows and made ready. Guy returned the greeting. 'Can I ask you, are you Guy of Waering?' The words snapped the rest of his wondering mind back into the moment. He could not hide his surprise at the question.

'Yes,' he replied. 'I am. How…' The old man looked to one of his sons.

'I told you,' He interrupted. 'I knew this was the leather of the Dun cow.' He turned to Guy, 'We hear of things all the way out here as well you know. People are talking about the Dun cow. Ha.' The old man did not try to hide his happiness. 'I had my suspicions before, but when I started polishing it I knew for sure. I have never seen a colour like it.' The old man chuckled to himself, 'And to think I thought of staining it with the beasts own blood.' He laughed some more. 'It's a good job we didn't have any.' The old man ducked into the tannery and emerged moment later with two squares of leather. One was raw and natural, the other had been polished into a wonderful grey brown colour that remained dull despite the polish, but someway vibrant. The old man smiled as he showed Guy, and Guy could not help but smile back. He was certainly enthusiastic about his work. 'It is almost ready.' He said flexing the polished piece. 'It will do.'

He pulled out a small hammer and nailed the two bits of leather to a post, one above the other and nodded to his son, who bought over a bow and a small quiver.

'Fire at the natural one first.' Guy took the bow confused and uncertain. 'Fire at it,' the old man repeated. Guy notched an arrow and carefully drew the bow back. The vambraces still made archery impossible to train, but he was only a dozen paces away, he hoped that he would hit it. He did and breathed a relieved sigh. The old man was rushing to the post. 'Come and see.' Guy lowered the bow and walked over to where the old man was pulling the arrow from the post. 'Look, less than quarter of an inch made it through the leather. It is incredible. Now fire at the polished one.'

The old man retreated, beckoning Guy with his hands. It took all of his effort again to hit the target, and while the arrow stuck it was loose. Perhaps he somehow tweaked the shot on release. 'Come see,' called the old man.

When Guy got there he could see that the arrow had somehow held on to the smallest penetration of the leather and it virtually fell into the old man's hands as he removed it and inspected the leather.

'Almost ready,' he repeated to himself. Guy was impressed and his face showed it. Perhaps his shot had not been so bad after all. The old man nodded to his sons who bought over a burlap bundle, both smiling with pride. Suddenly Guy felt bad. Perhaps he would not ask the old man to make him something more crude and rustic. He clearly knew what he was doing. At the old man's direction they removed the burlap and Guy saw his leather for the first time. He realised that he had actually gasped. This simply fed the old man's excitement further. 'Put it on.'

Guy let the old man's sons help pull it over his head. They had certainly improved that, it slipped easily over his shoulders with ornate reinforcements screaming quality at him. He lifted his arms as they secured it, and looked down. He found it hard to look past the colour, it was truly the most incredible colour he had seen. A matt grey, brown that someway had a shine. His chest was reinforced with a double layer of leather while there appeared to be muscles carved or moulded into the abdomen. The old man had even engraved his arms onto the left shoulder. He was very proud of his work.

'This is not what I asked for, and not what I paid for.' Guy's words bought immediate discomfort and a look of confusion between the sons. 'This is worth far more than the three silvers I paid. The old man nodded to his sons who ducked into the Tannery returning moments later with more leather.

'This is what you asked for,' he waved his hand dismissively 'and you paid too much for that.' He looked to Guy. That and the bracers, and in truth you would still have paid too much. Sometimes you have to let the leather speak to you, sometimes you should listen. This is what it told me.' Guy searched his body with his mind, counting up the gold coins he had left, and his silvers. He had eight gold coins left, and in his mind he decided seven was a good number.

'It is worth more than I paid.'

'Aye, maybe so, but this is the leather of the Dun cow. This alone will bring me more business.' Guy smiled. 'If you feel the need, give my boys a silver, they did all the physical work, but it is yours to take. If anyone likes it, send them my way.' Guy nodded and fished in a coinpurse for two silver coins happily handing them over to the two men. Guy had a secret smile to himself. These men were probably close to twice his age, but still were only the old man's sons. He congratulated them on their work as their beaming faces took the coins hungrily.

'You are attending the tournament, yes?' the old man asked. Guy nodded. 'You should wear it tonight, it would look good with green, tell them where you got it.' Guy smiled at the old man.

'I might just do that.'

The old man spotted the roll of leather on Guys back, and they talked about it. Guy had a couple of requests, and listened to the old man's suggestions, leaving it in his hands as his sons packaged up his prepared leather. Guy flung one bundle over his shoulder as the servant did the same. He clasped hands with the old man, leaving a gold coin in his palm.

He had collected his leather. Number two, meet the Knightmaker. He looked to the sky. It was still well before noon, they should arrive in good time. He did not want to leave them in a tavern for too long. It was a temptation that they may not fight, and from the sounds of it they would all need to focus.

An hour later as they passed through the city gates on their way to the *Last Stop Tavern*, Guy was hot and tired. The iron vambraces made the sack full of leather seem heavy, and Guy chastised himself for not asking the servant if there was another way they could have made the journey, an easier one. He did not want to get sweaty as he would not have the chance to bathe before the opening banquet.

It was only a little past noon when they arrived, as Guy pushed open the door he heard loud laughter and the words.

'I haven't had a solid shit for over a month.' The laughter boomed again, the unmistakable sound of the Knightmaker wanting to be noticed. All sound stopped as the door opened.

'Squire!' he boomed. 'Glad you could make it.'

The other person turned around. It was Hawkins. A flood of mixed emotions ran through him. He found himself happy to see that he was still alive, yet unhappy that he was there. They exchanged a curt nod as Guy sat and the servant disappeared into the shadows. There was wine on the table. Not a good sign. The Knightmaker called for a chicken each, some breads, and an ale for his squire. They ate as Sir Parcifal caught up with Hawkins. Despite the bravado that he was putting on Guy could see that the Knightmaker was happy to see Hawkins. Guy sat quietly as a squire should and considered how Hawkins' arrival would change the way things were going to be. Their loud conversation continued and they called for more wine. Guy was no longer concerned, he had seen the Knightmaker pour most of his into a skin on his belt. It was a pretence, it was the role the Knightmaker had chosen to play. Guy thought that he should get into character too. His chest felt tight, from nerves, from anticipation, from fear. He did not know which of them it was, but none of them were good. He took a breath and found his ball of energy, he visualised roots from his feet, and he searched for calm.

Step two was complete, he had met up with the Knightmaker. Step three, get ready to arrive. He would rather have been getting ready than be sat in an inn, but the Knightmaker seemed to be in no rush. He could get ready in his mind. He had been told to ignore everyone on the way. They would travel in silence, and with purpose, to the castle. He would make it appear as if his eyes were fixed on the Knightmaker, but instead his vision would be focussed beyond, on the lookout for any kind of threat. The Knightmaker had told him that there would have been many a fancy arrival with fanfares and waving knights and Lords. This was the king's tournament, it was in everyone's interest to be noticed. They were not going to do any of that, but the Knightmaker wanted it to be their arrival that people remembered. The Knightmaker explained the king's love of theatre and occasion. In times of peace, tournaments were the only way for warriors to make a name for themselves, and if people talked enough of these events, they would not be plotting, and hence not fighting. The king believed that tournaments could be used to settle disputes, and thus avoid conflict. He also saw it as a way of providing heroic moments for normal people to remember. Tournaments were a way of keeping the peace throughout the kingdom. The Knightmaker had spoken plenty of tournaments over the last few days, not just of the mechanics and the bouts, but the reasons behind them and their importance to Rodina.

49

'He's here,' said Hawkins in a voice just for them. The Knightmaker sank the remains of his goblet and declared in his booming voice that he had a tournament to attend. He tossed a silver on the table as he stood to leave. Guy gathered his leather and followed him out of the inn. When his eyes had adjusted to the light he saw the servant loading up his bundle of leather onto a cart that the stranger was driving. Charger was pulling it, and it looked like it contained a lot of kit. He walked over and rubbed his horse's nose to say hello. Guy felt an unfamiliar happiness at seeing Charger and he realised that he had missed him, missed him on an emotional level that surprised him.

Step three, get ready. He put his bundle on the cart and followed as it set off. The other three rode on the cart, he walked behind. Charger only had two paces that he could comfortably travel at, and he was not going eyeballs out, so it was a pace Guy could easily keep.

After a few minutes they pulled off the road and settled next to a stream.

'Right, let's get ready,' the Knightmaker called. The stranger wore his cloak, Hawkins looked fine enough in his travelling clothes, the servant had disappeared, no doubt halfway back to the castle already. 'You can take the vambraces off now. You can keep them though, a gift,' the Knightmaker laughed to himself.

As the Stranger and Hawkins set about dressing the Knightmaker in half armour Guy fished around in the cart for his own kit and outfit. It felt good not to wear the iron on his arms any more. He wrapped them in his dirty shirt and packed them away. He listened to the old man's advice and pulled out a good forest green shirt from his bag, and he took a pair of muted farmers trousers that were clean. He had even cleaned up his fighting boots before leaving. He stripped quickly to his small clothes and gave himself a quick wash in the stream, enjoying the freedom of his arms. He rubbed fragrant leaves on himself afterwards. He was to attend the opening banquet of the king's own tournament. He did not want to be remembered because he stank.

By the time he returned to the cart the other three were ready. The Knightmaker took a moment to look at him and examine the leather, before grunting in approval. Guy quickly sorted his kit before the Knightmaker gave his instructions for the journey. 'From now on I walk. Guy, you will walk behind me, you two on the cart behind. We ignore everyone, understood? We do not even look at anyone.' They nodded, he continued. 'We don't have time to fuck about. We are late for the banquet, but we do not hurry. When we get to the castle we head to our tent as if we have lived there this past year. These fuckers are in our home and do not deserve our recognition. Clear?' They all nodded again.

They set off, Guy fell in behind the Knightmaker, two steps behind, one to the left. Charger plodded behind. They did not walk fast, but they walked with purpose, ushered straight through the city gates by guards who clearly knew who they were, Sir Parcifal at least. By now the city had seen the arrival of many knights, and was used to moving aside. They did not have to break their stride once as they approached the castle, even in the busiest areas of the city. People just stood aside and looked on, mostly as silent as those that passed through. Guy felt it strange to be a part of such a thing, but he remained focused, he maintained his purpose and his role. He imagined how they must look striding through the city as if they owned it. Both of their faces still showed the result of their fight the other night. Guy tried to make himself as tall and imposing as he could, to add his part to the theatre. He was happy that he had kept it together. Not once did he directly meet another's eye.

As they approached the castle gates it was as if the guards had been made aware of the Knightmaker's intent, for as they stepped out to stop them, on seeing it was Sir Parcifal, they stood aside as they passed. For the briefest moment Guy lost concentration, as he wondered whether the Knightmaker had spoken to the guards beforehand.

'Sir Parcifal,' they said as they passed, almost with a bow. The Knightmaker was certainly saying *fuck the ceremony*, and Guy thought he might have been right. Perhaps theirs would be the arrival that was remembered. As they got closer to the castle the heavy throng of people fell quiet as they passed, and held murmured conversations once they had. Guy was glad to be in the castle, though it was barely quieter than the city. The tournament build up was in full swing and he could feel the anticipation. Men sparred for bets, minstrels wondered around singing tales of heroic deeds, there were people everywhere. The only one who did not stop to look at them was a woman chasing a chicken, her attention was required elsewhere. They strode with purpose past the tournament arena and through to the knight's quarters. Guy was much more aware of eyes on them inside the castle. There was more intent in the stares, it made him more alert.

When they approached the knight's quarters the guards again stepped aside so that they did not have to break stride. Their pavilion tent was first on the left and only about thirty feet away, but by time they got there, Guy had stepped ahead of the Knightmaker and pulled the flaps aside letting the Knightmaker stroll past his shield and straight into the tent. Guy slipped in behind him and, as discussed, Hawkins and the stranger unloaded the cart and prepared camp.

'Now that is how to make an entrance,' the Knightmaker congratulated himself. 'None of this fannying around with feathers and ponces. Even if we do not leave this tent, within the hour everyone will know we are here.'

As Guy and the Knightmaker shared a skin of his fruited water he could see that the stranger was doing most of the heavy work unloading the cart. Guy was glad in a way because he knew that his things would be handled carefully. Hawkins would see fit to drop or scuff his armour just to piss him off. Hawkins was obviously not yet back to full health. The Knightmaker talked quietly about how they would act at the banquet, and most importantly, whatever resentment he held towards the king must be put aside. He should treat him with respect, even if he sliced his balls off. Guy did not feel resentment towards the king. He was the king. He resented the situation, but not the man. He hoped he never had to find out whether this would be the case if his balls were in the king's hand, or more likely the hand of the poor fucker he had commanded to do it. He was told that in public the king must be addressed with the required etiquette. Guy had resolved to follow the Knightmaker's lead, and be as respectful as he could.

His heart was pounding in his chest again. The rest had allowed him to calm, but now that they were about to leave it flooded him with anticipation, fear, and excitement. He took a deep breath.

'I would keep your leather on,' the Knightmaker proclaimed. 'It might be hot in there, but it fits you well.' Guy nodded, he had not thought of getting changed, neither seemingly had the Knightmaker, for he was still in half armour when he stood. 'Hawkins, make your way to the stalls.' He flicked his head to the stranger, 'You stay here. Where there are knights there are thieves.' He nodded to the stranger and turned to Guy. 'Let's go. We walk, same as before.'

Guy stood, and took some breaths as he readied himself. He could feel Hawkins watching, probably laughing, but he did not notice that, it was not important. 'Ready?' Guy nodded. 'We go now.'

Guy pulled the flap aside allowing the Knightmaker to pass, quickly falling in behind him. It was quiet, a few squires and servants made busy, but the rest were at the banquet already. He could see people rushing to enter the castle further ahead, but they did not rush. They walked with purpose as dusk settled over the castle.

They were ushered through the main castle gates, but the Knightmaker knew where he was going and soon enough the servants and porters stopped trying to hurry them along and it was Sir Parcifal himself that opened the doors to the banquet hall without announcement as the king was addressing those present. Every head turned to face them.

'Sir Parcifal,' the king called with authority.

'Apologies, Your Grace, unexpected delays.'

Sir Parcifal's voice matched the king's in authority and respect. Guy Stood stoically as instructed, his mind was considering the Knightmaker's voice. He remembered the extent to which even being greeted by the man had intimidated him in the early days. That was just the Knightmaker though, he always spoke like that. He knew it, the king knew it, but he wondered how many others in the room would know it.

'You are just in time. Come, take your seats.' The king clapped his hands. 'I was just telling the good people of Rodina of a monstrous cow recently slayed in my woods. I fear many feel I exaggerate its size when I told them that a single flank would feed everyone here.'

As Guy made his way to his seat, which corresponded with their tent location on the main table, which ran from directly opposite the king's seat, he saw six servants struggling with a mighty platter, upon which was the pit roasted rear flank of the Dun Cow. It was the biggest piece of meat he had ever seen. They had left the relatively meat free cloven hoof on, and it achieved its purpose of adding to the wonder of it. People began to gasp when they saw the size of it. 'But as you can see...' the king added, 'there was no exaggeration.' The crowd muttered their amazement as the platter was set on a platform in front of the king's table. Only feet away, Guy marvelled at the smell. Seeing the flank showed just how much he had under estimated the size of the beast in his mind. The flank was easily longer than he was tall and the thigh was thicker than a two hundred year oak. He felt his chest tighten at the memory, but he quickly fought it, he had instructions to follow.

The king walked to the unfathomable joint of meat, was presented with a greatsword, which he took and held up for the crowd to see.

'I declare this tournament open,' he declared as he smoothly sliced the first chunk of meat. The crowd erupted in cheers. Sir Parcifal did not, and neither did Guy. He was not allowed. It was not difficult for him, he watched, hiding his awe, as the king brandished the legendary greatsword, the greatest sword in the whole of Rodina. If he reached past the Knightmaker he could touch it. It was simply magnificent. There were not many who could say that they had been that close to the legendary greatsword of Rodina. For a moment he envied the servants holding the velvet cushions upon which the sword was placed after being cleaned, for they got to carry it. Guy found himself making him the ridiculous promise that one day he would know what it felt like to hold it. His mind laughed at itself as a plate of meat was presented to him. It was from the slice cut by the king, the servants were only just getting the hang of carving such a hunk of meat. He had been served by the king at a banquet. He did not allow his mind to enjoy that moment, or any other.

The meal had passed successfully, he had not spoken to anyone, nor made eye contact with anyone other than the king. It was easier for him as he was simply a squire. If it was difficult for the Knightmaker, he did not show it, he went about eating his meal and drinking his wine as if he were alone. Whilst one of the closest knights to the royal table, he was in truth too far away to be involved in any conversation, but Guy noticed the king look at him several times, and it was always with a look of utter respect. He was getting better at seeing things without looking, and while there were no weapons present, other than those of the chevroned knights, he still found himself alert for potential threats. There had been some hard looks coming the Knightmaker's way, and not just from those displeased with his etiquette. There were some dangerous looking men around the table, and none seemed happy to see Sir Parcifal. He wouldn't care though, Guy thought to himself, he would consider it a compliment. He didn't seem to give a fuck what anyone thought of him. '*Then why the charade with the entrance?*' his mind asked. He did not let it search for an answer, he had to focus. He had to get through the night.

As the meal settled, and for some the wine and ale flowed, the king gave a rousing speech about the tournament and by the end had people, including many on his table hooting and hollering after each sentence. He did speak well though, had Guy not been under instruction he would have been hooting with the rest of them. It was his first real tournament, the king's words sang a truth and idealism that roused him. Keeping the words inside made him stronger, where most of the others were releasing it. It was that kind of superior feeling that the Knightmaker wanted him to display. For the briefest of moments it was not an act and it filled him with a feeling he was unfamiliar with. Pride, he thought.

50

The king raised his hand and silence fell almost immediately.

'This beast that we have eaten did not come without sacrifice.' He declared. 'Let us remember the men and women killed by the beast as they tried to defend their land.' There was a moment of silence. 'As a man, as your king, I am thankful on a personal level, for I was there when the beast was slayed. I am only here today thanks to the bravery of three men.' For a moment panic rose, the king was talking about him. 'Sir Gliddeon, please approach.'

The chevroned knight who had initially taken on the beast appeared from behind the king pushed in a wheeled chair towards the table. Though he wore full armour he did not hold himself well, and the chair told Guy that he could not walk. The cow had damaged him. A servant stepped forward with a jewelled golden dagger on a red velvet cushion. 'To thank you for your service and your sacrifice,' the king announced.

The knight almost seemed reluctant to take the dagger, it seemed to Guy that this was a retirement gift combined with a reward. He felt sympathy for the knight, his condition did not look to be good. He found himself hoping that he would recover.

'Sir Parcifal,' the king continued as Sir Gliddeon was wheeled away. For a moment Guy sensed a hint of uncertainty, but the Knightmaker stood and made the short distance to the king. 'Sir Parcifal, though you have not been in service for many years, when it went down, your first instinct was to protect me.' Guy watched the king and Sir Parcifal share a look. The king nodded his thanks. 'For this I offer my thanks. The king reached out his hand and Sir Parcifal clasped it. To anyone watching it was a simple handshake, but Guy was sure that he had seen something passed between them. The Knightmaker bowed and returned to his seat appearing unflustered.

'Master Guy,' the king called. His eyes flicked from the king's to the Knightmaker's whose indistinguishable nod saw him rising. 'For your heroism for taking on the beast that had just injured a king's own knight…' Guys mind raced, could he be knighted before the tournament? His heart was pounding in anticipation, he just hoped that he was keeping it together on the outside, inside he wasn't. 'For slaying the beast I present you with this.' He waved his hand to his side and saw two servants carrying a big iron cauldron. 'The porridge pot of Rodina.' Guy was not to be knighted, but smiled his thanks to the king. The king smiled back and nodded. Guy looked to the pot, it was an incredible gift. He would never again forget that he once cooked oats for the king. The king's theatrical nature had not been restrained, it was a hefty porridge pot that looked as if it would provide oats for a small army. Guy returned to his seat, hoping that he had control of his face. He was surprised and happy, but that had not been part of Sir Parcifal's plan. When the king withdrew Guy became more conscious of those looking at Sir Parcifal, and indeed those who were now looking at him. He was relieved when a steward approached and took them to the king.

'I could have knighted you for your deeds,' the king began, 'you would certainly have deserved it, but it had already been decided that you must win the tournament for Sir Parcifal here. I cannot interfere in justice.' The king shared a look with them both as Guy's mind tried to take in what he had just said. Being knighted by the king for saving his life, that would be far better than returning in white. 'It is something you must fight for,' the king continued. 'I trust you like your pot.'

'I do Your Grace,' Guy offered sincerely. It was a gift that had been considered, and while it may not be worth much in terms of coin, it would always remind him of his time with the king.

'I shall have it sent to Waering. Is there a message you would like to send with it?' Guy thought but for a second.

'No Your Grace, the pot itself will suffice. Thank you.'

He would not contact Phylissa again until he returned a knight. The king nodded and turned to the Knightmaker.

'Sir Parcifal, I apologise to you. I concluded things that are not true. You are a man of honour, and I have watched your training with Master Guy, it reaffirmed something that has occupied my mind for some time. We will talk when you have defended the bridge, but whether you win or lose I want you to train men for me, to defend me.'

'You have your king's own knights, Your Grace.'

'I do, and will continue to do so, but there may be a time when I am driven out and someone else calls themselves the king. Who would those knights defend then?' Sir Parcifal just looked at him, he knew the answer. They served the throne, not the man, the turquoise knights were the same. 'If that happens, who defends me, and what is right then, or if I am dead, my son, the rightful king? I want you to train men to defend the kingdom, not the king.'

'What about the Lords of the South, are they not your men?' Sir Parcifal asked.

'Aye, in theory they are, but would they leave the south to get my throne back?' The king did not expect an answer, the southerners were known for holding their own lands, not fighting the battles of others. 'I want a dozen teams of four that can also work together. I want exceptional warriors who do not know when to give up, like young Guy here. I want the best. I shall give you lands by the skywall, I shall give you gold. Do you have what I gave you?'

Sir Parcifal pulled something from a pocket. Guy knew that the king had given him something. The affirmation made him stronger. It was a seal, it looked to be blank.

'It is all down to you, from the seal to the men, to how you train them. There is no place for ceremony, I shall need warriors, and highly skilled ones at that. Think on it Sir Parcifal, you said yourself that the world has gone soft.'

The king returned to the banquet hall leaving the two of them with a handful of servants. The Knightmaker nodded his head away from the hall and they made their way back to camp in silence. They both had things to consider.

They passed the stranger and entered the tent. Guy had resolved not to talk first and was soon regretting it. There were so many things that he wanted answers to. The Knightmaker seemed to be able to apply more thought to his concerns, and was not up for speaking yet, though he did not let it look like anything had happened. Guy knew that his mask had slipped as soon as they had entered the tent.

The Knightmaker had still not spoken when Hawkins returned.

'Well that's fucked that,' he announced as he sat down. 'I was close to getting four for one on him to win when the king did his little award show. What the fuck?'

'I didn't know,' answered Sir Parcifal, giving no indication that he was concerned with other things. Concerned as he was with his own affairs, Guy was able to recognise the Knightmaker's composure, and figured that was why he was a good leader.

'There is normally not a lot of action on the squires, but there are two, possibly three that have a good shot of winning it.' He turned to Guy, 'You're not one of them,' he spat before he continued to the Knightmaker 'As soon as he got his pot, no one was interested.'

'Give it a day and I'm sure you'll be able to get three for one.' Guy looked on bemused. He did not have a clue what they were talking about. The Knightmaker turned to Guy. 'Do you still have the two gold I gave you from your help in the woods?' Guy found himself nodding. 'You did not spend it all on your fancy leather?' Guy tentatively shook his head. 'Good. Give it to Hawkins.' Hawkins looked flustered and was about to protest. 'He's one of us now.'

Silence fell. Guy still did not know what they were talking about, but that did not matter. The Knightmaker had said that he was one of them and it had knocked the stuffing out of him. In that moment, it meant more to him than his quest to become a knight, he had finally been accepted. The Knightmaker looked to Guy who fiddled through his pouches, then slid the heel from his boot to remove two mud encrusted gold. He looked at them for a moment in his hand before holding them out to Hawkins, who showed slight hesitation in taking them. Their eyes met briefly, but Guy barely knew what *he* was thinking, let alone Hawkins.

'As much as coin can be won by a knight via ransoms and prizes, there is more that can be won through betting. There is much pride on the tournament fields and often people will bet on the outcome of bouts. An observant man can make good coin.' During the next hour

Guy was reminded that he was still very much new to the world as he learnt about another side of tournament life. Sure, he had heard about gambling before, but dismissed it. It was a shady part of life. He never considered for a moment that it could provide coin for a tournament knight to get through the winter. He had always assumed that they went into the service of an earl or lord somewhere. He had found his mind showing him pictures of the Man of Cups, but they would have to wait for later, he was too busy trying to learn all he could. It was the first time he had seen Hawkins animated in his speech, it was the first time Hawkins had spoken to him without treating him like a pat he had just stepped in. If Guy had known it would only take two gold, he would have paid that price months ago.

Hawkins and the Knightmaker talked of making two gold into eight, or maybe twelve, throughout the tournament. It would be easier at the king's tournament as there was more money about. At some tournaments Hawkins would have to spread the coin far and wide in silvers and sometimes even coppers. There though, gold was king. Guy finally came to realise the role Hawkins played in the group, the gambler, the purveyor. Yes, he could look after himself, from the sounds of things a gambler needed to occasionally. It turned out that people did not like losing, and some more so than others.

During a pause in their recounting of stories the Knightmaker told Hawkins to swap with the stranger and take first stag. Where there are knights there are thieves. Guy settled on his rollmat and hoped that sleep would find him soon enough. As he lay down he realised that they had not done any training whatsoever that day. He had really wanted to, his arms felt so free after taking off the vambraces, he had looked forward to dancing with the stranger. He put it to one side, he could not change that. His mind instead thought back through the process. There was a lull after stage five, attending the banquet. He imagined that after the evening's events, whatever the next stages were going to be, that there might be some changes. What a day it had been. The excitement kept his mind awake far into the night, though there was no mischief to be found. The porridge pot that the king had given him would soon be making its way to Waering, and with it the story of how it came to

346

be. That in itself would be enough for Phylissa's hand he was sure. But she wanted him to return in white, and that is what he would do. Not for Phylissa, or Smith, or Little Ash, or even himself. He would return in white for love.

51

Guy awoke to what sounded like Hawkins receiving instruction from the Knightmaker. Their voices were muted, and Guy suspected that it was not just because he was sleeping. Hawkins had slipped through the flap in the tent before Guy sat up and stretched.

'He has gone to survey the damage,' the Knightmaker offered.

'How is he? You know the wound…' Guy gestured to his torso.

'He's still not right, tender, but better than he would have been without you.' Guy felt himself flush, but felt pride at the same time. 'Let us break our fast and await his return.'

Guy left the tent, passing the stranger who looked as if he was sleeping on a chair with his feet resting on a table. Guy nodded and headed through to the tournament area. The food that he collected was finer than he would have expected. The pork was fried in front of him, the eggs were fresh and the bread soft but crusty. He could just about feel the heat of the oven still in it, and found his mouth watering at the prospect. He gathered fresh fruit, honey and milk. A servant was needed to carry the hot food. The stranger swung his legs from the table as the servant placed the plates. They looked to have been made for the tournament alone. Guy thought to keep one for his house as he arranged the breads and fruit before finally placing a jug of milk he had hooked his finger around on the table. It had soon got heavy and his hand had cramped several times on the short journey. He had not spilt a drop though, and it had made him stronger. The smell of the fried pork bought the Knightmaker out of the tent and they all sat at the table eating and watching people pass them by. Some glanced their way, some tried to stare, but they ignored them all chatting shit between them. Well, Guy and the Knightmaker at least. It was all a show, the first act of the day. Guy was pleased to retreat into the pavilion after eating. He fished out a piece of leather and his knife. He wanted to keep himself busy while the Knightmaker started honking at those who passed.

Guy looked at the leather belt as he heard muted voices from outside, there was more that he wanted to do to it, but it was a start, and it would do what was required of it for now. He could always work on it later. It was then that the Knightmaker and Hawkins entered the tent, both taking a seat on a cot.

'The king's generosity has done us no favours,' Hawkins announced. It was still strange for Guy not to be sneered at by him. It still was not easy between them, but it was definitely different. 'People are cautious of you now. But we have a plan.'

'Most of the knights are out on the training fields now,' the Knightmaker continued. 'We will go and join them.' The Knightmaker paused for a moment. 'You will train with Hawkins.' He left the words hanging in the air for a moment, as if Guy was to fill in the meaning himself. 'You are to let Hawkins get the better of you. You are to show only half of your ability, and let Hawkins here reassure the onlookers that you have your flaws. You can offer attacks when he lets you, but go easy, no matter how bad he makes you look.' The Knightmaker's eyes bored into him. He meant that. Guy took a breath and nodded. The Knightmaker turned to Hawkins, 'The same goes for you, strike the body only.' Hawkins nodded, was there some reticence for his previous elbow injury? Probably just Guy dreaming again, but he liked to see the good in people.

'I have made this for you,' he said to Hawkins, 'to protect your…' he motioned with his head to Hawkins wound, 'just in case.' Hawkins took it and nodded. There was not a smile, but maybe a hint of respect.

'I would get yours if I were you. You are going to need it.'

As awkward and humiliating as the noon training session was, Guy was happy that he had played his part. Hawkins certainly had. He had made him look a fool many times, and Guy had made it appear to affect him more than it did. He could see the pain in Hawkins eyes as he attacked him, he was not as fast as he used to be, but he gave it his all.

The Knightmaker chastised him from time to time as he feigned pain from the blows. Hawkins though was true to his word and all the landed blows were to his body, the thick hide of the beast beneath his shirt absorbed most of the impct. All they really did was remind him of the bruises he wore beneath his leather. He was impressed with the leather, he liked it even more than the fancy piece he had. It was simple, yet effective, and he could move freely. Or at least he could if he had been allowed. The training hurt his pride more than his body, and he soon became aware of glances and laughter from those around. He was happy when the Knightmaker called halt, not so happy when he called him pathetic. He took his time to rise to his feet, favouring his ribs and breathing hard. He staggered behind Hawkins and the Knightmaker back to the tent.

'That will have done it,' announced Hawkins as the flap closed behind Guy. 'At the very least your own opponents will not consider you a threat. We might make some money on you yet.' Guy nodded and smiled, though he felt that he was not hiding the fact that he had not enjoyed it. Fuck it, he didn't want to hide it. He could see the reasons behind it, but he had felt like a braying ass out there.

As upset as he was with the noon training the early evening session was the opposite. He had danced with the stranger in the privacy of their usual courtyard. It was the first time in weeks that he could swing a stick without the vambraces, and the stranger let him go as fast as he wanted. As incredible as it had been to clash with the Knightmaker, dancing like he was with the stranger was the greatest feeling he could imagine. They danced for less than an hour before the Knightmaker called halt and gave him instructions for the following day, but more importantly, explained why. They returned via a tournament tavern within the castle walls where the Knightmaker put on a show of his own. Pretending to have supped more than he had, he issued challenges for knights to face him. But if he were fighting for his shield, they too would be fighting for something. To one knight he demanded that if he faced him and lost, he would win a night with his new bride, to others their armour and horse. He acted like an angry, drunk, has been. Guy could see without the Knightmaker saying that this would spread throughout the camp, and while some would be riled by his actions, others would take heed. They would not step up to challenge him with so much at stake.

The Knightmaker seemed to know exactly what to say to get the response he wanted and the whole show was as much about deterring people from facing him, as it was making some coin. He was glad Hawkins was not with them, for he did not quite have the same skill, and would probably upset someone a little too much. Guy was relieved when they left noisily as the Knightmaker wobbled on his feet. Guy was concerned that they would be met outside by someone looking to take advantage of the Knightmaker's drunkenness, but their journey back to the pavilion passed without event. Guy was happy to see that food had been collected while they had been out, and he enjoyed his meal as Hawkins informed the Knightmaker of the success of their plan. Guy tried to listen in, but he was hungry, and still had his dance with the stranger on his mind.

52

There was no public humiliation the following day, he was to simply hang around and take in the tournament. He was told not to speak to people, not to be noticed. That was easier said than done for someone of Guy's size. He was leaning on a fence looking out over the training ground when Hawkins approached.

'It is the first round of the melee today, I thought you would be watching.'

'I will later.' Hawkins looked out over the training field with him. It was full of activity, knights sparred for coin, others trained, and others still, learnt. These were the ones Guy found himself looking at.

'You start soon. Do you feel ready?' he continued, Guy sighed.

'I don't know. I have not practiced archery much recently.'

'That may be for the best. A poor performance in the archery would put you out of people's minds. Do you understand what I am saying?'

'Not really.'

'If you are not in people's minds, they will not be betting on you, they will be betting on other people. That means we can make more coin.' Guy simply nodded, this was more important than coin. He could not afford to fuck about, he needed every advantage he could get. He had to win the tournament. 'Imagine for instance if you were to enter the melee first. People would think that you had no chance. No one wins from going in first, especially among the squires.' Guy simply looked out over the training field and let the words hang in the air, he hoped awkwardly, but that was probably only for him.

Hawkins began telling him about some of the other squires who were out in the field, and some who were not. There were two big favourites, and one more who could possibly win. After the previous days show, Guy was no longer considered a threat for the spurs. Hawkins told him of their successes, their masters and anything else he could think of.

'How come you know so much about them?'

'If I am risking coin, I like to know what I can. Information is everything.'

'Isn't it risky to bet on me?'

'There is risk every time a bet is placed. As well as information you need big fucking balls.' He said as he grabbed his nuggets and laughed. The laugh was interrupted by a grimace that Hawkins tried to pretend never happened, but Guy had seen it. Before he could ask though, Hawkins cut in. 'The old woman told me it was you who stitched me up.' They shared an awkward glance before Guy looked away. This time he was sure that the words hung awkwardly for them both. 'Thank you.' continued Hawkins as he patted him awkwardly on the arm. 'And think about what I said.' Hawkins left and Guy stared out onto the field seeing too much but seeing nothing at all.

He made it over to the tournament area and watched a few melee bouts, exhibition jousts and saw his first tournament death in a vicious knife fight. These things would normally astound him, but he had things on his mind and did not enjoy them as he should. He had just started to make his way back to the knight's quarters when he heard a voice calling out.

'Hoy Big man.' He looked around, not just out of instinct, but also familiarity, and within a few seconds he saw Johnny emerge from the crowd waving. Guy felt a smile creep across his face.

'Johnny! What are you doing here?'

'Alright big man? The king's tournament… Sir Chandley would not miss this for all the coin in Rodina. He has a knight competing.' Guy laughed.

'I guess the wine needs protection.'

'Aye maybe, but he just loves tournaments, it is where he makes his coin, he finds rich fuckers to buy his wine at high prices. You have the archery tomorrow. I hope you do better than last time. Make sure you get a decent bow.' Guy laughed.

'I'm going to use my own.'

'Good man, me too.'

'You made the tournament?' Guy asked, sounding more surprised than he had intended.

'Nah, just the archery. Maybe next year.'

'It is good to see you.'

'You too big man. I have to get back, Sir Chandley is in high spirits already.'

'Tomorrow then.'

'Aye big man, tomorrow.'

The commotion of the tournament happening around him had gone for a moment. As it began to seep back into his consciousness he saw another familiar face moving past the crowd. He moved towards them, unsure entirely whether he was right but when they stopped and waited for Guy to approach, he knew. The servant was not in his usual burgundy tunic, perhaps he was finally enjoying a day when he was not in service. Guy asked a couple of things from the servant, he felt bad asking, but he had no one else. John did not seem to mind, and said that he would do what he could and meet him the day after the archery. As Guy continued his way to the knight's quarters, he could not shake the feeling that it had been wrong to ask John, but the truth was he simply had no other way, he wanted his bones cracked before his battle.

Training that night was for him and the Knightmaker, they both danced with the stranger in full armour, but he did not perform his usual dance, instead he adopted a different persona, a different style each time, first he danced with Guy, then the Knightmaker, and then Guy again. He estimated eight or nine different styles from the stranger until he got to dance with the Knightmaker. With the tournament due to start, it was not full on, but Guy was pleased that he could hold his own, or perhaps more correctly, he was pleased that the Knightmaker allowed him to hold his own. While Guy was operating at perhaps a little over three quarters of his ability, he imagined that for the Knightmaker it would unlikely be over half.

When he had called halt and removed his helm, Guy realised that the Knightmaker was gasping for breath as much as he was, but then he had been dancing with the stranger before.

'That was good,' he said between breaths clapping Guy on the shoulder.

They took some time to recover before removing their armour and piling it in the corner of the courtyard. They sat and drank, Guy fruit juice and water, the Knightmaker wine and water.

'Whatever Hawkins told you earlier, it is your choice to make,' the Knightmaker began. 'The important thing is that you win the tournament.' Guy nodded, he had seen some of the squires train, and Hawkins had pointed out those tipped to win. Guy could not compare himself to them, they had put in years of service as squires and had years of training. They had looked so good, and he had been made to look like a bag of shit. 'You are better than you think you are. You have it in you to beat all of them and a dozen more. I'd wager there are knights who would be hesitant to fight you. But that is what makes you who you are. You are not some pompous prick, you are the real thing. Remember why you are doing this, and decide what is best for you.' Guy looked up and caught the stranger's eye, who offered a very slight, but very deliberate nod. He agreed with the Knightmaker. The Knightmaker held his gaze, as if to affirm that he had meant what he said, before nodding when he was satisfied that Guy understood. Guy nodded back and watched as Sir Parcifal drained the skin of wine, splashing the last few dribbles over his shirt and face before standing to leave.

Guy followed, and once past the castle and into the tournament area, the Knightmaker transformed into a man who had supped too much, staggering and calling out knights as they passed. Once back at the pavilion he was sent to rest as the squire's tournament began the following morning. Sir Parcifal sat affront the tent with the stranger, supping wine and honking, Hawkins was nowhere to be seen.

Guy did not expect sleep to find him, but he rested his body and calmed his breathing while his mind struggled, not only with what to do, but whether he could. It was the dilemma Hawkins had set that occupied his mind, but the Knightmaker's words that circled in his head.

53

When he awoke he was rested but unresolved. In fact it was as if his mind had picked up where it left off when sleep had finally found him. There were so many chains of thought running through his mind, it was hard to focus on any one of them. He pulled on his running boots and set off through the knight's quarters and out towards the castle gates. A quick run would help calm his mind, and get him ready for the tournament. For a while some thoughts resisted, clinging to his mind as he ran, but soon they too faded and all that existed was the next four steps. He would not try to decide what to do, after all, he could not change what is meant to be. An easy excuse, but it worked and soon the morning air had cleared his mind, and he returned to the knight's quarters ready for the tournament, or at least, ready to accept that he was not ready.

After eating, he washed himself while the Knightmaker sat breaking his fast on a skinfull of wine, bringing attention to himself as other knights and squires prepared for their contests. Guy's mind was free enough to find itself considering his surprise that no one had confronted the Knightmaker about his behaviour. He had seen some who had to be restrained, and some wither away, pretending that they were not there. Guy wore his fancy leather and tied his bracers. He certainly looked the part, more so than he had last time he began a tournament. They would not be insulting what he wore this time. He was surprised at how calm he felt. He was just going to shoot some arrows. He had fired hundreds over the past few months, thousands probably. When he stretched the bow all that existed was the target, and until the iron vambraces came to be, the target was hit frequently, and his new bow… it filled him with joy just to think of it. He was confident that he could put in a display that would see him enter the melee in the last three places. By then half the field would be tired, and some of them eliminated. It was unusual for Guy to feel confident and he enjoyed it. He was more confident in his archery that he was with his chances in the melee, and it was the melee that mattered. Last squire standing would be knighted, simple as that.

Once dressed, Guy started stretching to prevent his mind from running away with itself again. The best arrows were fired with a quiet mind. He rolled his shoulders to ensure the leather fitted properly, twisted his body and bent his knees when the Knightmaker suddenly pulled the tents flap aside.

'I think it best you do not use my arms this time.' The tone of his voice was such that Guy knew there was an element of fondness to the words. Not that he could tell by looking at him, he was all business.

'You are probably right.'

'You have your own now. Will you use them?'

'No, my arms are for when I am a knight.'

'Fair enough,' the Knightmaker replied. It was as it should be.

'I will enter without arms.'

'Get yourself ready.'

The Knightmaker turned and left without another word.

'We go now.' boomed into the pavilion, Guy grabbed his bow, and was only half a dozen steps behind the Knightmaker as he left the tent. But the time they reached the entrance to the knight's quarter he had fallen in, two steps behind, one to the left. He walked with purpose towards the tournament area. It was busy, and that was just the competitor's area, knights and squires readied themselves as the joust was about to begin. They were ushered into a canvas corridor awaiting presentation, Guy had been the last to arrive. The Knightmaker had splashed wine on himself once more and acted as if he were trying to hide drunkenness.

Guy watched as one by one those in front of them were called forward and announced to the crowd. The crowd was excitable for the jousting, and cheered loudly for those squires that did not matter to them. When the Knightmaker and Guy were called forward there were more cheers than he would have imagined, but he also heard some knights and even some of the crowd honking at them. It sounded like much of it was aimed at Sir Parcifal, who ignored it, but some he recognised from the training grounds. Some were honking at him.

He listened all through the presentation ceremony before they filed out of the arena to applause that they had not earned. Guy noticed some of the squires milking the attention, he also noticed that the Knightmaker had kept on walking leaving him alone. This was part of the game that the Knightmaker was playing for his own event, he had bid him well earlier, and reminded him to do what he thought was best. He took a breath and headed over to the quartermaster to claim his quiver. He had to present the token as a man wrote his name and set of arrows. Number seven, green and gold. The quartermaster handed over the quiver, but Guy did not leave as expected, instead he held out his hand.

'The token.' The quartermaster looked at Guy, the token yet to be added to the pile of other submitted ones.

'It is customary…' the quartermaster began, but Guy cut him off.

'The token,' he repeated, 'Please.' He gave a look that, in his mind, said *'Don't make me go to the king about this,'* but he probably just looked as if he was constipated. The Quartermaster sighed and placed the token in Guys hand. 'Thank you,' he offered as he placed it back in his pouch. He would have the token on the mantelpiece in his private chambers in his House, and occasionally he and Phylissa would look at it and remember how it had bought them together.

He meandered over to the muster station, and it was probably ten minutes until a familiar voice called to him.

'Hoy Big man. How are you feeling?' Guy looked round and greeted Johnny.

'I feel good, you?'

'Aye, fucking top notch mate. It is not every day you get to play at the king's own tournament, even if I am only off in the fields.'

Twenty four archers gathered around the tournament master as the instructions were called out. A dozen arrows, two points for red, one point for white. One long arrow. The rankings would be combined and the lowest score would be the archery champion. Those knights that had qualified for the melee would enter in reverse order. Finish last, go in first. Finish first, go in last, simple.

Guy could feel excitement rise in his belly, but his calmness concerned him. He had still not decided what he was going to do. Sense was telling him to score as well as he could to give himself the best advantage in the melee. But the Knightmaker telling him he should easily kick all their arses was making him think. He had been all night, and he had realised that he had been looking at everything wrong. He had been comparing himself to the Knightmaker and the stranger, and felt that he was nowhere near their standard. If he were comparing himself to other squires and even some knights, from what he had seen, he felt that he could give a good account of himself. He had won the last tournament without using any offence. There was of course also the gold to consider. Guy wondered who in their right mind would bet on a squire's tournament anyway, but it seemed that it was not just the best warriors that were drawn to these events. The best gamblers were also present, and Hawkins had been away doing whatever he did. *Could he? Should he?* He knew the answer, but could not stop hearing the Knightmaker's words.

They were led to a space behind the main arena. It had its own fencing behind which stood spectators consisting of knights and staff of those taking part, and members of the public who had not got a spot for the jousting. They were probably disappointed as they heard the cheers as the first jousting knights of the day were introduced while the archers lined up in their designated places. Johnny was lined up at number three, but leaned over to wish him luck. Guy smiled and returned the sentiment. The others around him did their best to ignore him. The target before him was two sacks in the form of a man, a smaller red one representing the head, a larger white one forming the body. It was only about three dozen paces away and Guy knew that on his day he could sink the entire dozen into the red sack. He rolled his neck to cracks that his neighbours could not ignore. He felt them looking at him. It was his turn to ignore them. There were more announcements as Guy focussed all his attention on the targets, looking only at them until they became all that existed in his world. He controlled his breathing imagining how the arrows would fly. He had practiced this many times, he called it isolation.

When the horn sounded to start the tournament Guy remained still as the sound of arrows being loosed thrumped through the air. He had not decided what he was going to do yet, and he did not think of it then. All that occupied his mind was how his lack of movement would be pissing off the squire that always liked to shoot last. There was bound to be one of them with this weird quirk. Guy felt a smile rising within him as he waited for a few more arrows to hit their targets before drawing his first green and gold arrow slowly from the quiver.

He notched it and smoothly pulled back the string until it touched his ear. He could see only the target, his breathing was calm, his mind quiet, yet focussed. He loosed the arrow and it flew true, but lodged in the wooden plank a few inches high and left of the red target. He smoothly slid his next arrow from the quiver and repeated the process, this one landing high right. Another high centre, then low left. Despite the misses he was calm. If he scored with all the rest he could still get a decent position. As he drew the next arrow the Knightmaker appeared in his mind and he remembered who his master was. When the arrow landed low right he let out a frustrated sigh, and with each further arrow that failed to hit the target he got more and more animated in showing his frustration. When he finally sent his penultimate arrow into the centre of the white target he was aware that he had the attention of much of the crowd and some of the squires around him. Once he had sent his last arrow dead centre of the red target, he slung his bow over his shoulder and muttered to himself as the others finished off their arrows. For while he had been last to start he had been quick with his arrows and was the first to finish. Some seemed to take their time more than others and towards the end some of Guy's animated frustration was genuine. He was not happy with himself, and that was evident to anyone casting a glance in his direction, and when the horn sounded to signify the close of the target round he made to move off in disgust, but Johnny caught his arm and held him back as others made their way to the tournament master to be escorted to the long arrow.

'What's up big man?' Guy shrugged him off. 'It looks like you drew a box around his head.' He knew Johnny was trying to make him feel better, and he gave him a smile. 'You did that on purpose didn't you?' Guy looked round shushing him, hoping that no one else heard. 'You did, didn't you?'

Guy shushed him again and led him off to catch up with the others. They hung at the back of the group and Guy quietly told Johnny about Hawkins. Johnny laughed and told Guy that he had some balls. Guy continued to look as if he were frustrated as they lined up for the long arrow. The tournament master gave the rules as Guy kicked a stone, feeling eyes on him.

'This,' he said pointing to a rope staked to the ground, 'is the point from which we measure. Look behind you.' They did, even Guy. 'You have all that space in which to loose your arrow. You do not need to be anywhere near the rope. If you step over it you will automatically get twenty four points. So stay away. Longest arrow wins, you shoot in the order of your assigned numbers.' That meant Guy would shoot seventh. He watched with a disinterested look as the first arrows were loosed, Johnny who fired third held the lead for a while. He watched the westerners with interest, and it was one who took the lead with the shuffle he had learnt as a child, but a much smoother version than he had attempted last time. He had been looking forward to the long arrow. He had not fully tested his bow yet. He was confident he could beat what had gone so far.

When Guys turn came, all the other archers were still watching with interest. He took a breath, rolled his shoulders and slid the green and gold long arrow from his quiver. He could feel the eyes on him and hear some of the mutterings, but he did not care. His mind was focussed, he wanted to see what his bow could do. He took a couple of deep breaths and slowly pulled the string back as he sidestepped towards the line, planted his foot and as he pulled, power flowed through him. He released the arrow at just the right time sending it soaring high into the sky.

Before the arrow had peaked the horn sounded to indicate a foul. Guy watched the arrow as muffled laughter became less restrained. It was hard for him to follow, because if flew so high and so far, easily outdistancing any previous arrow. When it finally struck the ground he looked down to see half his foot over the line. He screamed in frustration, protesting with the tournament master. He stood firm though and Guy's arrow was not to be considered.

Guy through his act of annoyance watched over the rest of the arrows. The result did not concern him, he had fucked that up already. None got close to his arrow. Some of the bigger squires used power over technique to go ahead of the smaller competitors, Guy assumed that these would be some of his opponents in the melee. They looked more like swordsmen. Guy imagined that it must frustrate those more gifted archers when power beat their skill.

The tournament master announced that the results would be declared before the melee. Guy stood with his head in his hands as the rest of the squires began to make their way back to the castle. Johnny clapped him on the shoulder as the last of them left.

'Bad luck big man.' Guy nodded at him with a wink. 'Fucking good arrow though.' They set off behind the others as Johnny informed Guy that he was not of right mind. Guy found himself wondering if Johnny was right. *What the fuck was he doing?* By the time they had reached the quartermaster to return their quivers Guy no longer appeared frustrated, he looked despondent. Johnny gave him a friendly pat on the back as he left to return to Sir Chandley, no one else paid him any mind at all, except for the smug look he got from his old friend Jefferson as he stood with a group of three other squires.

Guy trudged back to the knight's quarters, even one who had not seen the archery would be able to see that things had not gone well. He finally relaxed when he let the flap of the pavilion close behind him. A smile crept across his face. He hoped two things, one, that Hawkins could now get some good odds, and two, that he would be able to do as the Knightmaker suggested he could, and kick all of their arses. At that moment he was not worried. He had made a choice, he could not change it now. It was maybe half an hour later when the Knightmaker burst into the tent.

'Last!' He boomed. Guy was taken aback initially, but then the Knightmaker winked at him. It did not make what followed any easier to take, but at least he knew. 'Fucking last.'

He did not get chance to figure out what he thought he knew as the Knightmaker launched into a shouted tirade at his incompetence. He had travelled all this way for nothing, he was a disgrace.

It was perhaps five minutes of abuse that he had to suffer before the Knightmaker stormed out and returned to his seat outside. It was another half an hour before he returned and explained that the tournament had stopped for noonshine, and that when he was shouting everyone was returning to the quarters. Guy smiled and nodded, but felt there was too much relief in his actions. The Knightmaker in full boom was intimidating, whether an act or not. Guy was happy that it was over and hoped that it would achieve what they wanted from it.

Instead of eating noonshine from the tournament camp, the Knightmaker led Guy to their courtyard where they ate in private in a shaded corner. The stranger joined them soon after.

'Is that what Hawkins told you to do?' the Knightmaker asked.

'No, he suggested finishing low in the order might help make more coin.' The Knightmaker laughed.

'You have some balls Guy of Waering, I'll give you that. Now you just have to win. Final training. Until the sun sets.'

54

They all dressed in armour, the stranger opted for full armour as well. Guy imagined that it was going to get heavy. The stranger came with a different approach each time. Sometimes the dances would last, other times they were over quickly, as if Guy had the skills to deal with that particular style. Again, the stranger moved between him and the Knightmaker as the afternoon wore on. He was glad of the breaks, it gave him the chance to take on water and recover his breath while he watched the Knightmaker take his turn.

As the sun lowered in the sky he danced with the stranger and the Knightmaker at the same time. He got tagged often, but his helm was only rung occasionally. It was difficult for Guy when both of them came at him because they were more organised than the squires had been in the tournament. It was if they knew what each other was about to do, and they used it to their advantage. Guy would use it to his. He had learnt more in the last few days than he had in months, but he was more than aware that it was only having been through the last few months that enabled him to learn as he did. He felt alive as he parried and dodged, quick on his feet and with sword. He knew that they could take him whenever they wanted, but they continued with a pace that meant he could just about keep up.

When the Knightmaker finally called halt as the sun sank from the sky he realised that Hawkins had arrived. The Knightmaker went to talk to him as Guy bent double trying to recover. He removed his helm and reached for the straps on his armour. He was hot inside and struggling for breath. They had been on him hard for some time. He was fucked.

They had tested him well that night, and even he knew that he had done well.

It took him a good five minutes to recover enough to pull his armour off and roll his weary shoulders. For a moment he thought of the springs in Waering where he could stretch out in the hot water, how he wished it could soak away his pain. He was rolling his neck looking for a crack that would not come when he noticed that the Knightmaker and Hawkins had finished talking and Hawkins was headed his way. There were no smiles, he was all business.

'Good work today.' He announced, 'We've got a chance. I have been working on a couple of people, I have won some coin and lost some coin, but these guys like to gamble. Between them I can get us some serious coin when you win.'

'When I win, you make it sound so easy.' Hawkins laughed, for the first time with Guy, not at him.

'You have really got no idea have you? I saw you just now, there are many knights who could not cope with that.'

'They were taking it easy on me,' Guy replied matter of factly.

'Maybe so, but that would have been too much for a lot of men. Yes there are some skilled fighters out there, but none who should beat you. They come from castles, not like you. They have skills, but do not know how what it is to fight.' Guy's mind reminded him that he had come from a castle, he could easily have been one of those boys. His mind asked why he wasn't, but he would have to think about that later. 'I'll tell you what would really help,' Hawkins continued, 'These guys are impulsive, if you seem to be struggling at the start I could push them up more.'

'What do you mean?' asked Guy. He thought he knew, but it would mean Hawkins had overlooked an important factor. He had to win. He could think of nothing else.

'Look, I know you are worried. You should be, it is no easy undertaking. But let's face it, the better squires will enter later, you could make it appear that you are less skilled than you are when the first few are out, you could let them push you around a little.'

'I need to win,' Guy said with more desperation in his voice than he intended to show.

'Aye, you do, else it is all for nothing. All I am asking is to see how you feel when you are out there. If you think that you can take it easy until six have entered, give it a shot. I'll get some good odds. If not, don't worry about it, we'll make do with what we have.' Guy nodded. 'But if you do decide to go easy, do not just switch, wait for someone to tag you, or something to happen that wakes you up. Remember there are people watching, we have to play the game.'

'Some game,' Guy said under his breath.

'Isn't it?' Hawkins said as he patted him on the arm and returned to the Knightmaker.

Guy still felt uncomfortable with the way Hawkins was with him now. It was going to take some getting used to. Guy watched, thinking of how absurd Hawkins' request was, as he spoke briefly with the Knightmaker before disappearing into the shadows. Guy realised he was shaking his head to himself. What was he thinking?

The Knightmaker left him to his thoughts as he and the stranger removed their armour piling it neatly in the corner. Guy carried his helm and chestplate over and started a pile of his own.

'You rest tomorrow, no training. You do whatever you do to get yourself ready.' The Knightmaker did not even look over as he spoke and pulled off his greaves setting them atop his pile. 'I have seen lots of squires over the years. None of them had balls like you do.' The Knightmaker enjoyed the freedom of movement the release from the armour gave him. 'Something is going to really have to fuck up for you not to win.' Guy looked up. 'Even the king must think so, or why keep such a stipulation after the cow.' Guy nodded, his mind swimming, but trying to retain the information. It just seemed so absurd that the king thought of him at all. 'Now that doesn't mean it will be easy, you need to be on it, no doubt, but remember people are watching. If they are to remember you, you have to do something special.' Guy looked up again as he finished his own pile and covered it in burlap. 'Give yourself a story to tell your woman.'

The Knightmaker had again splashed himself with wine and acted the drunkard throughout the evening. Guy made more of an effort to watch what was happening. To all who passed he appeared constantly drunk, obnoxious and arrogant. His words and his actions screamed confidence, his appearance did not. He saw many a confused knight try to figure him out. For a lot of knights, the drawbridge challenge represented another chance after being eliminated from the main tournament. It was a way for them to save face, which Guy was starting to learn was taken very seriously among knighted men. That, and they wanted to be seen. This was the last tournament of the year, and for many their last chance at securing employment for the winter. A good representation could lead to a good winter in service of a Lord or Earl, a bad showing and they would end up serving anyone who would give them a roof and food. Some knights approached and engaged the Knightmaker, others just looked at him. He knew that would not bother the Knightmaker in the least. If anything, it looked like he enjoyed these more. These were the ones that the Knightmaker tore apart. It always started the same.

'You want my shield? You come and take it. If you beat me, it is yours, and everything that comes with it. If I beat you, what will you give me?' Sometimes people made offers which the Knightmaker laughed at, sometimes they did not. The range of demands that the Knightmaker made varied depending on who it was. For some it was a night with their wife, for others, their mother, sometimes the Knightmaker told them that he was going to fuck *them*. This was Guy's favourite response. He would watch them crumble, and he knew they would dare not step up, sometimes he would watch them try and be defiant, but he knew they would not step up either. Were these the knights that would be more likely to win? Guy wondered. Was the Knightmaker eliminating threats before they even stepped up? Of course he was. He was also making it seem that challenging him was a good idea to other knights, perhaps those he felt were less skilled. At the end of the day though, confidence was not something knights were short of, and Guy learnt a lot from watching. It made him stronger.

Guy felt that he had identified two who would step up, risking their horse and armour, but he had identified many others who he felt would not step up, no matter how confident in their skills they were, the price was too high. The Knightmaker was fucking with their minds, and he did it with ease. He had laughed inside every time one of them wondered off dismissing him as a drunk, when in fact he was as sober as Guy could remember seeing him. Though he acted with bravado Guy had seen the Knightmaker change over the weeks at the castle. He could see beyond the act now, and he was even more fascinated by him.

Though he would have liked to carry on watching, he was tired and his mind was no longer holding information, he retired to the pavilion, leaving the Knightmaker to continue his negotiations while the stranger watched on. His mind was full, and he hoped it meant that sleep would find him swiftly, he did not want to think about what he did not know.

55

He crept out of the tent in the morning, he had woken to silence which meant it was early. He would have a little run to get his blood flowing. The stranger was sat in his seat, feet on the table. He nodded at Guy who responded with a nod of his own. Guy knew that he had been there all night, and wondered if he had slept. A knight's sleep, perhaps, with one eye open. The sun had barely risen above the horizon and this was Guy's favourite time for running. He was just about to start his slow wind up after passing the guards at the entrance to the knight's quarter when he spotted John the servant leaning against a gateway arch.

Guy stopped his run before it had begun and walked towards him.

'Good morning John.' He said with a smile.

'That matter you asked me about,' replied the servant without a smile. 'Follow me.'

Guy did without question. It was not until they were inside the castle walls, navigating dark narrow corridors, that the servant spoke again, filling Guy with intrigue. He explained that there was a copy of the book he was after in the king's library, and that someone would bring it to him. It was better they go early for many of the scholars and librarians worked at night. He added to the suspense by insisting that if anyone were to discover them, he was to cover the book with another. It was best people did not know that he was looking at that particular book. Guy had wanted to ask why, but was aware of his surroundings and kept conversation to a minimum. He also thought of how he was seen. He had never hidden his true self from the servant, and he did not now, but to other eyes he played. The Knightmaker had taught him more than he had realised.

Guy crouched through a door and found himself in an alcove in the king's library, the servant beckoned him to follow, and he did not have time to take in the magnificence of the place that he found himself in.

A huge domed glass roof let in the morning's first light, revealing wall after wall of books as the golden glow slowly spread. There were sections off the main chamber into the building itself. He had never seen so many books. The enormity caused a chasm in his chest, and his breath was tight. He followed the servant between shelves of books, and into a windowed alcove with cushioned seats and a stone table which had been scarred with graffiti over the years. Guy took a seat while the servant stood at the entrance to the alcove. He was conflicted, the servant had given him the impression that his presence would not be appreciated. The king's library was guarded by scribes, who were not keen on sharing the collection. A boy in a scarlet tunic approached, bringing with him two books. The smaller of the two he knew was the one he was after. It showed more signs of age and was practical where the other was a large ornate embossed leather affair with gold trim and edgings. His eyes searched as the servant placed the books on the table. He thought he could see enough of the faded title on the cover, yet still he reached for the book, flipping the front to reveal the title in script. *Healing practices of the Old World*. He closed it again and looked to John who had just finished talking with the servant.

'Read some of the other one first,' he told Guy, 'So that if I signal you can cover the one you read with it, and if anyone asks, you will know what you are looking at.' Guy nodded, opening the larger book and placing it over the smaller one. *Legendary Weapons*. He took a moment to enjoy the sheer quality of the book, and he realised that this was a copy specifically for the king's library. It was magnificent. Good thick paper and exquisite penmanship. He carefully thumbed through until he came to a picture, inked perfectly onto a page. The legendary flail. It lay on a wooden table upon which the remains of its last victim dripped. He carefully thumbed through until another picture caught his eye. The legendary greatsword. This picture was gilded in a golden sunbeam, the sword shone through. It was the sword that had carved the beast's flank a few nights before, it was the sword that he had been close to. He turned the page and began to read, fascinated. The sword had a history that could be traced back to the beginning of Rodina. He repeated his vow to himself that one day he would have a room of books, and a copy of Legendary weapons within it. No doubt it would not be as fine as the one he looked upon, but it would be the same. The same words, the same pictures.

The servant coughed and for a moment Guy saw a flash of emotion in him, fear. His eyes flicked to the table to make sure the other book was not visible, and as his eyes flicked back and fear started to fill his belly, the king looked into the alcove.

'Your Grace,' Guy offered.

'Master Guy.' Guy was flapping, and flustered words escaped him.

'I did not expect to see you here.'

'Can a man not wander his own library?' The king allowed himself a smile at Guy's expense. 'I like to come when it is quiet, it is one of my favourite places. All this knowledge,' he said spreading his arms, 'If I could know everything in here I would be a better king.'

The words hung in the air, amplified by the silence. After a moment Guy nodded, respectfully. There was nothing that he could say that would benefit the conversation.

'Are you a scholar yourself?' the king asked showing his diplomatic skills.

'I am a recent convert, you grace. I hope you do not mind my being here.'

'Of course not,' the king replied. 'Knowledge should be available to those who seek it.' He cast an eye at the book. 'Ah legendary weapons seventy one, there is quite a story for the long axe in this one. Number sixty three has a good history of the greatsword, though that is a fine picture.'

'Thank you, Your Grace.'

The king smiled a nod and continued on his way. Guy felt the relief that the servant showed, and finally when their eyes met Guy saw the smile. Yes, it was one of relief and not friendship, but they had shared a moment, and that was what Guy had wanted. He reached under legendary weapons and removed the smaller book as the servant kept watch once more. He held it for a moment, hoping that it might contain what he was looking for. He did not know for sure that it would, but he felt it did. He started flicking through, not entirely sure what he was seeking.

He saw sections on plants, on fixing bones, on illnesses. He stopped on a diagram. There had been a lot of simple factual diagrams throughout of the body, of plants, but this was different. It was a symbol, coloured scarlet. It reminded him of flames when he looked at it though there were no overt flames in the drawing. On the page opposite it had diagrams showing how it was drawn. A small horizontal, left to right; a longer vertical, downwards and a decreasing spiral reaching back halfway up the vertical. After looking for a moment, he flicked back a few pages to find the start of the chapter. *'Hands that heal.'* He preferred his burning hands, but nonetheless he had found what he was looking for. He wanted nothing more than to sit and absorb every word of every page, he would read it all day if he could, but he knew he did not have long, and set about greedily trying to obtain as much as he could, flicking from page to page feverishly scanning them. Perhaps if his eyes saw everything they would remember it, even if he did not.

He caught himself for a moment, embarrassed. Not just because of how he must look to the servant, but of how he looked to himself. He was taking what he could, and that was not his nature. Because of this he would likely end up with nothing. *Stay true to who you are.* Who had told him that? He could not remember, but that did not matter. What mattered was that someone had, and he ceased his frenzied search for information and instead returned to the pictures. There was another symbol that stood out, a single bolt of white lightning. Bright against a dark background. There were others, but they were more complex. He looked at the first and read the text close to it, but had only just started reading the text around the second one when the servant returned to collect the books. Guy had a final flick through a few pages, letting his eyes see them one more time before handing it over to the servant and thanking him. No sooner had he left and John nodded with his head for them to leave. Guy did not want to leave. The king himself had said that those who sought knowledge should be able to find it. He followed John though, perhaps he could go back. He knew that the knowledge was there, for now that would have to do. When they reached the alcove Guy realised that he had come through a secret entrance, and he could not hide his excitement as he ducked through it into the narrow corridor and waited for the servant to close the door behind them. He calmed himself as he followed John through a warren of narrow corridors. He suspected that they were taking such a convoluted route to confuse him, so that he would not be able to find his way back. By the time they left the castle walls, Guy had not the faintest idea how he would get back if he wanted to. The servant stopped near the gate where they had met. It was busier, the muster was open and food was being collected. The place was not fully awake, but it was certainly alive. Guy thanked John, and he meant it.

56

Though his stomach growled, he would have his run, he would collect the food on his return. He walked through the castle grounds to a small gate near the woods trying to commit to memory what he had read, once he started running he memorised the symbols drawing them in his mind. It relaxed him and cleared his mind which had so many questions. He ran steadily, finding the optimum pace. One question would not go away. Could he use it on himself?

He could not deny that drawing the pictures in his mind as he ran felt good. He could not feel heat in his hands, and perhaps his mind was playing tricks on him. The question teased his mind throughout the day, he had come close to asking the old woman as she cracked his bones, but remembered her last words about healing being for women and thought it best to exercise a little discretion. He did not want people to know that he had knowledge, or thought he did. He was relishing the opportunity to try it, to see if he could make his hands hot, but while he was not training, there was still much he had to do. He fed and watered himself well at noonshine, and drew the symbols in his mind while he stretched, before washing and heading off to see the knight's melee.

As a competitor he was able to find somewhere to lean out of sight and watched as they dismantled the tilts, drawing the symbols in his mind.

It had been a sight to behold as the knights went at each other with everything they had. There was no holding back. He had been reminded of the stakes when he saw one knight lose his life, and another who would likely never walk again. A Warhammer had given him an extra joint in his thigh, and he doubted he would ever forget the crack that pierced through every other sound. A moment of silence followed before the knight screamed and the crowd cheered. It was brutal, and he had learnt that there were more deaths in the king's tournament than any other. The stakes were higher. He had seen three men die on the field already and he had not been watching a lot of the tournament. On average there were seven deaths at the tournament, John had told him. Being a knight it seemed was a dangerous business, even in times of peace.

As he made his way back to the knight's quarters, he saw the servant waiting in the same archway as he had been that morning. Guy wondered over and John handed him a hessian wrapped bundle not much bigger than his boot. The servant was gone again before Guy had finished thanking him, not in the mood to chat.

As Guy continued through the quarters he was considering whether he had put John the servant out. He had not been himself when they met. Perhaps he had just been waiting a long time, and had other errands to run, though he was not wearing his tunic again. That was strange as, Guy remembered him saying that he was in service every day. Perhaps he finally had some time off and Guy was making him run errands. He was just starting to feel bad about it and questioning his own approach to servitude when he heard the Knightmaker's voice before he got close to the pavilion. He was acting the belligerent drunk, harassing anyone who passed. Guy nodded and ducked under the flap, pulling open the hessian package. Inside were two sets of leather vambraces that John had collected for him from the old leather worker. They were exactly what he had asked for, probably better. They were simple yet beautiful, they had been slightly polished to enhance the décor, the unmistakable grey brown hue of the beastly cow. He popped his head through the flap, and looked over at the Knightmaker and the stranger. While neither looked at him, they both knew he was there, and after a nod from the Knightmaker the stranger rose and entered the tent.

'I want to say thank you for everything you have done for me. I had these made for you.' He handed the stranger the smaller set. The stranger took them and felt the quality. He nodded his thanks, Guy smiled. Whatever had happened, whatever was to happen, he was thankful. He watched the stranger put them with his kit and nod again as he left the tent.

A moment later the Knightmaker bundled through the flap pretending to have supped more than he should. As soon as the flap had closed, the pretence ceased.

'Is everything all right?' he asked, not with concern, but Guy liked to think it was as close as he got.

'I wanted to give you these,' Guy said as he offered the vambraces. Even now, the Knightmaker's very presence intimidated him on some level. He had a speech planned to thank the Knightmaker, but that had gone to rat shit. 'To say thank you.'

The Knightmaker took the vambraces and examined them for longer than the stranger had, flexing the leather, sniffing it.

'From the beast?' Guy nodded. 'They are very good.'

An awkward silence developed, almost as if the Knightmaker knew there was more he wanted to say, but the words just weren't there. He remembered his time in Waering, and hoped that he was not about to propose to the Knightmaker with his next words. 'But your thanks will mean fuck all if you do not finish the job tomorrow.' Guy smiled inside, but knew the Knightmaker was not fucking around. 'You have the chance to do something special tomorrow. Not to buy a knighthood from an old drunk like me, but to earn it. You get to show that you are worthy.' The Knightmaker's words hit home. He was right. 'You are representing me tomorrow, but you also represent yourself. We both depend on your victory. Be the man you are meant to be.'

The Knightmaker turned to leave the tent, pausing briefly. 'Thank you.' He said waving the vambraces. He pulled open the tent, and in an instant transformed himself into an angry old drunk.

Guy sat for a moment, allowing the Knightmaker's words to absorb. He had been so caught up in his training that he had not even considered what the Knightmaker had said. While his spirits were lifted, he was also deflated. He had wanted to earn his knighthood from the Knightmaker. He wanted to be knighted by Sir Parcifal, the baddest fucker in all of Rodina. A smile crept over his face as he considered which Phylissa would prefer. It was a moot point anyway. If he did not win the tournament, the Knightmaker would not be able to knight anyone.

His mind raced with thoughts all evening as he collected food for the three of them. He had not seen Hawkins since he suggested fucking around in the melee. All kinds of thoughts and permutations danced unrestrained in his mind as mild panic began to set in. He had been stupid to think that it was not bothering him. He would have to fuck Hawkins off. He had to win, it was as simple as that. He could not afford to fuck around. Not when faced with the best squires in the kingdom.

He was relieved when the Knightmaker sent him to sleep. His mind had given him no answers, but had told him one thing. The next day was important, more so than he could understand, and he did not like that. What if he fucked up? He chose to lay on a rollmat thinking it strange that the floor was his preferred sleeping location after having dreamt of a cot for months when he was at Eastfield Manor. Now he had one, the floor called to him. He lay aback as his mind continued to contemplate unanswerable questions. An important day would be best met with a clear mind. He slowed his breathing until it was deep and calm, and drew the symbols in his mind aiming only to clear it. Slowly the questions, thoughts and fears faded until all he saw in his mind's eye was the symbol, horizontal, vertical, inward spiral, in scarlet. His hands had naturally come to rest on his body, right hand over his heart, left over his navel. He let calmness wash over him as he drew the symbol once more. A soft energy joined his hands, a heat. *Holy fuck!* Guy sat up and looked around making sure he was alone. Fear and wonder jolted through his body like it had the first time he had pulled back his foreskin. Panic, his body bristled. He looked at his hands, put them to his face. They felt no different to usual. He relaxed a little, managed a breath and placed his palms over his eyes and drew the symbol again. A surge of gentle energy pushed through into his mind, and he melted back to the floor and breathed deep breaths, and did not fight the energy. It calmed his mind, it would do him no harm. His hands naturally found their way back to his torso, as before. The energy flowed freely through his freshly cracked bones and he felt detached from his body and his mind, almost as if he were asleep, yet someway still aware floating in something made of nothing. There was only him.

Somewhere in his mind he remembered how the old woman had held his feet to the floor, grounding him. He could not hold his feet to the floor, instead he rolled his palms so that they rested on the ground, and instead of floating, and he connected himself with the world. It was then that sleep found him, in amongst the roots with a quiet mind.

57

The Knightmaker's foot nudged him.

'It's time.'

Guy took a moment before opening his eyes and stretching his spine to satisfying cracks. He propped himself up on his elbows. He had not even heard the Knightmaker come in. He rolled his neck allowing his body to wake. It was early and there was very little sound of activity outside the tent. He felt a calm satisfaction and a grin wanted to show itself. He imagined it would feel similar when he woke the morning after bedding Phylissa for the first time. He did not know whether it was because his hands had got hot, or whether it was because it was the day when he found out one way or another if he was to be knighted. He thought the former, because he was not gripped with the fear that he had felt the night before. His mind was serene, despite what was to come.

He made oats for the Knightmaker and the stranger, before being sent to wash the pot.

'It is good for you to be seen,' the Knightmaker had told him. 'Put a question in your opponents mind.'

He could feel the eyes on him as he scrubbed the pot in the designated washing area. Other squires were doing the same, but Guy did it with purpose. He paid no mind to anyone else, the Knightmaker would have been proud.

On his return, the Knightmaker led him to the courtyard where they had trained. It was nice to be away from the noise and business of the tournament grounds. Immediately the familiarisation relaxed his mind, and helped him to focus. He remembered his old plan. This was to be stage eleven, final preparations. For a moment he cast his mind back to see whether he had accomplished the steps to get there. He could not remember what they were, but he was there anyway. He did not know what was going to happen, so he could not be ready. He knew that though, and used it to make him stronger. When they arrived he could see his new armour had been laid out next to his training armour. He found himself looking at it, imagining how he would look in it, how quick he would be, but he had resolved that it was to be his knight's armour. He would wear his training armour in the melee.

'I have had your armour brought for you,' the Knightmaker announced as he saw Guy looking at it.

'Thank you, but I shall wear the training armour with your permission.'

'Will you now?' Guy knew him well enough to hear the joke in his voice, but still imagined how he would have cowered at such tones not all that long ago.

'I am familiar with it, it can take a beating, and besides…' he paused for effect, 'I don't want any of those fuckers to be the first to mark it.'

The Knightmaker's laugh boomed out, probably heard among the gathering crowd. The final rounds of the joust were to be held after their bout, so people had arrived early to get the best view they could for the afternoon's events.

'Fair enough, though someone must be the first.'

'Aye, but not them. I shall not give them the satisfaction.'

'That will please Hawkins.' The Knightmaker laughed again. 'Come, get yourself ready.'

The Knightmaker set about wrapping Guy's new armour in the hessian as Guy began to run up and down the courtyard. Its 120 foot length did not allow him to get into his full stride, but he did not need that now, he needed to get his heart pumping and his blood flowing. After a dozen or so there and backs his stopped in the middle of the courtyard and started stretching as he caught his breath, drawing the symbols in his mind as sweat started to bead on his forehead. He twisted his hips and rolled his shoulders until he was satisfied that he had full movement. He arched his back and stretched his arms high to the sky giving his entire body a final stretch and returned to the Knightmaker who was already dressed in his half armour.

The stranger fitted Guys armour, just as well as he had before and it gave Guy confidence. He had been hampered by poorly fitted armour in training many times, he would not be hampered that day.

The Knightmaker beckoned him to the courtyard with his sword, and they started a slow controlled dance, allowing Guy to get used to the movement. With the commencement of each dance the Knightmaker picked up the pace until Guy reached the point where he felt like they were going at it quite hard. The pace was fast and they both pivoted and turned regularly clashing with purpose until Guy was breathing hard.

'Now,' said the Knightmaker, grasping for breath, 'you know what is at stake here, and you know that none of it matters. Not the gold, not the king's rules. You came to me to become a knight, and now you have your chance. What matters is that you take it. You take it for your own reasons.' The Knightmaker paused, as if waiting for a response. Guy had become so immersed in the Knightmaker's little world that his mind seldom had the chance to think of his own reasons. He would not forget them though. Through everything, Phylissa was the one that had been driving him, to keep getting up, to keep hitting the rock, to make himself stronger. He was doing it for love. He would achieve it, or die trying. Guy nodded. 'Use the crowd, play to them. They do not know you, but you are not a ponce like most of them out there. They will like you, give them a show. Think about what Hawkins said,' the Knightmaker continued. 'You might surprise yourself at how good you are.' He paused again, not for a response, but to meet his eye. 'Now is your chance to go out there and be the man you were born to be.' There was silence as Guy held the Knightmaker's gaze. He was still breathing hard, his blood was pumping, and the Knightmaker's words echoed in his mind. Satisfied, the Knightmaker declared. 'We are already late. We go in two minutes. Get yourself ready.'

58

Guy took a final deep breath as they left the courtyard. He could feel the heat of his body inside the suit, he felt loose, his body was ready. It took most of his mind's effort to concentrate on keeping up with the Knightmaker who walked with pace and purpose. As they approached the muster someone stepped forward perhaps thinking of admonishing them for their timekeeping. A look from the Knightmaker encouraged him to change his mind and instead hurry them through as he signalled ahead. After coming dead last in the archery Guy was to be at the back anyway, the Knightmaker slowed, and they joined the procession as it entered the area and the bells rang out mid-day.

They filed out into the arena, Guy stood beside the Knightmaker at the end of the two dozen competitors. The sun beat down through the cloudless autumnal sky, radiating the colours of banners and bright clothes, and the smiles in the eyes of the common folk. The arena was vast, it was where the joust would conclude later and was half as wide as it was long. The Stands were full of the families and players from throughout Rodina, and the Royal enclosure was the grandest of all dominating the main stand. It was the only area where there was space, virtually every other seat was filled, and behind him the crowd spread up the grass banks that rose from the arena. It was good of the king to put the squires melee on such a day, it could easily be hidden among the knights qualifying bouts and have hardly any spectators. For some this would be as good as it ever got. Guy hoped that he would not be one of them.

The announcement of the archery result seemed to go on forever. Guy having been last was the first of the squires to head to the muster point for the melee, where the steward inspected his sword. It was his training sword. It was a further six places before the next squire came towards them.

'He is nothing,' muttered the Knightmaker as he approached. Guy stood still, maintaining his breathing, moving his little ball of energy throughout his body and drawing symbols in his mind. He would make sure that his body was still ready even after the longwinded ceremony.

'Watch this one,' the Knightmaker muttered as the tenth of the dozen knights approached. 'Very skilled, very technical.' Guy hoped that he appeared static to anyone who bothered to look. He knew the attention would be on the prize giving as they were down to the final three. Even though Guy was in his own zone, he allowed himself to smile as the king awarded Johnny with the third placed prize, before the final two squires for the melee made their way over. 'This one thinks he's already a knight,' the Knightmaker muttered finally.

As the crowds cheers subsided. He was happy for Johnny, almost proud on his behalf, but third place would not be good enough for Guy. He had to win.

Once the final squire and his knight joined the line, the introductions for the melee began, starting with the squire of Sir Desmond Lane, Lord of the Cornhills, who had only just joined the line. They stepped forward and milked the crowd of their cheers before leaving the arena, and so it went on, one squire at a time until only Sir Parcifal and Guy remained. The Herald announced them and Guy knew the cheers were because of Sir Parcifal as they stepped forwards.

'Let's get this done. Be the man you are meant to be,' the Knightmaker said before he departed. 'We go now.'

The words triggered something in Guy, something primal. He had heard those words many times over the months, usually just before a kicking. They filled his body with a mild fear that he used to make him stronger. Only once the Knightmaker had left did the horn sound to start the tournament. *Step 12, the melee.*

Guy was alone in the arena, and he could hear the crowd calling, some good, some bad, he thought he heard someone mention the

Dun Cow. He turned to face where the next competitor would enter and bounced on his feet a few times. He had kept his energy moving throughout, he was still ready, still loose. It was time to start the show.

He stood with his hand on the pommel of his sword, whose tip was aground in front of him, and waited like a sculpture. It was a long minute before the first squire entered, but Guy did not move as he approached. His mind was whirring with words, suggestions, temptations. It was not until the squire reached within a dozen paces that Guy moved his sword to the north east position. The crowd cheered and jeered in equal measure. They wanted action, but Guy simply stood waiting. The other squire seemed unsure, and when he finally launched an attack, Guy simply sidestepped away. Three different ways that he could have tagged him ran through his mind, but he hadn't, he had not even engaged him. He turned to meet him again, and parried as a strike came in. It was without finesse and without power, and he could have tagged him. He patted away the strikes and occasionally offered mild offence. He pretended like he was figuring out his opponent, his opponent was doing the same, though without the pretence. Guy did not detect a threat of any kind from this squire, instead he saw only opportunities to finish him that he did not take. He would see how he went. There were still ten to enter, but he would not have to fight them all.

They were only through half a dozen tentative exchanges when the third squire was announced. It all seemed a bit slow to Guy, but he was grateful, he would have more energy for later when it would be needed. Guy used their next exchange to leave the other squire facing the newly introduced combatant and made ready, hoping that they would engage each other. The new squire indeed engaged and they seemed equally matched, as Guy looked on, ready. He thought about getting involved, he certainly saw many openings that he could have used, but the other two looked keen to try and take each other out, perhaps there was some history. He left them to it.

When the fourth squire was announced he came out swinging and Guy let him drive him around the arena as he utilised his well-practiced defence. He thought of the Knightmaker briefly, he was letting this guy push him around so much that there was not one section of the crowd that had not seen him up close. It was controlled by Guy, not once was he ever in any danger, but it made the other squire look good, and gave the crowd something to get excited about.

Three more squires had entered by the time Guy allowed himself to be driven back towards the centre of the arena, He had seen them all pretty much together waving their swords at each other with no real contact being made. That was seven. One way or another Hawkins had got what he wanted, he just hoped it was worth it. He was driven back by another attack, but as he was about to place his foot his helm was clattered by another squire seeking to take advantage. Off balance his mind flipped into survival mode. It was instinct. He had been clattered so many times, he knew that he needed to relax into the fall. All he did was aim himself and hope for a good landing. He managed to roll and end up aknee, taking a moment to clear his ringing head. Out of his visor he saw a glint of metal to his half left, and dived into a roll to escape. His vision was blurred and his head was still to settle. He backed off, firmly in survival mode, unaware of the crowd's excitement. He moved away to the edge of the arena, away from most of the other squires. He was pursued though, by at least one. He had given himself those precious few seconds, enough to recover his bearings, enough to evaluate his situation. No more fucking around. This time as the over confident squire approached thinking to drive him further towards the crowds barriers, he pivoted and slammed the pommel of his sword into the advancing squires visor. He dropped, thrown backwards by his own momentum and did not move. There was no need for a yield. The squires visor wad badly dented. Guy threw his arms out and screamed. Frustration and anger escaped him, his head continued to clear and his balance recover. The crowd nearby erupted, and Guy gave them a little display whirling his sword as he turned to face an approaching squire. From what Guy could tell he had just entered, he would probably be one of the better swordsmen come to pick off easy prey. Guy showed with the intent of his first block and parry that he was not easy prey, he drove the attacker back a step. Guy filled that gap, stepping into an attack of his own. He was not going full out yet, and his attack was blocked and a lengthy exchange was entered into, until the squire stepped back, and offered a nod of respect before stepping back in. Again they travelled along the barrier by the common folk to cheers and hollering. Guy was starting to catch him with more intent, and was aware of times when he did not. He was letting the other squire know that he was there, but he was still well within his limits.

He took the opportunity to see how many other squires were left. He had not heard an announcement for a while as he and the other squire enjoyed their own personal battle, the others stayed mostly in a group. There were seven left, which meant another two had been eliminated. He could see how a group of three squires were ganging up on a single squire who held his own. He had a curved sword, the likes of which Guy had never seen and was quick with it. He was unable to mount much offence but aside from the occasional tag and stagger he was doing ok. He was the squire from the east he recalled. He must have been paying more attention than he thought during the introduction. He was caught on his shoulder by a blow that reminded him where he his attention should be. He exaggerated his stagger, before tagging the squire back on his helm. Guy did not think that he was exaggerating as he staggered backwards. Guy pushed him with his boot and sent him sprawling to cheers from the nearby section of the crowd. He heeded the Knightmaker's words and swung a blow at the prone squire. He escaped as Guy expected, but it got a response from the crowd, he spun his sword snapping it into ready, true north as he allowed the squire to get to his feet.

The crowd had an effect on the other squire, and he rushed in with an attack that Guy blocked and parried. He followed one of the castle dances that he had learned and their combination drew more cheers of excitement from the crowd. Again it ended with Guy ringing the squire's helm which sent him staggering back, retreating towards the centre of the arena. Guy followed tagging him at will as the crowd cheered each blow. The squire was trying to retreat into the crowd, Guy knew, but was caught by surprise when he mounted an attack and managed to turn Guy so that his back was to the battle, facing the crowd. He stepped forward ready to punish the squire. It was time to take him out.

As he was laying blows on the squire, ready to beat him into submission, out of the corner of his eye he saw alarm in the crowd. Immediately his senses kicked in, he could hear the sounds of battle of course, but there was a sound of approaching armour that sounded clearest. He bent his knees and pushed himself upwards, tucking his knees to his chest. Something caught his boots and knocked him off balance. The same thing also fell through the feet of the other squire and it was atop both of them that Guy landed hard to gasps from the crowd. Guy rolled and sprang to his feet as the other two tried to disentangle, throwing punches as they did so. Jefferson had tried his trick of diving at his legs again. Not his time. Guy stepped in and kicked the shiny helm of Jefferson, to let him know that he was there, and stepped back as the other squire rose unimpeded and turned to face him as Jefferson rolled afloor in agony. Guy considered taking him out, he was good, but strictly followed the rules of the dance, and Guy knew other dances that would see him lost, but he noticed three squires break away from the dwindling group heading towards them. Guy offered a nod, and received one in return before the other squire turned to parry a blow.

It got very messy very quickly and Guy had to take one out clattering his helm. He did not yield, and was not knocked out, but he was out of action for a while. It was just as well because a re-helmed Jefferson was joining the fray, heading straight for Guy. He had to give it to Jefferson, or Jeff as his mind liked to call him, at the previous tournament he had squires helping him, and again here. Perhaps there was a pecking order that he was not aware of. He started making a point of tagging Jeff as he and his mates came at him. Sometimes he had to go through one, sometimes two, to do it, but he started batting them off as if they were not there, each time sending Jefferson to the floor. He wasn't trying to take him out, he did not really know what he was doing. What he did know was that he was showing off, and that would do him no good. As an angered Jeff got to his feet, a little slower than before, Guy swung round connecting his elbow with helm, sending one of Jeff's mates to the ground again. In an instant the point of Guys sword was at the visor. The immediate yield meant that he was ready for the attack from behind and after their swords clashed a few times, Jeff's other mate lay flat aback with Guy's sword at his visor. Guy became aware of the crowd for the first time in a while, they were cheering and hollering like fanatics. Guy turned to face Jefferson and jolted into ready north west and his armour sang, bringing more cheers.

Jeff's remaining mate was being taken care of by the squire Guy had spent most of the day fighting, and the eastern squire had bought the yield from one of the two that were on him, and was on his way to getting another. Guy smiled in his suit. There was nowhere else for Jeff to run. Guy invited him on, and he obliged, confident in his abilities. It was mostly the usual castle dance, Jefferson threw in a few different moves to try and get an edge, but he was nothing compared to the stranger. Guy parried with ease and struck at will, each time tagging him harder, smiling inside his helm about calling him Jeff, he would hate that. His mate Jeff would be hurting the next day, Guy was going to make sure of that. He was deciding whether he wanted to make him yield, or knock him out when he heard a cheer indicating another submission. The Eastern squire stood above his freshly yielded opponent and surveyed the arena. Guy entered into another sequence that ended in him slamming his sword into Jefferson's codpiece. No matter how good his armour was, that would hurt like fuck. The crowd liked that move, and it was quickly followed by another cheer as Jeff's final mate gave a standing yield, such was the battering he was getting.

Guy watched and assessed the arena, the three of them looked at each other while Jeff rolled afloor. Guy shared a look with the eastern squire, as if to say, *'I'll finish Jeff and let's get on with it.'* Guy let Jefferson struggle to his feet, he could barely raise his sword as Guy landed an overhead blow in the centre of his helm which sent him crumpling to the floor again. Guy did not get the satisfaction of looking into the fucker's eyes as he gave his yield when he struggled to get to his feet. Guy had wanted that so much, but for him to admit he was defeated would have to be enough. He would feel that defeat for days in his body, longer in his mind.

He stood to face the remaining two, as Jefferson was helped from the arena. They had barely moved since he last looked, the three of them faced each other in a triangle, perhaps two dozen feet apart. They all stood waiting as the crowd ramped up the noise. They were certainly putting on a show thought Guy as he gulped as much air as he could into his body.

Almost in unison they made ready and slowly advanced. Guy's heart was pounding and his lungs were burning as he waited to see what happened next. He thought that the Eastern squire would be the first to make a move, but against which one of them? He was alert to the threat as they edged gingerly towards each other. To his half left, he saw that it was the other squire who flinched first, but the eastern squire who landed the strike. He had been wound so tightly, he exploded into action as soon as there was movement. The two of them went at it, and Guy did not know what to do. He felt like he should get involved, but how would that benefit him? He left them to it, gasping for air, recovering his strength. Whichever one of them came out of it, he would have had more chance to recover. He stayed ready, moving his sword through the positions, he was expecting them both to turn on him.

Expect the worst and hope for better, that was what his training with Sir Parcifal had taught him. The problem had been, that no matter how bad Guys expectations were, the Knightmaker had always found a way to make them worse. He kept light on his feet, finding himself going through some drills just to stay alert. The eastern squire was going at it. He was not as skilled or disciplined as the other squire, but he could fight. He watched for openings, signs of weakness, tiredness. He saw them all, and focussed on gulping air in him as he drew the bolt symbol in his mind. He, along with everyone else, watched as the eastern squire started dominating the other. He kept moving forwards pressuring, and no matter how skilled the squire may have been, cracks were beginning to show. He was relentless, but was not taking the opportunities. Even when he was struck it did not stop his forward momentum, and being on the back foot was starting to tire the other squire. It was a shame to see someone who was obviously skilled being battered into submission and it did not take long until just that happened.

He looked at the eastern squire while the defeated other left the arena under his own steam. He knew that each second they took was a second more recovery for his opponent, but it was also further recovery for him. Guy felt he should approach and give him as little recovery as possible, but the eastern squire had other ideas. To the delight of the crowd he spun his sword around in a solo dance that was well practiced. Guy stood for a moment, before entering into his own dance. He had spun the iron pole at the rock for long enough that the dance happened of its own accord. He did not have to think of it. In his mind he was aware that he was putting on a show for the crowd, he ended with a 'Hyu' snapping his armour in a way that even the Knightmaker would be proud of. The crowd's cheers told him he had won that one. Now he just had to gain the yield.

For a moment his mind realised how close he was. *One more to go.* It was as if the eastern squire sensed the lack of focus and he came at him with speed. Guy manged to block and pivot, and was more prepared when the eastern squire turned to face him again. He came at him with powerful blows, but nothing compared to the Knightmaker, and Guy settled into blocking and dodging many of them, both of them got in some strikes, but Guy was just exploring, he could see ways to take him out, but he wanted to see what the response was. He was not as skilled as the other squire, nor did he follow the dances moves as much. It was power and aggression that the eastern squire used. Guy started to feed the aggression by stepping away from, or dodging the attacks. Whilst tiring his opponent it also raised his frustration, and frustrated people made mistakes.

Guy soon realised that it was not just frustration that leads to mistakes, complacency did as well. He casually sidestepped another attack, but the Eastern squire was aware, and had learnt, bringing his curved sword around to the back of Guys leg. He crashed aback knocking the wind out of him. He shouldn't have fucked around, he shouldn't… He rolled away as the curved sword came down, rolling to safety but minus his sword as he scrambled to his feet favouring his leg. He gasped for air as his mind raced. He had to get his sword, but it was behind the other squire who he imagined to be smiling behind his visor. He had no option but to wait for him to make a move, but he was crouched and moving, showing the squire that he was ready. The eastern squire showed Guy that he still had his sword offering another display for the crowd. Guy tried to circle around the squire by moving from side to side, gradually moving further right each time closer to his sword. He did not fool his opponent though who simply stepped forward a few paces forcing Guy to retreat. His sword was gone, he needed another plan. He was not going to fuck it up after getting so close. All his attention was on the other squire, in that moment there was no crowd, no Knightmaker, no Phylissa even. There was only the two of them. The squire came at him, and while he dodged the initial blow he was tagged soon after and had to retreat. It took another three attempts, and three frenzied escapes before he managed to get into the position he had been looking for. He was up close against him after receiving a glancing blow to his pauldron. He planted his feet and pushed as hard as he could with both arms pushing the squire and his armour into the air.

He started to roll as he landed, but Guy was already moving to dive atop him and secure the sword arm. He grasped it with both hands as they rolled about on the floor until finally Guy was able to use his size and restrain the rest of him. He slammed the sword arm into the ground until his grip was released while the eastern squire threw punches with his free hand. Guy slammed the back of his gauntlet into the squire's helm and watched his head rock to the side, then as he recovered slammed the bottom of his fist into the front of the helm slamming his head against the floor. Guy flung the curved blade away then stood and beckoned up the squire, unaware that the crowd were in raptures.

The Eastern squire had his warrior blood well and truly awoken and once he had got his bearings launched at Guy. They grappled and threw punches, but it was becoming messy, Guy pushed him away to try and get some space, but he came right back at him. He was relentless. The third time he launched at Guy he was ready, slamming him with a straight arm as he stepped through him. The squire flipped a full circle before landing heavily on his back. Guy paused only for a moment as he tried to struggle to his feet, but could not get beyond all fours. Guy stepped in kicking him in the head so smoothly that his helm flew off and across the arena, and the squire landed on his back. He was barely conscious as Guy placed his foot on his chest and looked down at his bloodied face with respect. Guy looked up when he nodded his yield and the cheers of the crowd invaded his world again. He had done it. He punched both hands in the air and let out a triumphant scream.

He had won. He knew it, but did not understand it. He took a moment to look around, the king was applauding, the Knightmaker sat beside him in the Royal enclosure as if he had expected nothing else. He was sure that it he were to look closer he would get a nod. Further round in the stands he spotted Hawkins, he was not looking at him, instead involved in victorious conversations. He saluted the crowd, bowed to the king, and then turned and saluted the normal people to a cheer. Not knowing what else to do he turned to leave the arena.

59

There were not many friendly faces in the competitor's area, many of the defeated squires had departed and the jousting did not conclude until late afternoon. A few people slapped him on the back as he passed, even a couple of knights. He spoke briefly with the squire he had battled with for most of the contest and accepted his congratulations, wishing him luck as he departed. He wanted to pull off his helm and freely breathe. But a voice caught his attention.

'Fucking hells big man,' Johnny called as he approached, 'Fucking hells.'

Johnny was clearly pleased for him, and for a moment he allowed himself to be pleased as well. *He had done it.* He knew in his mind, that he would not comprehend it, and did not even try. That would come with time. He congratulated Johnny on his third place in the Archery and looked at the silver arrow he was keeping under his cloak.

'It should keep Sir Chandley happy for a while,' he smiled.

'Aye, and so it should. I must return to my camp. I need to get this armour off.'

'Aye, can I see you later?'

'Of course.'

'Fucking well done big man. I knew you could do it.'

They clasped arms and headed off in different directions, Guy's body started to feel heavy and sore after his efforts. One thing dominated his mind on the way back to the pavilion as he grinned inside his helm like the village lunatic. *He'd fucking done it.*

He composed himself as he approached the tent, the stranger was sat outside keeping watch. He pulled off his helm as he approached the balcony, the stranger nodded. It was one given with respect, but one that also told Guy that this was expected. There was something in his eyes, it was as close to a smile as he had seen. He ducked into the tent where a steaming tub dominated the centre of the room, he could smell herbs in the steam. The stranger pushed in behind him and helped him out of his armour. He could have done it himself, but with the stranger it was off in no time. Guy was grateful, his body was losing the excitement of the day and feeling slow and heavy. A bath was just what he needed. Once the armour was in a neat pile the stranger went to resume his watch and Guy peeled off the sweat soaked underclothes. He lowered himself into the tub with a sigh and let the hot water soothe his body.

It felt good. He drew symbols in his mind and felt even better. He could not get past the fact that he had done it, he had won the tournament, and would be knighted. He had not dared to think beyond this point and would not try now, instead he tried to relax his mind and enjoy his victory. *He'd fucking done it.*

When he had finished soaking in the tub the stranger was not in his usual spot, so Guy sat and kept watch, for where there are knights there are thieves. He tried to hide the grin as he sat there and people passed, probably happy that the Knightmaker was not there honking at them. All that consumed his mind was that he had done it, nothing past, nothing future and it was a delightful time for Guy as the sun lowered in the sky. The warm early autumnal colours pleased him, the slight breeze pleased him. Hells, someone could take a dump on his boots and that would probably please him too. Guy cared not, it had been some time since he had been pleased with anything other than seeing another day, and that did not usually last long. More than anything he was pleased with his sense of accomplishment, for no matter what anyone said, he had earnt this knighthood. Perhaps not through the years of servitude as many of the squires, but the old fashioned way with sweat, blood and hard fucking work.

Guy and the stranger were sat in silence together looking out over the knight's quarters. Guy was still unable to get his mind to contemplate anything other than the fact that he had done what he had needed to, and the satisfied grin was barely hidden. He had nothing to do until the Knightmaker returned, he had nothing to do anyway, he had done it. He could not return to Waering until he had been knighted, he felt trapped in a space between time. All he could do was wait for what was to happen.

'Hoy Big Man,' Johnny called. Guy looked up smiling. 'Can I come in?' Guy's eyes flicked to the strangers who nodded without moving his head.

'Of course. Do you want a drink?'

'Nah big man,' Johnny said as he approached, 'I have come to collect you for dinner. I hope you don't mind but I told Sir Chandley of your intent at the archery.' Mild panic made Guy's eyes flick to the strangers, but if he gave a fuck he did not show it. 'He did very well out of it, and has invited you to dine with him. Sir Parcifal is there already.' Guy looked to the stranger who nodded.

'Aye, should I change?' Guy looked at his casual clothing. Johnny laughed.

'No big man, this is just us. You are fine as you are.' Guy checked his belt, he felt naked without it, and pulled his shirt to cover it, standing ready to leave. 'Your man did good today,' Johnny said to the stranger who simply nodded in reply.

Guy walked with him as Johnny continued his enthusiastic recounting of the melee. It was good for Guy to hear, he had begun to wonder if it had been a dream, a fantasy of his mind, some of the parts he knew, others he did not. A feeling rose in him as he followed Johnny to the castle, he wasn't sure what it was, but it felt good.

Johnny led him through corridors and past guards deep into the castle, he could hear Sir Parcifal's booming laugh as they approached the room, a guard opened the door for them and the laughter stopped. Guy followed Johnny into the room and was immediately hit by the heat thrown off from the fire in the hearth. The room was small but lavish, silks hung from the walls, fine polished furniture and animal skin rugs adorned it.

'Here he is,' called out Sir Chandley, who from the sound of him had supped plenty. He hoped Sir Parcifal was being more cautious with the drawbridge challenge the following day. Sir Parcifal he had come to learn was adept at playing drunk. 'You really are a big fellow,' he continued. 'Johnny said you were big, but I did not appreciate just how big from watching the melee.' Guy felt as if he flushed and hoped it did not show. He was never comfortable when people talked of his size.

'Sir Chandley,' Guy offered in greeting, before nodding at the Knightmaker.

'Come, sit, and let us celebrate your victory.'

Sir Chandley beckoned a servant to fill some goblets with wine. 'It is my own vintage. Normally the king buys the best, but I keep some to one side.' He held out the goblets for the two squires. 'A toast,' he declared, 'to Guy, tournament champion of the squires, and to Johnny, the first non-westerner in half a dozen years to win a place in the archery; and to the knights who trained them.'

He raised his goblet and they all drank. Guy did not know much about wine, but assumed that it would be the best wine he had ever tasted. He caught the Knightmaker's eye, it was the first time he had seen him since the tournament, he nodded, and cracked the vaguest hint of a smile and Guy felt pride course through his body. He knew what was on the line, and he had come through, not only for himself, but for Sir Parcifal, and someway that meant more to him than the accomplishment of his own goal. Perhaps because he was yet to take in his victory, perhaps because of all the people in his life, the Knightmaker had become the one whose respect meant most.

'Johnny here told me that you fucked up the archery on purpose,' Sir Chandley continued. For a moment Guy had the same feeling of dread he had felt when Johnny had mentioned it earlier. 'As a result I have made a lot of coin. I turned a dozen into a gross.' He let those words sink in as he turned to the Knightmaker. 'I wish you had told me, I could have done the same for you.'

'We did ok.'

'I have no doubt. You should send your man to me tomorrow. I know men who like to gamble with much coin. Send him with two dozen. He can lose a dozen and win them, and more back.'

'Thank you. I shall send him to you in the morning.' Sir Chandley turned back to Guy.

'I was willing to risk a dozen gold on you. When you gamble you must expect not to see that coin again.' He tossed a pouch onto the table with a heavy clatter. 'This is for you, my original stake.' Guy looked at the pouch, and then to Sir Parcifal. He did not know what to do. Was he really being given a dozen gold? 'Well come on boy, take it. You are to be a knight, and a knight needs coin.'

'Sir Parcifal should have it.'

'Ha.' He fished out a gold from his pocket and flipped it towards Sir Parcifal who snatched it out of the air. 'You were right.' They shared a laugh at Guy's expense. 'This gold is for you. You earned it. Sir Parcifal will see me right tomorrow.' He nodded towards Sir Parcifal. 'There is a chance I can make more coin tomorrow than I did today, and yours was not the only bet I won.' He allowed himself a satisfied laugh. For all Hawkins' work and antics, Sir Chandley it seemed operated on another level all together. It was a level Guy felt he would never understand. Where so many people struggled for a single copper, Sir Chandley was throwing gold around as if it meant nothing. Take the gold boy, lest some servant clear it away.' Guy looked again to Sir Parcifal.

'Take the gold,' he offered with a reassuring nod. Guy was still reluctant, he did not want to be in anyone's debt.

'I have another one hundred and twenty two from your efforts. I have done well, it is only right that you take a share.' Guy reached for the pouch. He would split it with the others later. 'But promise me one thing.' Guy stopped his hand. He should have known there would be conditions. 'If you need work for the winter, come and work with me. I always need good knights to protect my wine and my grounds.' Guy looked at Sir Chandley, he was older than the Knightmaker, and nowhere near as intimidating, but he looked like he did not take any shit.

'I can't Sir Chandley. I have things I must do.'

'He has a woman to claim,' the Knightmaker interjected.

'A woman?' Sir Chandley looked at him, 'Well, let me say this then. Should you ever need work, think of me first. I pay good coin for the right men.' Guy nodded. He had not even thought about what came next. 'But the gold is yours. Take it before the food arrives.' Guy picked up the pouch and secured in in his belt.

'I don't know what to say. Thank you.'

'You earned it. It took balls to do that.' Guy looked to Johnny and nodded. 'And don't be thinking of giving any away. Johnny has been rewarded for bringing me the news.' Johnny grinned and nodded with a little too much enthusiasm.

'Thank you,' Guy repeated.

'No, thank you,' Sir Chandley offered. 'You have made this a very fruitful trip, and we still have Sir Parcifal to go tomorrow. How do you think you will fare old friend?' The Knightmaker became serious.

'I do not need my shield, but I'll be fucked if I am going to let anyone take it from me.'

The words hung in the air, Sir Chandley nodded, Guy and Johnny remained silent. The awkwardness stopped as the rear doors opened and servants bought in the food. They remained quiet as the servants fussed about, preparing the area and leaving the platters on the table.

'The king eats with the important people tonight, but he shares his food with us,' Sir Chandley proclaimed. 'Guy, have you ever tried swan?' Guy shook his head. Swans were the king's birds, anyone caught eating or killing one could lose their life, or at least their hands. 'Well, imagine a dog fucked a duck, its offspring would taste like swan.' Sir Chandley laughed at his own joke briefly, 'Come, let us eat, let us celebrate.'

They ate and drank late into the night and after a goblet of sweet wine, the sweetest smoothest liquid to ever pass Guy's lips, he sat back in his chair. He had long since given up trying to process anything from the day, besides, the wine was stopping his mind from working correctly. He knew he should try to stop it from swirling, to keep control, and he knew he wore a stupid grin on his face, and that he probably looked like Johnny, a stupid, happy young prick that had supped more than he should. Seeing Johnny like that made him laugh inside, or at least he thought it was inside. When he saw Johnny start to laugh with him he could not stop himself. The two of them sat giggling like idiots, but he did not care, he had fucking done it. His eyes closed and his head rested back on his chair. He breathed, it was all he could do. *He had fucking done it.*

Through the haze of the wine his ears heard the two knights talking. They had got serious like men who have supped sometimes do. It was Sir Chandley's voice.

'It is every knight's dream to be a kings own knight. You will have many suitors for your shield.'

'Aye, maybe.' The Knightmaker replied, 'Maybe not, for some the price will be too high.'

'How so?'

'These fuckers have been eying up my shield all week. Betting is not the only way a knight can make coin.'

'Indeed.'

'I'm not a tournament knight. When I fight, I fight.'

Sir Chandley laughed. 'I remember.'

'Aye. These fuckers do not know what war is. If they step onto that bridge, they will find out, and they know it.'

'Still, to be a king's own knight, many in our day gave their life to be one. I doubt it is any different today.'

'We'll see.'

When the Knightmaker roused Guy later, the first thing he noticed was that he was still grinning, he simply could not stop. His face was hurting from it. As the Knightmaker's face slowly came into focus, Guy saw that he was all business.

'We go now.'

The Knightmaker's words stirred Guy. Those words always had. They meant suck it up and get the fuck on with it. The control he had dismissed earlier returned and he shook away the haze before nodding to the Knightmaker that he was ready. Standing was not easy, but he managed to only smile in Johnny's direction when his wobble bought more giggles. He took a breath and straightened. He had not thought about getting back to their camp. The Knightmaker seemed in control as he opened the door, after bidding farewell to Sir Chandley, he even gave Johnny a nod. A guard stood to and escorted them through the castle. He remained two steps behind and one to the left of the Knightmaker and used all his concentration to do so. He knew it would be evident to anyone who saw them that he was drunk, and his grin was never far away. He managed to keep it together until the Guard left them at a castle entrance. He saw Sir Parcifal nod his thanks as he turned. They walked towards the gates and once through, and slightly away from the guards, the Knightmaker transformed into the drunk that he had been throughout the week, perhaps not so much an act as it had been on other nights.

'Let's give them a show.'

The fresh air had smacked Guy in the face like the world's biggest salmon, and he was naturally staggering, there was no acting required for Guy. Before long they were both weaving towards the knight's quarters, arms around each other's shoulders as the Knightmaker was spouting bollocks that Guy could not understand. Guy was vaguely aware that there were people about, and that they looked at them, but he allowed the Knightmaker to lead him back to the tent and the safety that it bought. He collapsed in a heap on the floor as they entered the tent, and unlike the Knightmaker, he was unable to switch off the performance. The Knightmaker forced him to drink two skins of water. Sleep found him quickly and deeply. He slept as he had spent most of the night, wearing a ridiculous grin.

60

Ittook more than a single nudge from the Knightmaker's boot to rouse him the following morning, and when he grunted his acknowledgment the Knightmaker nudged him again this time harder.

'Get up, we have a busy day. You don't want to miss your own knighthood. Fill the skins, wash yourself and get us some food.'

There was a part of Guy that wanted to sleep more, but a larger part, his bladder, that needed him to get up as a matter of urgency. His head throbbed as he sat up rubbing his eyes, they hurt too.

'Get busy, there is little over an hour until we needs be at the arena. Drink some water to clear your head.'

Guy crawled from his rollmat, feeling as if someone had poured honey in his ear and filled his head with it while he slept. He needed to piss more than anything, but a quick glance around provided no suitable receptacle. He gathered some skins and walked quickly to the river, each step hurt both his head and his overfull bladder. His body played tricks on him as he neared the river and he had to clench hard through the pain to prevent pissing himself. He pulled off his boots and trousers quicker than he had in a long time and strode into the waters finally releasing as he crouched. The relief was immense, and anyone who saw him would know exactly what he was doing. He cared not. All he was concerned with was relief. He moved upstream before ducking his head into the waters trying to awaken himself, and quickly scrubbed himself before pulling clothes onto his wet body and filling the skins from the water pump on the way back.

His head was still not right, but he did not need to be on form, he just had to get there. It was the Knightmaker's day to perform. He collected eggs, sliced pork and bread enough for four from the muster and returned to the tent where he found the Knightmaker being attended to by the stranger. It was unusual for the Knightmaker to be in full armour, he usually wore half armour over chain, but that day he was not for fucking around. If what Guy had read about previous drawbridge challenges was right, the Knightmaker would be lucky to survive. The Knightmaker did not look concerned.

'Hawkins,' he boomed. 'Get the food on so Guy can get ready.' Hawkins emerged from the tent, it was the first time Guy had seen him in a while. He nodded at him with a smile that said two things, one was, well done, the other, sympathy to his sufferings. He took the food from Guy and set to preparing their meal. Guy drank from a skin. 'Don't fuck about there, time is against us. Get yourself ready. Wear your knight's armour. This is a big day for you.'

Guy pushed into the tent to see his armour laid out for him. He usually preferred to prepare his own kit, but was grateful. He stripped from his wet clothes and started getting ready. He would not wear his chain or gambeson for his day was to be ceremonial. He pulled his leather around his body though, to protect him from the armour. The stranger finished up with the Knightmaker and went to help Guy. Between them he was ready in no time. The armour felt fantastic, a part of him thought that maybe he should have worn in in the melee, he could move so freely in it compared to his training armour. The smell of fried pork and eggs wafted inside the tent and he realised how hungry he was. He hoped that it would soak up the washiness that churned in his belly. He pushed through the flaps of the tent to be handed a plate almost immediately. He started filling his face as if he had not eaten for a week.

'Though you are to be knighted today, I have one more request of you. You will act as my squire today.'

'Of course,' Guy replied. 'What do I need to do?'

'Stand there and look mean, and feed me water when I require. Make people think twice about approaching. Your new armour will help, take your sword. I'll tell you if I need anything else.' Guy nodded as they shovelled food into their mouths. 'Hawkins, did you get what I asked for?'

'I did.'

He put his plate down before disappearing into the tent, emerging again with a pair of huge greatswords. 'Will these do?' The Knightmaker took one laughing.

'Aye, this will do.' The Knightmaker said as he examined one of them. The sword looked big, almost up to the Knightmaker's shoulder, and it looked heavy with its full blade. 'No one is going to want to fight with this.' Guy felt himself staring admiringly at the Knightmaker. He looked like a bad fucker, but he was smart. Drawbridge challenges were often for legendary weapons, and the challengers had to use a weapon of similar type. By choosing the greatsword, the Knightmaker was forcing anyone who challenged him to use the same, and there were not many in the kingdom for which the greatsword was the weapon of choice.

Despite Guy's best efforts he could not shake the haze in his head that the previous night's wine had left. He tried to listen as the Knightmaker gave him instructions for the day as they made their way to the tournament area, and he tried to listen as the stewards instructed him on the procedures and etiquette that were required. He hoped that someway his mind was taking everything in and he would be able to recall it later, but at that time he could not recall what he had been told. He found himself nodding and trying to look attentive, hoping that the Knightmaker would steer him where he needed to be.

He was glad when the instructions were over and he was left in the competitor's area to wait. It was busy, not as busy as the first days of the tournament, but there were plenty of knights and squires making ready. The tournament itself was complete, the champion would be crowned after Guy had been knighted, but this was the king's showcase day. The drawbridge challenge was the big event of the day, but there were any number of other bouts to happen between challenges.

He could hear the crowd as the jesters warmed them up with their acrobatics and juggling, his moment had almost arrived. It was not how he had dreamed it would be. He had always imagined being knighted by the Knightmaker, it would have meant more to him after his personal journey, but to be knighted by the king himself, he had never dreamed of such a thing. He wished his mind was not swimming in a haze of wine, he had wanted to be on top form for the ceremony, but he could not change what was. The main thing, he considered, was that it was happening at all. Sir Parcifal stood silently beside him, he too had been given instructions about his day, and indeed, had given instructions back. Perhaps the Knightmaker was reflecting on what lay ahead for him. Guy tried to consider what was about to happen, but in a moment that should see excitement rising in him there was nothing, just a thick head. He simply stood, not even paying attention to those around him, waiting to be called.

Finally the horns sounded, and Guy knew that the king would be making his way to the presentation area.

'When we go out there, we go out there with purpose. This is your fucking moment.'

The Knightmaker spoke so only he could hear. Guy nodded and following the Knightmaker's lead and pulled his helm on. He found himself taking a deep breath, and when the stewards beckoned them he followed the Knightmaker, with purpose, two steps behind, one to the left. He was glad that he had his helm on, especially once they entered the arena. Someway it had been transformed overnight. At one end of the arena a wall of over 30 feet had been constructed, it was probably twenty feet high, and held a raised drawbridge. He would discover later that a large trench had also been dug and filled with water to represent a moat. The transformation was astonishing. It sat to the left of where the king would sit, and would be where Guy would spend the rest of the day. If nothing else, it would give him a magnificent view of the other events. He had barely composed himself when they approached the presentation stage where the king was waiting, another fanfare erupted, and so did the crowd. Guy assumed that much of the cheering was for the actual tournament champion who followed behind, but he did not care. He suddenly felt a little self-conscious, as he stood before the king with purpose, or as much as he could muster, every eye in the arena on him. Even that faded as his head offered a distant throb. It took too much effort to keep the world in the visor of his helm to concern himself with much more, his mind made him feel vacant, and that was not how he had intended the day to be. It was the biggest day of his life, and emotion was distant. It did not seem right.

Finally the fanfare died down and the king's herald stepped forward and welcomed everyone to the final day of the tournament. Guy wished that he were not so close, for he spoke so that he could be heard by much of the crowd, and that was loud to Guy who stood only 6 feet away. He harped on about the tournament so far, and how the last day would eclipse them all. Guy doubted whether it was true, it was probably aimed more at rousing the crowd. Though as he reeled off some of the events, he found himself looking forward to seeing them, especially if Sir Parcifal held onto his shield, then he would be sat within the arena itself.

The Herald's big moment soon came to an end, had Guy been more of mind he would have appreciated how succinct the speech had been.

'And now,' he declared, 'show your appreciation for our champions with the victory presentations.' The crowd cheered and a steady drum beat started. This was Guy's cue. He removed his helm and tucked it beneath an arm. The light made his eyes blur and his body sway, but the freedom to breathe unrestricted air meant that he controlled it. He stepped forward to where the king had positioned himself and took a knee.

'Master Guy, congratulations on your victory. I have rarely seen a squire like you, but then I have rarely seen a knight like Sir Parcifal.' Guy nodded, he did not know what else to do. 'Had you not achieved a victory, I would have knighted you anyway for slaying the beast. It gives me great pleasure to knight you now,' the king said as if he were speaking to Guy alone. At that moment, the crowd did not exist, even Sir Parcifal was not in the moment. It was just him and the king. 'Sir Parcifal claims you will be one of the greatest knights Rodina has ever seen.' Guy looked at the king, still lost for words. Out of the corner of his eye he saw two servants approach with the legendary greatsword resting on two velvet cushions. He lowered his head.

The king took the sword, and touched it on each shoulder. 'Arise Sir Guy of Waering, Knight of Rodina. Your life is now governed by the knight's code.' Guy looked up before standing, he still felt no emotion, but saw some in the king's eyes.

'Thank you, Your Grace.'

A servant approached with another velvet cushion, on it sat a folded white silk cloak, which held a small red leather bound book, and on top of that, a set of golden spurs. The king lifted them from the cushion and held them out to Guy. He bowed as he took them.

'Congratulations Sir Guy.' As the silk touched his hands emotion suddenly returned to him, he had not been expecting to receive a white cloak, he could return to Waering as Phylissa had asked. He felt a lump in his throat.

'Thank you, Your Grace.' His words were thick with emotion.

'I shall see you at the champion's banquet tonight.' Guy nodded, fighting tears. It would not do to break down in front of so many people. He controlled his breathing. *He had fucking done it.*

61

He stood for a moment as the crowd cheered and applauded. He was about to step backwards to join Sir Parcifal, when a knight burst through the crowd and tossed a gauntlet at Guy's feet and the crowd gasped. Guy looked at the knight, still unable to muster any reaction. It was Sir Robert Young, the knight he had laid out back at the tournament in Rowansbrook, Jeff's master.

'How dare you interrupt the ceremony,' boomed the king's voice. It was intimidating indeed, but still not up to the Knightmaker's standards. Sir Young was taken aback. 'I shall not allow this challenge, but since you want to fight, you can be the first challenger to Sir Parcifal,' the king looked to the tournament champion, whose right it was to challenge first, 'if you have no objections.'

'None at all, Your Grace.'

Sir Young could not hide his anger, but knew better than to disobey the king. He nodded, and approached to collect his gauntlet.

'Another time boy,' he said to Guy, trying to intimidate him.

'Aye, but not today.'

The knight's face reddened from anger and he curled a lip at him. Guy could not help but smile and Sir Young hastily made his way through the presentation party as the crowd quietened. Guy calmly stepped back to stand beside Sir Parcifal as the announcement was made for the tournament.

'You did well,' the Knightmaker spoke quietly, 'Congratulations.' Guy nodded as he watched the tournament champion approach the king to receive a small chest which looked to be full of gold coins. It seemed that this was a tournament worth winning.

Guy watched as the knight received and enjoyed the acclaim of the crowd. He certainly knew how to work them. It was a different show to the one the Knightmaker had taught him. Guy was more aware of the shows people put on, now that he had been a part of one himself. In fact he still was, their day was not over. For the Knightmaker, it was yet to begin. He sorted himself out while the ceremony continued, regained his focus, or as much as he could, trying to remember the Knightmaker's instructions. Becoming a knight was only step one for the day. He would have to put it to one side, he would enjoy it later, but he had to focus. He owed the Knightmaker that much.

As the ceremony came to a close and the prizes had been handed out, the herald returned to encourage the crowd to celebrate the victors as they departed the arena. Guy raised his hand in acknowledgment, and followed the Knightmaker from the arena with purpose, leaving the others to milk the crowd.

Tournament stewards were waiting for them as they passed through the gate, waiting to finalise details with the Knightmaker. The tournament champion congratulated Guy as he passed. Guy thanked him, but it was clear his mind was on other things. Guy would seek him out at the banquet.

Sir Parcifal and Guy were led around the arena, behind the stalls to the newly constructed wall. While this was happening, all remaining knights were collecting in the arena itself raising the excitement of the crowd. Guy was pleased that the Knightmaker was a thorough man, he had the chance to grasp more detail of the instructions as the Knightmaker went through everything again as they walked. Out of view Guy walked beside him, his mind clearer, more able to focus, and put the Knightmaker's instructions in order.

The drawbridge was up, Guy and the Knightmaker stood behind it, alone. The rest of Rodina was on the other side as the herald announced the challenge and explained the rules to the knights and crowd alike. Guy realised he was breathing hard, his blood was flowing. He drew symbols in his mind to connect with the world.

'Let the challenge begin!' the king called, the crowd cheered as the drawbridge started to lower with the sound of rattling chains. Guy stood behind the Knightmaker, who waited until the bridge was fully lowered before stepping out onto it as the crowd went wild. He simply stood with his shield on his arm.

The king approached the drawbridge, stopping on the other side to face the assembled knights and crowd.

'Knights of Rodina.' He called, 'To be a king's own knight is the pinnacle of what you do. For reasons of a political nature, Sir Parcifal is to defend his Shield, the shield of the king's own knights. Should one of you claim the shield, you shall have the chance to become a king's own knight without the usual selection process.' He paused to let the words sink in, the crowd took the opportunity to roar with anticipation. 'Victory is gained through submission, incapacitation or by forcing your opponent from the drawbridge. Up to a dozen of you can challenge, and it is he who has the shield at the end of the day that will be the victor.' The king paused again, Guy had not even considered the idea of the Knightmaker being defeated, but if he were, it could be that the man who defeated him may lose the shield himself. He remembered reading of such occasions where legendary weapons were on the line. A man could only claim to have owned it, if they were declared the victor of the entire challenge. 'Sir Parcifal has chosen the weapons with which the contest will be fought. It is time to reveal what it is.'

That was Guy's cue. He picked up the greatsword and walked with purpose out and across the drawbridge, theatrically raising the sword before sticking it point first into the ground. To his delight the sword held, he had been fearful of it falling over, but the ground was soft enough to take it, and he had given it some power. He found himself bowing to the king before turning and taking up his position behind Sir Parcifal.

'The Greatsword,' announced the king. There were cheers from the crowd, but concerned looks from the knights as they looked around at each other, presumably looking for those that favoured the weapon. Guy knew that some would not even consider taking part with such a blade. It was big and heavy, cumbersome in the wrong hands. 'Normally it is the honour of the tournament champion to decide if they wish to be the first challenger, but on this occasion the first challenger has been determined. Sir Young, step up, let the drawbridge challenge commence.'

The crowd roared and Sir Robert Young was ushered forward by two turquoise knights. He did not look happy about it. As he approached the drawbridge he exchanged glances with the king who was returning to his viewing seat. Guy realised that the crowd were jeering, seemingly his public challenge had not gone down well with them either. The rest of the knights although dismissed had not moved, almost all of them remained to see the first challenge. As Sir Young approached the sword the Knightmaker strode out halfway across the drawbridge.

'You come for my shield. What do you offer me if I beat you?' the Knightmaker said. Guy could hear, but not many others would.

'I offer you fuck all. I am here because I have to be.' The Knightmaker stayed still, Guy imagined the discomfort Sir Young would be feeling. Even through his helm, he imagined the Knightmaker's eyes burning with contempt.

'If you offer me nothing, I shall have to take something.'

'You'll take nothing from me. You are nothing but a drunken has been. You don't deserve that shield, and your squire does not deserve to be knighted.' He spat on the floor.

'Perhaps, if I let you live, I shall take your ability to walk,' the Knightmaker said almost casually. 'I am not a man you want to disrespect.' Before Sir Young could answer the Knightmaker continued, this time in his booming voice. 'You want my shield? Come and get it.'

He turned away from the knight and walked back to Guy who had his sword ready. He could see Sir Young struggle to remove the huge blade from the ground. He smiled inside his helm when he finally pulled it free with a stagger. He heard some of the crowd laugh.

The Knightmaker took his sword and turned to face Sir Young who was gingerly swinging the sword to get a feel for its weight. The Knightmaker took three paces onto the bridge and swung his own sword a few times in a display that put the other knight to shame. Even from the other side of the drawbridge Guy could see anger in Sir Young's eyes. That was no way to start a contest. Anger clouded judgement, and you could not afford to do that against someone like Sir Parcifal. The angered knight took a breath and stepped onto the bridge, the Knightmaker allowing him half a dozen steps before starting to meet him.

'You want my shield?' he boomed. Sir Young took a wild swing with his sword, the Knightmaker stepped inside the arc of the blade, instead of striking with his own sword, he stamped on the side of Sir Young's knee, making it bend in a way it was not supposed to. He let out a scream, one which turned into the highest pitched noise Guy had ever heard a grown man make. He collapsed to the floor, sword clattering, as his hands went for his knee. He curled up, a foot or so from the edge of the drawbridge, in too much in pain to yield. The Knightmaker did not give him the chance, a two stepped approach saw the Knightmaker's boot connect with Sir Young's body, lifting him off the ground. As he landed the momentum took him over the edge of the drawbridge and he fell the four feet into the water below. 'Get off my bridge.' The Knightmaker boomed. Stewards rushed into the water to help the defeated knight out of the water, and potentially prevent him drowning. Losing the use of a leg, mixed with immense pain had stalled his movement, and he thrashed desperately raising his head to breathe between screams. 'Who's next?' The Knightmaker called. No one stepped forward. It was tradition for other events to take place to give the victor time to recover. Such was the brevity of the contest, preparations were not in place, and there was a break while the knights dispersed, and physicians carried the screaming Sir Young away on a blanket while the crowd showed their appreciation.

'I don't think that he will be tossing any more gauntlets for a while.' the Knightmaker said to Guy as he returned.

By the time Guy had finished setting up a table with chairs, fruit and water, and replaced the sword at the other end of the drawbridge an impromptu quarterstaff bout had begun. Guy stood beside the Knightmaker while he relaxed and watched. By the end of the bout Guy had decided that the quarterstaff was something he should learn. It was all about speed and footwork, he knew that if he could master it many would underestimate him, simply because of his size. When the bout had concluded without serious injury to either combatant, the king gave the tournament champion his opportunity to face the Knightmaker. He approached with much pomp and ceremony and stood at the far end of the drawbridge. The Knightmaker rose without sword and took three paces onto the bridge.

'If you come to challenge for my shield, what do you offer me should I win?'

'What did the last knight offer?'

'Nothing, and now he cannot walk.'

'You despatched him quickly.'

'He pissed me off.' It occurred to Guy that the champion was not one of the knights that Sir Parcifal had been abusing as they walked past.

'What would you like me to offer?'

'Your champion's prize.' The knight thought for a moment.

'How about half, that is a dozen gold. I could not return to my wife empty handed after winning such a tourney.'

'Fair enough,' the Knightmaker replied.

'I take it that will mean that I would suffer no unfortunate accidents, and we can put on a show for the people.'

'Aye.' The knight nodded.

'I shall return later to take your shield,' he declared loudly, and turned heading back to the arena. As champion he was given the choice, he had chosen to wait, and Guy could not blame him. Why take on a fresh Knightmaker, when in a few bouts time fatigue would have set in.

'Are there any other challengers?' the herald called. Guy looked over to the wings where some knights had collected. They shared looks between them, but after what Sir Parcifal had done to Sir Young there seemed a reluctance to step forward. After almost a minute, a knight stepped forward. He did not wear fancy armour and did not appear to be much older than Guy, he was certainly smaller. Guy could hear the murmur of the crowd even from where he stood. Where perhaps they had been expecting a famous knight to approach, instead they were faced with a young upstart. He approached with purpose though, and Guy knew Sir Parcifal would appreciate that. When he reached the other side of the drawbridge Sir Parcifal stood and took the three steps towards him.

'If you come to challenge for my shield, what do you offer me should I win?'

'Alas I have nothing to offer.'

'Then why are you here?'

'Sir Parcifal, you are one of the greatest knights Rodina has known. It would be an honour to touch swords with you.' The young knight was respectful, he heard the Knightmaker take a breath, 'Besides, after what you did to Sir Young, many others are reluctant to face you.'

'But not you?'

'I have nothing to lose, and besides, if I last a few minutes it might encourage others to step up.'

'What if I do not want others to step up?'

'I had not thought of that. I'm sorry, I was just trying to help.'

'What do you have to offer me, so that I do not hurt you?'

'Anything you like, my armour and horse, though they will not fetch much. I could offer you a year's service.' There was hope in his voice.

'I have no need of another mouth to feed.'

'Please Sir Parcifal, to say I touched swords with you would be the greatest thing to have happened in my life.' There was a pause.

'Three minutes, then you take a swim, and I will take your armour.'

'Thank you Sir Parcifal, thank you.' Guy wondered if the poor boy knew what he was letting himself in for. He struggled to pull the sword from the ground as Sir Parcifal returned and Guy handed him his sword.

'This one has balls,' Sir Parcifal said as he turned to face him. The sword was far too big for the young knight, but he wielded it with some proficiency and Sir Parcifal allowed a short exchange before ringing his helm. The young knight staggered back, gathered himself and came at him again. Sir Parcifal allowed the knight to drive him back a couple of paces before planting the pommel of the sword in his chest sending him to his arse. The young knight squirmed back, to make space to rise, but Sir Parcifal did not advance. After a couple more exchanges, true to his word Sir Parcifal sent the young knight into the moat with another blow to the helm. He crawled out of the moat under his own steam and the crowd gave a cheer as he stood on the other side.

'Thank you Sir Parcifal.' the young knight offered.

'My squire will collect your armour later.'

Sir Parcifal returned to his seat, hardly breathing heavily at all. 'That should bring some more out,' he said to Guy as he pulled off his helm and reached for a goblet.

413

Two more knights stepped up between an axe throwing contest and a three stage battle consisting of three minute contests with staff, flail and sword. The Knightmaker despatched both of them. Guy knew him well enough to know that he was not really being pushed. It seemed clear that Sir Parcifal's choice of weapon was limiting the effectiveness of those that stepped up. He had more forfeits to collect, he just hoped that he would remember who to collect them from. He hoped that the Knightmaker would tell him.

A trial by combat followed. From what Guy could make out a knight had been accused of treachery, and, as was his right, demanded that the matter be settled with arms. A chevroned knight was to be his opponent, and more knights both chevroned and turquoise were present as security. The difference in the intensity of fighting was immediately noticeable. Though tournament knights took their combat seriously, nothing compared to having your life on the line. The knight attacked with a fervour that showed his intent to survive, but though under pressure, the chevroned knight absorbed the attack. As the contest went on Guy felt bad for thinking that it was becoming the best contest of the day. The speed and ferocity as the exchanges went back and forth left his mouth agape, he was happy that his helm hid it. He was stunned for another reason shortly after, when two moves saw the knight's head hewn from his body. One created the opening, and Guy was sure he had seen the knight's eyes as the realisation hit that he was about to die. Traitor or not, that was how he would be remembered. Even the crowd were muted in response to the reminder that life can be taken away so quickly. There was a pause for noonshine and Guy tried to clear his mind as he prepared the Knightmaker's food.

62

Sir Parcifal had been in good spirits, he had beaten four knights without pushing himself and earnt himself some coin whilst doing so. Towards the end of the meal he saw the Knightmaker's face change, first he was all business, then something else, something worse. Guy looked round to see what had caused the change. A very regal looking man was approaching flanked by six knights, three on either side. It was an intimidating view. Guy glanced to the king's box, it was empty, the guards minimal. A murmur spread through the crowd as they too became aware of the approach. Guy wondered what the fuck was going on. Was it all going to kick off? Immediately he was ready, he knew Sir Parcifal would be, and he was sure the stranger would be around somewhere. But even then, three against six, they would be fucked. Guy found himself assessing the situation. These were not tournament knights, these looked like the kind of knights that whoever was approaching used to get shit done. He tried to control the panic, Sir Parcifal, though clearly angered remained calm, sat watching their approach. Guy looked on, remembering the Knightmaker's instructions to look intimidating. Without his helm on, he just hoped that it was not visible how much he was flapping. Should he stand, would that look more intimidating, or would it just make things worse? He would follow Sir Parcifal's lead. The relief that flooded him when the party came to a halt at the usual challenge point did not release the grip panic had on his heart. His breaths were short and shallow, but it was the best he could do.

'Come with me,' the Knightmaker said quietly. Guy stood, he knew his size was imposing, so he stood tall, but knew that even if he had been a dozen foot tall he would not look near as imposing as what faced him. He took the three steps out onto the drawbridge and stood beside the Knightmaker. Should he have stood behind him? Fuck it, if it was going to kick off, he would be in there before the Knightmaker.

'Sir Parcifal,' called out the smart man without armour, the one that had the power.

'My lord,' was the clipped reply of the Knightmaker. *A lord!* Guy's restricted heart was pumping harder. Where was the king? Where were the guards?

'Sir Parcifal,' the man replied with a *'what are we going to do with you'* tone.

'Do you want to challenge for my shield?'

'Me? Oh no. But it would be good to have one of my knights close to the king, if you know what I mean. No, I have come to show you by whose hand you die today.'

'Is that right?' How could the Knightmaker remain so calm Guy wondered. He did not think that he would be able to speak if required, let alone sound so calm and intimidating.

'You are an old man, and from what I hear quite the drunk. Had I known I would have sought you out before. But I think it is right that it happens here in front of everyone.'

The Knightmaker's gaze had not moved, his eyes firmly locked on the Lord's. If he was intimidated, he did not show it, but then he had half a dozen knights behind him. 'You caused me a lot of trouble and killed a lot of my men.'

'You still got what you were after,' the Knightmaker replied.

'I did. But you upset me, and now you pay. Your next challenger is going to be one of these fine gentlemen.' He waved his arms to the side. 'I will watch you die and he will take your shield.'

'And if I win, what do you have to offer?' The Lord laughed.

'Another challenger.'

'And when I beat him, what do you have to offer?' The Lord stopped laughing.

'*If* by some miracle you beat him I will offer you my forgiveness.'

'Your forgiveness?'

'Yes. You made my life difficult for some time. If neither of these men kill you I will forgive your sins against me.'

'I was following orders.'

'Even so, today you die.'

The Lord turned, five of his knights turned with him and followed as he took two dozen paces away, then turned back to face them. Sir Parcifal turned himself to collect his helm and sword.

'Who the fuck was that?' Guy found himself asking in a hushed tone.

'Lord Mountjoy, Lord of Northunderland. It appears that he is upset with me.' Guys mind went into overdrive, if he had bells in his mind, they would be ringing, and he did not like what he was realising. *The battle of Ashford.* That was where he recognised the name. *Holy fuck.* 'If he takes the shield, you must challenge immediately, Lord Mountjoy cannot have a man close to the king.' Sir Parcifal pulled on his helm, took the Greatsword and turned away. 'Immediately,' he repeated.

Guy's words failed him, his body failed him, his mind was failing him. He could do no more than watch as the Knightmaker strode out.

'You want my shield?' he boomed. 'You can't have my shield.' As the crowd started to cheer, the knight pulled the sword one handed from the ground and strode onto the drawbridge. He did not break pace as he swung his first blow as the two of them collided like stags. Where the other knights had struggled with the sword, this one did not, and Guy could tell that it was all the Knightmaker could do to deflect the attacks. Neither of them was fucking around, and within moments the Knightmaker was sent reeling by a blow, as the knight followed up he was met with resistance. The knight's attacks were relentless. The Knightmaker was unable to land any significant blows himself as he was too busy defending. This was unlike any contest he had seen, even the trial by combat, and all taking place on a 36 by 18 foot drawbridge. After several minutes of relentless attacks Sir Parcifal was starting to take more blows, his defence was starting to slow, and Guy feared the worst. The Knightmaker managed to step inside and the two ended up grappling, both too close to land a blow with the sword. The knight started pushing the Knightmaker back, he wasn't looking to push him off the bridge, he was there to kill him. It was Sir Parcifal, he noticed, that was steering them in that direction. Guy remembered their training, even with Guy's size it had been hard to shift Sir Parcifal, but the lord's man was doing it. Both were grunting and talking shit to each other, when suddenly the Knightmaker spun away from the grasp of the knight, who then had to stop his forward momentum to prevent himself toppling from the bridge. As he did the Knightmaker had spun away, and brought the sword around at great speed with a full body spin. It connected with the back of the knight's neck, and he fell face first into the moat, his arms out to the side, not moving. The Knightmaker let out a roar.

It did not concern Guy that a man had just lost his life only feet away from him, it was relief that was released in him. The relief did not even get to last for a moment. Before the Knightmaker's roar was finished, another of Lord Mountjoy's knights had started his approach. A dozen steps from the drawbridge he began to draw his own greatsword, the other had gone into the moat with the defeated knight. The stewards who tried to recover the knight protested, and then got themselves to safety once they realised that he was not going to stop.

'Same as before, if I go down, take my sword and challenge immediately.' Guy gave a nod. He did not know how convincing it was, or what use it would be him challenging. This knight was bigger than the previous knight, and his sword was sharp, not like the tournament blades. The tightness returned and he wanted to vomit. He had done that several times in his helm, and was not going to do it again, not on the day he was knighted. He composed himself as the Knightmaker stepped forward to meet his foe.

'Time to die old man,' the knight taunted. The Knightmaker went at him with a fury. Strike after strike. The big knight was unable to mount an attack of his own. Perhaps the Knightmaker thought that against a sharp blade offence was the best defence. The knight blocked or parried most of the strikes, occasionally a glancing blow would get through, but nothing that would cause any damage. Though the knight's defence was desperate, he did not look panicked. He was in control, and it worried Guy. The Knightmaker was fresh from battle, and he feared, would soon tire. The knight was just absorbing it. The Knightmaker seemed to miss a beat, and the knight was raising his sword to launch his own offensive blow. He took a strike to both sides of his ribs before he could lower his sword to block, and when he did the Knightmaker landed a blow to the helm. It glanced off the knight's thick pauldron on the way through, but still did enough to knock the knight on his arse. The Knightmaker stepped back, and this time he was gasping for breath.

The knight let out a roar of his own, one of frustration, but the crowd were going nuts. It was strange for Guy, to be aware of them, but be focussed only on Sir Parcifal's battle. The knight got to his feet and shook himself off. 'Is that all you have got old man?' the knight called, the anger plain in his voice. He charged at the Knightmaker who charged back. The knight made the first move, raising his sword high, Sir Parcifal started swinging from below, a long arced swing which rose to meet the downward strike as they met, Sir Parcifal followed through with the swing, spinning himself to meet it before catching the knight on the back of the shoulders. The knight scrambled to the floor at Guy's feet, unable to keep himself upright. Guy could end it right now, but he took a step back instead.

'Oh no,' called the Knightmaker, 'I have much more than that.' Guy watched the knight as anger rose within him, it forced his body to do the same, he turned to face the Knightmaker. 'Would you like some more?'

Whatever anger had been building in the knight snapped and he launched himself at Sir Parcifal, for the next couple of minutes it was the Knightmaker's turn to defend. He had riled the knight, and the attacks were with aggression. With aggression comes a lack of control, and Guy was beginning to see openings that the Knightmaker should take, but instead he took the assault and talked shit to the knight. He launched another powerful attack, but this time the Knightmaker did not block it, he had instead spun away. As the knight's unanswered strike took him off balance the Knightmaker struck the back of his head with the pommel of his sword sending him sprawling on the floor once again. Sir Parcifal did not even glance Guy's way, but turned to see the angered knight quickly getting up. Guy felt much better now the Knightmaker was back on his side of the bridge, it was as it should be.

The next time the knight launched at him, they entered an exchange that saw both of them attacking, and both of them defending. Both were landing occasional blows, but nothing too heavy and Sir Parcifal was having the better of the exchange. They both went to strike and their swords met, steel sliding on steel as they pushed against each other in a show of power. Both were holding off the other when the knight's knee struck firmly between Sir Parcifal's legs lifting him off the ground.

'Oooof.'

It was the first time he had heard such a noise from the Knightmaker. It was a sound that told everyone he had been hurt. He staggered back, naturally bent over. Panic flashed through Guys mind, such a position exposed the back of the neck, a strike there would not be able to be defended, and with a live blade… Fortunately the knight was still angered and instead opted to lift his boot and kick Sir Parcifal in the head. It was less of a swing of the boot, and more of a frustrated push, it did no real harm except remove Sir Parcifal's helm. It clattered to the floor rolling twice towards Guy. Panic rose again, as the knight raised his sword. He wanted to scream out, wanted to launch himself and push the Knightmaker out of the way, but he would never make it, his body was not moving. As the knight went in with the blow the Knightmaker pushed up, driving the pommel with as much as he could muster up at the knight's helm. It sent the knight to his back, but the Knightmaker kept moving, bringing the sword down, almost as if the drive upward was to set up his move. The sword struck below the heavy chest plate and into the knight pinning him to the drawbridge. The sword remained planted and wobbled with the force of the drive. The Knightmaker stood and let out a roar even greater than the last. Guy knew the crowd would be cheering, but all he could see was the sword standing upright as the knight clasped the blade in a vain attempt to pull it out. He could hear the knight's gasps as he tried to cling onto his life, he could hear the bubbles of blood in his throat.

'ENOUGH!' The whole arena fell into shocked silence. The king was on his feet, and as Guy looked up he noticed that another of Lord Mountjoy's knights had started approaching. In a quieter, but no less demanding tone the king continued, 'Lord Mountjoy, a word.'

Whatever was about to happen had been stopped. As the Lord started his approach to the king, relief finally began to swarm through Guy's body. For a moment he actually thought that he would have to go up there.

'This is *MY* bridge.' boomed the Knightmaker for the benefit of the crowd, and perhaps the king, for the attention was now on Sir

Parcifal, instead of the animated conversation between the king and Lord Mountjoy. The Knightmaker picked up the knights sword. 'I'm going to keep this sword,' he called out as he held it aloft and the crowd cheered, 'and the armour too.' He motioned at both fallen knights. The crowd cheered and called out his name as in the distance Lord Mountjoy's remaining knights were being led out of the arena, along with the Lord himself, by a dozen turquoise knights.

A bugle announced the herald, and the Knightmaker returned to his seat as the next bout was announced. It was to be North vs South. A dozen knights from each side would battle in a melee, captured knights could be ransomed, and the winners would be the first to gain a dozen yields or captures from the other team. Guy had decided to wait for the Knightmaker to speak first, and was watching as stewards and servants removed the bodies, or tried at least. It was proving difficult for them to remove the sword, it must have gone through the knight and embedded into the drawbridge itself. Guy watched the match, but his focus was on controlling his breathing and trying to gather himself. He was still standing, as the Knightmaker tried to recover from his exertions.

63

Guy had spent several minutes familiarising himself with the melee before him, trying to give his mind something to think about other than what had just occurred. Each team had a holding pen, if they were able to get a member of the other team into it, they would be able to ransom them later. It appeared to Guy that both lords were taking part, and several earls. It seemed to be more of an exhibition bout, which was a nice change of pace. There were no captures so far and all two dozen knights obeyed the rules in front of him.

Within half an hour the southerners had forced the yields of their opposition, and led the lord and his fellow captives away from the arena to negotiate their release. As the crowd settled, the tournament champion made his way from the Royal enclosure to the drawbridge. When he reached the other side of the drawbridge he stopped before the greatsword that had been recovered from the moat. Sir Parcifal took his customary three steps onto the drawbridge.

'You want to take my shield?' the Knightmaker said, loud enough to be heard by much of the crowd.

'I do,' the champion replied just as loud, before adding in quieter tones, 'Sir Parcifal, I have no interest in your shield. The king has sent me over to lighten the mood. I do however have an interest in my wellbeing.'

'You know the price,' the Knightmaker boomed.

'I do,' he called, 'Half of my winnings in return for my health.' He added quietly.

'I have changed my terms,' the Knightmaker continued in their own conversation. For a moment concern spread across the champion's face.

'I do not want half of your winnings. Two gold will suffice, one for my squire, and one for the first knight who faced me after we last spoke.' Relief and confusion replaced the champions concern.

'Of course.'

'And one more thing,' the Knightmaker continued. 'The young knight in question offered me his service for a year. I would ask that you take him into your service. He will serve you well I feel, and learn a lot.'

'It is done,' the champion replied. 'Let us put on a show for them and I will happily go into the water.' The Knightmaker nodded.

'Take the sword Sir Champion, and let us see what you have got.' The Knightmaker said for the effect of the crowd. The champion nodded, and when he reached for the sword the crowd began to cheer. Sir Parcifal turned to Guy who handed him his helm, and then his sword. When he turned to face the champion, they shared a respectful nod, and the champion came at him with a grunt of effort, more for the crowd's pleasure than anything else.

Their swords sang songs of steel as they parried, blocked and occasionally struck each other. The contest was fluid, despite the size of the swords, and it was clear that the two skilled knights were enjoying the contest. Rarely was a significant blow landed as they danced a simple yet elegant dance. He could hear them talking to each other as the contest went on, and more elaborate manoeuvres were undertaken. It reminded him of when he had seen the Knightmaker and the stranger dance. It was not up to that speed, but it was an enthralling contest which the kept the crowds attention.

The respectful bout continued for over quarter of an hour before the Knightmaker moved the battle towards the edge of the bridge. Seemingly desperate exchanges followed before the Knightmaker aimed a sweeping blow that left the champion no option but to step away to avoid it. Alas for the champion there was not enough space to step into and he tumbled from the drawbridge as the crowd whooped and hollered. The champion had been right, the whole place was jumping and in stark contrast to the end of the Knightmaker's previous bout. Their contest had lightened the mood as the king intended.

As the champion climbed the bank, the Knightmaker called him over, and they clasped arms as the crowd enjoyed the moment, cheering loudest when the champion raised Sir Parcifal's arm. Guy smiled from inside his own helm as he took the Knightmaker's sword on his return. He was breathing heavily, but Guy knew he would recover in a few minutes. It had not been an intense battle, but it had lasted a good time. Sir Parcifal sat, removed his helm and drank from the water jug as his breathing recovered. Guy remained standing as a knife fight was introduced by the herald, and two shirtless men emerged from the competitor's area.

The knife fight held Guys attention, the wary posturing made him think of snakes poised to attack. When they struck, it was with speed, and it was finely tuned reflexes that enabled them to dodge or parry the blow with their vambraced forearms. Knife fights were usually to first blood, but this being the king's tournament it was first to three. When the late afternoon sun caught their bodies at the right angles Guy was sure he could see scars from previous battles. It was well over five minutes before the first blood was drawn, one combatant caught on his side. A few minutes later the same man was caught again, this time across the stomach. It was not looking good for him, but very soon after his second wound he caused one of his own to his opponent's arm. A deep cut to his knife arm that soon had a stream of blood running from it. It was clearly inhibiting his movement and he went on the defensive. He only needed one counterstrike to claim victory. Within minutes though his arm was coated in a thick crimson mask, blood dripped freely from his elbow.

The other fighter was patient waiting for the right moment to take advantage, and before long had levelled the match drawing blood from his opponent's chest. The deciding blow came not long after, weakening from the loss of blood the reactions slowed just enough to allow another substantial slicing on the other side of his chest. The one who looked most likely to lose had become the victor. Guy glanced down at his own knife, dreaming but for a moment that he might be able to compete in such a bout. He would be too big a target, and though he may be quick, especially for his size, he would not be anywhere near quick enough for that kind of contest. He had enjoyed the bout though, there was something real and honest about drawing first blood to win. He told himself he would watch more of these contests.

The loser had been led off, and was already having his arm tended to by physicians at the side of the arena, the victor milked the crowd for a short time before heading back to the competitor's area, a physician rushing after him. There was a pause in proceedings, so Guy sat at the table with the Knightmaker to drink water and eat fruit, talking with the Knightmaker about the contest he had just seen.

'You have to be a crazy fucker to be a knife fighter,' was how the Knightmaker summed it up. Guy could not disagree. He looked at the sun, it was getting late, and the Knightmaker still had a potential five bouts to come. How would they fit those in before the banquet? Almost on cue, a procession of knights led by the tournament master filed out of the competitor's area lining up on the other side of the drawbridge. 'Here we go.' said the Knightmaker, Pull on your helm and come with me when I go.' Guy nodded as the king made his way towards the drawbridge.

Sir Parcifal stood, tucked his helm under his arm, and picked up his greatsword. Guy followed as he walked out onto the drawbridge, past his usual three paces, instead coming to a halt about three paces from the other side. Guy stood slightly behind him.

'Sir Parcifal has survived seven challengers to his shield. How many more wish to face him?' the king asked as he paced the line of knights. Guy looked down the line smiling inside his helm. There were many knights there, many who had suffered the Knightmaker's abuse over the last few days. This was where the Knightmaker's work would pay off. After his displays so far, those with whom he had negotiated would be unlikely to step up. The idea of Sir Parcifal fucking their wife, or even them, would be too high a price.

'Who's next?' boomed the Knightmaker. Many knights looked to the ground, other stared angrily, unwilling to pay the price the Knightmaker would demand. 'Come on you fuckers. Who wants my shield?'

No one moved, not the knights with nothing to lose, and especially those with something to lose.

'To be a king's own knight is a prize indeed. Will no one take up the challenge?' the king asked as he paced looking at each knight in turn, still no one stepped forward. 'I expect more from the knights of Rodina,' he continued. 'You will face a formidable opponent in Sir Parcifal, but this chance does not come often.' He paced the line again as the crowd began to grumble. 'Does no one have the courage to step forward?' Guy could see some battling with themselves, some perhaps angered by Sir Parcifal's demands, some perhaps shamed by the king's words. Not enough to step forward though.

'Sir Guy.' the king called as he turned to face him, 'Perhaps as the most recent knight in the kingdom you can remind us what it is to be a knight and provide Sir Parcifal with his final challenge, since none here wish to face him.' Guy's heart caught in his throat, and his blood ran cold. He felt for a moment like a deer as it looked down the wrong end of an arrow just before it was loosed. There was no way he would defy the king, but facing the Knightmaker was the last thing he wanted to do. It had been made perfectly clear that it could be very bad for your health.

'Go on boy, step forward,' he heard Sir Parcifal mutter. He could not move though, his mind frantically tried to process what was going on, and more to the point, how to avoid it. He could not face the Knightmaker, he did not want to face the Knightmaker. He did not want to get fucked up. 'Step forward, show them what a real knight looks like,' Sir Parcifal repeated. He took a breath, tried to compose himself, and found himself taking the three steps to the end of the drawbridge. The crowd's murmuring turned to cheers. The king gave them a moment.

'The final contest in the drawbridge challenge will see student against master. Let us see what kind of knight you will be Guy of Waering. Already you have shown yourself to have courage. The rest of you should stay and remind yourselves what is required to be a knight of Rodina.'

The king waved his hand and the tournament master ushered them away to the middle of the arena. 'Good luck Sir Guy,' the king offered before returning to his enclosure. Guy turned to face the Knightmaker who had his bad fucker face on.

'You want my shield?' he boomed for the crowd. 'Come and take it.'

'I don't want your shield,' Guy replied quietly.

'Maybe so, but you will put on a show for these fuckers that will remind them what a knight should be. What do you offer me if I win?'

'Whatever you want, everything I have if required, I would not be here without you.'

'What I want is for you to put on a show, and for you to finish your training. You may be a knight, but I have not finished with you yet.'

'Of course.'

'Just think of this as training, and you will be fine.' Guy relaxed a little, 'and think of this,' the Knightmaker continued, 'it will be me that gets to put the first dinks in your armour.'

'Aye, it is as it should be,' Guy smiled.

'Well come on then!' the Knightmaker boomed before returning to the other side of the drawbridge and pulling on his helm. Guy undid his belt and placed it carefully on the ground beside the drawbridge and pulled the greatsword from the ground waving it around, getting accustomed to its weight as the crowds anticipation began to bubble to the surface. He turned to face the Knightmaker who rapped his helm with his sword twice, and pretty hard. That was not a good sign, he regretted not wearing his gambeson and chain. A knight should always be ready. *We go now.* Guy made ready in North East and edged his way along the drawbridge. The Knightmaker came at him, he blocked the first blow, the second and third struck him either side, and he staggered backwards only just avoiding a strike to the head. They met again, this time he blocked three strikes before the Knightmaker's boot met his chest forcing him backwards falling on his arse. He immediately rolled away as the Knightmaker came in, avoiding the strike. This was familiar territory for Guy, and he had no time to worry about the crowd or the drawbridge.

When the Knightmaker was coming at him, the only thing he worried about was survival. He took a beating for several minutes as it took him a while to get used to the weight of the sword. It was heavier than the swords he had used before, but lighter than the iron bar that he had first learnt the moves to this dance with. He was panting inside his helm, but it was not unusual. He remembered his defence training, which had consisted of an hour of this kind of abuse, for while the Knightmaker was coming at him hard, he knew it was controlled and it was a dance they had shared many times before.

Gradually he got used to the sword, and soon was able to maintain the dance for longer intervals before taking a blow, or on occasion landing one himself, and it was not long until he began to enjoy the movement and the lightness of his armour. They battled back and forth with some intensity, the familiarity of their shared dance undoubtedly putting on a show for the crowd. He had been put on his arse a few times, and had thrown himself to the floor on occasion as their battle neared the edge of the drawbridge, once sweeping the Knightmaker's legs from under him as he rolled to safety. He waited for the Knightmaker to get back to his feet, and within a minute had his helm rung by a solid blow. He staggered backwards, stumbling as his vision blurred. When the Knightmaker came at him he was fully in survival mode, but the Knightmaker was only adding to the show. He came with moves that he knew Guy could block with his eyes shut, which was just as well. He could not remember being hit so hard. That would have left a mark on his helm for sure, one that he would never remove.

Their swords came together, as did they, as they pushed against each other. He could hear the Knightmaker breathing hard.

'We'll give it another few minutes, and then you will put me in the water.'

'What? No...' he did not get chance to finish the sentence before the Knightmaker's knee struck between his legs, and the pommel of his sword met his helm as he bent double. He was on the floor again desperately rolling to avoid the follow up blows. He finally struggled back to his feet. 'I can't, it is not right,' Guy protested.

The Knightmaker came at him again, they danced, Guy doing little more than surviving, as his vision slowly started returning some clarity as his warrior's blood gave him strength.

'You must. There is a lot of money at stake here.'

'I don't want to take your shield,' he said between blows.

'You are taking nothing. I am giving it to you. I was unable to knight you, but this I can do.'

Guy was unable to talk any more, partly because he did not know what to say, partly because his lungs were burning from the sustained effort and his head felt as if an axe was imbedded in it. As his vision cleared, he was better able to play his part in the dance, even as his mind raced like a freshly branded stallion. His mind was considering two things at once, the first being that he did not even want the shield, he wanted to get back to Phylissa. The second was more a memory returning from the haze of the previous night, as the Knightmaker talked to Sir Chandley, he remembered the Knightmaker saying that he would tap his helm twice if he was going to lose, so Sir Chandley could bet. Fuck, if that was the case it was likely that there would be more money on the line that he would see in his lifetime. He would have to put the Knightmaker in the water, but it was not right. They battled on, and the next time they were close to each other he heard Sir Parcifal talk.

'Soon I will deprive you of your sword, then you will send me off the bridge.' His voice was serious, Guy finished the sentence in his mind *'or I will hurt you.'*.

The bout continued, Guy was starting to land more shots, either the Knightmaker was tiring, or more likely, was letting him. He still had to work for them, but occasionally there were openings that were not there before. He was still getting tagged, but the tide was changing, this probably meant that he was about to lose his sword.

Though he was expecting it, when the sword was wrenched from his hands, he looked to follow it as it clattered to the floor. He had just driven Sir Parcifal back with a flurry of well landed blows. He had no idea how the Knightmaker had done it, but his sword had gone. The Knightmaker put both his hands in the air, and roared in celebration.

Fuck it. Guy took three quick steps towards the Knightmaker. 'I'm coming with you,' he said just before he drove his shoulder into the Knightmaker's chest, grabbing around his body, the momentum took them both off the bridge to the four foot drop into the artificial moat below them. He had never fallen so far in armour, and when they landed he regretted his decision to protect the Knightmaker by rolling them in the air so that the Knightmaker landed on top of him. It knocked the wind out of him, but as he gasped for air, his lungs filled with water, the weight of the Knightmaker kept his head below the water. He panicked for a moment as his lungs tried to expel the water only to take more on. *Was he to drown in two feet of water?* As his body began to convulse he sent a silent message to Phylissa. *'I did it.'*

64

Suddenly he was lifted, the Knightmaker's gauntlet grabbed the bottom of his helm. Water shot out of him into it, and as he gasped for air more sputtered out. It was the most painful thing he had ever experienced, but at the same time, he had never felt such relief. The Knightmaker slammed him on the back which forced a cough of more water before he vomited inside his helm. He had broken a promise to himself, but at least he was alive. He felt that he had been gasping for air for an eternity, the reality was different. It had been less than a minute since dragging him from the moat and the Knightmaker was telling him to get up. He forced himself up, for no other reason than that the Knightmaker had told him to, and for the first time in a long time became aware of the crowd as they cheered. He pulled off his helm and splashed water on his face before he climbed the shallow bank of the moat.

The Knightmaker helped him to his feet when he reached the top, and then raised his hand for the crowd. Guy was still in a shit state. His Lungs hurt like they had been punched from the inside, he could not catch his breath and his eyes were not working. All he saw was a swarm of faces all blurred together. When the Knightmaker lowered his arm, Guy grabbed his in turn and raised it for the crowd to an even greater cheer. The king was on his feet applauding from his box, the noble crowd followed, the common folk were already on their feet. Even the knights in the middle of the arena applauded.

'What a way to close the tournament,' the king called out in jubilation, 'Courage, skill at arms, and a level of determination that I have not seen in a long time, from both men.' He let the crowd applaud for a moment. 'Thank you to all our competitors,' he said as he waved his hand towards the assembled knights in the arena. 'Congratulations to our champions.' He let the crowd have another moment, 'The real winner today though is Rodina, and the great knights that protect her.' Another pause, 'Come back next year when the tournament will be… Legendary.' The crowd went nuts, the knights turned to the king, and the nobles got excited. Guy did not know what was going on. He finally collapsed to the floor and retched again, unsure where the liquid had come from. He gasped and retched until his eyes streamed and he had finally rid himself of the moats water. By the time his head had stopped spinning and the world returned to his awareness, the knights and nobles had gone, and the crowd were leaving. He looked up to see the Knightmaker, a couple of physicians, and some tournament officials in a group around him.

'Now that was a fucking show,' boomed the Knightmaker triumphantly as he pulled Guy to his feet.

Guy was still suffering, even after a soak in a tub had removed the rest of the moats grime. The armour and leather had prevented his body from being harmed on the outside, but inside he hurt, and he could feel one of his eyes closing. The helm had done its job, without it, the blow to the head would surely have killed him. There was a groove in the steel from the blow, but more worrying, the helm was dented slightly, on the reinforced area. It felt as if the force of the blow had slammed the helm into his head. His eye was flashing with pain, and he did not know what the fuck was going on. Words came at him from a distance, and his mind, though it had much to process, did not seem to be working. It was as if it was asleep for all but the most basic of functions. He was too fucked up to draw any symbols, let alone believe they helped. He just wanted to curl aball and wake up when he was better.

Unfortunately for Guy, he did not have that option, it was the champion's banquet, and he had to attend. It was taking all of his mental strength to even dress himself, grateful on some level that he did not have to choose. He only had one set of smart clothes. The Knightmaker had noticed that all was not well, taking his face in his hand and looking into Guys one good eye until he was certain that he had his attention.

'You are a knight now, you cannot afford to show any weakness. I once had a conversation with the king with an arrow in my back and he had no idea. Do you understand what I am saying?' He had to repeat the question before Guy nodded. 'Just be big and quiet and intimidating. Understand?' Guy nodded, unsure whether he really understood, but being big and quiet he could do. He would focus on that.

On the walk to the banquet hall Guy tried to convince himself that the fresh air was making him better, he failed, but commended himself for trying. The pain behind his eye was crippling, he was glad someway that his eye was swollen shut, he remembered how much it had hurt when he could still see through it. In the cool air of the evening he was starting to sweat, that did not bode well for the banquet hall rammed full of people. As they entered the castle Guy and the Knightmaker were led to a room off the main hall where the champions gathered before being announced. There were nine of them it total, which seemed like a lot to Guy, there must have been events he was not aware of. Stewards gave instructions that Guy did not understand, but he must have nodded in all the right places, he hoped that the Knightmaker had been listening.

King Thamas himself paid a visit, and spoke to each of them in turn. Guy was aware that he had spoken with him, but could not remember what was said. He tried to sort himself out, but the more he concentrated the more his head hurt, almost like some kind of punishment. He sat and focussed on his breathing as the king completed his circuit before heading into the hall to address his guests.

One of the stewards approached leaning in close to Guy, he must not have nodded in the right places, for a couple of fuzzy moments later he returned with a physician who, as the Knightmaker had done earlier, grabbed his face and looked into his one good eye. He opened a leather box case and rummaged for a moment with its contents before bringing out a vial filled with a thick purple liquid and held it to Guys lips.

'Drink this, it will perk you up, and see me after the meal.' Guy let him pour the vial's contents into his mouth and swallowed the bitter liquid, grateful that he knew it was bitter. The steward and physician were having a conversation that he could not hear when he felt the Knightmaker's rough hand grab his chin.

'Knight training, two hours. We go now.'

Guy took a breath, found himself preparing, it had become instinct over the past months. It meant the next two hours were all that existed, getting through them was all that mattered. Sir Parcifal pulled him to his feet and after a slight wobble he was able to follow him to the other side of the room. He was breathing, he could feel the liquid spreading from his belly. A moment later he was more aware of what he was seeing, but instead of seeing normally, it was as if he was seeing things from the back of his eye, it was an improvement.

When the cue was given for the door to be opened thoughts started in Guy's mind once more, as the sounds of the room and the king talking flooded through the curtain in the doorway. The sounds were distant, the same as his thoughts. It should have been one of the greatest nights of his life, attending the champion's banquet of the king's own tournament, as a champion. He would be asked about it for the rest of his life, he just hoped that he would remember some of it. As soon as he became aware that his thoughts had returned he focussed them on sorting himself out. Two hours, he could do that, he would do that, or die trying. In his mind somewhere he laughed at himself, which he took as a good sign.

He could hear polite applause as the king's welcome concluded. He wished he had heard it, it was not everyone who could say that they had heard the king speak, and every word should be savoured. As the applause died down the king's voice started again. Guy listened.

'There is still one unresolved matter of the day.' the king began, 'The drawbridge challenge. I have conferred with the tournament masters, and we have decided that whist the last contest does not deserve to have a loser. I declare Sir Guy the victor.' A euphoric cry from Sir Chandley in the crowd was quickly controlled before the king continued. 'A battle of such intensity, lasting almost an hour, defining the very essence of what knighthood should be, ending in the way it did... Both men deserve every credit, and Sir Parcifal will keep his shield. So join me in welcoming the first of our champions tonight, he faced eight foes as he defended his shield in the drawbridge challenge, a man who epitomises what it is to be a king's own knight, Sir Parcifal of Eastfield.' The Knightmaker stepped through the curtain to applause and cheers leaving Guy on his own. There was a pause before the king spoke again. A steward leant in close.

'You are to sit next to Sir Parcifal.' That seemed like important information, so Guy tried to remember it, repeating it in his mind until the king spoke again.

'Our next champion fills me with hope for the future, and is the other participant in that epic bout on the drawbridge. He is also the winner of the Golden Spurs and Rodina's latest knight, Sir Guy of Waering.' The steward pushed Guy forward. When he passed through the curtain, the light of the candles hurt his eye, and heat struck him like a giant pillow. He sucked it up and stepped forward as the applause made the room feel very small. The king clasped his arm and offered congratulations before he found himself standing for a moment.

'Thank you, Your Grace.'

He had to say that. No matter what the king's words would have been, that is what he would have said. He had done that. He stood a moment longer the heat making him sweat. There was something else he needed to do. Sit next to Sir Parcifal, he remembered, and approached his seat, grateful to sit down, and have the attention on someone else. What was it with him and meals like this? He hoped that he could get through this one as he had got through the one at Waering.

He sat in silence, somewhat dazed as the king introduced the rest of the champions. The tournament champion was next out and sat opposite the Knightmaker, clasping both their arms as he arrived at the table. Guy had liked him, and only wished he were in a better state so that he could tell him so. It would probably earn him a look from the Knightmaker, but it did not matter, he could not tell him anyway. It was taking all his focus to keep his eye open, and his awareness in the room. He was not aware of the finery of the room and its inhabitants, the silk banners that hung from walls, the polished ornate wood of the panels, and the fine clothes worn by the noble guests. He was not aware of the painted ceilings or the finest candelabras in the kingdom. He was aware that he was there, and that he had to get through the next two hours.

When the meal was served, Guy managed to regain his focus for long enough to register the size of it. The four rib section of the Dun cow. It looked as large as two doors side by side and the smell… His nose was working, one side of it anyway. He took that as another good sign and kept his awareness throughout the carving and his first taste of the meat. It was soft and bloody, melting to juice in his mouth. He knew that he would remember how it tasted and felt in his mouth. At least he would remember something.

Soon after eating, while some were still being served, Guy stood, a servant approached instantly.

'I need to piss,' he announced. Using all his resources, he followed the servant through a door, along a corridor and into a courtyard laden with troughs and rows of canvas cubicles fitted with wooden slats over a pit. He did not need one of those, but as he made his way to a trough he spilled his guts in spectacular fashion as the delicious cow and wine that he had foolishly drunk expelled themselves with such force a three foot puddle formed in front of him. He gasped for air as his eyes watered again, almost shocked as much as the servants, one of whom rushed over with a cloth which Guy used to wipe his drooling mouth.

Once he had recovered from the outburst he realised that it had actually bought him some relief. The effort had caused his head to hurt as if a steel heeled horse had just made contact, but in other ways he felt better, there was a clarity that was absent before. He thanked the servant for the cloth, and he knew that while he may have been the first, many others would spill their guts that night. As he pulled himself upright a servant began to scatter sand over his puddle, and by the time he had finished his piss you would never know there had been a pool of vomit there. Guy stepped around it though, he knew it was there, and headed back to the feast feeling confident that he could get through the rest of the banquet.

65

Guys form was visibly improved as he returned to the table, he felt more aware, and he felt more able. He even finished the meat of one of the champions more concerned with filling his belly with wine than the beast that Guy had killed. He savoured the taste all over again, and while it was no longer hot, it was as full of juice as it had been before. He could feel it in his belly, the flesh of the Dun cow, it made him stronger. For the first time since the drawbridge it did not require the entirety of his focus to simply be aware, he was able to relax and let his senses experience things that he hoped he would remember later.

He would remember the honeyed buns that were served just before the official element of the banquet ended and the king retired to his quarters. They were the sweetest things he had ever tasted, sweeter even than the ripest of fruit.

As the king passed through the curtain, Guy shared a look with the Knightmaker, he had done it, he had made it through the evening. He got one back that told him that they would leave soon enough, *we go again*. For the first time that night he felt a smile inside him. The tournament champion caught his eye before it could spread to his face.

'Congratulations Sir Guy, knight of Rodina.' He held out his hand. Guy took it, not knowing what else to do saying thank you as they hands moved towards each other. The champion pressed a gold coin into his hand. 'My forfeit to Sir Parcifal.' The knight nodded at him, Guy nodded back, hoping that it conveyed all the things he was unable to say. It was certainly a nod of respect.

The conversations continued around him as groups formed among the masses. Drinking and networking was how the rest of the evening would go. He was glad that the Knightmaker was not that sort of man, drinking aside. He knew well enough that the Knightmaker had no time for that kind of thing. Had he been feeling more with it Guy would have enjoyed watching, but all he wanted was to get out of there, and find some quiet.

A steward approached, leaning between them with a hand on each of their shoulders, he announced that the king had requested their presence. A mixture of relief and anxiety swept through Guy. He was sure that they would not be returning to the feast, and was glad to be getting out of there, yet concern grew that he would have to keep it together to speak to the king. He reassured himself that at least he was feeling better than before, and that the king would mostly be speaking to the Knightmaker. As long as he remembered his words, 'Thank you, Your Grace.'

He nodded to the table as he rose and followed the Knightmaker, breathing carefully. They passed through the curtain, and the further they moved away the cooler it became and the sounds of the banquet began to fade. His ears still felt wide open, but there was no longer the amount of noise to fill them.

They were led into a room which was dominated by a large stone table carved with a map of Rodina, the king was there and an elderly man in olive robes. There were several stone benches, tables for books and holes in the wall that were filled with scrolls.

'Come in, sit down,' the king was all business. Guy found himself attempting a small bow before he gratefully placed himself on a stone bench. The light was less harsh in the room, his pounding head was relieved to notice. 'Sir Parcifal, I apologise for Lord Mountjoy's behaviour this afternoon. I had thought all that was behind us.'

'It would appear not Your Grace.'

'It is now. He shall not bother you again.'

'Perhaps not directly.'

'You did well today, and put Sir Young and Lord Adler's complaint to the sword. The shield would have been yours regardless, you have been a great servant to Rodina.'

'Thank you, Your Grace.'

'I was wrong about you and your methods, your young knight here is testament to that. To win the squires tournament and then battle with you for almost an hour shows me that you have trained him to fight.'

'That is what knights do.'

'Aye, in your time, yes. Rodina has been at peace for almost twenty years. Yes there have been disputes and skirmishes, but there have been no wars. I am concerned that we are all becoming soft, and ill-equipped to deal with such conflicts.'

The king paused, looking thoughtful and as if he were trying to form the right words in his mind. 'I have been thinking of taking measures to correct this for some time, but it was not until this nonsense with Lord Adler came up… I have been watching you Edrick, even in your private sessions. I need someone to train knights who know how to fight, that will do whatever is necessary.' The Knightmaker looked as if he was about to say something, but thought better of it. 'I hear rumours of plots and troubles on the horizon, from those who were not present this week.'

'The East.'

'Exactly, the only competitor from the east was the squire. The peace with them has been delicate. I need a group of men who can train other men to fight, to do what is required.'

'You have the king's own knights,' the Knightmaker interrupted. The king let out a laugh of derision.

'Aye, I do, but their allegiance is to the throne. Besides, it is different to your day, these knights do not fight like they should. I think today showed that the king's own knights are not what they used to be. So few stepped up to challenge you and those who did, some of them should be nowhere near me. As I said, the entire kingdom is becoming soft.'

'Your army?'

'An army that has never seen war. No I need something different.' The king paused a moment as a thin framed man with darting eyes made his way over to them. 'This is Filip, my Lord Steward. No one other than those of us in this room, and my sons will know of this. I want you to recruit and train up the men. I need them to be leaders, I need them to be fighters, I need them to defend Rodina, no matter what the task.'

'Your Grace, I…'

'Edrick, I have known you a long time, but I am still your king. I could command this of you, but I would rather ask it. Filip will ensure you have everything you need, I have lands in the South where you can be based. Money is not an issue. I know you are not an extravagant man, so anything you need you shall have.'

'Your Grace...' the Knightmaker started.

'No Edrick, I have chosen you for this, think on it and join me for noonshine tomorrow with your answer.'

The king turned his gaze to Guy who had been listening, but pretending he was not there. It was not difficult with the way he was feeling.

'Sir Guy. You have impressed me with your attitude.' Seeing the swelling on his face added, 'that looks like some blow you took.'

'Thank you, Your Grace.'

Guy was gathering everything he could to focus on the king. He was sweating and his head throbbed like the inside of a bell, but the Knightmaker's words drove him on. 'I understand you have a woman waiting for you in Waering.'

'Thank you, Your Grace.' The king glanced at Sir Parcifal, who nodded back.

'I am going to send a rib bone from the beast back to Waering so they may hear of your deeds. Is there any message you would have me send?'

'Thank you, Your Grace,' Guy Started, 'But I shall deliver any messages myself on my return.' The king took a breath.

'I am afraid that you may have to delay your return. I have something I need you to do for me.' Guy looked up. His mind was suddenly clear, despite the pain. He had been waiting for this to be over, so that he may return to Waering with his white cloak, and golden spurs, to show Phylissa he was the man she wanted. That was how it was meant to be.

'Your Grace?'

'You have proved yourself a man of great integrity and desire. One who does not give up easily. I need someone like you for a very important job. Besides, the prize for beating Sir Parcifal was the opportunity to become a king's own knight. Fulfil this task, and you shall be one.'

The fire of frustration was starting to burn inside him. He did not want to be a king's own knight, he did not want any task. He just wanted to get back to Waering, and to his love. That was the whole point of him doing any of it. He could not even say his words.

'My son has not been seen, or heard of for almost six months.'

The king paused, the words were clearly not easy to say. 'I sent a messenger to track him down at the start of the summer, but have not received any word from him. I need someone who will not stop until he is found. My son is the holder of a legendary weapon, and he needs to return for next year's tournament. I need to remind him of his obligations, both to his father, and to Rodina.'

The king paused again, and Guy's mind took the chance to chastise his selfish thoughts. He could not turn down the king anyway, but a quest of such importance… Phylissa would wait. 'I need you to find him and bring him back.' Guy nodded.

'Thank you, Your Grace.' The king nodded back.

'I am sorry, Sir Guy, to keep you from your love, but it is your drive to get back to her that will bring my son back to me.' Guy and the king shared a look. There were many things that could have been going through Guy's mind, but he was not aware of any of them. He just knew that the king was right. 'I believe in love.' for a moment so did Guy. 'Come with Sir Parcifal tomorrow, and I will give you what information I have, and anything you need for the journey.' Guy nodded, his world slowly disintegrated in his mind. That was not how things were supposed to be.

'Your Grace,' Sir Parcifal started, 'It is inevitable that I am to do as you ask. I have one request, if I may.'

'Of course.'

'I shall need a sword.' The king nodded to the Lord Steward who reached into a velvet covered recess and bought out the Legendary Greatsword.

'Will this do?' Sir Parcifal nodded and carefully took it from the steward before turning to Guy.

'Take a knee.' Guy looked up in confusion. 'I was denied the opportunity to knight you myself, take a knee, so as I may do it now.' Guys good eye flicked to the king who nodded his consent and took a knee, his head bowed between the king and the Knightmaker. 'It gives me great honour to knight you Guy of Waering, you represent what a knight of Rodina should be.' He tapped the sword to each shoulder. 'Arise Sir Guy, knight of the realm, protector of what is good and right.' Guy looked up, as the sword was handed back to the steward. The king applauded.

'I like that. Knights of the realm. Return to me tomorrow, and we shall discuss the details.' As if on cue a servant entered the room. 'They will return you to the banquet.'

'Thank you, Your Grace, but I think there has been enough excitement for one day. We shall retire.' Sir Parcifal said with a bow.

'Take them back to their quarters,' the king instructed. Guy bowed and followed them out of the room, his head spinning in more ways than one as he gave everything to keep it together long enough to get to the pavilion.

The Stranger was sat with Hawkins, who was looking very pleased with himself. Sir Parcifal joined them, and set about filling his belly with wine. Guy excused himself and ducked into the tent laying on his rollmat without taking off his fancy clothes. He had made it through the night, and could finally allow sleep to find him. It was what he craved more than anything. If his head allowed, he would figure everything out when he woke up. He felt relief.

As throbbing pain in one side of his head forced sleep upon him, only one thought occupied his mind. *Find the king's Son, how the fuck was he going to do that?*

Lightning Source UK Ltd.
Milton Keynes UK
UKHW041500060619
343973UK00001B/47/P

9 781728 388533